Crusade

The battle against the Cursed Ones
continues in

Damned

**Also by Nancy Holder
and Debbie Viguié**

Wicked

Witch & Curse

Wicked 2

Legacy & Spellbound

Resurrection

Crusade

NANCY HOLDER
& DEBBIE VIGUIÉ

Simon Pulse

NEW YORK   LONDON   TORONTO   SYDNEY

SIMON PULSE

An imprint of Simon & Schuster Children's Publishing Division

1230 Avenue of the Americas, New York, NY 10020

First Simon Pulse paperback edition May 2011

Copyright © 2010 by Nancy Holder and Debbie Viguié

All rights reserved, including the right of reproduction in whole or in part in any form.

SIMON PULSE and colophon are registered trademarks of Simon & Schuster, Inc.

Also available in a Simon Pulse hardcover edition.

For information about special discounts for bulk purchases, please contact

Simon & Schuster Special Sales at 1-866-506-1949 or business@simonandschuster.com.

The Simon & Schuster Speakers Bureau can bring authors to your live event.

For more information or to book an event contact the Simon & Schuster Speakers Bureau

at 1-866-248-3049 or visit our website at www.simonspeakers.com.

Designed by Mike Rosamilia

The text of this book was set in Cochin.

Manufactured in the United States of America

2 4 6 8 10 9 7 5 3 1

The Library of Congress has cataloged the hardcover edition as follows:

Holder, Nancy.

Crusade / by Nancy Holder and Debbie Viguié—1st Simon Pulse hardcover ed.

p. cm.

Summary: An international team of six teenaged vampire hunters, trained in Salamanca, Spain, goes to New Orleans seeking to rescue team member Jenn's younger sister as the vampires escalate their efforts to take over the Earth.

ISBN 978-1-4169-9802-0 (hc)

[1. Vampires—Fiction. 2. Guerrilla warfare—Fiction. 3. Supernatural—Fiction.

4. Sisters—Fiction. 5. Horror stories.] I. Viguié, Debbie. II. Title.

PZ7.H70326Cru 2010

[Fic]—dc22

2010009094

ISBN 978-1-4169-9803-7 (pbk)

ISBN 978-1-4169-9808-2 (eBook)

To my daughter, Belle Holder. I would fight
a million vampires for you, my darling girl.
And I would beat them all.
—N. H.

To my father, Richard Reynolds, who continually
teaches me that there are things in this world
worth fighting for.
—D. V.

ACKNOWLEDGMENTS

I'm so grateful to everyone who has joined us on this crusade. A novel is a huge undertaking, and a new series is an even bigger one. Thank you to the legions who helped us on the journey, most especially our fantastic agent, Howard Morhaim, and our truly wonderful editor, Annette Pollert, as well as our Simon & Schuster family, including Bethany Buck, Mara Anastas, Paul Crichton, Taryn Rosada, Bess Braswell, Venessa Williams, Sammy Yuen, Mike Rosamilia, Katherine Devendorf, Karen Sherman, and Stacey Sakal. *Gracias* to Lawrence Schimel, who helped with the Spanish; any errors are ours. My deepest thanks and love to Debbie, my comrade in arms, my coauthor, and my dearest friend. My gratitude to Debbie's husband, Dr. Scott Viguié, who kept us both sane. Thanks also to Katie Menick, and to Kate McKean, also included in our literary representation. Thanks to my family, and to Richard Dean Anderson for starring in my favorite show. And *besitos* to my homegirls — Pam Escobedo, Amy Schricker, and Beth Hogan.

—N. H.

So many people have joined us in bringing *Crusade* to the world, and their tireless efforts have ensured that this story was all it could be. I would especially like to thank

Howard Morhaim, a great agent, and Annette Pollert, a wonderful editor, for their enthusiasm and support. Thank you to Nancy, the best collaborator anyone could ever wish for. Thank you as well to Belle Holder for her energy and encouragement. I would also like to thank my husband, Scott, my mother, Barbara, and my friends Calliope, Juliette, and Ann. I would fight vampires with you any day!

—D. V.

BOOK ONE
HADES

On a dark night,
kindled in love with yearnings~
oh, happy chance!
I went forth without being observed,
my house being now at rest.

—St. John of the Cross,
sixteenth-century mystic of Salamanca

CHAPTER ONE

For thousands of years the Cursed Ones hid in the shadows, fooling mankind into thinking they didn't exist. Then one day they just . . . stopped. Skeptics turned into believers one fateful dawn. And no one was ever safe again.

No one knows why they made themselves known. Why they chose a Valentine's Day in the early twenty-first century to reveal their presence. Some say it had something to do with the end of the world. Others that they simply grew tired of hiding.

I was twelve when Solomon, the leader of the vampires, first appeared on TV and lied through his fangs to all of us. Thirteen when the war broke out. Fifteen when the United States declared a truce . . . when, in reality, we surrendered, and the nightmare really began.

Even after that, many of us couldn't bring ourselves to actually say the word "vampire." It was as if once we admitted it, then we'd have to believe in extraterrestrials or government conspiracies, too. Or in witches and werewolves . . . in anything and everything that could destroy us. Because we could be destroyed. We lost something so precious—our faith that eventually everything would be all right. Because it wasn't all right . . . and few believed it ever would be again.

So among those of us who swore not to abandon all hope, vampires came to be called the Cursed Ones. We learned that it was the name given to them long ago by those few groups who knew of their existence yet never shared the knowledge. But the vampires weren't the cursed ones—we were. They had seduced us with their hypnotic smiles and talk of peaceful coexistence and immortality even as they had mounted a war against us. Then they sought to turn us into their slaves, and drink from rivers of our blood.

I'm nearly eighteen now, and I have learned something about myself I might never have known, if I'd been able to live an ordinary life.

But there is nothing ordinary about my life.

Nothing.

Including me.

—*from the diary of Jenn Leitner,*
discovered in the ashes

THE VILLAGE OF CUEVAS, SPAIN
TEAM SALAMANCA: JENN AND ANTONIO, SKYE AND HOLGAR, AND ERIKO AND JAMIE

Barely sunset, and death exploded all around Jenn Leitner.

It was a trap, she thought.

The sky crackled with flames; oily smoke choked the air and burned her lungs. Jenn struggled not to cough, fearing that the sound would expose her. On her elbows and knees, her dark auburn hair loose and falling into her eyes, she crawled from beneath the red-tiled roof of the medieval church as it collapsed in a crash of orange sparks. Fragments of tile, stone, and burning wood ricocheted toward the blood-colored moon, plummeting back down to the earth like bombs. She dug in her elbows and pushed forward with the toes of her boots, grunting as a large, fiery chunk of wood landed on her back with a sizzle. She fought to stay silent as the pain seared through her. Biting her lip hard, she tasted coppery blood as she rolled to extinguish the flames.

Next to her, Antonio de la Cruz hissed a warning. The scent of her blood would fill the night air, attracting the vampires they'd been sent to hunt—but who were hunting them instead. When Jenn was little, her grandmother had told her that sharks could smell a drop of blood in the water half a mile away. She hadn't gone in the ocean since. Cursed Ones could smell blood more than a mile away. With sharks you could choose to stay out of the water. With Cursed Ones it was different. You couldn't leave the planet. You were trapped.

Like we are now.

Antonio studied her with his deep-set Spanish eyes. Jenn gave her head a shake to let him know she was all right; she could keep going. She had no time to search through her jacket for the garlic-infused salve that would block the odor of her blood. She prayed that the stench of the burning buildings—and burning bodies—would cloak the scent long enough to allow them to escape.

Past the church grounds the oak trees were on fire, acorns popping, leaves igniting like tattered tissue paper. Smoke filled the inky night sky, smothering the faint glow of the moon, but the hellish light from the fires illuminated Jenn's and Antonio's every move. Combine that with her bleeding lip, and they were two very easy targets for the savage monsters bent on massacring the village.

Antonio stopped suddenly and held up a warning hand. She watched him closely. Wisps of his wild dark hair escaped from his knitted cap; his full eyebrows were raised slightly, and his jaw was clenched. Like her he was dressed all in black—black sweater, black cargo pants, black knee protectors, and black leather boots—and now coated with ash. She could see the glint of the small ruby-studded cross that he wore in his left ear. A gift, he had said, when she'd asked about it. His face had darkened when he'd answered her, and she knew there was more to that story. So much of Antonio was a mystery to her, as intriguing as the sharp planes and hollows of his face.

He was focused, listening. All Jenn could hear were the flames and the terrorized, outraged cries of the villagers from the surrounding houses and office buildings. Her world became Antonio's face and Antonio's hand, blotched with soot, and she tensed her muscles so she'd be ready to move again when his hand dropped. She wished she could stop shaking. Wished she would stop bleeding and hurting. Wished someone else could do the rescuing, instead of them.

But somewhere in the darkness the Cursed Ones were watching. She imagined them staring at her, and could almost hear their cruel laughter dancing in the acrid air.

Three vampires and six hunters stalked one another through the steamy inferno. *If the other hunters are still alive. If they escaped the burning church.*

Don't think about that now. Don't think at all. Wait. Watch.

Cuevas, a small Spanish town a couple of hours from their home, had been terrorized by a group of vampires for weeks, and their mayor had begged for help. Jenn was one of a group of trained vampire hunters called the Salamancans, graduates of the Academia Sagrado Corazón Contra los Malditos—Sacred Heart Academy Against the Cursed Ones—at the centuries-old University of Salamanca. Father Juan, their master, had sent them to Cuevas to rid it of the Cursed Ones.

Instead the vampires were hunting the hunters, as if they had known they were coming, as if they had lured them there. Jenn wondered how they'd known. Father Juan always sent the team out covertly. Was there a spy at the university? Had someone in Cuevas betrayed them?

Or is the Hunter's Manual right about all *vampires?*

Don't think.

Late that afternoon Jenn, Antonio, and the other hunters had parked in the woods and silently made their way to the church, where they waited, meditating or praying, and preparing for the battle ahead. The vampires appeared with the flat shadows of dusk, and in the literal blink of an eye — they moved faster than most people could see — they set fire to the stone ruins of the *castillo*, the brick-and-mortar shops of the nearby plaza, and the glass and steel of a handful of modern office buildings. Flower boxes lining the plaza, which had brimmed with pink and white geraniums, crackled like sparklers; windows shattered; car horns blared like Klaxons; and everywhere, everywhere, fires roared.

In their short two months' hunting together as a team, the Salamancans had fought greater numbers — once there had been as many as eleven — but those Cursed Ones had been newly converted. The younger the bloodsucker, the easier to defeat, as they would not have fully adapted to their new abilities . . . or their weaknesses.

Against older vampires, like the three lurking in the darkness, you could only hope they hadn't yet run up against

8

a hunter. That they would have grown so used to slaughtering the helpless that they would underestimate those who knew how to fight back.

But the Cuevas C.O.'s had struck first, which meant they knew what the six hunters were capable of. By the time Jenn and the other Salamancans had smelled smoke, there had only been time to rouse Antonio from his meditations in the chapel behind the altar and crawl outside.

Now they were exposed and vulnerable. And—

Jenn blinked. Antonio was no longer beside her. Panic wrapped around her heart, and she froze, unsure of what to do. Directly in front of her an oak tree shuddered inside its thick coat of fire, and a huge limb snapped off, cascading into the dirt with a *fwom*.

He left me here, she thought. *Oh, God.*

Breathe, she reminded herself, but as she inhaled, smoke filled her lungs, and she pressed her hand over her mouth. Her balance gave way, and she collapsed onto the dirt. Jenn grunted back a hacking cough. The welt on her back burned like a bull's-eye; she was a prime target. And alone.

Where are you, Antonio? she silently demanded. *How could you leave me?*

Tears welled. Jenn gave her head a hard shake. She had to hustle. If she didn't move, she would die a horrible death. She had seen vampires kill people. But he wouldn't let that happen to her. Would he?

Don't think. Just move.

Jenn's fingernails dug into the dirt as she lifted herself up. Commando-style she worked her way forward, scrambling to the left when another large oak branch cracked and fell toward her like a flaming spear. She had to get away from the collapsing buildings and the falling trees before she could think about going on the offensive.

There was a whisper of sound, a *shushshushshush*, and Jenn rolled farther to her left just as a vampire landed on his back beside her. His pale blue eyes were opened wide in a death mask, and his breath reeked of rotting blood. She thought he groaned a word, maybe a name.

Then all at once the vampire collapsed into dust and was scattered by the hot winds. *One down,* she thought, covering her mouth and nose to avoid inhaling any of the vampire's remains. The first time Jenn had seen that happen, she'd been unable to speak for over an hour. Now she couldn't help the triumphant smile that spread across her face.

Jenn struggled to her feet; Antonio stood a breath away, his eyes blazing, the stake that had killed the vampire still clenched in his hand. He towered over her, six feet to her five-five. As she reached out to touch his arm, a blood-curdling scream ripped through the night air, and she took off in its direction, expecting Antonio to do the same.

Instead his body hurtled past her, landing in a pile of burning branches and leaves.

"Antonio!" she screamed, then wheeled around in a fighter's stance, facing off against the vampire who had tossed him through the air like one might toss loose change onto a counter. The Cursed One was tall and bulky, grinning so that his fangs gleamed in the firelight. His face was covered in blood. Her stomach lurched, and she tried not to think about how many of the villagers were already dead.

Jenn swiftly grabbed a stake from the quiver on her belt, gripping it in her right hand, and ripped open a Velcro pocket with her left to retrieve a cross. She desperately wanted to look back at Antonio. She dared not.

The vampire sneered at her and snarled in a thick Leonese-Spanish accent, "*Pobrecita*, I can hear the frightened beating of your heart. Just like the rabbit in the trap."

He slashed her across the cheek with his talonlike nails before leaping back in a dizzying blur. Jenn felt the blood running hot and sticky down her cheek before she felt the sting.

Jenn circled him warily. *I'm a hunter,* she reminded herself, but the hand around her stake was shaking badly. Surely he could see it. If he attacked, there was a good chance she wouldn't be quick enough. The specialized training she had received at the academy had taught her how to anticipate a vampire's moves even when she couldn't see them. They moved so fast, the Cursed Ones. Father Juan said that they moved faster than man could sin. He said they could kill you and you would never know it had happened, but if you had been a brave and just person, the angels would tell you all about it, in song.

I'm not brave.

She took a deep breath and turned her head slightly to the side. Her best bet at tracking him was not to look directly at him. Movement was most effectively caught out of the corner of one's eyes. She had learned that at the academy, and it had saved her before. Maybe it would again.

But maybe not.

The vampire stayed visible, stalling, but more likely toying with her before he made his kill. Some vampires were matadors, drawing out the death dance like a ritual. For others the hunt was a means to an end—fresh human blood, pumped by a still-beating heart.

Movement in the shadows caught her eyes. Jenn fought not to react as one of the other hunters—*the* Hunter, Eriko Sakamoto—crept toward the vampire, her tiny frame belying her superior strength. Dressed in night hues like Jenn and Antonio, she wore a turtleneck, leather pants, and thick-soled boots that Velcroed halfway up her calves. Her short, gelled hair made her look like a tribal warrior. Fresh streaks of soot were smeared on her high, golden cheekbones.

The sound of the fires masked any noise from her approach. Eriko caught Jenn's eye, and Jenn began to edge to the right, placing the vampire between them.

"Hunters . . . *jóvenes* . . . you're nothing special after all," the Cursed One snarled.

"We're special enough to turn you to dust," Jenn growled, trying to hold the vampire's attention. She focused on his fangs instead of his eyes, so as not to be mesmerized by him. That was one of the first rules of survival—to resist the Cursed Ones' hypnotic gaze, designed to put their prey in thrall. "You'd better say your prayers. You're about to die."

The vampire scoffed, weaving closer, seemingly unaware that a hunter advanced behind him with her stake poised. The smell of Jenn's blood cloaked the subtler scent of unharmed human flesh.

"Prayer is for mortals," he said, "who must beg some deity to save them. And as we know, those prayers always go unanswered."

"Always?" Jenn asked, feeling the blood oozing down her cheek. The vampire stared at it as if he hadn't drunk in centuries.

"Always," he replied.

Eriko kept her distance, and Jenn had a terrible thought: *She's using me as bait.* Jenn began to back away, and the vampire made a show of taking a step toward her. Her hands were slick with sweat—from the heat, from her fear—and her grip on the stake began to slip. She worked her fingers around it. The vampire snickered.

Jenn took another step backward, her boot crunching

down on something. Her stomach lurched as sparks flew upward. What if it was Antonio?

She couldn't stop herself from glancing down. It was only a branch. The vampire launched himself at her with a hiss.

"No!" Jenn shrieked, falling backward.

The vampire landed on top of her, his eyes filled with bloodlust. His fangs were long and curved; she flailed, forgetting all her training, every maneuver that could save her. His breath stank of fresh blood, and she heard herself whimper.

Antonio.

Then, suddenly, the Cursed One was gone. Jenn pulled herself into a crouch, aware that she'd lost her cross. Eriko had yanked the vampire to his feet and was on his back, legs wrapped around his waist. He batted at her as she laced her fingers underneath his chin, forcing back his head. He hissed and grabbed her ankles, trying to peel her off him.

"Jenn, stake him," Eriko shouted. "Now!"

Jenn blinked. She took two steps forward, and then she stopped for a fraction of an instant. Just stopped.

She could no longer see Eriko or the vampire. They were moving too fast for her to track. She lunged forward, stabbing at the air. There was no contact. She caught flashes, blurs, but not enough to give her a target. Through her exhaustion Jenn kept swinging, as her mind raced. If Eriko died, it would be on Jenn's head.

Then she saw them. The vampire had been forced to his knees, and Eriko stood behind him, her hands still laced beneath his chin. Jenn ran to stake him as Eriko flashed her a fierce smile and twisted off his head. His headless body held its shape; Eriko threw the head into the advancing flames. It was something Jenn could never have done; she didn't have Eriko's superhuman strength.

"At least someone's prayers were answered," Eriko said, panting, as the body disintegrated. She trotted toward a crumbling stone wall to their left, which marked the north end of the church's cemetery. "Let's keep moving."

Jenn looked back to where she had last seen Antonio, but he wasn't there. Another surge of panic washed over her as she raced toward the spot. He was simply *gone*. He wouldn't have just abandoned them, though; he couldn't have *left*.

"Antonio!" Jenn screamed. "Wait, Eriko. Antonio!"

"*Sí,*" he called. "*Sí,* Jenn."

Antonio pushed through the burning brush a few yards away, wisps of smoke curling from his charred clothes as he batted at them. His hands were blackened and peeling.

She ran to him and then stood hesitantly in front of him, frightened and ashamed of her doubts. "Are you okay?" she asked.

He nodded grimly. "I will be."

She began to shake. "I was worried. I thought . . ." She trailed off. It didn't matter what she had thought. All that mattered was that he was alive and there.

15

"You didn't think I would leave you?" Antonio questioned, his gaze intense as he reached out to cup her cheek with his hand. "I was coming to help you and Eriko." Then his soft expression flickered, and she saw his despair. He hid it well . . . though not well enough, at least for someone so focused on him as she was. The shadow in his eyes spoke of something he had refused to share with her—his deepest wound.

His darkest secret.

Tears stung her eyes. Jenn loved Antonio, and she wanted to trust him. But trust was something she'd left behind two years ago when she'd crossed the threshold of the university. She'd had to learn not to trust her eyes, her mind, or even her heart. Every time she forgot that, she nearly got herself killed.

"*Ay, no,*" Antonio whispered, gazing at her. "I would never leave you."

Antonio stroked her cheek with his thumb, and she closed her eyes, leaning into the touch. Calloused, velvet. When his lips brushed hers, she returned the kiss with a sob. She threw her arms around his neck and clung to him. His lips were soft and yielding against hers, and the taste of him mixed with the faint metallic flavor of the blood in her mouth.

Leaning against Antonio, she whimpered, wanting more. Then, suddenly, he *was* gone.

Jenn opened her eyes and saw Antonio hunched over

a few feet away, eyes glowing and fangs protruding. Eriko strode up beside Jenn, a thick stake clasped in her hand. One throw and she could kill him.

"Estoy bien," Antonio growled deep in his throat. He wiped something dark off of his lips and onto his black cargo pants.

Her blood.

"Eriko, I'm all right," he said in English.

His deep voice always made Jenn shiver, but with fear or desire she was never quite sure. Sometimes when they were kissing she would forget, just for a moment, all that kept them apart.

Antonio was a vampire.

She forced herself to take a good look: the gleaming teeth, the hungry, feral look that had crept into his eyes, the way the muscles in his face contorted as he tried to overcome his bloodlust. He didn't like her to see it, but she needed to. She needed to remember so that she could protect herself—and him.

Some vampires claimed to be able to control their cravings, but Antonio de la Cruz was the only one she had ever met who could actually manage it. Years of meditation, study, and prayer had given him the strength he needed. Or so he claimed.

But deep inside Jenn knew that every moment they spent together was eroding that strength. One day he wouldn't pull away, and then she would have to kill him. If she could. Or one of the other hunters would. Like Eriko. Or Jamie—

"Good," Eriko said. "One down." But she didn't lower the stake. Muscular and petite, Eriko was a couple of years younger and a couple of inches shorter than Jenn. When they had graduated from the academy two months before, Eriko had been chosen from their class to receive the sacred elixir that bequeathed astounding speed and strength. The elixir was so difficult to make, there was only enough for one Hunter, capital *H*. Their leader.

"Antonio killed one too," Jenn said.

Eriko raised a brow and glanced at Antonio, who nodded. His face was returning to normal. "There were only three, right? We're nearly done."

"Three's what we were told," Jenn said, relaxing only slightly. She pulled out her garlic salve and quickly applied it to her cheek and lip.

Eriko sighed and pressed the fingertips of her free hand against the spiky stubble of her hair. "The villagers might have miscounted. It wouldn't be the first time that happened."

Jenn swallowed hard. "I'm sorry, Eriko," she said. "I didn't back you up."

Eriko shrugged. "You don't have the power I do, Jenn. You did fine."

But Jenn knew she hadn't. She had panicked. She'd been more worried about Antonio than anyone else, including herself.

Eriko looked past her to Antonio. "Antonio, on the other hand . . ."

"He was burned," Jenn said, angry and defensive at the implication. "Look at his hands."

"Bloody hell, that was all arseways," a familiar voice fumed. Jenn turned as two figures approached. One was tall, with a nearly shaved head and heavy tattoos on his arms and neck, which made him look like a demon in the firelight. The turtleneck he had been wearing was gone, and only an undershirt remained. That was Jamie O'Leary.

For once the girl at his side didn't disagree. From her black battle clothes—padded jacket, leggings, thigh-high boots—to her white-blond Rasta braids, to the silver crescent-moon ring on her thumb, Skye York was covered with soot except where tears had cut paths down her pale cheeks.

Skye made circles in the air with her hand while muttering an incantation with the Latin refrain "*desino*." Cease. One by one the fires in her vicinity were extinguished.

"Cursers all dead?" Jamie asked, gazing around. He looked at Antonio. "The ones we're *allowed* to kill?" he added pointedly.

"There's one more," Eriko said. "I got one, Antonio got one, and that leaves—"

"None," Jamie interrupted. "I got one on my way out of the church." He showed them his singed palms. "Staked him through the back with a piece of burning timber. It was good and long and caught him in the heart."

19

"That's great; we're done, then," Eriko said, grinning at her fighting partner. Jamie grinned back, clearly relishing that both of them had managed kills. They hadn't been near each other when the church went up in flame, but they had still caused the most damage. Energy practically sizzled between the two. They did seem to belong together, somehow.

After fasting, praying, and working magicks, Father Juan had matched them into fighting pairs, insisting that each fulfilled some complicated balance of yin and yang, light and dark.

Strength and weakness.

Jenn was paired with Antonio, much to her relief. Eriko and Jamie were matched, and they pushed each other hard and themselves harder. Skye and Holgar were the third pair, and they had a quiet closeness with each other that was enviable.

Like Jenn, Jamie had no special gifts or powers. But his ferocity and the fighting skills drilled into him by his family during his childhood in Belfast more than made up for it.

Eriko seemed unaware of the way Jamie looked at her. . . . It went beyond a Hunter-hunter relationship. It must have been obvious to Skye, too, as she turned away to concentrate on her incantations. Their gothy witch carried a torch for Jamie, and Jamie had no clue. Jenn wasn't sure if the other team members knew, or if she was the only one who had figured it out. She felt both sorry for Skye and, frankly, bewildered, because Jamie was a jerk. He made no secret of his desire to be elsewhere; he didn't even believe that there should be a team of hunters. Jamie was only there because Father Juan had asked him to stay in Salamanca and serve the cause. If it hadn't been for his deeply ingrained loyalty to his church, Jenn was sure that even Jamie's attraction to Eriko wouldn't be enough to keep him from going home.

Finished with her incantation for the fires, Skye gently touched Jamie's palms, and his skin began to heal. Her delicate face nearly glowed as she infused him with her nurturing energy. Jamie sighed with pleasure but said nothing.

Skye turned next to Antonio. Moving into position while the sun was still up had weakened his system. He held out his hands, palms up, and Skye moved her hands over them and whispered in ancient Latin. Jenn felt herself relax slightly. She hated it when Antonio came close to fire. Fire was one of the few things that could kill a vampire. Vampires could also be killed by sunlight, a wooden stake through the heart, and decapitation.

"How many dead, *brujita*?" Antonio asked softly, calling Skye "little witch," as he flexed his fingers. "Villagers?"

Skye shook her head, her Rasta braids swaying down her back. "At least fifty. When the fires started, the vampires killed the first few people who tried to escape the burning buildings. The rest were so afraid . . ." Her voice broke.

"Some of them stayed inside their homes and burned to death," Jenn bitterly finished for her, sick knots twisting her stomach. "Then we failed."

Eriko shook her head. "No one would be alive if we hadn't come."

"And about that," Jamie said, spitting into the dirt. "How the bloody hell did they know—"

"Where's Holgar?" Skye asked, glancing around for her fighting partner.

"Fried, extra crispy if we're lucky," Jamie muttered.

"Sorry to say it, Irish, but my ears weren't burned off," Holgar quipped, limping toward the group. His clothes hung in tatters from his body. Gaping wounds on his chest and legs had already begun to scab over. Holgar's hands were bloodied, though whether it was his or someone else's, Jenn couldn't tell.

Jamie swore under his breath, but Jenn only could make out ". . . bloody werewolf."

Jamie made no secret of the fact that there was one thing he hated even more than Cursed Ones: werewolves. The world at large had not been forced to accept the existence of humans who transformed into beasts at the full moon, but Jamie's people in Ireland had witnessed their savagery firsthand. As far as he was concerned, vampires were the enemy, and werewolves were their treacherous accomplices. When the vampires had revealed themselves to humanity, the werewolves had elected to remain hidden, passing as ordinary humans. There were few enough of them that they could pull it off, and they kept their numbers low by bearing few pups. They allied themselves with the vampires, who kept their secret in return. It was an evil bargain, and as far as Jamie was concerned, proved why they should be wiped out. They had destroyed the world, and for that they should be erased from existence. No exceptions, no mercy. Both Holgar and Antonio watched their backs around him, and Jenn wished Father Juan would release Jamie from his promise to remain with the team. When you were fighting for your life, you had to know that everyone on your side would come to your rescue.

Of course, no one can count on me, either. Jenn swallowed hard as the shame gnawed at her.

"Father Juan wanted us to check in as soon as we were done," Skye reminded the group.

"Yeah, to see if we survived this bloody trap," Jamie said. He narrowed his eyes. "Oh, come on now. You're all thinking the same thing. Someone told the C.O.'s we were coming. We were ambushed." He looked directly at Antonio. Antonio raised his chin and stared back stonily. The tension was as thick as the smoke had been earlier.

"Father Juan," Eriko said into her cell phone. "*Hai.* We're all fine. *Hai, hai.*" Jenn knew Eriko was tired. She was lapsing into Japanese and bowing her head with each syllable.

Jamie shifted his glare from Antonio to Holgar, and then to her. Jenn knew he didn't like her, either. Loathed her, more accurately. Because of Antonio. And for that Jamie had to watch *his* back, at least around Jenn's fighting partner.

"What happened to you?" Jenn asked Holgar. She noticed Antonio had moved a few steps away and was covering his mouth with his hand. The smell of blood on Holgar was great.

"Vampire. It was a bad time of it, but I finally got a stake through him."

"Feckin' hell," Jamie swore.

"Excuse me?" Holgar asked, clearly puzzled by Jamie's reaction.

"That makes four, not three," Antonio said quietly.

Instantly they were all on alert. Jenn yanked another stake from the quiver at her belt and spun to face the darkness. She fished in a pocket for another cross. They always carried multiples of each weapon. "Do you think there are any more?" she whispered.

There was a moment of silence, broken only by Eriko's occasional reply to their master as she continued to relay information.

"Only vampire I can smell is ours," Holgar said after a minute.

"I don't hear anything," Antonio added.

Skye cast a short seeing spell. "I think there were only four," she confirmed.

They all relaxed slightly. Antonio stooped down and picked up a charred piece of wood that had been part of the church. He drove it into the ground as though driving a stake into the heart of the earth itself. From a pocket of his cargo pants he drew a pennant. The thick white silk was emblazoned with a red cross consisting of four curved arms of equal length—the cross of the original Crusaders. A blue knight's helmet crowned with three white feathers—the color for the Virgin, the feathers to honor the Trinity—perched on the top arm of the Cross. Below, the word "Salamanca" was stitched in a font reminiscent of Spain's Moorish roots. It was the ancient crest of the Salamanca Hunter. The hunters wore matching patches on their left shoulders, which could be covered over with Velcro flaps.

"This town is under our protection," Antonio announced as he fastened the flag to the stake. "The hunters of Salamanca." Then he stepped back and made the sign of the cross over the pennant and then himself. It was a strange and miraculous thing that Antonio could do so, given that crosses made other vampires burn. As the only other practicing Catholic in the group, Jamie gritted his teeth, then did the same. As a White Witch, Skye was nominally Wiccan, and Eriko was Buddhist. Jenn's roots were Bavarian, and her family had long ago stopped thinking of themselves as Catholic. They weren't anything. As for Holgar, she had no clue what he believed. The rest of them bowed their heads briefly in respect of the flag.

Team Salamanca, victorious. But as Jenn stared at the flag, she thought of all the dead and dying in Cuevas and couldn't help but wonder how she could protect anyone else when she couldn't even protect herself or her teammates.

A breeze picked up, and the flag fluttered defiantly, a symbol of all that had been fought for and lost—the hunters who had gone before and those who would come after. *God help us all,* Jenn thought.

CHAPTER TWO

Lost and searching
Cursed and undying
A race in need
The vampire breed
Let us show kindness
Offer respectful silence
And give each heart
As our perfect part

CUEVAS
TEAM SALAMANCA

Jenn felt a mixture of pride and shame as she stared at the makeshift flag planted in the bloodied soil. Aware of a gaze on her, she glanced up. Antonio's eyes blazed with intensity, zeal for the mission of the team. He never wavered, and she loved him and envied him for it.

"Is it wise to leave a calling card like that?" Skye asked nervously, breaking the silence. Their presence at the university was a secret—though not well kept, as many of the locals had started to request their assistance. The Spanish government knew of their existence but did not openly acknowledge them, explaining away the activity at the University of Salamanca as a small garrison of mixed Spanish military forces. In a way that was true. Three of their teachers were Spanish military officers. The three taught many of the combat classes; one of them, Felipe Santasiero, had also been Jenn's Spanish tutor.

As for the real Spanish armed forces, those who knew the truth resented the Salamancans, calling them *las pulgas* — the fleas. General Maldonaldo of the Spanish army feared them. A conservative man, he knew the Salamancans used magicks . . . and magicks, he believed, were the work of the Devil. The Devil was alive in all the bloodshed and mayhem; General Maldonaldo did not wish *el diablo* to drink any more Spanish blood. He would never have accepted that Father Juan shared that wish.

Jenn shifted her weight as she looked at the pennant. Her back was throbbing. "If planting our flag in the dust of dead Cursed Ones makes the C.O.'s even a little bit afraid of us, I'm all for it."

"Unless it's a code," Jamie said. "Like, 'Got the memo, thanks. Still not dead.'"

"Jamie, *please*. He's one of us." Skye glanced over at Antonio. "I've thrown the runes. We can trust him."

"Most vampires stink, and Antonio doesn't," Holgar said in his Danish accent, making as if to sniff the air. "Besides, he saved my life." He looked at Jamie. "Yours, too. Last time we were out. That is, how you say in English, 'sweet.' And sweeter for you, Jamie, since your life means so much to you."

"Down, boy," Skye murmured, placing a hand on Holgar's forearm. "We're all on edge. But it does seem like they were expecting us."

"Cast magicks when you get back," Eriko suggested. "You and Father Juan together. Perhaps you can scry the source of a leak. We may simply have been unlucky."

"Born under a bad star," Jamie said. He grimaced at Holgar. "Or a bad full moon."

Holgar sighed. "It's not wise to *bait* a werewolf."

Jamie showed his teeth, then spat in the ashes. "Fine. You know I'd love to *rabbit* on, but I'm jacked."

Skye pursed her lips, and Eriko nodded. Jenn was at a loss. Two years at the academy and two months as team-mates, and Jenn still couldn't keep up with a lot of what Jamie said. It was bad enough that Skye had a thick Cockney accent, Antonio liberally laced his English with Spanish, Eriko swore in Japanese, and Holgar had a tendency to talk to himself in a series of growls, howls, and yips that only a dog, or another werewolf, could understand. With Jamie it was somehow worse. She understood the words he used but couldn't even begin to fathom half their meanings.

"He wants to go," Skye said, by way of translation. "He's tired. We all are." Skye the peacemaker.

Tacitly agreeing to drop their hostilities, the six fanned out, walking in a circular formation in the event that there were more vampires. Skye had put out the fires in the houses visible from the plaza area. Slowly, people began to congregate, some emerging from the forest where they had sought refuge. When they saw the hunters, they broke into a chorus of cheers. Men in jeans and business suits, girls Jenn's age all fashion-forward and trendy. A guy in a *Hellboy* T-shirt held up his cell phone, filming them.

"Bloody hell," Jamie said. "They'll be wanting us to pose and sign autographs."

"We should do it," Skye said. "You know there's a lot of hunter haters out there."

"That's in America, not Spain," Holgar insisted.

"I need a smoke," Jamie said.

"Antonio, you should get out of here," Eriko cautioned. So far no civilians had ever discovered Antonio was a vampire—most of the time you couldn't tell just by looking at him—but there was no reason to take unnecessary chances. The smell of blood from something as small as a paper cut could bring on the bloodlust, which would make his fangs grow and his eyes flash red.

"I'll be at the van," Antonio said, turning to go.

Jenn trotted up beside him, and his sharp features softened. He took her hand and squeezed it, not too hard. He could have shattered every bone if he wanted to. He was even stronger than Eriko.

Behind them the cheers grew louder. The survivors were rejoicing. Soon they would grow more sober, as some of their wounded joined the ranks of their dead. Jenn had seen it before. It would be worse this time; so much of the town had been burned. It would take a long time to rebuild. She felt guilty at her relief that she wouldn't have to help clean up and help them start over. She didn't know anything about creating, but thanks to the academy she knew a lot about destroying.

"I'm glad you're not hurt," Jenn told him, trying to shut out the sounds of cheers that were growing in strength behind them. "When I saw you land in those flames—"

"Jamie's right," he interrupted her, the red glow of bloodlust back in his eyes. A thrill skittered up her spine. His fangs were beginning to lengthen.

"He's right to mistrust me," he went on. "And he's right to think there is a traitor among us, or a spy at the Academia. Someone told those vampires we were coming. We were *very* lucky none of us were killed."

"Well, none of us were," she reminded him, swallowing hard.

"Not *yet*," he replied, his voice rough and deep. And his eyes glowed full on at her beneath the glistening silver rays of the Spanish moon.

She lowered her gaze and trudged to their white

Mercedes-Benz Vito van. Skye's protective spells had kept the van hidden from strangers and untouched by fire. The oak grove it was parked in, on the other hand, had been half consumed, and much of the smoldering remains would be nothing but ash by dawn.

Antonio slid behind the wheel, and a couple of minutes later when the others joined them, Jenn found herself wedged between Holgar and him. *It's like those old horror movies I used to watch with Papa Che when I was little: werewolves and vampires,* she thought, and instantly felt very silly and even more guilty.

In the backseat Jamie lounged between Eriko and Skye, and he was snoring loudly before they were back on the road.

"Can't you do anything about that?" Antonio asked through gritted teeth. His hearing was sharper than theirs, which made him a great lookout.

And could make him an even better traitor. . . .

Skye muttered a spell, and silence descended. Jamie was still snoring; they just couldn't hear it anymore. Then the witch did some work on Jenn's back and mercifully took away the pain. Jenn wearily closed her eyes, bone tired, yet as wired as if she had drunk twenty cups of the thick Torrefacto-roasted Spanish coffee she'd become addicted to. She wished she had some now to wash down the dust and soot and blood that coated her tongue and mouth. Even more than that she wished that she could sleep like Jamie.

Jamie was the only one who was able to sleep through

sheer force of will. He said it was good to rest at every opportunity, because you never knew when and where violence would erupt—something he had learned from his IRA family in Northern Ireland. His parents were dead, savaged a few years before by local Belfast werewolves who were working with the Cursed Ones—who, Jamie claimed, were working with the English. The older hatreds were still there; so were the warriors fighting for the cause of a united Ireland free of English rule. Though Jamie wanted to, the group never went after werewolves, only vampires.

Jamie had mad fighting skills, but just like the rest of them, he'd still had to train hard to become a hunter. Modern weaponry was forbidden, mostly because it was ineffective against a vampire. To kill one of them you had to move in close and risk your life. Jamie had been training with his grandfather to be a gunsmith before he left to study at the academy. The only thing the Salamancans were likely to kill with a gun was each other. Given the tension between team members, fear gnawed inside her that someday it might actually come down to that.

"Gracias, brujita," Antonio said to Skye as Jenn sighed and moved her shoulders, indicating that Skye's magicks had soothed her burns. Thank you, little witch. Skye liked it when he called her that. Skye had sensed magickal power emanating from Father Juan, so she had told him that she was a witch. A White Witch, in fact, one of many White Witches who considered themselves Wiccan followers of the

Goddess. There were Dark Witches, too, called warlocks by some, who followed the God in his many evil aspects and practiced dark magicks. Both branches of Witchery tried to stay off the radar of the common people, and White Witchery had gone underground, fearing the vampires would exploit them as they had the werewolves and force them to become allies. Some vampires sought out witches to use as weapons; others wanted to wipe them out because witches could detect the presence of vampires. Skye was the only witch at the academy, and at first she had tried to hide her magickal skills from the others. White Witches were healers, not fighters. And so she was an anomaly.

But Antonio had welcomed her. And had explained his belief that fighting was a form of healing—just as weeping was a form of prayer.

She liked the way he thought, and she was fascinated by his ardent belief in his Catholic religion. His devotion to the Virgin Mary was like her devotion to the Goddess. He believed many things that she didn't, such as the concept of sin and the necessity of salvation—but the purity and simplicity of his faith charmed her. Skye liked that. She liked *him*. She had assured Jenn over and over that Antonio really was a man—a vampire—they could trust. Every spell she had cast to judge him had shown that. But maybe vampires could manipulate the magickal forces of the universe—just as they had manipulated the human race. *We want to live in peace. We want to be your friends. We drink the blood of animals.*

The road twisted and turned through the Spanish countryside, trees and brush weaving shadows in the high beams of the van. Unlike Jenn's home in California, there were no streetlights, just incredible, inky darkness. Antonio could see better than anyone else in the van, but even he had his limits. She glanced at him nervously, but he kept his eyes straight ahead.

Beside Jenn, Holgar licked his wounds. She tried not to grimace, but it was disgusting. Holgar's body healed itself much faster than a human's could, and he often helped it along by cleansing his injuries as his wild brethren did. She knew it even made Antonio a little sick, and he had had a lot longer — over sixty years — to become accustomed to such things.

In the backseat Eriko and Skye were talking quietly. Both of them were upset about how many villagers they had lost, and they were puzzling over the apparent ambush. Jenn was upset too, but her mind was occupied with other worries.

She had hesitated. She hadn't been up to the fight. She didn't belong. She knew it. There were six in their team, six Salamancan hunters. Of those six, four had superhuman abilities.

Holgar's wolf nature had been revealed during their first semester of training when, though locked away by Father Juan, his raging howls had pierced the night of a particularly bright full moon. Plus, one day he'd forgotten and licked his wounds after a training drill.

The students had learned of Skye's witch nature soon

after that, as if no one saw any point in trying to hide just how much of the supernatural was present in their currently unnatural world.

Jenn had braced herself for even more shocking revelations . . . but even with that, she hadn't been prepared for the most stunning disclosure of all:

Antonio.

No one had known about Antonio until the night of graduation, when he was paired with Jenn to go on a vampire hunt—their final exam. By then, her crush on him had transformed into a deep longing. Her sense of betrayal was enormous when she'd found out that he was, in essence, the same kind of monster she had sworn to kill. Everything she had learned about vampires in her classes, from her teachers, and in the Hunter's Manual, insisted that all vampires were evil. Cursed Ones, who must never be shown mercy. And then to discover that the guy she wanted was so very, very much the wrong guy for her—or for anyone with a beating heart, and a soul . . .

But then to learn that he'd been studying to become a priest before he had been "converted," as it was called, and that even if he'd still been human, he would be off-limits to her . . .

Don't brood. You're tired. You do this when you're exhausted. It was like her mini-vacation into despair. Like hitting her head against a wall because it felt so good when she stopped.

The last supernatural member of the cohort was Eriko.

As the Hunter, Eriko had the incredible power born from drinking the elixir.

The last two members of the team, she and Jamie, were ordinary humans. With the exception of Antonio, Jamie had more combat experience than all of them combined. The Irish hothead was a vicious street fighter, and he had a gift for strategy—where to strike to cause the most damage and confusion. That was why, Jenn suspected, no one pushed to get him thrown off the team. Jamie did nothing but quarrel, argue, and accuse, but they needed him.

So that left her. Just Jenn. That was how she thought of herself—nothing special. She brought nothing distinctive to the group—no street smarts, no extraordinary abilities, and even her Spanish was the weakest. More than once she had thought that for the good of all she should leave. Every time, though, Father Juan had stopped her. Secretly, she was grateful. A lone hunter was an easy target and an easy kill. Even if she survived her first night alone, where would she go?

It was a crazy, mismatched group, but these were crazy times.

Jenn had applied for entrance into the academy as soon as she had heard there was a special school that trained people—young people—to fight vampires. Such schools had apparently been in existence for centuries, but they had fulfilled a different purpose—to train one Hunter to battle the vampires in each local town or region. In her History of Vampirism class, Jenn had learned that during the Dark

Ages many of these schools had been lost, and even the academies themselves had lost track of each other until each thought it was alone. Each surviving academy continued to train single Hunters, often regarded as a knight or a saint or both, who would protect his—or her—small territory. The Hunter of Salamanca had protected the university, the town, and the nearby villages.

Then the vampires had revealed themselves to humanity. Their spokesperson, Solomon—young and rock-star hot, with red hair like Jenn's—had stood beside the president of the United States and offered his hand in friendship. Solomon hinted that the vampires had access to the secret of their own immortality, and that they would share it if they were treated as "global partners."

"As equals," Solomon declared.

And the United States president—old, gray, tired-looking—had taken Solomon's hand. Celebrities rushed to party with the vampires and to be photographed and interviewed with them. Talk shows booked vampires to boost their ratings. Movie stars married them. Politicians and corporations courted them. It had all happened so fast. It had all been so exciting.

Solomon was so charming, affable, and *funny*. Jenn's girlfriends at school had hung his picture in their lockers and used it as wallpaper on their laptops. Vampire avatars and icons sprung up all over social networking sites. Vampires were completely, totally cool.

Then Nina, the president's teenage daughter, was kidnapped. The search for her was intense, and Solomon and the vampires dedicated themselves to finding her . . . or so they claimed. People prayed, generals threatened, and the first lady wept and begged Nina's captors to release her daughter.

When Nina finally surfaced, her kidnappers showed her on live TV. She had been changed into a vampire. "Converted," in vampire jargon. The CIA joined forces with other intelligence groups to figure out where Nina was, and located her in a remote village near the Arctic Circle, where it was dark nearly all the time. The Marines went in, along with a camera crew, and people saw how savage vampires could be as they attacked the human liberators. Instead of handsome Solomon, whose followers drank blood from blood bags and butcher shops, these vampires ripped open the throats of armed soldiers. Blood gushed and sprayed.

Sergeant Mark Vandeven carried Nina to safety. As soon as he set her down, she attacked him. Corporal Alan Taliaferro staked her through the heart, and everyone who was watching saw what happened to vampires when they died.

Corporal Taliaferro was interviewed afterward. He was hollow-eyed and shaken.

"She was a monster," the marine was quoted as saying. "There was no girl there anymore, just a demon."

Solomon claimed a radical fringe group had converted her. He insisted that these "renegades" must have forced Nina to drink from one of them, a violation of all that most vampires held sacred. To decent vampires, sharing their blood with a human was a sacred act, and the human had to be willing.

"The mortal must *ask* to be converted," Solomon explained on national TV. "It's very much like the Christian notion of Holy Communion." Sensing how terrified many of his new allies had become, he went on to remind his viewers that a vampire bite couldn't convert a human; not one or two or even a dozen bites. A human had to drink the blood of one already reborn into immortality.

"Willingly," he'd added. "This was a senseless tragedy, and it had nothing to do with civilized vampires like us."

But too many people saw the marine's interview on YouTube—*monster, demon*; the haunted look in his eyes said even more than his words. A few weeks after the video went up, his body was found drained of blood, and slowly many came to realize that there were no decent vampires.

It was then that regular Americans began to call vampires "the Cursed Ones." It was once a phrase written in ancient, musty books safeguarded by a few aware elite, then passed on to people like Jenn—hunters who had dedicated themselves to destroying the Cursed Ones. The name caught on, becoming truncated—"C.O.'s," "Cursers"—and instead of being viewed as exotic newcomers, vampires were finally regarded as the enemy.

The United States declared war against the Cursed Ones and demanded that its allies around the world do the same. Many did. Some didn't. Governments didn't trust each other. Some took advantage of the chaos and declared war on their human enemies.

The U.S. president was assassinated.

Worldwide war broke out, horrible war. The Cursed Ones were impossibly fast and strong. Armies fell, both to Cursers and to other nations; special-ops forces were obliterated. Dozens of smaller cities and towns around the world were destroyed in the fighting. And when it had become obvious that humanity was going to lose, the new president of the United States—young, sexy, and ambitious—declared a truce with the vampires. Several other nations followed suit, with Spain being one of the holdouts.

But it was a truce without honor. And while many people chose to believe that it had all been a tragic mistake, others knew that the real war—the cold war—had only just begun.

In the back of the van Skye and Eriko had fallen silent. Holgar had finally stopped licking his wounds, and they bounced along the road in the darkness. Jenn fought the urge to ask Antonio how much farther until they were home at the university. It was like a family car trip from hell.

Her throat tightened at the thought. She couldn't help but wonder how her family was, back in Berkeley, California. There was still so much wrong between her parents and her. She remembered the sick feeling that had clenched her stomach, the sheer anger, when her father had come home from his new job, all excited, spouting pro-vampire propaganda as if he really believed it.

"Three vampires just joined our division," he told the family at the dinner table. "And they're really great guys. They're practically just like us."

"You can't believe that," she'd said. "They're not like us at all. They can't even work during the day."

"We have people working all kinds of hours," he'd replied defensively.

"They're *not* people," Jenn had countered.

And there'd been a fight—the first of many. Her mother would go pale. Her sister, Heather, would cry. And Jenn would push away from the dinner table and slam the door to her room—if her father didn't send her there first.

Then one night there'd been a crack in his façade. He'd blurted, "You're going to get us in trouble," and she knew then that *he* knew he was working with monsters. He was just pretending, so they could get by.

Jenn stormed off to her room so ashamed of him, and so afraid. She'd wept into her pillow and fantasized about running away. But where could she go?

Later, he'd knocked softly on her door, opening it before she could tell him to go away. He had looked small as he stood on the threshold. Helpless. Gazing at her, he had reached out a hand. She started to get up, thinking that they were going to be honest with each other. Finally.

"You have to behave," her father said, and his words were sharp. "You can't be like this. You're part of this family."

Then he'd shut the door. She'd stared after him, unable

to believe that her father could say something like that to her. He had been raised by parents who fought for what they believed in, literally. Her grandparents, who had fought the oppressors of the people before, distrusted the Cursed Ones, and Jenn didn't know how her father could just dismiss the evidence, pretend that everything was okay when it wasn't.

Word slowly spread about the covert vampire-hunter academies. A lot of the information was wrong. But Jenn listened hard, and figured out what was right. There was one school in the United States, in Portland, Oregon, and it was full. All the other countries with anti-vampire schools only accepted students who were native-born—except for the school in Spain. It was housed on the grounds of the University of Salamanca, one of the oldest universities of Europe. For centuries academic students had flocked to Salamanca for an education superior to all else in Europe.

Until the war against the Cursed Ones, only the Catholic Church had known of the existence of the Academia Sagrado Corazón Contra los Malditos. During the war the University of Salamanca itself had closed its doors, and they'd never opened again. But inside the vast complex of buildings both ancient and modern, the Sacred Heart Academy beckoned a new kind of student, and everyone who wanted to fight vampires was welcome—everyone who qualified, that is.

Jenn still wasn't sure how she had managed to get in— and less sure how she had pulled off graduating. Of the ninety students who had composed her cohort, only thirty had made it to graduation. The others had flunked out or been killed. Their final exam was held on New Year's Eve; their test, to wipe out a vampire nest made up of nine Cursed Ones. Of the thirty students, fifteen died that night.

That left fifteen waiting to find out who would be declared the Hunter of Salamanca. There had been a Hunter for centuries, who guarded the area around Salamanca, defending the city, the university, and nearby villages from attacks from *los Malditos*—the Cursed Ones. Through the centuries, Salamanca's Hunters had not had much to do. The near-constant religious purges of heretics and foreigners made it difficult for Cursed Ones to avoid scrutiny, so they left the area alone. Other parts of the world were not so lucky.

But now that the Cursed Ones were waging war on humanity, something had to change. Father Juan was able to distill only enough magickal essence to create one dose of the sacred elixir, said to make a human nearly as strong as a *Maldito*, and nearly as fast. This he gave to Eriko, whom he decreed was his chosen Hunter.

Then he broke with tradition and gave the Hunter a team of warriors to support her campaign against the ancient enemy—a team of five, who would be called "hunters" with a lowercase *h*. The world at large was only beginning to find out about these venerable fighters and didn't understand the difference between *the* Hunter and *a* hunter.

But for the five chosen to back Eriko, there was a huge difference. The other nine would remain at the school if they wished, helping to train the new class of ninety.

When Jamie realized he hadn't been selected as the Hunter, he had exploded with fury. Skye had paled, frightened, as well she might be—she was being ordered to fight vampires without benefit of the elixir. Holgar had appeared to take the news in stride, declaring that with or without the elixir, he was glad for the chance to "rip some fangboys apart."

As a vampire, Antonio had not expected to be chosen as the Hunter, and Father Juan had already told him that he was assembling a team. Later, Antonio had told Jenn that he had asked to be her fighting partner so that he could watch her back.

As for Jenn herself, when Eriko had been picked, she had realized that she herself hadn't expected to be chosen — not really, not deep down. It was a blow. She had, in essence, lied to herself. She believed in the cause, but not in herself.

"There is a reason that you're here," Father Juan had told her. "Each of you has a path. Each of you is a light in these new Dark Ages. Some shine brighter now. For some, there must be a cooler wind first, and then . . ."

He had trailed off, and blessed her and the others, even though only two of them believed in Catholic blessings.

Then Father Juan had outfitted them and armed them, and their new lives had started. They were hunters.

She wished her father could have understood. What would he say if he could see her now, see the fighter she had become? Tears stung her eyes.

Not now, she thought, clenching her fists. She made herself think about the strong men in her life—her grandfather, whom she called Papa Che after his idol, the freedom fighter Che Guevara. Antonio.

Antonio, who was *not* a man.

"Jenn?" Antonio asked. She slid her glance at him, embarrassed because he could read her so easily. He could always tell when she was wrestling with some private problem.

She shrugged. "I'm fine," she said, which pretty much was code that she didn't want to share with everyone else.

"Bien," he said, indicating that he understood. But he kept glancing at her, his face illuminated by the dashboard lights. Sometimes she wondered if he was reading her mind, or her heart. Maybe vampires could do that. There was a lot about vampires people didn't know.

A lot about Antonio that Jenn didn't know. Except that, when he whispered her name, she believed he really loved her.

After a time her exhaustion and the warmth of the car heater lulled her to sleep. She dreamed about her family's trip to Big Sur, before the vampire war; about taking her sister's hand and strolling beside the rolling waves without going in the water.

There are sharks, her dream self told Heather.

"Jenn, we're home," Antonio murmured.

She jerked up her head as the van rolled through the wrought-iron gates of the university entrance. Statues of saints posed on high, arched walls. Crosses, mounted six years ago to keep out vampires, glittered in the moonlight. Behind the gingerbread plaster the new class was sleeping, or maybe cramming for exams in Beginning Leadership, Spanish, or Cold Reading, taught by Señor Sousi, who was the weirdest man Jenn had ever met. Jenn was supposed to help out with sparring in Beginning Krav Maga tomorrow, training the young students who could very well replace any or all of the members of her team . . . if the students themselves lived long enough.

Antonio parked in the space beside the chapel, and the others piled out. Father Juan, dressed in a priest's clerical suit and collar, walked down the steps toward them. The priest was trim with silvery strands woven through his blue-black hair.

"Hey, Father, I got a bone to pick with you," Jamie half shouted at Father Juan, but the priest walked past him. "They *knew* . . . hey!" Jamie yelled.

Holgar got out, leaving the door open for her. Jenn unfolded herself, frowning as Father Juan neared the van. Usually he would have met them inside the chapel, to bless them after their battle and lead them in prayer to give thanks for their safety. Instead he approached the open passenger door, face grim.

"*¿Padre?*" Antonio said, leaning in Jenn's direction.

"Jenn, I need to talk with you privately," Father Juan said somberly.

Jenn glanced at Antonio, who looked as puzzled as she did.

"What?" she asked nervously as she climbed out and followed Father Juan. Her mind raced. Had Eriko told him that Jenn had choked during their mission? Maybe he was going to tell her she was off the team because they couldn't depend on her. Or that Antonio *was* a traitor.

No. Never. That can't be it.

Near a large stone statue of St. John of the Cross, Father Juan stopped, turned, and put a hand on her shoulder. Jenn looked up into his dark brown eyes, and fear rippled through her.

"What's wrong?" she asked, her mouth suddenly dry.

Antonio stared at Jenn and Father Juan, tuning out Jamie's angry tirade and Skye's attempts to placate him, and focused on their conversation. He wasn't concerned with the niceties of things like privacy. He wouldn't allow what was rude and what wasn't to get in the way of doing his job.

Which was to destroy as many vampires as he could.

And to keep Jenn from getting hurt.

Though some nights he thought the biggest danger to her wasn't from the vampires she hunted but from him, the one she didn't. He had wanted her so badly when they'd been kissing back in Cuevas. The desire had flooded through him, filling him with an intense need to really taste her, feed off her, to drain her dry.

Just remembering made the thirst worse, and he felt the sharpness of his fangs pressing against his lower lip.

"I'm so sorry," Father Juan was saying to Jenn. "It's your grandfather. It was his heart, very sudden. Your grandmother is asking for you. Your family wants you home for the funeral."

Ah, no, Jenn, Antonio thought, crossing himself. He knew she adored her Papa Che. It was because of him that she had entered the Academia.

He saw Jenn's knees start to buckle, and he shot into motion. Father Juan reached out to support her, but Antonio beat him to it. She fell into his arms, and he gathered her up, easily.

"Mi amor," he whispered. My love. *"Ay, mi amor."*

She sobbed against him, and his heart ached for her.

And his fangs lengthened.

"Jenn should stay in California," Antonio said, as he and Father Juan sat at a wood table in a small tapas bar a few blocks from Madrid International Airport, having just put her on a plane. The floor was tiled in squares of black and white, like a chessboard. The vampire and the priest had passed many hours together playing chess and other games—war games, mind games.

Jazzy flamenco-flavored pop music bounced along Antonio's nerves. Two armed Spanish soldiers sat at a nearby table, glancing over at Antonio and Father Juan and muttering in low voices. They hadn't noticed that Antonio cast no reflection in the window framing Antonio and Father Juan's table, but when his vampiric hearing alerted him of their interest, he changed seats with the priest. It had been careless of him not to pay attention in the first place. He

49

knew he was distracted with his worries about Jenn.

The soldiers recognized from the embroidered patch on his jacket sleeve he was one of the Salamanca hunters. Teams of hunters were new, but the symbol of the Salamanca Hunter was ancient. Many in the military approved of the independent bands of vampire hunters scattered through-out the world. But others, like these two, feared the hunters' independence and wanted them to serve as a branch of the armed forces or be branded as renegades.

There were few other patrons at the bar; since the war and the "truce," people no longer ventured out at night if there was no pressing need. Spain had never signed the treaty; people's loyalties were questioned—to vampires, to mankind. As she always had, Spain harbored many secrets about faith and belief, complicity and honor. She stood as a beacon . . . or a bonfire.

The world is drowning in fear, Antonio thought. So was his world. For two years he had rarely let Jenn Leitner out of his sight. Until he had confessed how he felt, she hadn't known it, would never have guessed that he spent endless nights outside her window, keeping vigil, study-ing the shadows. Why Jenn? Why the California girl who doubted herself at every turn, insisted that she was noth-ing special? He didn't know how she had beamed light into the shadows of his soul. She *was* special. He knew it as fully as he knew that without her—as without blood—he would wither into dust.

And now she was flying back to the States. Thousands of

kilometers would part them for who knew how long. All while there was a traitor in their midst. What if Jenn was their target? What if she was doing exactly what they wanted, leaving the safety of Salamanca, and the safety of *him*?

What if she is the traitor? She has sympathy for one vampire, why not others?

Angry at himself for such doubt, Antonio shook his head as though the action alone could clear it of the unwelcome thoughts. Jenn cared for him despite what he was, not because of it. That was the truth he clung to every time he lost himself in her eyes. Still, there was a part of him that doubted. Continually.

"She should stay away," he insisted, more forcefully than he had meant to. Because he also knew that they weren't safe together. Not any longer. The more time they spent with each other, the more difficult he found it to control himself.

Father Juan raised an eyebrow, and Antonio dropped his gaze. Two small glasses of *sol y sombra* sat at Antonio's and Father Juan's elbows. Half brandy, half licorice-flavored anisette; Antonio sipped his out of companionship for the man across from him. Father Francisco, Juan's predecessor as master of the university chapel, had granted Antonio sanctuary half a century ago. Father Francisco had kept Antonio hidden, praying with him for release from the vampirism. When Father Juan had taken his place, he had brought Antonio back into the light of community. Father Juan had encouraged him to continue his theological studies. Another war, years earlier, had interrupted those studies — World War II.

Antonio had been "converted," as it was called, in a forest in 1941. He'd run with his sire for less than a year, until shame and horror sent him fleeing from the vampire's nest located in Madrid, and back into the arms of the Church.

It had almost seemed like a second chance, and the studies had helped him feel almost human. All that changed, though, when the university became a busy training ground for vampire Hunters. There had been five graduating classes at the academy, and each time Antonio had masqueraded as a student. When Father Juan and other masters around the world had decided to break with tradition and train groups of hunters to work together, Antonio had had his doubts. But when the hunter band was formed—Jenn's band—he had joined it, at Father Juan's request.

"She'll be back," Father Juan said. "She's one of us." He lifted his glass and turned to the soldiers at the other table. *"A la gente,"* he called to them. To the people.

The soldiers hoisted their glasses. *"A la gente."* The two looked tired, as well they should. It was exhausting to be on the losing side.

"I wish to God that she'd stay home," Antonio muttered.

Father Juan smiled sadly at him. "You're such a puzzle to me, my son. You're older than my grandfather, and yet parts of you are still very much nineteen."

"She's nearly eighteen," Antonio said. "Too young for this."

"You've fought alongside eighteen-year-olds before," Father Juan countered. "In that other war."

"And they died," Antonio said in a tight, hushed voice. "By the thousands."

"Then protect her," Father Juan said. "With all your soul."

Antonio huffed. "We still don't know if I have a soul."

"I know you do." It was an old conversation, one Antonio figured they would have until he died the Final Death—if that day ever came. Likely, it would. There was a price on his head. Among his own kind he was a traitor. To his sire he was a Judas.

"So how did the Cursed Ones know we were going to Cuevas?" Antonio asked, circling back to their original topic.

Although it was generally known in the region that there was a team of hunters covertly sent out on missions to defeat marauding vampires, the grateful citizens kept their mouths closed. Father Juan received dozens of pleas for help and responded to as many as he could. Antonio had listened with wistful amusement to one of Juan's pep talks to the team, in which he compared the hunters to Robin Hood or Zorro—do-gooders fighting established authority on behalf of the oppressed. So Antonio had imagined himself, up to the night he had been converted.

"The vampires in Cuevas knew we were coming. They lay in wait for us. *Do* we have a spy?" he pressed.

With a sigh Father Juan held up his *sol y sombra*—sun and shadow—to the light and studied the amber liquid. "I don't know. I've worked with Skye, cast runes, summoned visions, but nothing has been clear."

"Skye is a strong witch," Antonio ventured.

"*Sí,*" Father Juan said. "And as you know, once upon a time so was I, serving both God and Goddess until the time of choosing. I've worked magicks our little witch has never dreamed of, but even I can't tell you if we have a spy."

"Jamie thinks I'm the one." Antonio said. "Maybe I am. If somehow the other vampires can read my mind, track me—"

The priest frowned. "But you can't track *them*, or read *their* minds."

"I'm different. The stench of the grave is not upon me. I live inside a *church*. One look at a cross and most of them are vomiting." He ran his fingertip around the rim of his glass, his mood growing ever more somber. "Padre, hear my confession. When I kissed her last night, I wanted . . ." He turned his head, ashamed.

"It's past time for you to feed. You used to be so good about it, 'Tonio." Father Juan leaned forward on his elbows, his young, suntanned face etched with worry lines. "Twice a month, the first and third Fridays. For decades. That was your promise."

Antonio's shame grew. For decades he had drunk the blood of willing human donors, who knew what he was and honored his struggle to stay true to his faith and his lost humanity. Animal blood could not sustain a vampire, though many lied that it did. He remembered watching all the telecasts where Solomon told the world that vampires fed on cattle, pigs, sheep. Antonio wished it were so, but only human blood could sustain them.

Ever since Jenn had entered the Academia, he had

half starved himself, imagining what she would think, how she would *feel*, if she ever saw him feed. In the eyes of the Church, love was a miracle. The holiness of love inspired ordinary men and women to act like angels. It lifted them on wings closer to God.

But the thought of Jenn's love for him made him dizzy, as if he were falling into a bottomless pit.

"That was your promise," Father Juan emphasized. "To stop yourself from bloodlust and the frenzy of the curse. I help you all I can, with prayer and magick. But you must help yourself, you know."

"I know." Antonio gazed up at the moon. Witches honored the moon as the Goddess in all her faces. For Antonio the moon wore the face of the Blessed Virgin. But tonight she looked like Jenn.

I told her I would never leave her, he thought. When he was young, he had left Lita, his first love, to die. He had sworn he would not do the same to Jenn. *But perhaps Jenn has left me.*

In that case she is free.

Twenty minutes later they were back in the car; two hours later they pulled through the gates of the university. Eriko, Holgar, Jamie, and Skye erupted from the chapel and ran toward the van.

Something happened to Jenn's plane, Antonio thought, as he rolled down his window and stuck out his head. "Is it Jenn?" he shouted.

"It's not Jenn," Skye yelled back, "but it's bad!"

*   *   *

Eriko led the way back into the chapel, and everyone assembled near the altar under the crucifix. Eriko thought the statue was macabre in the extreme. She didn't like looking at Jesus dying in terrible pain, so she kept her back toward it as she told Father Juan the terrible news: During the previous twenty-four hours, three Hunters had been slaughtered by vampires.

"Three?" Father Juan murmured, crossing himself. He looked shaken. *"Que descansen en paz."*

Antonio crossed himself and echoed Father Juan, but in Latin: *Requiescat in pace.* Rest in peace. They all fought for humanity. But in the end, hunters fought for their lives. Alone.

His jaw clamped with anger, Jamie crossed himself.

"We received e-mails," Eriko told Father Juan, bowing slightly. "They were copied to me." As the Hunter, Eriko was the official commander of the team.

"Was it an organized attack?" Father Juan asked. "Did you get e-mails from any other Hunters?"

"I don't know if they were organized. Perhaps some e-mails were sent only to you. Maybe someone called."

No one knew how many Hunters there were in the world. There was no confederation of Hunters—or of their teachers or confidantes. Some had chosen to make themselves known to a few other Hunters; others remained anonymous. Secrecy gave them a chance at a longer life. Last year's Salamancan Hunter had lasted less than twenty-four hours after drinking the sacred elixir. The vampires had lain in wait, eager to take him down.

Cursers went after anyone they knew trained to fight them. That was one reason Father Juan had given her a team.

"Their governments probably sold 'em out," Jamie bit off, "to appease the suckers." He looked as if he wanted to spit on the floor, but would never do such a crude thing in their chapel.

"That's why it's so important to be in a group," Skye said, nervously picking at a piece of lint on her gray sweater.

"*Ja,*" Holgar agreed. "Like a pack."

"Hardly," Jamie retorted. "We're not animals. At least, the rest of us aren't." He sneered at Holgar.

Even when we are talking about the deaths of Hunters, we fight, Eriko thought pensively. But she said nothing.

"I'll say Mass for them," Father Juan announced. "In one hour, if anyone cares to attend."

"I'll assist you," Antonio said.

Eriko didn't want to go. Her joints ached, she was tired, and she had no desire to think about death any more that day. But she realized that the ritual might serve to unite the team, and sighing, pondered whether it was her duty to attend.

She looked at the others. They were angry and frightened. Antonio's eyes were closed, his forehead furrowed, and his lips silently moving. He was praying fervently. For an instant her heart softened. Then it hardened again. He was a monster. He didn't belong on their team or at the academy. But again she said nothing.

I'm a terrible leader. She ticked her gaze toward Father Juan, who was watching her. *Does he know that?*

CHAPTER THREE

*The war was a war like no other—for the vampires
had no standing armies, as we did. Stealthy, menacing,
they seemed to materialize out of nowhere, like
mist; they ambushed our soldiers and tore out their
throats. Our best hope against them were special-
forces teams—the U.S. Navy SEALs, the British
Special Forces, the Israeli Mossad, and the secretive
special-ops teams of Japan, Kenya, Australia, and
a dozen other countries who brought their long-
standing hatreds and mistrust to the fight. There
were accusations of conspiracies, collaboration, and
back-room treaties with the vampires in exchange
for protection. Instead of banding together against a
common foe, humanity fragmented.*

That was where we came in.

—from the diary of Jenn Leitner

Berkeley, California
Jenn and Heather

For a miracle, it didn't rain during the funeral. It should have rained—that was what happened in the movies whenever someone important died. There wasn't a cloud in the sky, though, and the sun shone down so hot Jenn could feel the skin on her arms starting to burn. *Antonio wouldn't be able to take it,* she thought. She spent so much time awake at night, hunting, hiding, that she was pale for a California girl. Next to her Jenn's younger sister, Heather, looked like a bronzed goddess with her shining blond hair, perfect tan, and gleaming white teeth.

Mourners stood in clusters around the grave site. More in keeping with her images of funerals, most of them wore black. Her parents and their friends, other family members, and aging hippies who had known and loved the great Charles Leitner—revolutionary to some, terrorist to others. Jenn's grandmother Esther stood alone, still fiercely proud, eyes like steel and chin firm and steady.

Jenn and Heather pressed shoulder to shoulder, leaning on each other for support. Even after two years, some things never changed. *And some things will never be the same,* she thought as she gazed at the coffin. While she was in Spain studying to be a hunter, she had thought often of her family. After a few months her mother had forgiven her for leaving, or so it seemed, and began to send her small care packages. Heather had written a dozen times. Of all of them, though, Jenn had missed Papa Che the most. And he was gone.

She glanced away from the coffin, an all too familiar symbol of death, natural or otherwise. She let her gaze linger on each face, many well known to her, others seen only in pictures. Her best friend, Brooke, wasn't there. But why should she be? Jenn hadn't even told her she was leaving America to join the academy in Spain.

At last her eyes fell on three men who were out of place. They were neither family nor friends nor admirers. Dressed in black suits and sunglasses, they stared steadily at her grandmother in a way that pierced Jenn's sorrow and creeped her out. Almost as though he sensed her gaze, the tallest of the three turned and stared back, and she forced herself to look away.

Her grandfather was being laid to rest in a beautiful old cemetery with plenty of grass and trees. The birds were singing. It was so lovely and peaceful that it was almost possible to forget that this was a place of death and sorrow.

Almost.

She had seen half a dozen freshly disturbed graves as she walked from the car to the grave site. She knew no one had dug them up. The dead were alive and well in Berkeley.

Usually vampire sires waited for their fledglings to wake up, in order to teach them what they needed to know about their new existence. Here, though, the new vampires had been buried; they'd revived alone, inside their coffins. They had then clawed their way out.

That was not good.

Either the siring vampires were completely reckless, or they didn't know what they were doing. *Or they're converting too many to take care of them all,* she thought with a shudder. *But why convert so many? To overrun us?*

The result was that there were a lot of new vampires in the area, and worse, they were vampires without mentors, which meant that they would kill anything that crossed their path. Smart vampires would only drink lightly from their victims, leaving them alive to feed from another day. Stupid vampires decimated their food supply and were then forced to move.

If the number of opened graves in this one cemetery was any indication, there were enough stupid vampires running around to put the entire population of Berkeley in serious danger.

Of course, the "good" vampires would argue that this chaos had been caused by the unnecessary war that America had started. Solomon was on record as saying that if the war had not happened, "lawless vampire gangs" wouldn't be preying on the human population. It was humanity's fault for lumping all vampires together, America's fault for being so aggressive.

An aging hippie with a guitar had finished singing a

soulful hymn, and the minister rose to his feet. "Dear brothers and sisters," he began.

Jenn gave Heather's hand a squeeze as her sister began to sob. Tears streamed down her own face, but at the academy she had learned how to keep it together so that she could live to fight another day. Standing beside Papa Che's casket was a battle of its own.

The minister extolled Papa Che's virtues, carefully choosing his words around the more sensitive topics. At last he spoke about surviving family, and for a moment Jenn thought Heather was going to completely collapse.

Jenn tried to listen, but other thoughts crowded in. She worried about the empty graves; she worried about Heather living in a land where Cursed Ones were so numerous; she imagined what they would say someday at her funeral. She shuddered. Hunters had a notoriously short life span. To be just a few months out of the academy and still alive made her an old-timer. She had beat the curve, but there was no reason to believe her luck would continue to hold. If there was one thing that Papa Che's funeral proved, it was that sooner or later luck ran out. Sooner or later everyone died of something.

Jenn wondered if that was the real reason the nine surviving members of her class who had not been chosen to be hunters had remained at the academy. If in reality they were being kept as backups in case she and the others died. The nine had been invited to teach the new class of recruits, and all of them had agreed. That had seemed odd. Though most were Spaniards, not all of them were. True, they hadn't received the elixir, and vampires loved to chase down hunters. They said hunters' blood tasted the sweetest. Did the nine stay because they were safer behind the university walls?

It had also struck her as strange that there was only one Spaniard in her hunting team—Antonio, a vampire. But Father Juan had assured her that all was as it should be.

"You know that in addition to saying my prayers, I threw my runes," he told her. "All signs and portents pointed to you six. For reasons, as I have told you before, that will be made clear."

Maybe Father Juan already knew when and how each of them would die.

Finally, the service ended. People began to walk to their cars to make the drive to her grandmother's house. Jenn watched the slow procession of vehicles with a faint, ironic grimace. Her grandparents had managed to stay under the radar for years, forced to be cautious because of the outstanding warrants for their "acts of social justice" when they were young—breaking into military installations and burning the records needed to draft young men into service, bombing the headquarters of corporations that built tanks and missiles and developed biological weapons like nerve gas. Now Jenn's father and her two uncles were handing out maps with detailed directions to everyone at the funeral.

Jenn glanced nervously toward the men in the black suits and sunglasses. Most of the men in attendance were wearing some kind of black suit, but these three stood straight and tall and had positioned themselves in such a way that they could watch everyone, keep track of comings and goings. The warrior in her saw the warrior in them — they were on guard, as if they expected an attack of some kind. They reminded her of her team back in Salamanca, and she had no doubt that they were dangerous.

The tallest of the three, silver-haired and strong-jawed, started walking toward the casket. His sunglasses prevented her from getting a really good sense of him. Jenn tried to gently untangle herself from Heather, who was hugging her tightly and sobbing.

Before she could manage to free herself, the man headed straight for her grandmother. Gramma was still wanted by the law, as her grandfather had been. In her gut Jenn knew the man worked for the government.

Leave her alone, Jenn thought, and eased Heather away.

"Hey," she said, taking a step forward.

The man extended his hand, and to Jenn's surprise her grandmother took it. Jenn stopped, watched.

"Hello, Esther," the man said in a twangy Southern accent.

"Hello, Greg." Esther Leitner's voice was sad and calm.

"I'm deeply sorry for your loss. We all are." The other two men had edged closer. Jenn tensed, reminding herself the code the Salamancans lived by forbade her to harm other human beings. But if they tried to arrest Gramma at Papa Che's funeral . . . well, she was pretty sure even Father Juan wouldn't blame her for her actions.

"Thank you." Her grandmother inclined her head, regally, like a queen.

"I'm going to miss him. He was a cunning opponent," Greg added.

"He felt the same way about you," Jenn's grandmother replied.

Greg nodded and then turned to go. When he saw Jenn, he stopped.

"You have big shoes to fill."

Startled, Jenn stared at him, lips parting, at a loss for words. He took off his sunglasses and stared at her with piercing gray eyes. She dropped her gaze and saw that he was wearing a black Crusaders' cross, like the red one on her shoulder patch and the Salamanca banner. From a distance it hadn't shown against his black tie.

"Many of us are praying you can fill them," he said, his words barely more than a whisper.

He left, and the other two silently trailed after in his wake. Bewildered, Jenn turned her attention to her grandmother, who was watching them go.

"Are you okay, Gramma?" Jenn asked, realizing how stupid that sounded.

Her grandmother nodded. "I'll miss Che until the day

I die, but he wouldn't want me to fall to pieces. He would want me to soldier on." Tears glimmered in her eyes but didn't fall.

"Who were those men?"

"Ghosts of the past, visions of the future," she murmured. Jenn frowned, and Esther cupped her cheek. At the same time Jenn felt the memory of Antonio's touch, like a reflection in a mirror.

"Very scary men," her grandmother added. "They work for the government, tracking criminals."

Just as Jenn had suspected. She didn't know why they had left peacefully instead of handcuffing her grandmother and hauling her off to prison. She was grateful, though.

Her grandmother nodded. "He chased us for years, but he came to pay his respects."

Jenn marveled at how different the world was. She couldn't imagine a vampire shaking hands with the widow of a fallen foe.

"I'm going to miss him so much," Jenn said, more tears spilling down her cheeks.

"He was very proud of you."

Esther put her arms around Jenn. Jenn sank into them, so tired and scared, and grief-stricken down to her soul. She had never realized how much she depended on her grandfather, that she had believed that things really would be all right because Papa Che would take care of them. But he was gone.

Her grandmother let her cry long enough to soak her black blouse; then she eased Jenn away with the same gentle insistence that Jenn had used with Heather. She wiped Jenn's eyes with her fingertips, and actually smiled.

Together they walked toward the black limousine that would take them to her grandparents' house. Heather and their parents and a couple other family members were already inside.

Esther threaded her arm through Jenn's. "Now, why don't you tell me all about this boy you're in love with. The one back in Spain."

Jenn stared at her grandmother in amazement. She hadn't breathed a word about Antonio to her family. She hadn't told anyone how she felt about him—not even Father Juan.

"How did you know there's a guy?"

Esther smiled. "The day I met Charles, a friend of mine took a picture of me. I still have it. I had the same look in my eyes that you have now."

"Oh." Jenn didn't believe her. With every step they were walking away from Papa Che's grave. She wanted to run back and throw her arms around the casket and cry forever. There was no way she looked like a girl in love.

Her grandmother kept smiling at her, waiting.

"His name is Antonio," Jenn admitted, flushing even as she said his name out loud.

"And why isn't he here?"

"He wanted to come," Jenn said. "But he's a hunter. I told him to stay in case there was . . . work."

"Very noble of you," Esther said. Then her eyes glittered, like when Papa Che would tease her and call her Essie. "But next time a young man volunteers to come and meet your family, you say yes."

She'll do it. I know she will.

Heather was sitting alone on one of the bar stools; she'd been holding the same plate of food for over an hour without touching anything on it. She wasn't hungry, but everyone kept pushing food on her. It was as though they all were at a loss after the funeral, and they needed something to focus on. Apparently whether or not she ate or drank anything was the top of the list.

Heather stared at her sister. Nobody was forcing food on Jenn. She was only two years older, and yet everyone treated her like an adult. A few knew why she'd been gone for two years—that she'd gone to Spain to train. That now she hunted vampires.

Vampires.

Dead and yet not. Unlike Papa Che, who would never walk the earth again or hug her or tell her that she could be whatever she wanted to be. It was unfair and still unbelievable in some ways. When she was little and would wake from a nightmare, everyone would tell her there were no such things as monsters. She still remembered the last time someone had told her that. It was the night before the whole world changed.

She and Jenn had been spending a few days with Papa Che and Gramma when the Cursed Ones went public. Their parents had gone away for their anniversary—Valentine's Day. Heather remembered waking before dawn to hear the phone ringing. She'd known something was wrong, really known, deep down inside. It was the first time she had ever felt like that, and she wished it had been the last.

Her uncle had called from Boston to tell them to turn on the news. A minute later she and Jenn had joined Papa Che and Gramma in the family room, staring at the television, as vampires addressed the world from the United Nations building in New York. Jenn had squeezed her hand until she couldn't feel her fingers. Her grandparents had looked ashen as the cameras got a close-up of bloodred eyes and flashing fangs.

Peace. That had been the message of the day. Solomon, the vampire who had done all the speaking, had been beautiful and charismatic like some sort of movie star, with gelled red hair, perfect teeth, and a dark suit with no tie.

The thing that had always struck Heather, though, was what her grandfather, who had the symbol for peace tattooed on his shoulder, had said when they'd finally turned off the television.

Papa Che had turned to Gramma and said quietly, "Peace is a lie."

"Heather, eat up," one of her uncles said as he walked by.

Heather sighed and watched Jenn, who stood across the room, talking quietly with one of Papa Che's friends.

Heather remembered the day that Jenn had left home, and the terrible fight. Correction: the last of the terrible fights. Jenn and Daddy had been at it forever. Heather had known that someday he'd drive her away, just as she had known on that Valentine's Day that the world had ended.

Frantically, Heather had stuffed underwear, her tooth-brush, her cell phone, and the three hundred dollars she'd been saving for her winter formal into her backpack, and blasted out of the house after her big sister.

But their mom had caught up with her in their Volvo, and Heather found herself grounded for a month. Forbidden to mention Jenn's name. Told to tell her parents if Jenn contacted her.

Her mom had never caught up with Jenn that day. Heather wasn't even sure she had really tried.

"How are you?" Tiffany, one of her best friends, asked, sitting down beside her on a matching oak bar stool. Blond with caramel highlights and blue-eyed, Tiffany was wearing a baggy black skirt and a lacy shirt of a totally different shade of black. Not her own clothes. Black was not Tiffany's color.

As an answer Heather let all the air out of her lungs.

"Do you want that food?"

"No."

Tiffany grabbed the plate and tossed it in the trash. "Done."

Heather stared down at her hands and wondered what she should do with them now. She finally folded them in her lap.

"This sucks," Tiffany said. Heather nodded, and they sat quietly together for a while.

All around them people were moving, talking, as if by keeping in motion they wouldn't have to think too much. The doorbell rang, and soon more men carrying flowers came parading through the front door. Heather fought the urge to sneeze as they moved too close to her. Her throat began to constrict slightly with the beginnings of an asthma attack, and she wished she hadn't forgotten her inhaler on the counter of the bathroom sink at home. Her mom sometimes carried a backup in her purse, but the tiny black clutch probably hadn't had room for it. She thought about asking, but she was afraid her dad would overhear and yell at her for forgetting it in the first place.

"I haven't seen your sister in forever." Tiffany wrinkled her nose, suddenly breaking the silence.

"Yeah," Heather said vaguely. She didn't want to discuss Jenn with Tiffany.

"You should talk to her, tell her she's wrong about the v-folk," Tiffany said anyway.

Heather rolled her big blue eyes. Tiffany, and half the girls at school, thought that vampires were romantic. Called them "v-folk" like they were fairies or mermaids or something. They all walked around wearing clothes with necklines that practically screamed, *Bite me!*

Tiffany fingered the silver bat necklace she always wore. The bat had a heart dangling from its claws. Girls like Tiffany wore them to symbolize that they weren't interested in regular guys; they were holding out for v-guys.

Heather glanced up and saw Jenn headed in their direction. Heather ducked her head, embarrassed. Whether Tiffany knew it or not, the necklace she wore was a total diss of everything Jenn stood for. Jenn fought vampires. She would never fall in love with one.

Heather took a deep breath. This was it. Tiffany might not see what vampires really were, and Heather's parents might believe the vampires only wanted peace, but like Jenn she knew better. Like Jenn it was time she did something about it.

"Hi, Tiffany," Jenn said. "Heather, Mom wants to know if—"

"Take me with you," Heather burst out.

Both girls turned to look at her in bewilderment. Jenn's pale face got whiter.

Heather rolled her eyes at her own lameness. "To Salamanca, when you go back."

"What?" Tiffany asked, actually standing up.

Jenn just stared at her through narrowed eyes. Then she gave her head a quick shake.

"I want to do what you do," Heather said, hearing the desperation in her own voice.

"Tiffany, sorry, sister business," Jenn said. "Give us a sec?"

"Um, sure," Tiffany said, backing away, trying to catch Heather's gaze. "Whatever."

"I'm all packed," Heather whispered fiercely. "I started getting ready as soon as I knew you were coming back. *Please.* I'll train hard. I promise."

"No, you won't," an angry voice said behind her.

Heather spun around to see her father towering over her, rage burning in his eyes. With his high forehead and hazel eyes Dad looked like his father, Papa Che, but Dad was nothing like him.

"You will not."

Tiffany moved even farther away, clearly not wanting any part in a family confrontation, and headed for the table laden with finger sandwiches and cheese cubes. Some friend.

"But, Dad—"

"No. We're done."

Heather knew that once he said that, there was no reasoning with him. She must have been on another planet to dream he'd say yes.

Jenn must have either forgotten that, or else she didn't care. "If she wants to go, that should be her decision. I was her age when I began my studies."

"Studies?" He set his jaw. "Your studies go against everything your mother and I believe."

"You still don't get it, do you?" Jenn said, the fury in her voice matching their father's. "We're in a war."

"No, *you're* in a war. And you're fighting for the wrong side. My war is over."

Heather gripped the edge of her stool tightly, her chest constricting more. She hoped her father couldn't hear the slight wheeze as she breathed.

"Wake up, Dad. Take a look around you. People are getting killed by vampires every day. Worse than that, they're getting converted. Do you have any idea how many empty graves there were in that cemetery, graves that should have bodies in them?" Jenn asked.

Her father blinked. Maybe he hadn't noticed. "That doesn't prove—"

"That's enough."

Heather jumped. Her grandmother, fists on her hips, had her feet planted wide apart. She looked the way she had in all the old pictures of her and Papa Che when they were young. Rushing off to blow up a bank or something—

"Let me talk to Jenn," Gramma Esther said. She stared down their father. His face grim and tight, he walked away.

But not very far.

"I didn't mean to get into it with him," Jenn murmured, abashed.

"You might not have meant to, but you did," Esther retorted bluntly. "Your father's a fool; you know that. Nothing you say is going to change his mind, either, so there's no use fighting today."

"You're right," Jenn said.

"Of course I am." She turned and looked at Heather. "Heather, come on, you should eat something. You're going to waste away."

Heather threw her hands up in frustration.

"I'll make sure she eats," Jenn said.

Esther nodded as though that was a satisfactory answer and then turned to look at two grizzled old men who were preparing to leave.

"Bobby, Jinx," she called to them. "I'll walk you out."

She took a half step and then reached into the pocket of her dress and pulled out an inhaler. Without a word she handed it to Heather before heading toward the door.

Heather took the inhaler and puffed on it, relaxing slightly as the medication went to work and breathing became easier. She was grateful to her grandmother for having an inhaler and giving it to her without making a show. At the same time she had to wonder if maybe everyone was right to treat her like she couldn't take care of herself.

I'll never forget an inhaler again, she vowed. *Ever.*

Jenn sat down on the stool Tiffany had vacated and made a quarter turn to face her squarely. "Are you serious about this?" she asked quietly.

Heather nodded. "I want to go with you. Things aren't the same here since you left. I don't mean with Mom and Dad; I mean with this place. Did you know that San Francisco is a stronghold for the Cursed Ones? They've taken over the city. Nothing happens without their permission."

Jenn's eyes grew wide. San Francisco was only a twenty-minute drive from Berkeley. "No, I didn't," she whispered.

"Well, it's true. It's like that all over the States. The vampires are taking over the government. They hardly even hide it. I keep waiting for Solomon to be 'elected' president." Her hands shook as she made air quotes.

"We've heard that it's bad here," Jenn said slowly. "But I had no idea." She swallowed. "All those graves—"

"I saw them too," Heather said. She cleared her throat. It was getting hard to breathe again. She was too tense. "Jenn, Daddy keeps saying that Solomon's going to restore peace and that we have to do everything we can to help him."

"Oh, God, he's gotten worse," Jenn blurted, then winced. "Sorry."

"No, you're right." Heather had to take another puff on the inhaler. Her heart was pounding. "It's like he's been brainwashed. He says if we aren't part of the solution, then we're part of the problem."

"Like me."

Heather could hear the hurt in Jenn's voice. And the anger. She felt it herself. Their father was acting so stupid.

"He says you guys are like Gramma and Papa Che. They did all kinds of things that were wrong, and no good ever came of it. All they did was hurt their family."

"Daddy had a bad childhood," Jenn said, though she was gritting her teeth. "Always hiding, on the run."

"So did we. I *remember* the fighting. All day long on TV I heard the bullets, and the bombs, and . . . and . . ." She closed her eyes. "And I remember hearing Daddy yelling at Mom to stop causing trouble."

"The war never came to San Francisco," Jenn reminded her. "But we knew we were fighting Cursed Ones. For Daddy everybody was the enemy. He never knew he had uncles until Che's brothers forced Che and Gramma to tell him. Think what that would do to a little boy."

"I can't believe you're taking his side," Heather said, stung.

Jenn's lips parted. "I can't believe I am either. But . . . now that I know what it feels like, the running, the hiding, the uncertainty, maybe I understand him a little better. He's scared. He's been scared all his life."

"Well, so am I. And at least I'm trying to deal with it."

Jenn paused and looked at Heather, really looked. Her brows lifted, as if she were seeing Heather for the first time. Heather seized the moment.

"Please, Jenn, I don't want to stay here. I'm afraid to." It was true. She hadn't been into the city in six months. Things were changing. She didn't go out at night anymore.

The last time she'd gone out—to the mall, to see a movie—she and Lucy Padgett had been chased by a vampire. She was sure that he hadn't wanted to kill them, or he would have. He was just trying to scare them because he could. Because he liked it.

The thought of fighting a vampire terrified her, but if she went to the academy, maybe she could learn how to protect herself. Maybe she wouldn't be so afraid. Maybe she could be more like Jenn.

"Please, Jenn." Heather let a tear trickle down her cheek as she grabbed her sister's hand.

"Let me think about it," Jenn said after a few moments. "Even if I can convince Mom and Dad, I'm going to have to get permission from my master."

Heather sighed. "I have to get out of here."

"Why is this so important to you?" Jenn asked. "If it's because I did it, then you should rethink this. It takes a lot of hard work to survive the training."

Heather stared at the floor. She suddenly felt lightheaded. She was afraid she might fall off the stool and the breath would be knocked right out of her.

"I just feel like if I don't get out of here now, I never will."

She closed her mouth, hoping Jenn wouldn't ask her anything more. Heather wasn't ready yet to tell her about the nightmares. The ones where she saw . . .

. . . where she saw . . .

She forced away the horrible images.

Oh, God, Jenn, please, she thought, clenching her fists. *You're so good at saving people. Please, save me, too.*

Jenn stared long and hard at her little sister. She wanted to protect her, just like when they were kids. She couldn't, though. If she had learned anything the last two years, it was that. She couldn't protect Heather if she enrolled in the academy. On the other hand, she certainly couldn't watch out for her from another continent. Especially if their father was still so blind to the truth, and most especially if San Francisco had truly fallen to the vampires.

Heather stared at her with desperation in her eyes. Jenn's gut told her that Heather was hiding something, but she knew better than to push.

"Let me think about it," she said, and she did think about it. She thought about the images on the Net and on TV, of soldiers in America—in Washington, D.C., and Seattle, and Chicago, and L.A.—fighting hand-to-hand with vampires, staking them; of all the failed weapons designed to hurtle stakes like spears at vampires; of scientists endlessly droning about what was real about vampires, and what was myth: Sunlight *did* burn them; they *could* die by beheading, burning, or staking. They *did* have to drink human blood. They *were* physically superior. They *did* force people to "convert."

And they *were* winning the war.

She remembered the days before the United States had called a truce. There had been food rationing, and days she had to stay home from school because of possible attacks. She remembered hearing that friends of Gramma and Papa Che had died trying to invade a vampire stronghold . . . and died horribly.

Her father had lived through all that too. He remembered that too. And his response was to cave in to the enemy, to vote for politicians who wanted to end the war, and to tell her mother not to sell art in her gallery that might be construed as hostile to the Cursed Ones. It was so wrong.

She had to give Heather other choices.

As the afternoon wore on, people started to leave. Finally, only family and her grandparents' closest friends were left. Jenn took the opportunity to slip off by herself for a few minutes.

She wound up in Papa Che's study and sat down in his chair, closing her eyes as she pictured him, hunched over the keyboard of his computer. The room smelled like him, and it brought fresh tears to her eyes.

She pulled her cell phone out of her pocket. Father Juan had told her to call whenever despite the time difference, and she was incredibly grateful as she dialed his private number.

He answered on the third ring. "Jenn, are you okay?"

She could tell she hadn't woken him up. He and the

others were almost as nocturnal as the vampires they hunted.

"I'm fine," she said, closing her eyes, imagining herself back in Spain and far away from Berkeley. "Sort of."

"How was the funeral?" His voice was kind.

"Good. Although there were a lot of empty graves at the cemetery."

There was silence for a moment, and then Juan said, "Not good."

"Exactly what I thought. My sister told me that San Francisco has become a vampire stronghold. The local government is compromised. Did you know that?"

"I'd heard rumors, but I wasn't sure. Most of the reports we get from the States are hard to sort out. There is so much propaganda and censoring, we don't know what is true."

She thought about telling him about the government agents at the funeral. But she and Father Juan dealt with vampires, not law enforcement types.

"Heather, my sister, wants to come back with me to Salamanca. She begged me. She wants to become a hunter. She said she doesn't feel safe here anymore."

"Becoming a hunter is not a decision to make in haste," Father Juan said. "And it's the wrong thing to do if one wishes to feel safe."

"I tried to tell her that."

"And?"

"I think there's something else going on with her, but . . .

she said the vampires are becoming such a problem here that she's scared."

"Many sisters are scared," Father Juan pointed out, his voice unreadable.

"Yeah, but this one's mine," Jenn said with a sigh.

Father Juan took a moment. Then he said, "Have you told her about Holgar? Or Skye? Does she truly know what your world is like?"

"No, but I know what *her* world is like," Jenn replied. "And ours is better."

There was another pause.

"If she wishes to study, as you did, she would be welcome at the Academia."

"But I'm . . . busy back home with missions. I—I'm afraid I won't be able to look out for her," Jenn confessed. "Protect her."

"You can't. You have duties, as you say."

"Then what should I do?" she asked, trying not to let her frustration show.

"Hide her away and pray for her safety, or let her choose her own path and learn to protect herself."

"What are you saying?" Jenn pressed. "Please—"

"It is your decision, and hers. Not mine. But she is welcome."

"Okay. All right," Jenn said. "I should go now."

"Be safe," he said.

"Thank you. And . . . thank you for saying she can come."

"Jenn," he said.

She waited. He didn't say anything more. For a moment she thought the call had been disconnected, but then she heard him sigh very softly.

"Father?" She heard the anxiety in her voice.

Silence.

"Father Juan?"

"It's all right," he said finally.

"Something's wrong."

"We're handling it," he replied. "Be with your family."

You are my family, she thought as she hung up. Then she stood.

A rustle of cloth startled her; she glanced toward the landing just in time to see the edge of a dark coat before it disappeared. She hurried to the doorway as her father descended the stairs.

Did he hear me? she wondered.

She shook her head. He couldn't have. If he had, he would have barged in and started yelling. That was what he did when he was afraid: yelled and screamed and stormed around. God, he was going to freak when he found out she was taking Heather with her.

Oh, God, she realized. *I am taking her. He'll never forgive me for that.*

She took a deep breath and thought of what her grandmother had said earlier. Time enough to fight tomorrow. Here, and in Spain.

SAN FRANCISCO
AURORA AND LORIEN

Aurora smiled at Lorien, the vampire lord of San Francisco, as he bowed low at the doorway of his lavish art deco penthouse apartment. She could smell his fear as easily as she could read the surprise on his truly beautiful face. He hadn't known she was in town, hadn't expected her at his party. The other vampires, dressed up for their gathering in couture gowns and tuxes, all followed his lead, giving way as she strolled across a floor tiled in jade. She was wearing scarlet, her favorite color; it set off her jet-black hair so nicely.

A white marble fountain of a naked woman pouring water from a jar trickled in the respectful silence. Some of the vampires knew who she was; others were openly curious. She heard the whispers: *Aurora, Sergio's former lover. Yes, Sergio is Lorien's sire. I don't know why she's here. There's a vendetta . . . secret plan . . . no, I don't know . . . and I don't think Solomon does either.*

But you didn't hear any of that from me.

In her four-inch heels she glided slowly to the window. She had learned centuries before that among those who could move with blinding speed, nothing aroused fear as one who moved slowly. The lights on the Golden Gate Bridge glittered like embers, and she admired the view.

"My lady Aurora, to what do we owe this unexpected

honor?" Lorien asked, his tone smooth yet deferential.

She kept her back to him. On another night she would have drawn out his anticipation, played with him a little. He was one of Sergio's fledglings, not hers. That alone, in her estimation, was reason enough to torment him. Ordinarily, she would not have passed up the opportunity. The night was far from ordinary, though.

She turned . . . *slowly*, and pinned him with her stare. She extended her arm and pointed toward the window. "There, across the bay, lies an enemy to us all. I'm here to take her out."

The vampires murmured among themselves, excitement and bloodlust flickering across their faces as they waited for her to continue. Instead Aurora glanced at a cage in the corner. A human girl huddled inside, limp and raglike, half dead. Pathetic. Lorien was allowing his followers to grow decadent, drinking from caged animals who could never hope to protect themselves. His vampires would forget how to hunt.

She turned back to the window. It was no matter. Lorien's life was hers to give or take when and if she chose. Sergio would be angry, but she could handle her old lover. Besides, Lorien was of no real concern to her; there, in the darkness, was one who was.

"Who is this enemy?" Lorien asked.

Aurora smiled. "A Hunter. From Salamanca."

Behind her there was an instant buzz of voices. All

vampires aspired to drink from a Hunter—the more clever the opponent, the sweeter the kill.

"Are you sure?" someone asked, and she looked from the window into the gathering. A tall, very handsome vampire shrank from her steady gaze. Aurora made a personal promise to herself to kill him before she left San Francisco.

Her icy silence was her answer.

"The Salamancans? I've heard of them," Lorien said nervously, obviously trying to smooth over his guest's faux pas and curry favor with Aurora. "They have one of those new hunter teams."

That drew murmurs. Aurora preened. "Yes, a team," she repeated. "Hunters are dangerous, not for the few pitiful kills they manage before being destroyed, but for the inspiration they provide."

That alone was worth crossing an ocean to snuff out. Let Sergio dare to do better. Let him find the traitor among the Salamancans—his own fledgling, Antonio. Sergio had no idea Antonio was still alive, much less that he had fallen so low as to aid and abet human beings.

Antonio de la Cruz was the true Cursed One. For when he was found, no god would show him mercy, whether he or she reigned above or below ground, in heaven or in hell. *She* certainly wouldn't, when she delivered him to secure her position in the new world order that was so soon to come.

"Not soon enough," she said aloud, as Lorien smiled at her quizzically. He was pretty, but he was an idiot.

Maybe Sergio wouldn't notice if she staked Lorien out of his misery. But he would certainly take notice when she delivered Antonio de la Cruz to their liege lord. Ah, yes, he would notice *that*.

She smiled at the window, as if she could see her own reflection. But of course she had lost it, over five hundred years ago. In a dungeon . . .

CHAPTER FOUR

We offer only peace and love
We will watch you from above
Trust us, love us, all we ask
Mankind's welfare our only task
We who dwell within the night
We who hold unyielding might
We can free you from your cares
Untangle your feet from all life's snares

AD 1490, TOLEDO, SPAIN
AURORA DEL CARMEN MONTOYA
DE LA MOLINA ABREGÓN

"Mujer," whispered the young, pockmarked guard as he unlocked her cell. The door squealed, and the rats, startled, scurried into the hay. "Woman."

He looked at her, then dropped his gaze as he stuffed the key into the pocket of his filthy smock. His dark eyes were ringed and sunken, proof that the Inquisition had robbed him of the ability to sleep. His distress meant that he still had a conscience and, God willing, a soul. "Prepare yourself. The Grand Inquisitor himself is coming." His gaunt face paled as he crossed himself.

"Ay, Dios me guarda," she whispered, unable to do the same. Her wrists were chained together and attached to a rusty stake in the center of the floor. As she tried to rise to a kneeling position, her soiled, unbleached shift caught beneath her knees. She jerked, and the guard reached toward her as if to help, then pulled his hands back as footfalls echoed in the corridor.

With a groan she tumbled back down on her sore hip, trembling with terror. Still the footfalls echoed; she jerked her head, her long black hair tangling between her fingers.

"I'm so sorry," the young man whispered. "If I could help . . ." He smelled of garlic and meat. Were it not for the chains, she would have lunged at him as if he himself were food. She couldn't remember her last meal. She was starving.

"He is coming," the man said. He pulled the key out of his pocket and stared at it. There were sores on his fingers, chilblains from the cold. "If I could, I would, believe me. . . ."

"Oh, please, *por favor*, get me out of here! Save me!"

She threw herself at him, grabbing at his hand. The key fell into the straw, and she groped for it. Her mind raced in a crazed fantasy where she found the key, opened the lock, and raced down the corridor to the cells where they kept her mother and the little ones, then to her older brothers and her sister Maria Luisa, and—

The guard gasped and sank to his knees beside her. She froze, and the shadow of Torquemada, the Grand Inquisitor of all Spain, fell across her like a net made of frozen iron. She stilled her hands, knowing the key was still there but that it was a useless piece of metal and nothing more.

It was said that Torquemada could read the minds of his prisoners, then break them down to speak the truth—that they were witches, or blasphemers, or Jews who had only pretended to convert to Christianity.

Jews like Aurora and her family.

Queen Isabella herself had invited Tomás de Torquemada to begin his reign of terror, and blessed and praised him for it. Aurora's father had spoken against the arrests and the resultant confessions and public executions—claiming that the god of his own understanding was a god of love. For daring to question the wisdom of the queen and the methods of God's servant, Torquemada, Diego Abregón had been declared a heretic and imprisoned, his lands taken by the Church. But during torture he had shouted not to the Virgin for her sweet intercession, but to the god of the Hebrews. He was declared a Marrano, a Jew who had only pretended to embrace the One True Faith. A liar, corrupting the city of Toledo with his unchristian ways. After being forced to witness his fiery death, Diego's wife and children had been thrown into Torquemada's dungeons.

And now Torquemada had come for Aurora, Diego's oldest daughter.

"Mi hija," said a low, deep voice. Aurora's stomach lurched, and bile flooded her mouth. That terrible voice had gloated as the flames crackled around her father, warning Satan that the ranks of his earthly minions were being thinned as Diego's bones fell to ash. Aurora tried to swallow the acid down and began to cough.

Torquemada: madman, monster, demon.

"Leave us," he said to the guard. The man jumped to his feet and scampered away, leaving Aurora to face the Grand Inquisitor alone.

The key was still in the straw. It was still *there*. If she could find it and ram it into his eye, if she could cut her throat with it . . .

"Raise your head, my daughter," he said silkily. "Do not fear me."

Aurora sobbed once, hard. "And why should I not?"

"Only the guilty need fear God. If you are not guilty . . ."

Guilty of being a Jew? Guilty of loving my faith and my heritage?

She kept her head lowered as tears rolled down her cheeks. Then something hit the back of her right hand.

Small, beautifully wrought, it was a crucifix with a cluster of rubies in the center, to honor the blood of Christ—her own; she had bribed one of the guards with the necklace in exchange for news of her mother.

"I return this to you," he said. "It was taken in error."

She closed her hand around the cross. Was this a generous act? Could it be God had softened Torquemada's heart?

She dared to look up. A torch burned on the wall behind the Grand Inquisitor, blurring her vision. He wore a black hooded robe with a white stole across his shoulders. Shrouded by darkness, his long face swam before her, but from the folds of his hood his eyes blazed as if he were burning from the inside out. And then he smiled. His teeth were scraggly and black, and his head looked like a skull. Her heart stuttered.

"Taken in error, because you were told that your mother was still alive," he concluded.

There was no air in the room. No thoughts in her head or feeling in her body.

She stared at him as he made the sign of the cross over her with his arthritic fingers, the talons of a demon. She couldn't remember how to speak. She could only stare at him in mute horror.

"Your mother confessed, as I knew she would, that she was a converso in name only. That, like your father, she had accepted baptism into the Catholic faith only to keep your family living off the fat of the land here in Toledo. That she had worshipped in the Jewish way, and had kept her house according to Jewish customs."

"No," Aurora said. He was trying to trick her. She would not confess—pitting her word against that of her mother. Catalina Elena, her beautiful *madre*, could still be alive.

"She forbade you to make the sign of the cross in her home. She would not allow you to mix meat and milk. You never ate pork."

Aurora clutched her hands together, digging her fingernails into her palms. These were lies. Her mother had served pork often, in full view of the servants. And they had all eaten it, silently asking God for forgiveness, and forgiving each other. They had prayed in the Catholic way. It was only on Fridays, on Shabbat, that they'd allowed any trace of their true beliefs into their home—they'd lit candles, and prayed once to Adonai. And then, for every other hour of their lives, they'd lived as Christians.

"We eat pork," she said. "Bring me some, for the love of God; I am starving."

He ignored her. "The Church has been watching. For fifty years the Abregón family has been under our scrutiny. Ever since the Jewish rebellion led fifty years ago by your great-grandfather—"

She shook her head, surer now that he was trying to frighten her into exposing her family.

Then Torquemada reached into the pocket of his robe and tossed a handful of glittering gold and delicate silver onto the straw. Eight crucifixes. She recognized each one. The larger ones had belonged to her three brothers, and the more delicate ones to her sisters. The smallest one, adorned with roses, was her little sister Elizabeta's, the *infanta* only four years old.

"You are the last," he said, dropping to one knee beside her as she began to heave. "But each soul answers to God. You may save yourself, my daughter. With my help."

He laid his hand on the crown of her head. Under its weight she collapsed facedown into the straw, and everything went black.

"He'll win," someone said. "And you will die in agony."

Aurora opened her eyes to darkness. Wet straw clung to her cheek as she turned her head. A man sat beside her. Like Torquemada he wore a monk's hooded robe. He was wrapped in darkness, the shadows shifting and spreading like a pool of black water, of which he was a part. Narrowing her eyes, she tried to make out his features, but she could not.

"*Buenas tardes,*" the figure said. His voice was low and soft, and she had trouble hearing it. "Yes, I am really here."

"*Por Dios,*" she whispered, cringing. "Please, please don't hurt me."

There was silence. Then the figure laughed. "You think I'm one of Torquemada's minions."

She caught her breath. "And you . . . are not?"

"I am not."

"Then . . . who . . . ?" And then she feared that he had come to attack her. She was an unmarried virgin, and the guards had said things, threatened things. . . .

Weak as she was, she balled her fists, ready to fight him. Her siblings' crucifixes were gathered in her right hand. If she screamed, would anyone come to help her? Or would others simply gather in her cell to join in the torment?

"Come no closer, or you will die," she warned.

"Ah," he said, sounding amused. "I have been watching you, Aurora. I find you special. Do you know what your name means? 'Dawn.' I have not seen one in centuries."

She shook, not understanding him, seeing only a man in her cell who meant to do her harm.

"I'll kill you," she promised him.

"I was right. You have the heart of a fighter."

"I—I do."

"I walk the dungeon at night, looking for those I can . . . help. And I *can* help you, Aurora."

"I will gouge out your eyes and—and ruin your manhood."

He was silent a moment. "Perhaps, in time, you will be strong enough to fight back. But for now . . ." He seemed to raise a hand, darkness against darkness.

And suddenly she knew: He was to be feared more than Torquemada.

"No!" she wailed. "No, please, don't hurt me! For the love of God, I beg you!"

Then he pulled her against his chest, wrapping himself around her, muffling her screams. He was as cold as the grave. His icy hand came over her mouth, and his other hand held her by the back of the head. She beat her fists against his chest.

He cut off her air supply, and she stopped hitting him, instead fighting wildly for air. The world dissolved into dots and blurs; her eyes rolled back, and she slumped into his arms. He loosened his hold slightly, and she began to suck air into her lungs, smelling him—the world—oranges, and roses, and pine trees. His arms were sinewy, his chest broad and muscular.

"Listen to me, Aurora Abregón," he whispered. "They are coming for you. They saved you for last, because you are the most beautiful of all the Abregóns. They will torture you even if you beg to confess. To appease their vengeful God they will ruin you, and disfigure you, and then they will burn you. Your family is gone. You are alone."

Gasping, Aurora let out a heavy sob. She shook her head and burst into tears. He covered her mouth with his hand again, and her body spasmed. Weakened as she was, she had no strength left to fight him. And yet defiance burned like a flame inside her.

"I can end your torment," he said, "in one of two ways. If you wish to live, nod your head. If you wish to die, do nothing."

Too exhausted to move, she lay still. He sighed and lowered his lips to her neck. A searing chill moved through her skin and crept into her blood. It burned. She didn't know what he was doing, but she whimpered.

He moved his lips to her ear, and he hissed. Then he ran his lips along the crown of her hair, as the world spun and cracked, and she knew herself to be in terrible danger.

"Do you wish to live?" he whispered.

Aurora nodded. Desperately.

BERKELEY
JENN AND HEATHER

As Heather quietly watched her pack Jenn couldn't help but feel that she'd made a terrible mess of things. Curled on her bed, Jenn's little sister looked young and vulnerable, dressed in her yellow ducky pajamas and green socks, a can of root beer cradled against her chest. Heather's eyes were swollen from crying. Both girls were exhausted. The day had been very long, and the fight with their father had taken a toll on all of them. Driving back from the funeral, their dad hadn't said three words to Jenn. Heather had kept looking from her father to Jenn and back again. Their mother had stared out the window, either oblivious or pretending not to know what was going on. Jenn wasn't sure how her mom had been able to ignore the tension.

Jenn folded the black dress she had borrowed from Skye for the funeral and placed it between her extra pair of skinny-leg black jeans and the black T-shirt and leggings she usually wore to bed. She hadn't worn pajamas since she'd arrived at the academy. If they were summoned in an emergency, she was one step closer to being dressed for battle.

She added her little toiletry bag, then replaced her stakes and vials of holy water. Her weapons had to be close at hand; back in Spain no hunter ever left the academy's grounds unarmed. It was ten o'clock at night in Berkeley; she thought of the empty graves and wondered how many newly made vampires would rise from their graves that night, tearing out the throats of their victims more like werewolves than vampires, because they had no mentoring sire to show them how to drink.

I can't do anything about that tonight, Jenn thought, ripping open the Velcro pockets of her cargo pants in a methodical pattern, top down, *rip rip rip.* She stuffed in a couple more glow-in-the-dark plastic crucifixes and checked the water level on both the plastic and glass bottles of holy water—glass was for throwing, since the vials would shatter on impact. The prepeeled garlic cloves were turning brown in their airtight containers, but they wouldn't lose their pungent power for at least another week.

She slid a six-inch stake into a long pocket along her hip. She'd whittled it out of a branch from a tree in their backyard in the predawn hours before the funeral, when she'd been too wired to sleep. She'd have to throw it away when she got to the San Francisco airport; she had no checked luggage, and it would be considered a weapon.

"That thing's so short," Heather said, sipping her root beer. "You'd have to get pretty close to, um . . ." She made stabbing motions.

"Drive a stake through the vampire's heart," Jenn finished for her. "Yup. Pretty darn close."

Heather's eyes widened, and her mouth dropped open. The look of hero worship on her face embarrassed Jenn. She felt like a fraud. She *was* a fraud. She had nearly gotten Eriko killed.

Maybe I should stay here, she thought. *I could teach Heather how to fight, and we could try to defend San Francisco together.* But that wasn't what she was really thinking. She was spooked, badly, and when she got back to Spain, she needed to sit down with Father Juan and tell him what was in her heart—she was afraid she was going to get someone killed. It would be a relief to confide in him. Confession, they said, was good for the soul. But would it be good for her life span? What if, instead of reassuring her, he kicked her out?

Exhaling, she hefted the bag over her shoulder, and Heather jerked, setting down her root beer.

"You're not leaving *now*?" she asked shrilly.

"It's dark," Jenn replied as she deposited the bag beside the closed bedroom door; then, realizing that she was talking like a hunter, she added, "so the vampires are out. It's too dangerous."

Heather glanced at the window. "Tiffany might be out

with one of them right now, letting him . . ." She ran her hands through her silky blond hair. "Tiffany's family has joined a Talk Together Team."

"No way," Jenn said, frowning at her. Talk Together Teams were groups of humans and vampires who met to try to "bridge the gap"—to explain away the war and the fact that vampires killed people and drank their blood. When they'd heard about them in Salamanca, no one had believed it. Then they'd seen posters plastered on the walls of the ancient Spanish city announcing *Grupos de Paz*—Peace Groups—which were essentially the same thing.

"That's crazy. That's just . . . beyond insane," Jenn said, sitting down on her bed. She picked up her field jacket, the one with the Salamanca patch, and decided she should conceal it in her duffel bag. The Velcro patch might come unfastened, revealing her as anti-vampire. If people were into Talk Together Teams around here, hunters would not be welcome.

"Daddy," Heather began, and then she glanced at the door and lowered her voice. "He says they're only getting rid of the people who attack them."

"Like me," Jenn said. "I know he's furious that Gramma Esther called Father Juan to tell me about Papa Che. He hates me."

"Oh, no, he doesn't." She looked again at their closed door and put her arms around her knees. "He doesn't believe in what you're doing, but he loves you. Like he loves Gramma and . . . and Papa Che."

Jenn remembered overhearing arguments between her father and his parents—more often with Papa Che than with Esther. Jenn's grandparents had been underground since before her dad's birth, always running and hiding, like escaped prisoners eluding hunting hounds. Her father had hated his life—he could still recite the string of fake names he'd had to use, and after a couple of glasses of wine he'd recount some of the lies he'd been forced to tell: that he'd transferred in from a school in Mexico, where his father had worked for a gas company. That his transcripts had been lost in the mail.

It seemed like every time he'd begun to make friends at school, get on the football team, fall in love, Che would get word from the underground that "the Man" had picked up their scent again . . . and the Leitners would leave town in the middle of the night. When Jenn's father had turned eighteen, he'd refused to run any more.

And no one had ever come for his parents . . . until the great Che Leitner was dead.

Sometimes Jenn wondered if that had made him even more bitter—that all the hiding had been for nothing. What had he thought of the men at the funeral?

Jenn sat down on the bed and took a sip of Heather's root beer. Tears welled in her little sister's eyes.

"You have to try to make him understand how dangerous the vampires really are," Jenn said.

Heather raked her hands through her thick hair. "Why

would Daddy listen to me? I'm the baby. The one who doesn't know what she's talking about. *You're* the smart one." She reached for Jenn's hand. "You *have* to take me back with you."

Jenn gave it a little squeeze. "Do you even have a passport?"

Heather frowned. "No. I thought you guys could get me, you know, clearance or something."

Maybe Father Juan could do something like that. Jenn had no idea; she'd have to talk to him again. But to smuggle Heather out of the country against her parents' wishes . . . maybe it was going too far.

But the world had gone too far. The war had changed everything.

"We have to make Daddy listen to us." Jenn pulled back the blanket and comforter on her bed. "He's kind of doing to you what Papa Che did to him, you know? Making decisions for you based on his ideals, forcing you to live in fear."

"Except we're not running and we *should* be," Heather muttered. "Running for our lives."

I can't argue with you there, Jenn thought angrily.

She pulled back the covers, lay back in her bed, and stared at the ceiling. Her mind worked furiously; she thought about the team. Heather would freak if and when she met Antonio. That almost made her smile as she drowsed but never really slept. She was too wide awake and too troubled—and too out of her element. The bed felt too soft, and the house was too quiet. Salamanca was her home now.

"What is it like?" Heather asked, startling Jenn.

"What's what like?"

"The academy."

Jenn sighed. "You know all those movies where they show you what boot camp is like if you join the army?"

"It's like that?"

"Worse," Jenn said.

"Why did you go?"

"To get my own room."

A pillow sailed through the darkness and landed on Jenn's head. Fortunately, she had been expecting it. She suppressed a laugh as she hurled it back at Heather.

Jenn threw it a little too hard and felt guilty when Heather grunted at the impact. For just a moment, though, it was like the last several years had been some terrible nightmare. She didn't know how many times they had lain awake as children, talking in hushed voices to avoid waking their parents.

There had been so many dreams. Jenn remembered the endless talks about things like homecoming and Christmas presents and what their weddings were going to be like.

And their wedding nights. An image of Antonio blossomed in her mind. God, was she insane? He was a *vampire*.

"Seriously, why?" Heather asked, distracting her. Jenn blinked, trying to remember what they were talking about. "Why did you go to the academy?"

"There were a lot of reasons. It seemed heroic, romantic.

I think I wanted to be like Papa Che and Gramma—to change the world, or at least save it." She smiled grimly. "And it didn't hurt that it made Dad angry."

"He really, really loves you," Heather insisted.

Jenn flipped onto her side. "He has a strange way of showing it."

"He told me once that you were fearless."

Shocked, Jenn fought the urge to burst into insane laughter. *Fearless? Me?* It was absurd. She was a bundle of fear.

"Dad's a big fan of fear," Jenn replied. "Fear keeps you from doing dangerous things. Keeps you 'safe.'"

"That is totally like something he would say." Heather fluffed up her pillow. "What do you learn at the academy? Do you have uniforms? What about coed dorms? Are the boys cute?"

Jenn sighed. She had been hoping for a decent night's sleep, but that clearly wasn't in the cards.

It was a Monday, and her father commuted into San Francisco on the BART train to his job as a software engineer. Jenn's mother used to own an art gallery, but it had been shut down at the end of the war because some of the canvases had been found to be "inflammatory." There had been a few protests in her favor, but people had far more pressing issues than someone's "boutique business," as one local politician had termed it.

Now she did volunteer work, taking meals to shut-ins, some of whom had been wounded in the fighting. Jenn's father didn't like her doing it; it seemed "provocative." There were other, "less political" things she could do if she wanted to be helpful.

She asked the girls to come with her for the day, and Jenn said yes because she wanted to spend time with her mom, and also to make sure she was safe. Heather had been allowed to stay home from school, so she went too. The streets were littered with posters about Talking Together Teams and curfews. Soldiers in khaki with submachine guns stared stonily at the pedestrians and the cars. The U.S. government was collaborating with the enemy because it insisted that a truce had been reached and that the two races, vampire and human, were living in peace. But the presence of these human vampire lackeys, keeping that peace while their vampire masters stayed out of the sun, told the lie. It was said that Solomon had promised the new president that he could become a vampire after he pushed through the legislation Solomon wanted—such as making it a capital offense to so much as enter the lair of a sleeping vampire.

At a stoplight Jenn locked gazes with a soldier who couldn't be much older than she was; his eyes looked dead, and mean. Cursed Ones had done that. She hated them.

It began to rain; around noon Jenn's mother tried to call her husband to see if he wanted her to pick him up so he wouldn't have to take BART in the bad weather. He didn't answer his cell, which was unusual, and Jenn saw how nervous it made her mom. She started talking fast, almost babbling with fear, and Jenn was relieved when it was time to go home.

Jenn found her father in the den, sitting in his old leather recliner. He was watching TV, and he held a glass of something brown that smelled like alcohol. Jenn guessed that it was Scotch.

"You're home early," Jenn's mother said, relief clear in her voice.

"Yeah, our meeting was canceled," he replied vaguely. "There didn't seem much point in sticking around."

"Oh." She kissed him and went into the kitchen to make dinner. Heather loitered, obviously wanting to talk about going to Spain, but he asked her to help her mother so he could speak to Jenn alone.

"Jenn." Her father patted the arm of the brown-and-white-checked couch, which sat at a right angle to his recliner. He took a sip from his glass, then drained it.

She sat down and watched him closely. He looked strained, tired.

"I gave you up for dead when you left," he said abruptly.

She bit her lip, not sure what to say in response.

"I knew where you were going, what you planned to do. You didn't do a very good job of hiding your trail."

"Then why didn't you try to stop me?" she asked quietly.

"I knew that if you stayed, it was just a matter of time before you said or did something that would put all of us at risk. Your mother, your sister . . . I couldn't protect you all."

"But you figured you could keep them safe without me around?" she asked, struggling to keep the pain out of her voice.

"I'm sorry."

Jenn knew she should say something, apologize too for running away, or at the very least accept his apology and offer him forgiveness. More than one conversation with him had gone badly, though, because she didn't know when to keep her mouth shut. She finally just nodded, hoping it was enough of a response.

"I never wanted you girls to grow up with the constant fear that I did. I just wanted you to be safe."

"I know," she said.

"When you left, I was sure you would be killed. I resigned myself to it. Seeing you at the funeral, I was proud of you. You've become so much like your grandmother. You've got her strength."

"Thank you," Jenn said, blinking back tears.

"And I realized I needed to tell you something. You're right . . . about the vampires. You always were."

Jenn stared at her father in shock. He had finally admitted it, but it seemed so sudden. She looked again at the pain in his eyes and the glass clutched tightly in his fist. "Dad—"

"Something happened today." He set the empty glass

down on a side table and wiped his forehead. "Do you remember Tom Phillips?"

"A little. He had a German shepherd named Gunther."

"Yes." He chewed the inside of his cheek. And then he looked at her. Hard. Tears welled in his eyes. "They said he'd been in a car accident."

"Oh."

"But his wife called." He shook his head. "It was something else. Not an accident." He leaned toward her. "An *attack*." His face crumpled. "And he was so good to them. So . . . loyal."

Jenn waited, sensing that there was more.

"What we do at work . . . It's a database." Her father dropped his voice to a whisper. "Of . . . undesirables. And I guess there was someone on it Tom was trying to protect. And *they* found out and . . ." He buried his face in his hands. "I can't believe it. If they did that to him, then no one is safe."

Now you know, she thought. *Now you believe.*

"I'm sorry, Daddy." She reached for him, but he didn't see her. He drew in a deep breath and let it out in long, painful bursts.

Then he got up and sat beside her on the couch. His face was gray, and heavily lined, as if he had aged terribly in the last three minutes, or maybe he'd just grown up.

"So I'm going to meet them tonight."

"Them?" she repeated.

He frowned slightly, as if he wanted her to figure out what he was trying to say so he wouldn't have to.

"The group Tom was protecting," he whispered. "Some people connected to the . . . *situation*. People who think that, ah . . . who don't agree . . ." He locked gazes with her. "*You* know what I mean."

Part of her was thrilled. Her father was getting involved, finally. He was going to take up where Che had left off. She could feel it.

But part of her was afraid for him. He wasn't as strong as she was.

"Dad, no, they'll be watched. The Cursed Ones —"

"Shh. I don't want your mother to know. But if I don't come back —"

"Dad, have you lost your mind?" Jenn asked in a low voice. "There's no way you can do this. No. No, I won't let you go."

"I told Tom's wife I would. Tom's . . . widow." Her father got up and began to pace. "I've been wrong, all along. I thought if we were helpful, if we gave them what they wanted, then they wouldn't hurt us. But . . ."

He stopped pacing and went to the window, drawing back the curtain. "There's about an hour and a half of daylight left. It's only fifteen minutes by car. That gives me an hour to talk to them."

"Then I'm going with you." By the expression of relief on his face, Jenn realized that that was what he'd wanted but had been reluctant to ask. Father and daughter—united in common purpose. Now she *had* to step up, act like a hunter, serve as protector. There was no backup this time. She was the first—and last—line of defense.

"Thank you," he said, giving her a hug. "I knew I could count on you."

"Yes, Dad." She licked her lips, torn by her conflicting emotions. Such intense pride in him. Even greater fear *for* him. And the realization that she could help protect him, keep him safe. And he knew it. He knew it. Years of anger burned away in an instant.

She said fiercely, "You can count on me."

CHAPTER FIVE

Salamanca Hunter's Manual:
The Supreme Enemy
The vampire is cunning. Like the Fallen Angel himself, he will try to beguile you, to charm you. He will try to convince you that he is nothing more than a human being blessed with special gifts and talents. He will entice you with stories of endless life, and ridicule your belief in a judgment hereafter, where your soul hangs in the balance. Do not believe him. He is a demon, and a liar.

(translated from the Spanish)

Salamanca, Spain
Salamancan hunters: Antonio, Holgar, Skye, Eriko, and Jamie

Holgar was having a nightmare. He knew it was a nightmare, but he couldn't pull himself out of it. He never could.

They were racing, playing, hunting rabbits. Holgar was twelve and in human form, running in a pair of shorts and nothing else. His bare feet flew across the rocks, impervious to their sharpness. His father loped alongside him in wolf form.

There was a sudden flash of orange in the trees. A hunter. The blond-haired man was sighting down his rifle at a deer. Wary, Holgar turned to change course, but his father didn't turn with him or slow down. Instead he accelerated, body streaking through the trees as he targeted the man.

Holgar shouted. The man turned, and his father ripped out the hunter's throat. Holgar ran forward, but it was too late. The man was dead, and his father was licking at the blood as it bubbled from his throat, whining with the pleasure of it.

"Nej!" Holgar shouted.

Holgar woke up with a howl, shook himself, and looked toward the door. Jamie was standing there, arms folded across his chest, wearing his perpetual scowl. Skye stood at his side, a hand on his arm as though ready to pull him back.

"Having one of those dog dreams?" Jamie taunted.

"Don't," Skye murmured.

Holgar shrugged and swung his legs over the side of his bed. His baggy sweatpants felt constrictive compared to the freedom of running in one's own skin. Sweat beaded on his chest and shoulders. He pressed his fingers to his head, trying to reorient himself. Holgar hated morning; most wolves did. He glanced out his narrow window and could see nothing but inky blackness. It had to be early.

"Haven't you heard it's best to let sleeping dogs lie?" he growled.

"Love to, but Master calls," Jamie answered.

"What's wrong?" Holgar snapped awake. Father Juan never called for them this early. Since hunters needed to be nocturnal, classes at the academy hadn't even started until ten a.m. most days. It was a schedule they had all stayed with upon graduation.

"We don't know," Skye said.

Holgar grabbed a shirt from his trunk and pulled it on with a grimace. It was two sizes too large, and he'd washed it dozens of times, but he still hated the feel of it against his skin. Where he was from, young wolves ran virtually naked until their fifth birthday. Then, as they were introduced to the rest of the world, they were forced to wear clothes when they walked among normal humans. Most of them spent the rest of their lives wishing they could have continued in their natural state.

"Let's go," Holgar said.

"We're to meet in his office," Skye said.

"What do werewolves dream of?" Jamie asked, not budging from the doorway.

Holgar couldn't tell if the Irishman was actually curious or if he was just trying to bait him again. "Weresheep."

Skye snickered, and Jamie continued to glower. "Let's go see what he wants," Holgar said, pushing past them and down the hallway.

The other two fell in behind him as they walked down the long corridor of the faculty dormitory. They passed rooms belonging to priests and instructors, including Father Juan's room. Holgar breathed in deeply and could tell by the staleness of the scent that Father Juan hadn't been in his room for hours. He whined deep in his throat, convinced that wasn't a good sign.

After graduation the team had moved out of the student dormitory, making way for the incoming hopefuls. Holgar and Antonio had been the only two who hadn't had to change rooms, since they had already been separated out from the other students.

Holgar hadn't minded, realizing it was as much for his protection as for that of the other students. When he had arrived at the academy, only Father Juan had known he was a werewolf. After his unfortunate howling at the moon, word had spread quickly that there was a werewolf at the academy, and it wasn't long before most of the students knew it was Holgar. Being able to point to one monster in their midst kept them from looking for others. Holgar had suspected there was something, though, about the soft-spoken Antonio that merited him living in the building with priests and faculty instead of students. One night he'd actually been downwind of Antonio on a training exercise and smelled the merest hint of death. That was when he knew why Antonio was also segregated.

Holgar had no great love for vampires, and he soon discovered that neither did Antonio. Holgar had kept Antonio's secret. Clearly those running the academy knew what he was and wanted him alive. Holgar knew what it was like to live with a dark side that couldn't be controlled, and he appreciated having Antonio as a sparring partner. Even in their human form werewolves were stronger than normal humans. In return for his discretion, the vampire helped him hone his fighting skills. The rest of the students walked carefully around Holgar, but none had known what Antonio was until graduation night.

They passed Eriko's room, everything neatly arranged, a brass Buddha sitting on her bureau. She was already gone, but her scent hung thick and heavy in the air. She had left within the last couple of minutes.

Each person's scent was unique and made up of so many factors. It was a combination of shampoo, shaving cream, soap, toothpaste, laundry detergent, deodorant, even the fabric of a person's clothes or the type of shoes they were wearing. Leather, plastic, canvas, rubber, each had a distinctive odor. Then there was a person's diet. Certain types of foods, particularly garlic and onion, could be excreted by the skin for days or even weeks. No amount of mouthwash could take care of that. Illness, perspiration, and chemical changes in the body all had an impact. Subtle changes could be recognized and compensated for, but if you wanted to throw a werewolf off your scent, it was simple—switch your shampoo for one with a more pungent odor, change to a deodorant usually used by the opposite sex, and start adding garlic to your food. Or smoking like a chimney, like Jamie.

They left the dormitory and crossed a cobblestone courtyard lined with statues and crosses to one of the administrative buildings. Inside they found Father Juan pacing in his office. It was a beautiful room, with centuries-old wood paneling cut to look as if it had been folded, and an ebony desk inlaid with mother of pearl. The modern chrome and black-leather office chair was wildly out of place. A stained-glass window panel depicting St. John of the Cross communing with Jesus hung on the wall. Holgar had to agree with the majority that Father Juan, with his high cheekbones, sloping forehead, and large, slightly sunken eyes, resembled the saint very closely.

Regarding the gossip that he was the reincarnation of the man, Holgar was quite skeptical. But there was no denying that Father Juan was a strange one. He seemed to cultivate a persona of weirdness, at least by Holgar's standards. On Father Juan's desk sat a copy of Bernini's statue of St. Theresa of Avila in mystical ecstasy, head thrown back, lips parted, as a chubby cupid of an angel grinned at her, preparing to stab her with the little burning spear in his hand. On other occasions Holgar, a modern, lusty Scandinavian, had inwardly chortled at the rampant sexuality of the piece. There was nothing mystical about what she was feeling. Catholics, as a group, were tremendously repressed, he thought. Look at Antonio.

But today Holgar knew something was going on, and no silent laughter burbled up from him.

Eriko and Antonio were sitting quietly, open curiosity on both their faces. Holgar, Jamie, and Skye took their seats. That left two chairs vacant, one for Father Juan and the one Jenn normally occupied. She was still in the States at her grandfather's funeral. Holgar missed her. She had an interesting way of viewing the world, and he was certain she could be a great hunter if she just eased up on herself a bit.

Father Juan turned, surveyed the team briefly, and then sat down. He leaned across his desk, folding his hands together. "We have a problem."

None of them said a word. If there hadn't been a problem, the priest wouldn't have awakened them.

"You already know there's a team of scientists working on a weapon that will help our side in this war. I've had news about it."

"Please tell us, *sensei*," Eriko said, bobbing her head.

"Yeah, there isn't much kills a Curser," Jamie noted. "If we've got something new, that'd be six kinds of bloody great."

"Is it an artificial sunlight weapon?" Skye asked.

"Or a poisonous gas like weaponized garlic essence?" Holgar suggested.

"I'd be happy with a bomb that exploded wooden shrapnel," Jamie put in.

Father Juan almost smiled. "Actually, it's a virus."

"You mean like the flu?" Jamie snorted disbelievingly.

Father Juan's expression did not waver. "*Sí*. I don't have all the facts, but apparently the virus will attack blood cells of a certain kind."

"Vampiric kind?" Skye asked.

"Yes." Father Juan's voice caught. "It must be injected."

"Injected," Jamie said. "As in . . . you give the Curser a *jab*?"

"How long does it take?" Eriko cut in.

"They're not sure yet." Father Juan looked at them. "It must be administered under the skin."

Skye wrinkled her nose. "That doesn't sound like much of a weapon."

"You could make a tranquilizer gun out of it, but that would only affect one vampire at a time, if you could hit them with the dart," Holgar noted. "It's not much better than staking them."

Father Juan took a deep breath. "No, but if what they have actually works, then the next step is to figure out if there's a way to infect vampires en masse as opposed to one at a time."

Holgar glanced at Antonio. If that was true, then the virus could kill their vampire as well. The thought must have occurred to the others—Eriko and Skye exchanged uneasy glances, and Jamie grinned from ear to ear.

"They'd been moving the lab twice a week to keep from being found," Father Juan continued. "But the most recent batch of virus—the most promising to date—was stolen two days ago, before it could be tested. Most of the scientists involved were killed in the attack."

Jamie pounded a fist into the side of his chair, while Antonio solemnly made the sign of the cross. Skye looked down at the ground, and the muscle along Eriko's jaw began to twitch. Holgar folded his arms across his chest. There had to be more, or the priest wouldn't have woken them.

"So the Cursers have it," Jamie noted. "They probably destroyed it, yeah?"

"We don't know," Father Juan said. He frowned slightly. "No one from the government wanted to tell me much of anything. But that much I did get. We know that *los Malditos* are not one cohesive, organized enemy. They're fighting among themselves, just as we humans find ourselves divided. One group could refine the gas and use it against another group."

"Fine, then, let's leave 'em to it," Jamie said.

"My son, think," Father Juan reproved him. "And listen."

They all leaned forward at the same time, and Holgar bit back a laugh. Even though they were constantly at odds with each other, they were a pack. For a group where everyone stoutly proclaimed their individuality, they all moved alike, fought alike, and often thought alike. They might not want to admit it, but each had a deep-seated need to belong—one that he shared. Holgar was just more aware of it, having an innate instinct to align himself and his actions with the group.

"The army thinks the Cursed Ones have plans to study the virus and develop a vaccine," Father Juan said.

"Making them stronger," Jamie mused. "It's always like that. Your foe learns from fighting you." He flashed a look at Eriko.

"So, Father, why are you telling us this now?" Skye asked.

"The Spanish army has intelligence about where the Cursed Ones have taken the virus," Father Juan replied.

"And the government needs somebody to get it back?" Holgar guessed.

"What, *us*?" Jamie cried.

"*Anno, sensei* . . ." Eriko's face clouded as she lapsed into Japanese, which she did whenever she was nervous. Holgar knew Eriko didn't want to argue with Father Juan. "We're not . . . James Bond types, Master. We hunt vampires. We don't do things like this." She bowed her head. "Please excuse me. I don't wish to be rude, but . . ."

"She's right," Jamie said. "This isn't what we do. We *hunt*."

Father Juan inclined his head and leaned forward in his chair. Holgar was watching the interactions in the room with a close eye. Eriko might be the designated alpha of their pack, but Father Juan was their actual principal. Holgar had wondered, on occasion, if Eriko had been the proper choice to become the Hunter. Of course, everyone in the room except Father Juan thought *they* should have been given the elixir. They'd all come to the academy expecting to be chosen.

"You know there is talk in the Spanish military about shutting us down," Father Juan ventured. "They fear our independence and what having us around might someday cost them. It's the days of Francisco Franco all over again, when he did whatever he had to do to keep Spain out of World War Two. Spain never declared war against the Allies or the Germans. By officially remaining neutral, Franco saved thousands, if not hundreds of thousands, of Spanish lives."

"And he turned Spain into a ruthless dictatorship in the process," Antonio murmured. "What kind of life was that?"

Father Juan's somber expression softened. "You lived, Antonio. And you fought against Hitler with the Free French Forces."

"And got converted for his thanks," Skye reminded the priest. That was all they really knew—that Antonio had fought for the Allies, and that a vampire had attacked him while he was running from the Germans.

"Probably saved him from permanent slaughter," Jamie said, grunting, as if the statement cost him dearly. "Dying, you know." No doubt he wished that Antonio's sire had left well enough alone.

"It's World War Two all over again," Antonio muttered. "Nations are bowing to the conqueror in order to spare their people. Our own government wants us to stop fighting its worst enemy. It didn't work then. It won't work now."

"Just like England did to *my* folk," Jamie said. "Toss us Irish to the . . . wolves." He crossed his arms and shook his head. "No way, Father. If they don't like us, let 'em get their own virus. We're not their bleedin' errand boys. This whole thing is bollocksed up."

"Agreed, Jamie, but I don't see that we have a choice," Father Juan countered. "We need the military's support. And this is a weapon that could win the war. If it works."

"And if it doesn't work?" Eriko asked.

"My guess is we won't live long enough to care," Holgar said.

"It's not about the weapon," Antonio said. "It's about buying us more time with the military, no?"

"The weapon *is* valuable," Father Juan said. "Even if it can only kill one vampire at a time."

"I guess you're right. I mean, until we develop a machine gun that shoots wooden bullets, it's the only bit of tech we've got." Jamie smiled sourly at Antonio.

"Woof," Holgar drawled.

"Yeah, what about that?" Jamie asked. "Any danger to other supernaturals or plain old humans?"

"They won't know until they can test it." Father Juan pushed back from his chair. "The virus is more complicated than it sounds. And our side wants it back."

"They're not our side," Jamie said. "And speaking of, there's a traitor around here, and you know it, Father." He stared at Antonio. "Himself's probably going to zoom off now, e-mail his sire, and—"

In a flash Antonio leaped across the room to Jamie's chair and wrapped a hand around the Irishman's throat. Antonio snarled, and his eyes began to glow with red-hot fury.

"No soy el traidor," Antonio said with clenched teeth, fangs beginning to extend.

"Get the bloody hell off me!" Jamie choked out, moving to slam his knee into Antonio's chest—except Antonio flashed away, and Jamie tumbled out of his chair and onto the floor.

"Enough!" Father Juan shouted, jumping to his feet. He made motions, and Holgar sensed a bloom of calm flooding the room. The good father had cast a magick spell to lower tensions. Sometimes they worked on the unruly Salamanca pack.

Often they didn't.

"We don't have time to waste; we've already lost two days," Father Juan said. "This is what I am *telling* you to do." He paused. "And . . . there's more."

"*Now* what?" Jamie cried, getting to his feet.

Father Juan looked supremely uncomfortable. Holgar braced himself. His thoughts turned to Jenn, and he tightened his grip on the armrest of his chair.

"The scientist who was spearheading the project was among the survivors. He hid in a freezer in the lab, and they missed him."

"Sure they didn't turn him into a Curser?" Jamie asked, glancing pointedly at Antonio.

"He's checked out," Father Juan replied. "He can verify if we find the right virus. So . . . you're going to take him along."

"You want us to take a civilian on a hunt?" Holgar blurted.

Eriko blanched. *"Anno, sensei . . . ,"* she said again.

"You're civilians. All of you," Father Juan replied. "And yes, that is what I want." Father Juan checked his watch.

"I've arranged a meeting with the scientist. His name is Dr. Michael Sherman. Antonio will have to stay out of the sun. He'll catch up with you later."

Antonio dipped his head in assent.

Father Juan sat back down at his desk. "Grab some breakfast, and get your gear."

"Gomenasai . . ." Eriko murmured, then stood and bowed low. *"Hai, hai, sensei,"* she said. "Yes, Father Juan."

"Yes?" Jamie blinked. "Eri, this is insanity. This is not our job."

"Jamie-*kun*," she replied softly. "It is my choice to do as our master wishes. I am the Hunter."

And that settled that.

They rose as one, but as soon as they exited Father Juan's office, they scattered in different directions. Holgar knew where the others were heading. Antonio would go to the chapel to pray and meditate. Skye would go outside to cast a circle and perform protection rituals. Eriko was off for the gym to warm up her muscles. Jamie would go to his room to break things in a fury, then pack and triple-check his arsenal.

For his part Holgar headed straight for the kitchen.

Once there he found a cranky priest named Manuel. The elderly man was rotund, with jowls stereotypical of his position — that of cook.

"Father Juan never listens to me. He wakes me and insists I make enough food for all who are going out. Every time I tell him that only you will come to eat what I prepare, and every time he tells me I must prepare food anyway."

"Ja, tak. Sorry for the trouble," Holgar said.

Manuel shrugged. *"Vale, vale.* You are the easy one; it's the others who are difficult."

He handed Holgar a plate of raw venison. Out of

deference to him, Holgar took it to the empty dining room to eat. Most people at the school couldn't stomach eating with him at mealtimes. He was intensely grateful, though, that Manuel respected his diet.

Werewolves could eat cooked meat, but it wasn't pleasant. It often gave them a stomachache. Their intestinal tracts were designed to process fresh, raw food. Anything more than a few hours old or cooked for any length of time tasted rotten.

Since no one was around to watch, he picked up the meat with his hands and ate it that way. He tried to take his time and savor the flavor, though, instead of just wolfing it down. So to speak.

Finished, he politely returned his plate to the kitchen. Manuel made the sign of the cross over him as he accepted the empty plate, and Holgar nodded his head in thanks. Like many Scandinavians, Holgar was nominally Lutheran, but if his family worshipped anything, it was the moon. He was rather like little Skye in that respect. He smiled at the thought of the English girl. His smile fell as his thoughts turned to the mission. Jamie was right. This was not why they had come to Salamanca.

Burping philosophically, he returned to his room, where he gathered vials of holy water, a dozen wooden stakes, and a small container of garlic-flavored mints that had once been a novelty item and were now highly prized for their ability to repel vampires. He hung a four-inch wooden cross around his neck at the last. It had been a gift from Father

Juan upon his graduation from the academy. The center of the cross had a lamb carved into it, while the arms of the cross ended in intricately carved wolf heads. A wolf serving the Lamb of God instead of devouring Him. The priest had a wicked sense of humor, which he mostly kept under wraps but often expressed around Holgar. There was something of the wolf about Father Juan that often made Holgar feel akin to him.

Satisfied, Holgar made his way to the chapel. Antonio was kneeling at the prayer rail in the first pew, and Holgar took a seat two rows back. He was close enough to make his presence felt but not so close that he was intruding. He closed his eyes and waited.

I wonder if we'll see Jenn again, Holgar thought. There were wagers throughout the military about how long the team of Salamanca hunters would last. Today they might make someone very wealthy.

Berkeley
Heather and Jenn

Heather was terrified. She knew her sister and her father were going somewhere. She had overheard them talking. She was sick with worry, and the twisting in her stomach told her she was right to feel that way. Her first reaction was to try and follow them in her mom's car. But her mom had sharp ears and would probably catch her in the act.

You're worried for nothing, she told herself. She didn't believe it, though. If she was going to act, it had to be now, before Jenn finished in the bathroom. Heather grabbed her inhaler and stuffed it into the front pocket of her jeans and then made her way to the brass-cat key holder by the back door. She grabbed the spare set of keys to her father's car, a dark blue Toyota Camry, and slipped into the garage, closing the door behind her.

Before she could give it too much thought, Heather unlocked the trunk with the button on the key remote. In the dim light she could see the bright yellow handle and the pictogram explaining how to open the trunk from the inside. She had always been curious about that as a kid. She wished more than anything that she had tested it out to see if it actually worked. There was no time, though, so she climbed into the trunk, squeezed her eyes closed, and pulled the lid shut.

She immediately felt claustrophobic, and her throat began to tighten. She started to twist to reach the inhaler in her pocket, when she heard the garage door open and close. She lay still, afraid that if she moved, they would discover her.

"You're sure?" she heard her father ask, his voice muffled.

"Absolutely," Jenn answered.

Heather bit her lip. She'd spent her childhood listening to her parents and Jenn as they talked. She knew that her father was upset and nervous. She also knew that despite her confident answer Jenn was frightened. That realization strengthened Heather's terror, and her hand found the cord and wrapped around it, ready to yank it and escape the trunk even if meant facing the two of them.

How do you think you can go to Spain and learn to fight vampires if you can't spend one minute in a small space without freaking out? she asked herself. Heather took a deep breath and let go of the cord just as the engine roared to life. The car vibrated against her right cheek where it was pressed against the carpet of the trunk floor.

The Camry began to roll backward. She braced herself as the car turned and then lurched forward. It was too late to turn back. Once they were fully in motion, she began to fumble for her inhaler again. She managed to fish it out of her pocket, and she breathed in as deeply as she could.

The medication began to take effect just as they accelerated onto what had to be the freeway. The car bounced, and Heather's head and shoulder slammed into the roof. She tasted blood in her mouth where she bit her tongue, and panic shot through her. Vampires could smell blood a long way away. What if they found them? How many vampires could Jenn fight off? Had she just gotten the three of them killed?

Tears filled her eyes as terror overwhelmed her. She thought of everything she could lose: her father, her sister, her life. *I'll never be a wife or a mother,* she realized. *I won't go to college, never graduate from high school. I'll never go to prom.* The last thought seemed so absurd in light of everything else that she stopped crying. *Keep it together. Be more like Jenn.*

By the time they got off the freeway, her tongue had stopped bleeding, and she was a little calmer. The car made a series of quick turns until the motion and the warmth of the trunk made her nauseous. She pressed her hand to her mouth, trying not to vomit. The chemical aftertaste of her inhaler made it worse.

At last the car came to a stop. She desperately wanted to pull the handle, roll out, and find someplace to hurl. Instead Heather forced herself to lie still, listening as the doors opened and feeling the car rise slightly as her father and sister got out.

"Stay close," she heard Jenn say.

"The sun's still up," her father answered.

"Not for much longer."

"How do you know?"

"I can feel it," Jenn said.

Jenn's words punched through Heather's waves of nausea, and a chill skittered up her back. Jenn had been fighting vampires so long she was starting to sound like one. Sudden panic flooded her. *Maybe Jenn is one.* Heather forced herself to take a deep breath. *Jenn was at the funeral, out in the daylight. There's no way she's a vampire. Then again, what do we really know about them? They say they can't turn into bats, but Cousin Tina's friend Mary said her sister saw one change.*

She suddenly realized she could no longer hear her father and Jenn talking. She strained her ears but didn't hear a sound. Grimacing, she pulled the escape cord, and the trunk unlocked with a click. *It worked!* As a tiny spark of victory warmed her insides, she lifted the lid ever so slightly so she could glance outside.

The world seemed shrouded in fog, and what sunlight there was disappeared long before it reached the ground. She sucked in her breath and threw the trunk lid up and scrambled out, sucking in lungfuls of the clean, cool air until her nausea subsided.

She couldn't see Jenn or her father anywhere. Why would they have come here so close to sunset with the fog rolling in? Her father knew better, and Jenn —

Heather gasped. Jenn had left before the vampires took over the city. She probably didn't know why they had chosen San Francisco as one of their headquarters. It wasn't that they could control access by monitoring the bridges. It wasn't that the town's leaders had given it to them without a fight. It was the fog. When the fog rolled in thick off the bay, vampires could come out while the sun was still up.

And it couldn't be foggier.

CHAPTER SIX

Come to us, children of the light
We have seen and heard your plight
Let us take you by the hand
Vampire and human together stand
Your struggles have been long and dear
But that's all done now we are here
Strife will cease through every land
Divided we fall, united we stand

MADRID, SPAIN
SALAMANCAN HUNTERS: ANTONIO, HOLGAR,
SKYE, ERIKO, AND JAMIE

Night had fallen; Eriko called once they had reached their objective and requested that Antonio join them. The scientist was being cared for in a church by sympathetic priests known to Father Juan. Sharing Jamie's mistrust of the entire mission, Antonio wondered who exactly had approached their master and asked for their help.

Antonio parked in a lot and walked through Retiro Park, passing by the Fountain of the Fallen Angel. Lucifer, angel of light, had just been banished from heaven, and he was plummeting to hell, wings outstretched, arms spread in dismay. Around the base of the fountain, faces of evil leered at the pedestrians, spewing water. The fountain was older than Antonio, and when he had seen it as a child on his special visit to Madrid to make his first confession, it had terrified him. Crossing himself now, he skirted around it, filled with intense feelings of displeasure.

Spain, will you tumble from paradise as well? Will you eventually capitulate, as so many other countries have done? Appease the vampires by pretending they've retracted their fangs and no long tear out the throats of your children?

A little ways beyond the park stood the church, a small but pretty building of baroque plaster with a bell tower. All its arched windows had been boarded up. There was a sign on the door that read WE SERVE ALL WHO ARE CALLED TO THE LORD.

Antonio walked around the side, in search of the rectory, and was escorted by a young, somber priest into a little room designed for prayer and meditation. There was a carved stone font beside the door, and he dipped his fingers in and blessed himself—the only vampire he knew who could do so.

In an alcove a statue of St. John of the Cross with bowed head seemed to be praying for those who entered into the sparsely furnished room. Votive candles flickered before the figure, and the saint looked almost as if he were smiling. Antonio found that meaningful, as if the patron of their Academia was accompanying the group on their mission.

The other four Salamancans sat on sofas and in stuffed chairs. Swathed in a gray wrap sweater and a matching knitted cap, Skye flashed him a grateful smile, and the rest nodded their heads, acknowledging his arrival. They were bundled against the cold. An electric heater ticked; hot air whirred. Madrid in late February was cold and damp, even for Holgar. Luckily, it had not snowed.

Sitting on the edge of a mahogany desk, a second young priest nodded at Antonio, who nodded back. The priest had a goatee, giving him a slightly satanic cast. And standing beside the desk had to be the man they had traveled to meet.

Antonio could have snapped the scientist in half. Somehow the man managed to embody every stereotype his profession had to offer. He was skinny and short, with pale-brown hair and watery blue eyes hidden behind a pair of thick glasses with black rims. Forty, maybe, but probably younger. And rather anxious, from the way his eyes darted around the room.

"I'm Father Luis," the priest said to Antonio. "And this is Dr. Michael Sherman."

"*Hola. ¿Cómo estás? Er, ¿están?*" the man asked in pained Spanish.

"You're not Spanish, Mick; speak English," Jamie growled.

"Sorry, thank you," Michael said, noticeably relaxing.

"American?" Antonio asked in surprise.

"Yes." Dr. Sherman nodded. "From the University of Maryland. Or, I was."

"What are you doing over here?" Holgar asked.

The scientist pushed up his glasses. "Well, you may remember from your biology classes that . . ."

"Skip all the fancy talk," Jamie said. "Some of us have been too busy saving the world to go to school."

Eriko flushed, and Antonio waited politely.

"Very well." Dr. Sherman raised his chin. "I've spent several years working on finding a complete cure for leukemia, which is a cancer of the blood. I realized that with my research it might be possible to actually *create* a strain of leukemia, one that could be injected into vampires, which would cause their bodies to destroy them from the inside out."

Holgar whistled low.

Michael sneezed. "Sorry, I have allergies." He pulled a packet of tissues out of his pocket and blew his nose. Then he spent a second examining the contents.

Jamie blinked and looked at the group as if to say, *And we've entrusted technology to this dolt?*

"I think he wants to know why you were doing that here and not working at home," Skye said gently. "In America."

Sherman looked around for a trash can. Spotting the one beside Father Luis's desk, he made a ball of his tissue and aimed it at the rim. It fell on the floor, well short of its target.

Skye tittered.

"Sherman-*sensei*, please excuse us," Eriko said, shooting her a scowl. "We don't mean to be rude."

"Oh," he said, "that's all right. I was told that you're a bit . . . exuberant. He smiled eagerly. "Like special-ops guys, only . . . younger."

"That being a relative term," Holgar replied, and Antonio smiled faintly.

Dr. Sherman frowned quizzically. Then he shrugged. "Well, anyway, I had approached . . . certain people . . . in my government, but they said they weren't interested. That same night my lab—the one in America—was destroyed. I was supposed to have been in it working, but I had gone outside to get some fresh air. When I went back into the building and saw what had happened, I ran."

The hunters looked at one another, aware that one of their own was alone in hostile territory. Jamie clenched his teeth and mouthed a curse, and Holgar cast Antonio a sympathetic glance.

"So you came here?" Antonio asked. "To Spain?"

Sherman nodded, gazing into the distance as if at a place they couldn't see, or maybe a time he'd rather forget. "Yes, I'd heard that Spain hadn't just rolled over and played dead. I was right." He bowed his head, as if personally thanking them.

Antonio couldn't help but think of Jenn, who had also fled to Spain from America so that she could join the cause and destroy vampires. He sighed. Thoughts of Jenn always disrupted his concentration.

"Let me tell you about *this* attack," Sherman said. "I went into the freezer for some cultures. Then I heard breaking and crashing, so I hid there until it was quiet and it seemed safe. When I came out"—his voice dropped—"everyone . . . was dead."

Antonio glanced at Jamie, whose jaw was tightly clenched. He read the Irishman's body language: *Dead like we're gonna be if we go on this feckin' jaunt.* Dead like those three Hunters. Were they being set up?

Sherman sniffed and wiped his nose with another tissue. He was fighting off some sort of infection. To Antonio's vampire senses it was offensive. Infection tainted the blood, and the smell of it was repulsive to vampires. Holgar twisted uncomfortably in his seat, and Antonio couldn't help but wonder if the werewolf smelled it too. That infection could have been what saved the scientist's life during the most recent attack. No vampire would have willingly drunk from him, and they were probably too busy draining the others to go and find him in the icebox and snap his neck.

Antonio dropped his head and coughed into his hand. The mere thought of feeding was causing him to change. He half listened as Dr. Sherman continued to explain about the virus. If it really worked, humanity could win the war. And then what? As sure as Antonio was that the sun would continue to rise and set, he was certain that, if given a chance, Jamie would use the virus to kill him.

Not if I kill him first. The thought rose in him as it had many other times, but this time it took more effort to dispel. One day the hotheaded Irishman would make a move against him or Holgar, and what then?

The priest started speaking, and Antonio forced himself to pay attention.

"When I phoned your master to tell him that you and Dr. Sherman had arrived, he told me to tell you to leave in three hours, and that you should be prepared."

"Can't we rest and leave tomorrow night?" the scientist begged. He looked at the others. "I've been through a lot."

"We don't want to lose time," Antonio replied flatly.

The man looked haggard, and Antonio wondered just how sick he was.

"But surely a few more hours wouldn't hurt. We could strike early tomorrow evening." Dr. Sherman emphasized the word "strike" as if he were trying to sound like someone in special ops. Antonio couldn't fathom taking him with them. He supposed they had to, but it bordered on absurdity.

Antonio glanced toward Eriko, hoping the Hunter would

back him up. It was Jamie, though, who met his eyes. The Irishman smiled grimly.

"Right there with you, Spain," Jamie muttered.

OAKLAND, CALIFORNIA
JENN AND HEATHER

Everywhere Jenn looked, the Oakland hills were blanketed with layers of white mist. Eight miles east of San Francisco, Oakland shared the same weather patterns, including heavy fog. This fog had set in as soon as the rain had stopped, covering the landscape with a white shroud. Winding through the hills above, Oakland's older houses, some of them Victorian and all of them well maintained, lined narrow streets. While a majority of the city had been abandoned years before to gangs, the houses up on the hills had always kept their value and status.

Jenn and her father had parked in a small park-and-drive lot where Bay Area commuters could meet and pile into one car for ride shares into the city. The lot was deserted, what with everyone wanting to get home before dark. Jenn didn't blame them.

The feeling of isolation was almost overwhelming as she and her father left the car and began climbing a steep slope. Jenn breathed in deep of the cold air and after a minute turned and looked down to admire the view. But the rest of Oakland and the bay itself were obscured by the thick fog.

Even their car, a hundred feet away, had been swallowed up by it. *Like a ghost,* the thought came, unbidden.

She had missed the fog and the crispness of the air. She had missed a lot of things about home. So many times she had dreamed about what it would be like to come back. But in her dreams Papa Che was alive, greeting her as a hero, as a peer. In her dreams there were no vampires . . . except Antonio.

She wished she could have told Heather about Antonio, that she was in love, and that the guy was gorgeous and strong and caring. Jenn couldn't tell her that Antonio was a vampire. She couldn't tell anyone in her family. It would just confuse the issue and make them question the cause that much more. Their side couldn't afford that, especially not over a single vampire, even if he was her boyfriend, sort of.

The truth was that no one knew why Antonio had the strength to do what he did. Antonio was convinced it was God. Jenn just didn't know. What she did know was that no one, not even Antonio, had heard of any other vampire who'd betrayed his kind and fought for good.

She stumbled over a bit of uneven sidewalk, a souvenir from the quake of '89. She regained her footing and shook herself mentally. *Focus!* It scared her when she zoned out like that. Still, at least it was daylight, but it wasn't good all the same. Especially not when her father walked beside her and she had promised to protect him.

She stared at her father as he climbed the hill beside her. He was tense. His hands were clenched into fists, and a tiny muscle in his jaw spasmed repeatedly. He was taking a huge risk to help out his friend's family, and he was scared. She knew how hard it had to be for him.

"You're doing the right thing, Dad," she said, careful to keep her voice barely more than a whisper. Even though it was well before sunset, one never knew who might be listening who was sympathetic to the other side.

"I hope so," he murmured.

They passed a dozen more large, upscale homes; the fog swirled around them, occasionally revealing bits of Queen Anne gingerbread, private hedges, and, in one case, two gray stone lions flanking a cobblestone walkway. It was like seeing mixed-up pieces of a jigsaw puzzle. Then the fog descended in earnest, obscuring everything.

Her father came to a stop. He reached out and put his hand on a white picket fence and just stood for a moment, as though lost in thought.

"There's no other way," he groaned.

"What is it?" Jenn asked, scanning the street around them for signs that they were being watched. She strained all her senses. All she saw was white on white on white. "Dad?"

Her father swung open the gate. She remained on high alert. She had to protect him. She couldn't let anything happen to him.

From the direction they had come, she heard the sound of shoes slapping against concrete. Someone was running toward them.

"They're . . . I thought we were meeting inside," her dad murmured.

"Dad! Go through the gate," she hissed.

"I . . . oh, *Jenn* . . ."

"Dad?" Something was terribly wrong. "Dad?"

He groaned again. The unseen runner kept coming, footfalls pounding harder and louder. Alarmed, Jenn slid a stake out of her quiver with her right hand. Hunters weren't supposed to kill humans. *What if it's a spy or a sentry? What if they know what Dad looks like, because of work?* She wrapped her fingers around the stake, wishing she had a gun. Adrenaline rushed through her, making her senses pop, heightening her awareness.

Her father walked through the open gate. She reached for him, but fog washed between them, obscuring him from her view.

"Dad, we have to get out of here," she said, wheeling back around the way they had come. The sound grew louder. Someone was deliberately heading for them. Her heartbeat raced. It could just be a jogger. But who would go for a run in a fog bank?

"No. I promised," he said.

"Dad, wait. Don't go anywhere."

She waited, poised, muscles thrumming. She could hear

his quiet footsteps behind her and the pounding footfalls of the person racing toward her.

Jenn planted her feet and prepared herself for battle.

Closer.

Jenn raised her stake high, fear racing through her. What if it was a cop with a gun? Or a soldier with an Uzi? What if this house was a known meeting place for the Resistance? They couldn't be caught. Her dad couldn't be identified. If he was seen with the people his coworker had died to protect, he would be killed too. *And Mom and Heather.*

I can't kill a human. Unless I'm absolutely sure that I'm in danger.

She could hear the runner's ragged breathing and strained to make out a figure. The stranger was only steps away, but the fog was too thick for her to see who it was.

Stop and identify yourself, Jenn wanted to call, but she couldn't risk being heard if there were others.

Closer.

She pulled back her arm, preparing to plunge the stake into the stranger's chest if need be, knowing it would be a violation of every vow she had taken. She wanted to yell at her father to run. The figure of a girl loomed suddenly in front of her, and Jenn began to swing her stake. Then saw her face.

Heather!

"Behind you!" Heather shrieked.

Jenn spun around, her arm still in motion. A woman

rushed her; Jenn thought she saw a flash of fangs as she plunged the stake into her heart.

"Oh, my God, oh, God!" her father yelled, and Heather screamed.

Horror washed over Jenn. It was still daylight. She had just killed a human being.

But in the next moment the woman collapsed into a pile of swirling dust as Heather screamed and screamed.

Vampire? In daylight?

Five more vampires, eyes glowing in the fog, faced her. Her dad darted to her right, heaving, one hand pressed over his eyes and the other across his chest. Behind her Jenn could hear the familiar wheezing sound as Heather succumbed to an asthma attack.

Jenn took a step backward as the vampires fanned out, advancing on them. Vampires. In daylight.

She blinked. "How . . . ?"

A tall one — sporting the classic vampire look right down to the slicked-back hair and the black cloak — smiled at her. "You know the wonderful thing about thick San Francisco fog? It diffuses the sunlight so that it doesn't touch us."

Fog? Fog! That's why San Francisco is a stronghold. That's why the vampires are running wild. And the people — her gaze ticked toward her father, standing with his shoulders slumped and his hands covering his eyes like a two-year-old who didn't want to see something scary. *The people know!*

She threw a vial of holy water so hard that it broke

against the Dracula wannabe's forehead. He howled and began clawing at his eyes. Three of the other vampires shrank back, while the fifth, a thin blond man, came at Jenn. Her hands flew to her pockets. With her left she threw a bottle of olive oil that had been blessed by the Pope to the ground in front of her, and with her right she struck a match against her jeans and dropped it onto the oil. A moment later the oil caught on fire just as the vampire lunged at her. He shrieked as the flames engulfed his shoes and pants.

He fell to the ground and tried to roll to smother the flames but only managed to catch the pants of his blinded companion on fire as well.

"Dad, get Heather and run!" Jenn yelled, heart pounding out of her chest. She had only one other vial of oil, and soon the fire on the ground would die out. There were three vampires left, and from the way they watched her quietly, patiently, she knew they were the smartest of the group.

Jenn pulled another stake from her pocket and gripped it tight. Her hands were slick with sweat, and even she could smell the stench of fear coming off of her. Her mind slipped back to Spain, to the burning church, her hesitation . . .

Stop it! You're better than that, better than this.

The flames engulfed the two injured vampires, and they were soon reduced to dust. Their companions were unfazed.

She took the remaining bottle of oil and smashed it against the wooden picket fence that surrounded the yard. Jenn lit another match and dropped it, and a flame sprang to life. Fueled by the oil, the fire burned hot and fast. Soon it would surround the vampires.

She took a step back. One of the three vampires, an older-looking female, glanced uncomfortably at the burning fence. Jenn dug more stakes out of the pockets of her cargo pants and risked a glance at her father, who was frozen with fear. Someone had betrayed them.

"Are the people we need to help inside the house?" she shouted to him.

He shook his head slowly. She had never seen such a strange expression on his face, or any other person's face — shame, fear, and . . . loathing. She jerked her head, bewildered.

"There were never people inside the house," he said, his voice barely loud enough to hear over the crackle of the flames.

"What?" she asked, even more confused.

"He said, there were never people inside the house," a throaty female voice purred from behind her.

Jenn spun around and came face-to-face with evil. She wore a plunging red cashmere sweater and black leather trousers that hugged her thighs. Black hair tumbled down her back, and she looked like a femme fatale out of an old film noir. Only this woman had wicked-looking fangs and super strength. She held Heather by the throat with one hand. Jenn watched as her sister struggled feebly against her grip, gasping for air.

"Heather," Jenn croaked, reaching out a hand. "Oh, God, Heather."

Feet barely touching the ground, Heather stared at her with enormous blue eyes. Her mouth worked, but no words came out.

"There are only vampires in that house," the woman said, smiling.

"That's not . . . true," Jenn said, frantically trying to figure out if she could stake the Cursed One before the Cursed One killed Heather. Wondering if the people in the house were alive, or if they'd been butchered in the surprise attack.

The Cursed One cocked her head. Her eyes glowed through the fog as Jenn tracked her every movement, her hunter training coming back to her despite her terror. One slash, one bite, and Heather could be dead.

"It doesn't matter. Daddy dearest said you were going to help some people. And you are. Her, I presume," the vampire said, giving Heather a little shake. Heather whimpered.

"Dad, what is she talking about?" Jenn blurted, without taking her eyes off her sister and the Cursed One.

There was silence.

"Tell her," the vampire said, "about the bargain you made."

More silence.

"What bargain, Dad?" Jenn asked.

Her father's voice was shaking so hard she could barely hear him when he spoke. "Jenn . . . Jennifer . . . I had to save Heather. I did it so they would leave her and your mother and me alone. "

"What did you promise them in return?" Jenn demanded, eyeing the vampire, listening to Heather's labored breathing.

"Tell her," the vampire insisted. She smiled brilliantly at Jenn.

There was another silence, this one longer than the previous two.

When he finally spoke, her father's voice was cold, detached. "You. I promised them I would deliver you."

BOOK TWO
HEL

In darkness and secure,
By the secret ladder, disguised~
oh, happy chance!~
In darkness and in concealment,
my house being now at rest.

—St. John of the Cross,
sixteenth-century mystic of Salamanca

CHAPTER SEVEN

We are the hunters. Steeped in tradition from a time
when vampires were considered a local, not a global,
menace, Hunters were once trained by their masters
and set against the Cursed One, or Cursed Ones, that
threatened the Hunter's hometown, or village, or tribe.
In the prime of youth we served our people—and our
people only—one Hunter set apart, revered, rewarded.
     Now that has changed.
                              —from the diary of Jenn Leitner

MADRID
ANTONIO, HOLGAR, JAMIE, ERIKO, SKYE,
AND DR. MICHAEL SHERMAN

According to Father Juan's source, the vampires who had stolen the virus had set up their own laboratory underneath the

Biblioteca Nacional de España, on the Paseo de Recoletos. The library was first founded by King Philip V in 1712; half a million books had been confiscated from civilians during the Spanish civil war of the 1930s alone, locked away inside its vaults to preserve the valuable texts from the ravages of war. Antonio had told Skye a lot about the history of the area, brushing only lightly on his own personal history.

Skye shared Antonio's unease about the mission: If the Cursed Ones were so brazen as to set up a laboratory in the subbasement of a public building, they had to have friends in high places. For all she knew, this "mission" could be a trap, arranged to get rid of the thorny problem of a Spanish team of hunters. Together with Father Juan, Skye had thrown the runes and consulted numerous other arcana, searching for auguries to predict the outcome of their mission. Neither she nor the strange holy man who was so conversant in the matters of the Craft had been able to foretell what lay in store for the hunters. Father Juan had apologized, and assured her he would pray.

But Skye was a child of the Goddess and had never had much reason to believe the Christian God would intercede on her behalf.

And so, she had turned to . . . other places, for help. But there was no answer there, either, and she worried that by going outside the sacred circle of her team, she had revealed too much about the Salamancans' plans and made them even more vulnerable.

Guilt-ridden, she almost told Father Juan everything then, looking for absolution in the event that she died. But her fear kept her silent, and she decided that she would carry her secrets to the grave.

Holgar whistled low in admiration as they entered the building, which to Skye's mind resembled a Greek temple. The sheer accumulation of knowledge was staggering. The massive library housed rare books that were centuries old, and Skye was certain that many of the tantalizing spell books believed by witches to be lost were stashed with all the books the Spanish government had deemed too danger-ous for their people.

And speaking of danger . . .

Weapons hidden in their clothes — short swords in scab-bards beneath bulky coats, the ingredients for Molotov cocktails taped to their legs — the Salamancans and their "civilian," the scientist with the bad breath, passed stack after stack of volumes bound in burgundy and hunter green with titles stamped in gold. Skye couldn't help but wonder if any of the books held clues that could help them fight their hidden war. Did any of them even mention the word "vampire" without immediately attaching it to the word "myth"? The histories of what had happened — the *accurate* histories — had yet to be written.

She had been little when the Cursed Ones had made their presence known. She remembered being amazed and frightened and fascinated all at once. It was one of the only times her parents ever permitted the television to be on at home. They said it was only for keeping up with important news in the mundane world and not for rotting her brain.

A group of vampires had called a press conference at the United Nations building in New York City. Their leader was the stunningly handsome Solomon. There, in full view of the world, Solomon had revealed the truth about his kind. Well, a version of the truth, at any rate. With some others he had shown off his glowing eyes and fangs for the cameras while swearing that vampires only fed off the blood of animals, usually obtained from butcher shops and rarely from the animals themselves. It had all seemed so civilized. They spoke of peace, of a world deeply divided, and how it was time for everyone to come together in a spirit of harmony.

The thing that she had remembered most, though, was that while she and her sister had been shocked, her parents hadn't been. She had often speculated since then that they had known of the existence of the Cursed Ones long before that.

Skye glanced toward Antonio, who was quietly walking beside Eriko beneath the fluorescent lights. The vampires said they wanted to live in peace, but he was the only one who had ever demonstrated that he could live and work with humans. He was fascinating, and she often said prayers that he and Jenn could find happiness together.

Holgar was even more exotic. No group of were-wolves had come forward, the way the Cursed Ones had, to announce that they existed and they, too, wanted to live in peace. Despite her life as a White Witch, holding all nature as sacred even after Holgar had come forward at the academy, Skye had found it almost more difficult to accept that werewolves were real. They had managed to mostly keep themselves concealed, hiding their ways from humans and often their identities, as well. Werewolves were shape shifters; on the full moon Holgar actually changed into a hairy beast. And even when human, he had bizarre habits—swiping at enemies with his fingernails as though they were claws, drinking from streams by dipping his face to the water and lapping it with his tongue, and the full-body growl that seemed to vibrate the air around him.

Antonio always acted like a person. That had been how the vampires had lulled everyone into a false sense of security—they didn't seem all that different. Vampires attracted groupies, fan clubs, middle-aged women and young girls swooning over them. People who grew fangs and whose eyes glowed? That had seemed kind of . . . kinky. People who turned into monsters? That was something to fear.

At first Skye had feared Holgar. Unlike Antonio, he was hard to read. His easy laughter and broad grin hid something dark that frightened her. Antonio had been converted as a young man and had memories of what it was to be human. Holgar had been born a wolf and knew nothing of what life was like for those who were not.

She had learned, though, how to read his body language

and how to react to him. She had felt like an idiot at first, occasionally stroking him as she would a dog and murmuring banalities. The first time she had accidentally told him he was a good boy, she had been mortified. Instead of getting angry, though, he had brushed his arm against hers in what she knew to be a sign of affection. That was what Jamie didn't get about Holgar. Jamie was constantly trying to put him down by referring to him as an animal. To Holgar there was no insult in that.

She stayed close to her partner as the Salamancans moved toward the left side of the cavernous reading room, past a row of archaic world globes decorated with little faces puffing winds across the oceans. Oblivious that hunters walked in their midst, people were seated at dark wood tables, reading, coats and scarves draped over chairs. Two little boys were giggling as they played a handheld video game, quieting as the elderly woman across from them glared and cleared her throat. The library would be closing soon; they were lucky that it was open after dark and they could just walk in.

Next to her, Skye felt Holgar tense.

"Easy," she whispered, putting a hand on his arm, feeling the vibration of his muscles against her fingers. "What is it?"

"Fear. This place reeks of it." He sniffed the air and grimaced.

"Most places do these days." Her smile was sad.

"*Nej, min lille heks*, not like this." He was switching into Danish, calling her his little witch. "Something is rotten, and it's not in the state of Denmark." And he was paraphrasing *Hamlet*. His tension communicated itself to her.

"I smell it too," Antonio said quietly, moving up beside them. "Something is different here."

"What?" Skye asked.

"Bloody hell, isn't it obvious?" Jamie hissed, turning around to glare at them all.

Skye shook her head.

Eriko was already several steps ahead and either didn't hear them or didn't care to be part of the conversation.

"Why don't you enlighten us, Irish," Holgar said with a low growl.

Jamie nodded toward a group of college students poring over stacks of math textbooks and asking each other the occasional question. "Resistance meeting."

"What? They're studying," Skye argued.

"That's what it looks like," Jamie said. "But they're also communicating."

As Skye watched, a pale girl wearing her black hair back with a scarlet headband wrote something down on her notebook, and the dark-skinned guy next to her, in a Real Madrid football sweatshirt, glanced at it. Real Madrid tapped twice with his pencil on the table. Headband nodded almost imperceptibly and then erased whatever it was she had written.

"Nice," Holgar said in admiration.

Skye glanced around the library with new eyes. There were a lot of solitary readers at tables and in overstuffed chairs, but others were clustered in groups of three and four. How many of them were praying for a miracle and risking their lives to make it happen for others? She shook her head in awe.

"Let's not draw more attention to them," Antonio said, pushing forward to follow Eriko, who was almost out of sight.

The rest fell in behind him, and Skye tried to keep her eyes on the ground lest she stare too long at any one group of people. She moved her hand slowly. It wasn't exactly a cloaking spell; the hunters could still be seen. If it worked, though, it would ensure that people wouldn't be interested in them when they did see them.

The magicks Skye had practiced with her family growing up were minor compared to what she had been called upon to cast since coming to Salamanca. She spent as much time with Father Juan as she could, learning new magicks, more defensive spells. He had even taught her a couple of spells used to attack, but she was too afraid to use them. It was wrong—that was what her upbringing had taught her. The more time passed, though, and the more the vampires took over, the more she wondered if that was her parents talking and not her.

What did Skye believe? Some days she wasn't sure.

They finally caught up to Eriko toward the back of the

building; she was scrutinizing a blank wooden wall. A tall bookcase obscured the hunters from view of others in the library as they clustered around her. The Hunter reached out a hand and patted the smooth, dark wood. According to their contact there was a secret passage in that wall that led into the chambers beneath the library. Skye could barely keep herself together. What if it was really a burglar alarm? Or a secret alarm that sounded below stairs, alerting the Cursed Ones that they were coming?

"Where is it?" Jamie hissed.

Skye waved her hand in a spell of seeing, but it didn't work.

"I can smell the difference in the air," Antonio insisted. "It has to be here."

"I agree," Holgar added. He stepped forward, and put his nose to the wall, pressing his face against it, so that his nose was squished. He yipped softly.

Skye glanced quickly around to make sure they weren't drawing attention. Fortunately, there was no one else in sight. Holgar walked slowly, nose sniffing like a dog's. Finally he stopped and took several deep breaths in one spot and then stepped back. "It's here," he said, tracing his finger down a seemingly blank portion of wall. "This is the opening."

"Are you sure?" Michael asked, his voice too loud in the silence that surrounded them.

Skye jumped. She had almost forgotten that the nerdy

little scientist was with them. He had followed behind submissively, quietly.

"*Ja,*" Holgar said.

The man frowned. "But I don't see anything."

"I trust his nose," Jamie snapped. "If he says it's here, it's here."

Skye was impressed that Jamie was backing Holgar up, especially given that Jamie didn't trust the rest of Holgar at all.

"Father Juan said there was a hidden spring," Eriko reminded them. "The door opens with pressure."

"Anyone know where?" Michael nervously pushed up his glasses.

"*Vale, vale,*" Antonio murmured, as he knelt and ran his fingers along the base of the wall. "There is a slight depression here. I can't see it, but I can feel it."

"So push the bloody thing," Jamie urged.

Antonio did.

A section of the wall slid silently open to reveal dark, brooding blackness.

And evil, Skye thought with a shudder.

OAKLAND
JENN, HEATHER, AND AURORA

Jenn turned to her father in shock. It couldn't be true. Her father would never lure her here to be killed. His guilt, though, was written on his face. "I lost you a long time ago," he said. "In the end it was the right decision to make."

She wanted to scream and lash out at him. But she was a hunter, and she was facing down four vampires. Shivering in horror, she swallowed back bile and forced herself to assess the situation. The fire had consumed all the oil-drenched wood and was burning out. The rest of the fence had absorbed too much moisture from the fog to burn. The vampires at her back were about to spring.

And her father was slowly backing away, abandoning both her *and* Heather, the daughter he had done all this for.

Think, Jenn! she commanded herself, swiveling back to the vampire who held Heather. The black-haired woman exuded power, and Jenn knew instinctively that she was far more dangerous than the three vampires behind Jenn combined.

"What are you doing so far from your home and your team, little Hunter?" the woman purred.

Jenn lifted her chin in defiance.

The woman tightened her grip on Heather's throat.

"Jenn!" Heather squeaked involuntarily.

"Jenn, is it? Just Jenn?" the vampire mocked.

Jenn felt her face flush. She told herself the Cursed One couldn't read her thoughts, didn't know that was what she called herself.

"And who am I going to have the pleasure of staking?" Jenn asked, forcing bravado into her voice.

The Cursed One laughed. "Well, you can have a try at Nick, Dora, and Kyle behind you. However, if you want to know *my* name, it will cost you."

Jenn didn't like it. They were trained never to get into a discussion with vampires. It was dangerous. Not only could they mesmerize people, but they could also distract you while others crept up behind you.

Just like the three that were behind Jenn. She sensed, though, that they wouldn't make their move until the woman in front of her commanded it. So Jenn kept her back to them and faced her true adversary, the one who was threatening her sister.

"Cost me what?" Jenn asked, careful not to look the Cursed One directly in the eyes to avoid being charmed. Jenn was stalling for time, though, while she tried to figure out how to get her and Heather out of the mess alive. To attack without a plan against such an opponent was suicide.

"Much."

Something cold and hard settled in Jenn's stomach. She and Heather were going to die. There was no way around that. Nothing she could do would stop it. She was one hunter, low on weapons, against four vampires and a human who had betrayed her. She shoved her hands into her pockets and pulled out two small crosses.

The vampire only smirked at her, then snapped the fingers on her free hand; suddenly, one of the Cursed Ones who had stood behind Jenn appeared in front of her. Jenn took advantage of her own surprise to jump backward, and then she spun around, stabbing the crosses into the eyes of both of the remaining vampires, taking *them* by surprise.

They fell to the ground, screaming and smoking as their eyes burned. It wouldn't kill them, but it would slow them down, giving her the time she needed.

Jenn pivoted on her left foot and flung the crosses at the leader and the other vampire. The guy reached up and batted away both crosses and then howled in pain.

A beam of light sliced through the fog and hit the ground right in front of the woman's foot. She jerked and jumped backward. The fog was thinning; little shafts of light started to open up in several places. The sun was setting, and once it did, all would be lost.

Jenn leaped forward, like a tiger closing in for a kill. All she had to do was knock the vampire into one of those shafts of light.

The woman snarled and hurled Heather as if she were weightless toward the guy with the burned hand. He caught Heather and tossed her over his shoulder.

"No!" Jenn shouted. "No!"

"Jenn, help me!" Heather shrieked, flailing and kicking. "Oh, my God!"

"Come along, Nick. It's time to go," the woman said.

"Wait, you said you'd spare my daughter," Jenn's father called out, arms raised toward Heather. His daughter . . . as if Jenn were just . . .

. . . nobody.

"Be grateful I'm sparing *you*," the woman shot back.

Jenn pulled the remaining stakes from her pockets and hurled them one after the other, but the woman dodged them with ease. She smiled at Jenn, and Jenn's blood turned to ice. "If you want your sister, come and get her. She'll be waiting for you in New Orleans. Otherwise, I'll convert her myself at Mardi Gras. See you. That is, if Dora and Kyle don't kill you first."

And then she, Nick, and Heather disappeared into the remaining fog.

Jenn gasped and spun around. The two blinded vampires were regaining their feet, their eyes still healing. They hissed angrily. Her father took off running back toward the car, and Jenn let him go.

She was out of stakes. She grabbed the charred part of the fence, but it crumbled to ash in her hands. She looked around, desperate to find something she could use to kill them. She was running out of time—and then she was just running.

Reeling, she looked left, right, searching for a place to launch an attack. All her training kicked in, and she ran, changing course every few steps to try and keep them guessing. Vampires were fast, but these were injured, and she had only a few seconds to get away, to find someplace to make her stand.

A house blurred past in the milky whiteness, then some

bushes, and then another house. She cut across a well-mowed lawn and exited on a different street. Everything looked suddenly familiar. Blinking, she turned to the right and began to race downhill, which was faster and easier, but she risked falling. Where was she?

Suddenly it snapped into place. Trestle Glen. That was the street her best friend, Brooke, had lived on for years. She hadn't seen Brooke since she left for Salamanca. Hadn't even had a chance to say good-bye to her before she left, and they had been friends since kindergarten. Brooke had always been the voice of reason. Deep down she knew she hadn't called Brooke before she left because Brooke would have been able to talk her out of going.

Jenn poured on extra speed. Unlike her sister, Jenn was used to massive physical exertion, and she didn't have the asthma that plagued Heather. She thought of her little sister wheezing and gasping for air as she had chased after Jenn. Heather could never survive the Academia, no matter how much either of them wanted it. Jenn had been foolish to think for even a second that Heather could withstand the rigors of the training.

But she has the heart for it, Jenn argued with herself. Heather had saved her life, warning her just in time about the vampire that was sneaking up behind her, ready to kill her, while their father stood silent.

He watched.

White-hot anger flooded her, driving her on faster and

faster. She had heard of it happening, family members selling each other out. But she had never thought it could happen in her family, no matter what bad blood existed. It wasn't the Leitner way. Or so she had thought. Nothing would ever make her betray her own flesh and blood.

The fog still pressed in, but it was thinning rapidly. Would it dissipate in time to kill her pursuers or drive them underground to shelter? She hoped so, but she doubted it. The sun was setting; she could feel it as surely as she felt the pounding of her own heart.

The heart that beat for Antonio.

Even though his couldn't beat for her.

She was sick with fear that she would never see him or Heather again. She had to do everything in her power to save herself and her sister. And to do that, she was going to have to endanger her oldest friend.

Brooke's house came into view, and Jenn put on a fresh burst of speed. She leaped up the steps to the front door and pounded on it, spurning the doorbell for something to hit.

She heard footsteps within, and a moment later the door opened and Brooke stood, blinking at her in shock. Brooke's big green eyes widened, and she gave a squeal of joy. "Oh, my God! Jenn, is it really you?"

Jenn threw her arms around Brooke, a choking sob escaping her. Her friend hugged her back before breaking away and pulling her into the white-and-black marbled foyer. The house was almost as familiar to Jenn as the one she had grown up in. She had to turn it into a fortress where she could make a stand. Straight ahead, a wood staircase with a floral runner led up to the bedrooms. To the left was the dining room and the kitchen, with a set of stairs that led down to the garage. Off to the right was the living room, where they had watched hours of movies, played on the piano, had pillow fights, and told each other their deepest secrets. The familiar odor of Brooke's parents' cigarette smoke lingered in the air. Once upon a time Jenn's biggest worry in life had been dying of cancer from secondhand smoke. It seemed forever had passed since then, like her memories were all stories Jenn had heard about somebody else's life.

Brooke squeezed her wrists, pulling her toward the living room, but Jenn stood her ground. Oblivious, Brooke kept pulling at her. "What happened to you? All your parents would ever say was that you had gone away to school. I knew that couldn't be true, though. You wouldn't have left without telling me or texting, calling, something," Brooke said, bewilderment and hurt in her eyes.

"I'm so sorry," Jenn said, looking back over her shoulder in the direction of the foyer. "I don't have time for explanations. I need your help."

"Why? What's going on?" Brooke's voice rose, alarmed.

"There's no time. It was stupid to come here. I had nowhere else to turn, and you popped into my mind." Jenn was babbling, but she couldn't stop herself. The vampires could be just outside the front door now. She had to pull it together.

"Simon, something's wrong," Brooke said, dragging Jenn into the living room.

A tall, lanky, dark-blond guy around their age, wearing a black button-down shirt and jeans, stood up from the couch. Brooke crossed to him, and he put an arm around her shoulder.

Whoa, Brooke's got a boyfriend and he's a hottie, Jenn thought. It was totally inappropriate, but he'd startled her.

"This is Simon. Sy, this is my best friend in the entire world."

"Hey," he said. "Are you okay?"

Jenn was panting, but she took a deep breath and shook her head. "I'm being chased."

"Who by?" Brooke asked in alarm.

"Show me who. I'll kick their ass," Simon said.

Oxygen rushed into her lungs as she leaned forward. She just needed a moment to catch her breath.

"You can't," she said. "They're vampires. They'll only be about a minute behind."

Brooke chuckled and rolled her emerald eyes. "Well, then, Simon will kick their asses."

"No, you can't," Jenn began. Then she stopped abruptly as her eyes fell on the necklace Brooke was wearing. It was a bat with a heart clutched in its claws. Girls wore that when they were holding out for vampire boyfriends. But

Brooke clearly already had a boyfriend, so what . . . ?

She locked eyes with Simon, and he smiled.

"Oh, no," Jenn whispered, backing furiously away.

"What's wrong?" Brooke asked. Then she looked down at her necklace. "It's cool. Simon's cool. Jeez, did they totally brainwash you while you were away?"

Jenn turned, praying she could reach the door first. Something grabbed her ponytail and yanked hard enough to pull her off her feet and send her crashing down onto the floor on her back.

She gasped as all the wind was knocked out of her. She stared up at Simon and heard him chuckle low in his throat. Maybe he was savoring the irony: She had been running away from vampires, and now she was locked in with one of them.

Savoring the irony, or anticipating a fresh kill.

CHAPTER EIGHT

Never again will you be alone
This we pledge with blood and bone
So lay you down in peace to rest
Join the ranks of the blessed
And while you're dreaming in your bed
Remember us, the proud undead
Answer you now the siren call
Into every life, night must fall

OAKLAND
HEATHER

Heather lay in the darkness and wondered where she was. Her lungs were aching, and she was struggling for every breath. She was afraid to move to get her inhaler until she figured out what was happening.

A metallic smell like tin foil surrounded her; she could see nothing but blackness. She remembered being thrown over the vampire's back. Then she must have fainted, because she couldn't remember anything after that. How long had she been unconscious?

A door opened; voices drifted toward her. She lay still and tried to make out what they were saying.

"Who knows why she does anything, dude," a guy's voice said. He sounded like a surfer.

"It's a mistake, taunting a hunter like that." Another guy—this one sounded older and grumpier. "And why'd she throw down the gauntlet and tell her where to find little sis?"

Relief washed over Heather. *Jenn is alive.* Jenn knew where she was, and she would find her and save her and kill the vampire who had done this to her.

"She must have some sort of plan."

"I think she's just being a careless, arrogant idiot."

"Don't seem like that type to me. She's smart, that one. Way smarter than us."

"You calling me stupid?"

"Nah, bro, I'm just saying she's like some kind of genius."

"Listen! Do you hear that?"

Silence descended, and all Heather could hear was her own wheezing breaths. She wanted her inhaler so badly, but she didn't dare move to get it.

"That's the girl breathing, dude."

"What's wrong with her?"

"Asthma."

"Asthma," the older, grumpier one said sarcastically. "What a crock. That's just an excuse to get out of doing any real work."

"No, asthma's, like, serious. My sister had it. She used to wake up in the middle of the night, like, strangling. My mom took her to the emergency room a bunch of times. I thought it was going to kill her," the surfer said earnestly.

"Did it?"

"Nah, I killed her instead. You know, after I was converted."

"Nice."

Heather clamped her hand over her mouth to keep from screaming. Terror washed over her. *Jenn, get me out of here!* she begged silently, tears pouring down her cheeks.

"Let's get her on the plane and then go hunt some dinner," the older one said.

"You'll have to go without me. *She* wants me to go with her to New Orleans."

"No way. *You?* Why?"

"Maybe she thinks I'm hot."

"Yeah, right. As if."

The ground shifted suddenly beneath her, and she felt like she was being hoisted into the air. Suddenly the platform under her right hand dropped downward and then stopped so abruptly her teeth slammed together with a clacking sound, and pain exploded in her skull.

"Hey, man, careful!"

Then there was forward movement, and she realized she must be in some sort of box. *They're going to put me in with the cargo!* she thought, panic flooding her. *Maybe if I scream for help, someone will hear me and come running. Then what? The vampires will just kill them and I'll be no better off.*

They carried her up what felt like a ramp and then set the box down roughly. A crack of light appeared near her knee, and by it she saw bars. She wasn't in a box; she was in a cage like an animal. They had thrown a black tarp over it to keep out the light. She saw beige carpet on the floor outside. So, not the cargo storage, which relieved her a little bit. She heard retreating footsteps and then after a minute nothing else.

She felt for her inhaler and jerked it out of her pocket. A couple of puffs and the medication began to ease the constriction in her chest and throat.

As her breathing became easier, other thoughts crowded her mind. Chief among them was wondering what had happened to Jenn. What her captors had said led her to believe her sister was alive. But was she, and if so, what kind of shape was she in?

Heather had been thrilled when she saw Jenn fight the three vampires. Her sister was amazing, like every super-heroine, but even better. She hoped that she was safe, and while she desperately wanted Jenn to find her and rescue her, part of her was terrified that if Jenn tried, then she would be killed. Heather couldn't live with Jenn's death on her head.

From there her thoughts turned to their father, and rage filled her. If Jenn's death would be on anyone's head, it would be his. How could he have done that to his own daughter?

How could he do that to us?

Shifting in her cage, she shivered as something sick twisted inside her. She strained her ears but could hear nothing. The patch of carpet outside the cage remained unchanged. Still she knew, somehow, that the woman, the vampire who had taken her, approached.

A door slammed; she heard the sound of an engine, and a moment later the plane lurched forward. They rolled for a few minutes and then stopped again. The engines built up a steady whine, and then the plane shot ahead. One bump, two, and then they were soaring skyward at a steep angle.

Heather slid to the back of her cage. She could feel the bars pressing into her spine, and she gritted her teeth. After what seemed a lifetime, the plane finally began to level out.

Suddenly the tarp was ripped off of her cage, and she blinked furiously in the sudden brightness. She was on board some sort of fancy corporate jet. She glanced upward and saw the woman vampire smirking down at her, hands on her hips. Her lips gleamed a brilliant red; Heather prayed that it was lipstick.

"It's time for the in-flight meal," she said, tongue licking her lips. Her eyes were the same color as her mouth and glowed with a ruby light. Smiling wickedly, she gave Heather a little wink that sent chills up her spine. Then she reached for the door of the cage.

Heather took one look at her fangs and began to scream.

MADRID
SKYE, ERIKO, JAMIE, ANTONIO, HOLGAR, AND DR. MICHAEL SHERMAN

Facing the hidden doorway, Skye reared back from the darkness. "I don't want to go in there," she muttered. "I can feel . . . something."

"You can do it, witchy," Jamie said, turning on a flashlight and shining it into the dark. "See, no bogeyman, at least none that we didn't bring with us."

Antonio had just about had enough of Jamie's insults and insinuations. He balled his hands into fists and squeezed until he cut his own palms open with his fingernails. The scent of blood did nothing to calm him down. Next to him Holgar stiffened and threw him a quick glance as he, too, reacted to the smell.

And that actually made Antonio relax, because, after all, Jamie was right. They were the bogeyman. Maybe it was time to stop running from that truth and embrace it.

He shook his head. It was the monster part of him that was talking. It wasn't the seminarian who loved God or the man who loved Jenn. It was the monster who loved blood and death and carnage. He couldn't let it take control, not now, not ever.

"I'm the Hunter. I'll go first," Eriko whispered.

Her face was inscrutable, and it was impossible to tell whether she was talking to him, to Jamie, or to the group at large. She stepped forward into the inky darkness, and Jamie trailed right behind her, like a puppy, with an unlit cigarette dangling from his mouth.

Skye followed with Holgar. That left Antonio, whose hunting partner was in the States, alone. It fell to him, then, to watch out for Michael Sherman. From the way the scientist was sweating, Antonio could tell that he loved the dark even less than Skye.

He put a hand on the man's shoulder and felt the frightened pounding of the blood in his veins. The stench of fear from the conspirators throughout the library was as nothing to the fear coming off the man beside him.

Antonio winced, wishing there was something he could say or do to calm the geeky scientist. With the smell of his fear—and his illness—so strong, they would come under detection far sooner. Antonio should have asked Skye to put a spell on Dr. Sherman, a sort of magickal muscle relaxer.

You could mesmerize him. The voice came from somewhere deep inside of him, somewhere he didn't like to go. He rejected it instantly, but it only came back tenfold. *You would be saving his life, and Skye's and the others. What's the difference whether Skye puts a spell on him or you do, just so long as he calms down a bit?*

"What's wrong?" Sherman cried, staring at him in panic.

Antonio realized he was shaking. Many times—dozens, a hundred—he had caught himself starting to mesmerize Jenn. It was like the vampiric version of coming on to her—enticing her, lowering her defenses. He had sworn he would never, ever do that to her. And so he tried not to do it to anybody, except other vampires. "Nothing," he said.

The man didn't believe him. Sherman turned ash white and began shaking too. Antonio had seen the reaction dozens of times from soldiers on the battlefield and from men faced with monsters.

He could do something about it. And, he admitted, he should.

"Nothing is wrong," Antonio murmured, staring deeply into the man's eyes.

Confusion flitted across the man's face. "Are you sure?"

Antonio reached out and put a hand on Sherman's shoulder. Laserlike, he locked his gaze. To give more force to the charm, he let the monster out, just a little bit. He could feel his teeth lengthening, knew his eyes were changing. Sherman stared at him, fascinated, as some stared at snakes that were about to attack them.

"Listen to me, *professor*," Antonio said, his voice a whisper. "There is nothing wrong. You are not afraid of going in there. Only by going in there will you be safe. You must find the virus. You can save the world. You must . . . trust . . . me."

"I must . . . ," Sherman said, his face now slightly slack and his eyes unfocused.

". . . trust me."

"Yes." Sherman's breath was rank.

"Good, then come with me now," Antonio said, taking a step forward into darkness.

Sherman followed.

Oakland
Jenn

"Jenn, oh my God, did you trip?" Brooke cried.

On her back in Brooke's living room Jenn stared up into Simon's evil red eyes and knew that she was dead unless she could get away from him. The very first thing they taught at Salamanca, before they taught street fighting or tactics or anything else, was how to run and how to escape.

Jenn's fighting skills might have been only mediocre, but one thing she knew how to do was get away. The vampire leering at her expected her to try and stand up, or roll to the side. She did neither. She pushed off from the ground with her arms and legs and did a backward somersault, nailing him in the face with her knees as she did so.

Even a centuries-old vampire couldn't keep himself from reacting when something hit him in the face, even if no pain or damage was inflicted. It was primal, the last vestige of the human he had once been.

So Simon jerked his head backward and stood up, backing away from her. It was the split second she needed to finish her roll, spring to her feet, and race for the staircase.

"Jenn, stop!" Brooke yelled, still in the living room. "It's really okay!"

Behind her she heard a shout of surprise followed by laughter. Simon had expected her to try for the front door again and assumed she had chosen poorly in making for the stairs. But she knew this house well, hopefully better than he did.

At the top of the staircase she turned left and flew into Brooke's father's home office. With relief she saw that it was the same as when she'd snuck in with Brooke to play hide-and-go-seek when they were kids. The same old-fashioned wooden kitchen chair sat in front of the desk, its back a square of eighteen-inch long slats. He had always claimed the hard chair was better for his back than the cushy one sitting in the corner piled high with books, his ashtray, and a pack of Marlboros. He used to say the wood chair saved his posture, and his cigarettes saved his sanity. Brooke had begged both her parents to quit, to save their lungs.

As Jenn laid hands on the chair, she hoped it would save her life.

She knocked it over and put her booted foot down on it. She grasped the first slat and yanked hard. For a moment she didn't think she was strong enough. Then the wood groaned and finally gave way with a crack. She ripped it free and then moved on to the next slat. It gave way more easily than the first. She grabbed the third, ripped it free, and heard the front door open and then close.

She froze, listening for a sound, but heard none. Had the other vampires finally caught up to her? She gathered the three stakes in her hand. She didn't have time to get more. There were three vampires.

Three vampires, three stakes. It had to be enough.

Don't miss, Jenn.

She heard the stair third from the top creak once, twice.

Two vampires upstairs. That left one downstairs. Probably Simon. Would he hurt Brooke?

Jenn wedged herself into the gap between two bookcases that were to the right of the door, and waited. She heard the door to Brooke's room open. Next she heard them checking the guest room.

She held one stake in her right hand and two in her left and tried to still her breathing. The door swung all the way open. The first vampire, Kyle, strode into the room, eyes forward. Dora followed, and Jenn leaped out. She plunged the stake into Dora's heart and ran out of the room through the resulting cloud of dust. She jumped to the side and dropped to the floor. When Kyle ran out, she tripped him.

Vampires could move at blinding speed, but gravity treated them the same as any other creature of the same mass. Right before the Curser hit the ground, she was able to angle the stake under his heart.

She coughed as dust choked her and filled her lungs. She rolled over onto her hands and knees, retching and trying not to think about it. She managed to drag herself to her feet after a few seconds, wiping her mouth on her sleeve. She still clutched the final stake in her hand.

Two down.

Brooke's boyfriend to go.

Jenn crept down the stairs, avoiding the one with the creak, and tried to angle her head to see into the living room without being seen. Brooke and her vampire boyfriend were both standing, staring her way. Brooke's eyes were huge, and she clung to the vampire, who had his arms around her.

"Simon, what is going on?" Brooke was saying.

"No clue. She's totally bought all the BS about us," Simon replied.

Jenn had one stake left. She advanced slowly. Then Brooke spotted her and gave a little cry.

"Brooke, step away from him!" Jenn yelled. "Right now."

"No! Are you crazy?"

"Move *away*," Jenn said.

Brooke took a step in front of him, as if to protect him. Over Brooke's head Simon grinned at Jenn, and chills ran down her spine.

"He loves me," Brooke insisted. "We're going to get married."

"Married?"

The vampire shrugged. "You know what they say. 'Till death do us part.'"

Before Jenn could react, he reached forward and grabbed Brooke. He twisted her head sideways—Jenn heard the crack—and sunk his fangs into her throat.

"No!" Jenn screamed.

Simon threw Brooke's body to the floor. Her eyes were open, lifeless.

"Well, what do you know, I guess they're right," he said, making a show of licking Brooke's blood from his lips.

He took a defensive stance, expecting her to attack him. Instead Jenn ran. He had just fed. That would give him a boost, while she was tiring. She bolted from the room and fled to the kitchen. The kitchen had an island in the middle of it, and the side facing the dining room had shelves running the length of it. On these shelves Brooke's mother stored her cooking oils.

Jenn swept olive oil, vegetable oil, truffle oil, macadamia nut oil, and several other bottles onto the floor, where they shattered, spilling their contents all across the kitchen.

The vampire appeared in the doorway and made a *tsk-*

ing sound. "The mother-in-law is not going to be happy. What a mess you've made. Remind me never to eat your cooking."

He approached, coming around the island, and Jenn backed up until she slammed into the counter. She opened one of the drawers and grabbed a butcher knife, flinging it at him.

He dodged it with ease. Her hand closed around another, and he dodged it as well. Her seeking hands yanked out two steak knives. She threw first one, then the other, while her free hand felt frantically in the drawer. It had to be there; it just had to be.

As he batted away the knives, her hand finally closed on a Bic lighter and a pack of Brooke's mom's cigarettes. She clicked the lighter on, swept the flame along the ground, and then leaped up onto the counter.

The oil caught fire instantly; in the space of time it took Simon to figure out why she had jumped onto the counter, he was ablaze. With a shout Simon leaped free of the room, stumbled into the foyer, and rolled to extinguish himself. Jenn jumped down and ran after him. Then she flung herself onto him. The flames burned; she ignored the pain and fought.

He bucked hard, throwing her sideways. She hit her head hard on the banister, and the room swam in her vision for a moment as he finished slapping at himself, putting out the fire. He tried to stand, but his legs were badly burned.

He crawled toward the living room. Away from her.

Afraid of her. She had to press her advantage. Dazed, Jenn forced herself upright, but promptly fell over, too dizzy to keep her footing.

She still had the stake clutched under her arm. Digging in her elbows, she crawled after him. Blood was rolling down the side of her face like sweat, and she shook her head to keep it from getting in her eyes.

Grunting, panting, she pulled herself to her hands and knees, hands and feet sliding on the marble tile. Bright red splatters of her own blood stained the white of the tile alongside the streaks of ash that the vampire was leaving.

She pushed forward, knowing that if she couldn't kill him within the next few seconds, she was dead.

In the living room she grabbed on to the piano and hoisted herself to her feet. Jenn launched herself at Simon and fell on top of him just as he flopped over onto his back.

She straddled him and slammed her boots down, one on each of his arms. He stared up at her with wide, terrified eyes. She pulled the stake from under her arm and pressed it against his chest.

"Who is she?" Jenn roared.

"Who?" he asked, confusion mingling with the fear in his crimson eyes. His fangs extended, and he hissed.

Jenn shook her head, and drops of her blood splattered across his chest and the carpet. His eyes darkened to a deep bloodred of their own. "She, the vampire."

"Dora?"

"No, *her*. Your leader. She ambushed me. She kidnapped my sister."

He shook his head, tongue darting to catch the drops of Jenn's blood—to get sustenance, fuel, energy. So he could kill her.

"Answer me!" Jenn shrieked.

"I don't know who you mean!" he shouted in turn.

"Yes, you do!" she yelled at him. "You live here. You have to know who she is." But she wasn't certain of that. He hadn't come here with the others. He'd been with Brooke. Still, he'd identified the vampire named Dora.

"You *do* know," she said more firmly.

"Sorry." He grinned at her. "Guess your sister's toast. Too bad. Too, too bad."

He was stalling for time, trying to get her to look at him, attempting to mesmerize her.

"No," she grunted, panting. She tore her gaze away. "Tell me."

Jenn dug the stake in harder until he began to bleed.

"The one who took my sister. Tell me *now*."

She pushed deeper. An inch or two more and she would pierce his heart, and he would turn to dust. If he knew, he would break and say the name. Had to. He wouldn't sacrifice himself out of loyalty. Vampires weren't like that.

Just ask Brooke.

"Aurora, her name is Aurora," the vampire gasped. "I'll help you track her; you need me. We can leave and—"

"I need you dead," she said coldly.

Jenn shoved the stake into his heart, and he turned to ash. She collapsed onto the floor and found herself staring into dead green eyes. Brooke lay on the ground where Simon had thrown her. The bat necklace lay in a pool of Brooke's blood. And lying there, her own blood dripping into Brooke's, she remembered all the good times they had shared. She remembered how happy Brooke had looked just minutes ago, when she had introduced her boyfriend. Everything she was, everything she could have been, had been taken away in a moment. Because Jenn had sought sanctuary in her home. Because Jenn had been attacked. Because her own father had betrayed her.

Jenn felt her heart break. Aurora was right. Learning her name had cost Jenn dearly.

CHAPTER NINE

Salamanca Hunter's Manual: The Mission
Remember this: Your charge, against all others, is to destroy your foe. You are a protector of God's creatures. Thus you are given dispensation to commit lesser evils, to thwart the greater. Fight with valor and honor when you are able, but sacrifice them both rather than risk defeat.

(translated from the Spanish)

OAKLAND
JENN

Too late to do any good, the fire alarm suddenly went off, startling Jenn to her feet. She reeled and put out a hand to steady herself on the back of the couch. She stared for a moment more at Brooke. Then she took a deep breath. There was nothing she could do for the dead; she could only focus on helping the living.

Hopefully that was Heather.

She staggered into the kitchen, where she stamped out the fire, already nearly out. She grabbed a chair and pushed the button on the smoke detector, but it didn't stop blaring. The sound filled her ears and had to be audible to the neighbors. If it went much longer, someone was bound to call the fire department. She ripped it loose from the ceiling and yanked out the batteries.

As silence reigned, her thoughts turned to escaping. She thought of her bag packed and ready to go back at her parents' house. She didn't want to have to go back there, but she needed the bag, which contained both her passport and driver's license. She had left with her dad in a hurry, leaving behind everything that wasn't immediately usable as a weapon.

She reached for the phone. She'd call a cab. She paused. A taxi driver could get her to her parents' house but couldn't help her get the things she needed from inside. She picked up the phone and dialed her grandparents' number.

"Hello?" her grandmother answered.

"It's Jenn. I need help."

"What's wrong?"

"Gramma, I can't talk now. *I need help.*"

"Okay. I'm here." There was no hesitation, no second-guessing. Her grandmother's years in the countercultural revolution had reasserted themselves. Jenn sagged with relief, nearly bursting into tears.

"I have to get to the airport, but I need a ride, and I need my things from my house."

"Where are you? I'll come pick you up and then we can get your things."

"No, we can't do that," Jenn said, willing herself not to cry. "Gramma, you have to get to the house fast. You have to see if Mom's okay. Gramma . . ." Now she did cry. Just as quickly, she forced herself to stop.

"Tell me *something*," her grandmother pleaded.

"Oh, Gramma, oh *God*," she whispered. "Dad . . . gave me up to some vampires."

"*What?*"

Jenn forced herself to keep talking. "So—so they'd leave the rest of you alone. But Heather got caught in the crossfire, and th-they kidnapped her."

There was a beat. Then her grandmother said steadily, "Go on."

"They're taking her to New Orleans. I'm going after them. But I need my duffel bag from my room at home, and I can't risk going there."

"Got it." She could tell her grandmother was keeping rigid control.

"It's packed. I'm in Oakland, on Trestle Glen. Do you

remember . . . do you . . . Brooke's house . . ." She started crying again. "Gramma, hurry. God, *please*."

"I'll be there in an hour," her grandmother said, and then, "If you're hurt or injured, wash up. Change your clothes. If anyone comes, leave. Is this a landline?"

"Yes. My cell's at the house."

"We have to hang up. It can be traced. If you have to leave, go to the nearest gas station. I'll find you there."

"Okay."

"Jenn, I'm coming."

"Thank you," Jenn murmured, ending the call.

Jenn walked around the charred spot on the floor. She took off her clothes and washed herself in the bathroom off the kitchen, then raided the folded clothes in the laundry room for something to wear of Brooke's—a jog bra that was a little too big, a black turtleneck sweater, jeans that were too long, underwear. There was a beach towel there too. Eyes averted, she draped it over Brooke.

Then she tried to clean up the evidence, but it was hopeless. Jenn's blood and her fingerprints were everywhere. Weirdly, the vampire's would be too. It was possible that the authorities could find her prints in a database—they'd fingerprinted everyone at her high school before she'd dropped out and gone to Spain—but somehow she doubted that Simon's would show up. There was no way of even knowing how old he was or where he was from. They might try to pin Brooke's murder on her. *Another reason never to come here again.*

Night had fallen; she checked the garage for concealed vampires, realizing she should have done it right away. Both cars were missing. She hoped Brooke's parents wouldn't come home before Gramma arrived. She felt so sorry for them, so terribly sorry. And for herself.

She thought about risking another call on the landline and contacting Father Juan, but he was on automatic dial on her cell phone, and she was too rattled to remember his number. Same with Antonio. With all of them.

I'm alone here. I'm alone.

Wearily, she sank onto the bottom stair of the landing. In forty minutes she heard a car pull up outside. She peeked out the living room window and recognized her grandmother's old green Jeep.

Ducking her head, she ran to the car and slid into the passenger seat.

"Thank you, Gr . . ." She turned to look at her grandmother, and the word died on her tongue.

She had never seen such naked rage on a face before. Her grandmother's eyes burned a brilliant blue, almost as though they were on fire. Jenn shivered.

"Your bag is on the backseat," her grandmother said.

"Thank you. Did you—was there any trouble?"

"No trouble at all." Her knuckles on the wheel were white.

"Was . . . was Dad there?"

"No. Your mother is leaving with me. I'll call you once

191

we're settled. She and I," she added, as if for emphasis.

"Oh, Gramma." Jenn swallowed hard.

"Do it later, sweetie," her grandmother said. She lifted her chin. "That's what *I'm* going to do."

Jenn nodded, and they rode in silence. It began to drizzle. They were halfway to Oakland Airport before her grandmother spoke again.

"You won't be able to get anywhere near New Orleans. The Cursed Ones have the city locked down tight. I checked with some old friends. Nearest airport I could get you into is Biloxi. From there it's about seventy-five miles. You'll have to hitchhike. Don't bother trying to rent a car. You have to have permits these days to get in and out of Louisiana, and you won't be able to get one, so you'll have to sneak over the border. I've half a mind to come with you."

Jenn shook her head. "I need to know that you're safe. You and Mom." She wondered if she would ever see them again. Or her father.

They were going to kill me. And he knew it. My father. My own father.

Her grandmother gave her a hard stare. "Child, nobody is safe, not anymore. You of all people should know that."

Jenn bit her lip, trying not to recall the image of Brooke lying dead. "I know that, but—"

"Don't worry. I've found something more useful I can do. There's a resistance movement, and they need people with experience. You don't need to drag my ancient carcass around like some damn albatross."

Jenn was too shocked to protest.

"I don't have people in New Orleans. I did, but they're gone."

Jenn almost asked whether they had left or were dead, and then realized that she really didn't want to hear the answer. Instead she nodded.

"Don't trust anyone. Be polite, friendly. It doesn't hurt to play dumb from time to time. There are people in this country who'll still underestimate you if you're quiet . . . or a woman. Use that to your advantage. Try never to be more than half an hour away from food, water, or medical help. Have you called your people yet?"

"No, not yet." She'd meant to first thing but had blanked out.

"Well, do it now. You never know who's going to be listening in on your private conversation when you're out in public."

Jenn reached around and grabbed her duffel bag. She pulled her cell phone out of it and pressed one for Father Juan. He picked up on the second ring.

"Jenn, are you all right?" he asked, his voice laced with tension.

"No. I mean, physically I'm okay, but I've got big trouble," she admitted.

"What's happened?"

She told him the whole story. "My father betrayed me, sold me out to the vampires," Jenn finished, unable to keep the raw grief out of her voice.

"*Ay, mi'ja*, I am sorry," Father Juan said.

"We're all real sorry, Padre. You coming to help or not?" her grandmother interrupted, loud enough for him to hear.

Father Juan grunted. "Your grandmother?"

Jenn smiled through her tears. "How did you guess?"

"Tell her that she has the ears of a fox. Of course we will come help. The team is out on a mission. We'll head for New Orleans as soon as they return, and rendezvous with you there."

"*Gracias*," Jenn whispered.

"*Vaya con Dios*," he replied. "Call me. Stay in touch."

"I will," she promised.

"Jenn, be careful. Very careful."

"*Sí, mi maestro*." It was beginning to dawn on her what lay ahead. Her hand around the phone began to shake again. "Please say hello to everyone."

"*Vale*, you know that I will."

Her throat tightened, and she nodded, even though he couldn't see her. Disconnecting, she turned to her grandmother. "They'll meet me in New Orleans."

She nodded. "You give that young man of yours a kiss from me and tell him I'll break his legs if he hurts you."

From the look on her face Jenn knew that she wasn't kidding.

They pulled off the freeway into a gas station, and the signs for the airport flashed overhead. Her grandmother yanked a money belt from underneath her seat and handed it to Jenn, ceaselessly scanning their surroundings. This was what her father's life had been like. On the run. Watching. Hiding.

No, I won't excuse his treachery. I will never, ever forgive him.

"What is this?" Jenn asked.

"Money, enough to get you where you need to go and then some," her grandmother replied grimly. "When you're in trouble, you can never have too much cash on hand."

"Thank you," Jenn said.

"Don't thank me. Just go get your sister back."

"I will," Jenn vowed, wrapping the money belt around her waist underneath her shirt as her grandmother rolled back onto the road that led to the airport.

Two minutes later they pulled up outside the terminal. "Here's your e-ticket. And here's a fake ID." All business, her grandmother handed her a printed confirmation and a California driver's license issued to Jacqueline Simmons. The picture looked like one of Jenn's old school pictures. The e-ticket was for Jacqueline Simmons.

"But how—"

"I've had documents for your whole family standing by, in case it ever came to something like this. I've been updating them every year since the war broke out." Gramma Esther's features hardened. "Of course I figured your father would be . . ." Her voice caught, and she clamped her jaw shut. Then she exhaled.

"By the looks of your pupils you may have a mild concussion. If you can't see a doctor, at least keep yourself awake for the next twelve hours."

Jenn leaned over, kissed her on the cheek, then grabbed her duffel bag and stepped out onto the curb. As much as she hated the idea, she checked her bag through so that she wouldn't have to dump all the stakes. She just hoped that the vials of holy water would survive the trip.

Staying awake on the plane turned out to be a lot easier said than done. She watched the movie, a cheesy love story, in an effort to keep herself awake. Half a dozen times she caught herself just dozing off and jerked up her head, fear making her heart pound.

Just keep it together, Jenn, she coached herself.

Once the plane landed in Biloxi, she was relieved to find her bag circling the baggage carousel. An armed soldier stood beside a poster featuring a man in a hard hat smiling at a woman unfurling a set of blueprints. The woman's canine teeth were very slightly elongated. WELCOME TO MISSISSIPPI. WE'RE ON THE MOVE!

Walking past the soldier, she grabbed her bag, then showed her matching claim check to an airport security official in a white shirt and navy blue trousers who was eyeing everyone as they left. The official studied her for a beat, then waved her on.

Outside, she caught sight of a guard tower. As casually as she could, she pulled out her phone and called Father Juan again. He sounded worried, but he told her everything was fine.

Hoisting her duffel over her shoulder, she glanced toward the taxi stand, but the sign read IN-STATE DESTINATIONS ONLY. She blanched and turned to look at her fellow travelers.

"Oh, golly," she said, striking a pose and putting on a Southern accent. "Excuse me, y'all, but is anyone heading toward Louisiana? My *maw-maw* just called and told me she couldn't make it." She fluttered her lashes. "I just don't have the faintest idea what I should do."

A dozen people shifted away from her. A guy with a beard leered at her and opened his mouth to speak.

Before the letch could get a word out, a middle-aged woman wearing a bright blue sweater decorated with teddy bears holding American flags glared at the man and stepped between Jenn and him. She flashed Jenn a kind but concerned smile.

"Land's sake, honey," she said. "You shouldn't be doing this kind of thing. My husband, Oral, and I will be happy to take you."

"Why, thank you kindly, ma'am," Jenn drawled. "I surely cannot tell you how grateful I am. It's so scary being out here by myself."

"Don't you worry," the woman said. "Oral's gone to get the car. Where are your people, sugar?"

"Just outside New Orleans," she replied boldly. The woman paled visibly; the letch frowned, and several of the onlookers traded looks.

"We'll get you as close as we can," the woman said, sounding a little strained.

"Thank you," Jenn said.

A moment later she found herself squeezed into the uncomfortable backseat of a red and white Mini Cooper between two massive mounds of luggage. As the car pulled away from the curb, she hoped that the driver didn't get lost on the way to Louisiana. Or attacked.

MADRID
SKYE, HOLGAR, ERIKO, JAMIE, ANTONIO, AND DR. MICHAEL SHERMAN

Eriko stepped carefully into the blackness on the other side of the reading room wall, the light from the flashlight barely illuminating her path. She didn't like anything about the mission. She didn't like Dr. Sherman, who was bringing up the rear with Antonio. He was too jittery to be trusted.

"How can you tell if someone's a vampire?" Eriko heard him ask.

"They have no heartbeat," Antonio said.

"That's all?"

"Unless they're hungry," Antonio replied. "Haven't you ever seen a vampire?"

"Actually, no." Sherman looked sheepish. "My work's been done with computer simulations. The next step is subjects. We've been hoping your people might help with that."

Eriko was offended, but tried not to show it. She had not become the Hunter to round up test subjects. Still, if this American could find a good way to kill them . . .

She came to a staircase, long unused. The brass railing was caked with dust and cobwebs, and it angled down steeply into a seemingly endless chasm.

"Down the rabbit hole," Skye murmured, and Eriko held up a hand for silence.

They all filed wordlessly down, light on the balls of their feet. Eriko began to wonder if there was a landing or a floor, or if they were going to the hell Father Juan believed in.

It felt a little like what she imagined hell would. Her muscles were sore. She ached from head to toe. Bending her knees as she walked downstairs was excruciating. The elixir gave her great strength, speed, and healing abilities. It worked, however, only with the body she already had. That meant that the muscle buildup was overpowering for her frame, and she often found herself waking in the middle of the night with crippling pain. And it was getting progressively worse.

At last they came to the bottom of the stairs. Light was coming from somewhere past a long corridor. There was enough of it that Eriko could shut off her flashlight. Vampires could see well enough in total darkness, but they could see better with the lights on, like humans. Lucky for her team, who would not inadvertently announce their position with flashlight beams.

The others grouped quietly behind her, waiting for her to do something, waiting for her to lead them. It was not the heroic life of the single samurai that she had envisioned when studying and training to try for the reward of the sacred elixir. After the hideous deaths of her two best friends, Yuki and Mara, she hadn't wanted friends. She had focused all her energy on one objective — becoming the Hunter, walking alone as an emissary of revenge. She had been the strongest, the stealthiest, seeing herself as a solitary ninja.

She had never envisioned herself as a team leader.

They crept silently down the hallway. Eriko signaled for Antonio to go first and for Holgar to bring up the rear. She wanted to see what was coming at her and to know what was following her.

The light grew brighter as they moved down the corridor. Through square glass windows cut into double doors of steel, she and Antonio could see into a large room filled with men and women — maybe vampires — in lab coats, and more scientific equipment than she had ever seen before in one place. Big machines with wires and buttons, glass tubes, and a huge microscope or maybe a laser. Wooden tables holding steel clamps and stacks of petri dishes. It looked like a crazy science-fiction movie set. It also seemed pretty sophisticated to have been set up quickly, but the haphazard placement of some of the machines indicated that some haste had been involved.

She made a gesture to Dr. Sherman, who came up beside her and peered carefully through the window. He studied the room for a moment, then whispered, "There." He pointed at a small refrigerator with a glass front panel, on a far table to the left of where they stood. Inside it she could see a rack of vials with clear liquid.

"Are you sure?" she dared to whisper, even though vampires had superior hearing.

"They look like mine," he whispered back. "Lavender caps, green labels."

As if on cue, one of the women in the room put on blue rubber gloves and a hood with a plastic mask, then crossed to the refrigerator. Eriko tracked her, detecting fear in her movements as she drew closer to the refrigerator. It was obvious that she was afraid of what was inside.

Eriko's arms and hands began to shake, but whether from exhilaration or exhaustion she didn't know. Her heart trip-hammered; it jittered out of rhythm when she was under strain. And she hurt all over. But that couldn't matter now.

Taking a deep breath, she met the eyes of each of the others in turn. She gave a quick nod. This was the moment. They had gone over it a thousand times. And one glance at the room had told her that their plan should work.

Making a fist, she indicated that they should all get ready. When she opened her fist, that would be their go signal. Then she found peace within herself, ready to face death if need be, and almost welcoming it through the haze of her pain.

Eriko's fist opened, and Antonio sauntered into the room calmly, quietly, as though he had every right to be there. He had no lab coat, but not all the vampires in the lab wore them, either. Because he had no heartbeat, no one bothered to look up at first. By that time he had stationed himself just behind and to the left of the refrigerator. He took a quick look around—scores of laptops on wooden lab tables, a more robust mainframe computer, banks of equipment that looked to his untrained eye like oscilloscopes and ste-reo speakers, rows and rows of test tubes and a couple of giant centrifuges, and microscopes galore. So much high-tech equipment, capable of such incredible things. Where did magick end and science begin?

He counted fourteen vampires in the room. He won-dered if there were more in another room. Surely they'd surround such a prize with more security forces.

For one wild moment he wondered if he could simply open the refrigerator, grab the vials, and take them out the same way he'd walked in. But soon—any second now, in fact—he fully expected someone to realize that he didn't belong there.

He turned and nodded once toward the hallway, where the rest of his team was concealed. While he'd been doing recon, they'd been preparing for their entrance.

The primary signal was not his to give.

Adelante, he urged Eriko, his leader. Let's get it going.

Then Jamie burst into the room, a Molotov cocktail in each hand. With a shriek he tossed them at the far wall right into a bank of the speakerlike objects.

The explosion rocked the room and nearly threw Jamie off his feet. Antonio managed to stand his ground. Moments later the other hunters poured into the room, each stopping only long enough to behead the vampires who crossed their paths, using short swords pulled from scabbards on their backs.

Sherman flew over to Antonio's side, eyes bulging, but still far calmer than he had been earlier.

"Get the virus," Antonio said, without explaining why he wasn't going to get it himself. "I'll cover you."

Antonio heard a high, piercing cry. Eriko was staking one vampire even as another threw itself at her. As he had anticipated, more were streaming into the room from a door in the northeast corner.

Holgar roared as Skye's attempt at a fireball singed the hair on his head as it whizzed by his ear. He howled, ducking, and shot across the room, knocking over a lab bench. A laptop smashed to the concrete floor.

Three vampires raced toward Antonio; he braced himself for their attack as two more *Malditos* sealed off metal double doors—which had to be the main entrance to the laboratory. The only escape lay back the way they had come.

The first vampire reached Antonio. Antonio moved with lightning speed to the side and then, with all his strength, drove the stake through the C.O.'s back into his heart.

Eriko leaped into the battle to help him face the two remaining vampires. They fought back and forth, both sides seeking the upper hand, until finally Antonio staked Eriko's vampire, then turned and did the same to the other one.

"What are you doing?" Antonio demanded, as he watched the scientist insert a syringe into one of the vials from the refrigerator.

The small man was standing in a tripod formation, legs spread wide apart, holding a syringe in his hand. "Making sure it's the real thing. I need someone to test it on."

That didn't make sense. Sherman had already said he'd never tested it on a real vampire. But at that very moment, a *Maldito* was rushing toward Antonio. So he stepped out of the way and then tripped him, following him to the ground to shove his knee against the vampire's throat.

"Then do it!" he bellowed.

The man dropped beside them and injected the vampire in the throat. Antonio tried not to wince at the proximity of the deadly virus. He suddenly realized that there were too many questions he hadn't asked, like if the disease could spread from one vampire to another.

The vampire shouted and began to writhe. Sherman shouted, "Yes!"

Antonio felt his spirits rise . . . and then drop.

Nothing else happened. The vampire lay still, blinking up at him. Antonio looked at the scientist, who was staring intently at his test subject. The smell of infection coming off him nearly made Antonio gag. That was when Antonio realized what was wrong with the man.

"You were studying leukemia because you have it."

"First my father, then my daughter, now me," Sherman affirmed.

Around them all was chaos, and it seemed so absurd that they sat quietly, like a tableau in a Christmas pageant. The vampire didn't struggle, as though sensing that if he did, Antonio would kill him in a heartbeat.

"It doesn't work," Sherman said finally, looking chagrined.

No virus. For a single moment Antonio felt a surge of relief almost amounting to joy. Then he staked the vampire and stood and turned to report to Eriko, but she'd seen the demonstration. She nodded but didn't say anything as she staked another vampire.

"Retreat!" she shouted. "Now! Go, go, go!"

Antonio turned back just in time to see Sherman, his face covered in blood, grabbed by a tall vampire and heaved across the room as if he were weightless. He yelled, then smashed hard into the wall. Antonio staked the vampire and then dashed over to the man, falling to his knees beside him.

The scientist was dead. His eyes were frozen in abject terror, and he had no pulse nor breath. *Why feed from diseased blood instead of just breaking his neck?* Antonio wondered. There was blood near the two marks on Michael's neck where he had been bitten. But that didn't explain the blood on his mouth.

A terrible suspicion filled Antonio, and he pried wide the scientist's mouth. Blood coated his tongue well. Antonio sniffed. It wasn't his blood; it was someone else's.

Dios, no! Has he been converted? he wondered. *I heard his beating heart. Didn't I?*

Antonio couldn't take that chance. He yanked a stake out of one of his pockets and readied to plunge it into Dr. Sherman's heart.

An explosion rocked the sealed door to the laboratory. The blast threw Antonio to the far wall and knocked the stake from his hand. A moment later a dozen men dressed in all-black body armor, wearing gas masks and carrying crossbows, emerged from the smoke. They spotted the inert scientist and immediately headed in his direction. One of the men tossed his weapon to another, hoisted Sherman's corpse over his shoulder, and disappeared back into the smoke.

The other men seemed to melt into it as well until only one remained. A black Jerusalem cross hung from his neck, the black bleeding into the black of his clothes so that Antonio almost didn't see it. The man looked at him and raised his hand in a salute, and then he, too, stepped into the rolling plumes and vanished.

"Let's blow," Holgar roared.

"Something we can agree on," he heard Jamie shout.

They made it to the passageway and took the stairs toward the secret entrance into the library. Antonio ran backward, keeping his eye on the lab, and prepared to take out anyone who was following them.

It took him a minute to realize that nobody was.

Upstairs, alarms were going off.

"We've got to get out of here," Eriko told them. "Now."

EN ROUTE TO NEW ORLEANS, LOUISIANA
HEATHER

Heather lay in her cage, wet with sweat and limp with blood loss. The pain was excruciating, and she curled her knees up tighter to her chest. She could still feel Aurora's teeth sinking into her neck. The pain had been unlike anything she had ever experienced. It had been dwarfed, though, by the horror of the forced intimacy.

Aurora's arms had been like steel as they wrapped around her, pulling her close and holding her tight. For just a moment her lips had been whisper soft on Heather's skin. It had tickled right before she bit her. Then there had been the feeling of being torn apart—not just skin, but mind and soul as well. She had felt the blood pumping from her into Aurora, and she had screamed and cried and begged for death.

It had seemed to last for nearly half an hour, but she

knew that couldn't be. Jenn had told her that a vampire could drain a human of blood completely in five seconds. She wasn't dead. She could feel that with every painful heartbeat and agonized breath. It had to have been only a second, even though it had felt like a lifetime.

When Aurora was finished with her, the vampire had made a purring sound and then dropped her back onto the floor of her cage. Heather didn't know how long she had lain like that, curled up. She did know that at some point someone—she thought it might have been the vampire with the dead asthmatic sister—had shoved a bowl of what smelled like taco meat into her cage. She couldn't have lifted her head to eat it if she'd wanted to.

The smell of the meat made her nauseous, and it dawned on her that they were planning on keeping her alive, at least for a while. Which meant that Aurora or someone else would take her blood again, against her will. Last year Tiffany had told Heather that you couldn't turn into a vampire just by getting bitten. Heather hadn't wanted to know why she was so certain. Solomon had said the same thing on TV, but Heather hadn't believed him. He was a vampire. A Cursed One, like Jenn called them. A lying monster, just like Aurora.

But now she hoped that that was the truth. She would rather die than become a vampire. She wasn't sure if she believed in heaven, but being a vampire would be a living hell.

I'd kill myself first, she thought. For the first time in her life she prayed.

Please, God, let me die first.

She heard murmured voices and gleaned that they would soon be arriving in New Orleans, and that the city was a vampire stronghold, even more so than San Francisco.

Below the plane, slumbering in their houses, the good people of America dreamed on. Good people who did nothing to stop the vampires. Good people who spoke of peace and treaties. Good people who thought that fighting was never the answer. Good people who thought talking and learning more about their enemy was the answer.

"Good" people like her father, who sacrificed family members to the vampires in exchange for protection.

Those good people could go to hell. Because of them she was locked in a cage like an animal, suffering for the amusement and feeding of demonic beings that shouldn't be real. And she had no idea what had become of Jenn. Terrible images of Jenn's possible last moments flooded her mind, and her chest began to tighten, painfully so. She couldn't succumb to an asthma attack now.

If I ever get out of here, I'll kill every last vampire, she promised herself, lying there in a pool of her own blood and sweat and vomit. *If I ever get out of here, I'll kill my father and every other man who allows this to happen to his daughter.* And the thought gave her strength, and she stopped praying that God would let her die and started praying that He would let her live.

CHAPTER TEN

Brothers and sisters one and all
There are those who would see us fall
They would kill us in our beds
And part us forever from our heads
This violence cannot continue on
Until all that's good in life is gone
These are the monsters you should fear
Kill ye the Hunters both far and near

JUST OUTSIDE BILOXI, MISSISSIPPI
JENN

"Have some biscuits, sugar," Modean Bethune said to Jenn.

Jenn and the Bethunes were seated at a table in the Pecan Grove Pie Shop, which was across the parking lot from the motel the Bethunes had checked into an hour earlier. Their Mini Cooper was empty of all their luggage. The border between Mississippi and Louisiana had been shut down for at least the rest of the day. Something about a security breach that Jenn didn't understand. It had been on the news, and the long line of cars stretched down the highway, slowly turning back around, proved the truth of it.

A newscaster was repeating the information on the TV that hung from the ceiling above a coffee dispenser. The sound had been turned low, and Jenn couldn't hear what she was saying. This kind of thing didn't happen in Spain. She was about to run screaming from the restaurant, steal a car, drive into the wilderness, and cross the border illegally. The Bethunes were philosophical. By their reactions, she saw that this kind of thing happened fairly frequently. They'd immediately checked into the motel and gotten her an adjoining room. She was already making her plans to sneak out after they fell asleep and make a run for it.

"Good thing you gave your ivy plants a good watering before we left," Oral said to Modean.

She nodded. "Jackie, darlin', you need to eat." Jenn was using the fake name on her papers. Jacqueline Simmons.

"Excuse me a moment, Miz Bethune," she said sweetly. "I am just so plumb worried about my *maw-maw*." She held up her cell phone. "I'm going to call her one more time."

"You do that, honey," Modean said, as Oral, who was just too large to be the owner of a Mini Cooper, took the last two biscuits and plopped them on his own plate. Modean gave him a look, which he pretended not to see.

Jenn walked briskly out of the restaurant and put another call through to Father Juan. He answered at once.

"Jenn, good news. We're on our way," he said. "There's a priest in New Orleans trying to put us in contact with a band of fighters there."

"Hunters?" she asked hopefully.

"Not exactly. Not like us," he replied. "Keep your phone on. When I find out more, I'll let you know." He paused. "Have they reopened the border?"

"No."

"Stay there until it opens."

"Father, no," she pleaded. "I can't just *sit* here eating grits."

"You will eat them," he insisted. "And then you will go to sleep in your hotel room. And you will rest while you have the chance. And then you will let the Bethunes drive you into Louisiana."

"But—"

"I'm your master," he reminded her. "Do you want me to put the Hunter on, so she can order you to do as I say?"

Through the plate glass window, Modean waved at her and pointed to the waitress who was setting down large plates loaded with meat loaf and mashed potatoes. Oral smiled at the waitress and held up an empty glass, which had once contained sweet iced tea.

"Stay with those people. They need to cross the border too," Father Juan said. "Think with your head, not your heart."

"But Aurora's got Heather."

"And she said she would keep Heather alive until Mardi Gras. If something happens to you, we'll have to rescue you. *Escúchame*," he said sternly as she prepared to argue. "We're going to land at the airport *in* New Orleans. We have no border to cross. Just several to fly over. Don't make this harder for us."

She drew a deep breath. "All right."

"*Bueno*. Jamie, there is no smoking in here," he said away from the phone. "Jenn. I know that you don't believe in prayer, but I do, and I'm praying."

"Thank you." Her throat was tight, and her eyes welled with tears. "Oh, God, Father Juan."

"Ah, a prayer after all," he said softly. "God willing, we'll see each other soon."

She could practically feel him making the sign of the cross over her. He hung up first. She glanced through the window again. Oral Bethune lifted up Jenn's plate, as if to warn her that her food was getting cold. Holding up a finger, she dialed her grandmother next. The call went straight to voice mail.

"I'm okay," was all she said. If someone got hold of her grandmother's phone, they wouldn't be able to learn anything about where Jenn was.

She stood outside for a few moments, collecting herself. Then she went back into the restaurant and sat down, aware that the volume on the TV had been cranked up. The same news anchor was on the screen. Both of the Bethunes had stopped eating, and their eyes were glued to the set.

". . . And so, to repeat, the border between Mississippi and Louisiana will be closed for at least another twenty-four hours."

"No," Jenn whispered. "No, please."

"Good thing I brought a good book," Modean said, "and my knitting."

"I wonder if they have Pay Per View," Oral replied. "Jackie, what kind of movies do you like to watch?"

The evening dragged on. After dinner they watched a spy thriller in the Bethunes' room. Then Oral announced that he was tired, and Modean took that as her cue to move the party into Jenn's room. Over canned soda and musty ice cubes from a noisy ice machine, she talked for hours about nothing, really, until she moved to go back to her room via the door that connected them.

One hand on the knob, she glanced over at Jenn. Her face softened. "It's not your *maw-maw* you're worried about," she said, "is it?"

Jenn shook her head. Modean smiled sadly at her. "These are hard times, but things are going to get better."

"Yes, ma'am." Jenn cleared her throat. "I know."

"Once our government and Solomon's people weed out the bad apples, everything will be back to normal."

Are you crazy? Jenn wanted to shout at this woman in her teddy bear sweater. But she maintained her composure and folded her hands in her lap.

"That day can't come soon enough," she declared.

"It'll be here before you know it." Modean blew her a little kiss. "You're just as sweet as sugar, Jackie."

"Thank you, ma'am," she replied.

By the time Modean left, Jenn was exhausted by worrying and playacting. She clutched the cheap toothbrush she'd gotten from the front desk and washed up. Then she lay down on the bed. The room deodorizer smelled like bubble gum. Her heart thudded.

I'll never relax enough to fall asleep, she thought.

But Jenn did. And she dreamed:

Antonio stood beneath a lacy canopy of orange leaves and white blossoms. He was wearing a white shirt and white trousers, with a broad red silk sash worn low on his hips. He was barefoot. His curly hair grazed his earlobes, and his skin was golden brown. There were freckles across his nose, and his ruby earring caught sunset colors blazing across the sky.

An ocean washed the shoreline behind him. Reaching up, he plucked an orange and pushed his fingertips into the orange skin; then he pulled it apart. Inside, the fruit was orange speckled with red.

"This is a blood orange," he said. "There are no apples in this garden." He held it out to her. "Taste."

Her dream self appeared. She was wearing a white gauze spaghetti-strap nightgown, and her dark hair was gathered up loosely with a strip of ivory silk. As she took the orange from him, his fingers brushed hers. They were warm.

"If I take this and eat, will I be like you?" she asked him.

His smile faded. "There is no one like me," he replied.

Then the sun fell into the ocean and the black sky lit up like a bonfire. Blue moonlight on his hair, his eyes gleaming scarlet, he opened his mouth wide, and his fangs—

Jenn bolted upright, gasping. Bathed in sweat, she pulled up her legs and wrapped her arms around them. Trembling, she rested her forehead against them. A nightmare, just a nightmare.

Or had it been the sweetest of dreams?

MADRID
FATHER JUAN, JAMIE, SKYE, ERIKO, HOLGAR, AND ANTONIO

"Tell me again why we're doing this," Jamie grumbled at Father Juan as he plopped down beside the salt-and-pepper-headed priest in his clerical collar and handed him the coffee the good father had requested. The entire team sat in Madrid International Airport, awaiting their flight to

216

JFK Airport in New York City. To avoid detection they were scattered at three different gates, and Jamie had roundly protested being separated from Eriko. He'd argued that no one on earth would figure the girl in the auburn bob wig and enormous sunglasses to be Eriko Sakamoto, the Salamanca Hunter. Jamie had covered up the majority of his tatts with a black sweater and leather jacket, and a loose black knitted cap pulled low over his brow. He looked so highfalutin, he doubted his own ma would recognize him. If she had still been alive.

After the Cuevas mission their pictures had ended up online. Their YouTube hits were in the millions. Fortunately, all the cell-phone video was blurry.

So what if the airport security were wandering about, keeping sketch over the lambs about to board planes for places other than Spain? They surely wouldn't realize that the Salamancans were about to quit the continent.

In addition, with the help of witchy Skye, the good father had placed hocus-pocus on their doctored passports, giving whoever touched the documents a feeling of goodwill toward the passport's holder. The magicks would work better on some than others—as was the case with all defensive weapons—but between that and Father Juan weaving spells as often as other Catholic priests actually *prayed*, like priests were supposed to, Jamie saw no reason why he couldn't watch over his partner.

"Sit down, Jamie," Father Juan ordered him. Jamie's

master had been texting; Jamie tried to read the words off the phone, but the father slipped it back into his jacket pocket and took the coffee from Jamie's half-gloved hand. Jamie knew what was up; they all did: There were two teams in Russia, up against some monster vampire there named Dantalion, who was torturing hunters to death and worse. They had been begging Father Juan for help. It never ended.

But instead of going there, where they could do some good, the Salamancans were bound on yet another fool's errand in the opposite direction. Another one doomed to failure.

Jamie seethed.

Father Juan glanced up at him, every hair in place, face cleanly shaven, heavy brows and deep-set eyes betraying nothing of his inner turmoil, which Jamie knew had been increasing during the many, many text messages he had been trading with Russia. They all knew it. If he wasn't praying, he was working his beads, sending up prayers to the Blessed Mother. Or the Goddess, or whoever he really worshipped. Jamie was beginning to wonder about Father Juan's brand of Catholicism. All right, then, not beginning to wonder. He'd wondered about it all along.

"Siéntate," Father Juan ordered him. Sit. "You pace worse than Holgar."

Rolling his eyes, Jamie flopped into the empty black plastic-and-chrome chair beside the priest. "At least I don't walk in a circle three times and sniff my own arse before I sit down," he grumped. He knit his blond brows and cocked his head. "New York," he prompted. "New Orleans. This is all arseways."

"Shh," Juan murmured, as he pried the plastic lid off his coffee and took a sip, all showy nonchalance and ease. "We've discussed this. Jenn's alone, and her sister has been taken."

"Heather, you said her name was? You know the chit's dead," Jamie snapped. He stared into his own cup, seeing his own family there. His own sister, torn apart before his eyes by werewolves when he was ten. Seeing the faces of the vampires who had cornered her in the alley outside their parish church so the wolves could get at her. Jamie, screaming at his priest, Father Patrick, to do something, anything, when all Father Pat could do was hold him back so that he wouldn't die that night too. Maeve, his sweet girl, shredded, as the wolves howled and the vampires doubled over, hissing and chortling. And none to help. No revenge taken, still, after years.

There'd been no Hunter in Belfast. No one to stand up to the monsters who terrorized the streets. And why was that, when every fecking *village* in England had a Hunter? The *capital* of Northern Ireland, with three million souls begging for help, and no one to champion them?

At the gritty, working-class graveyard, as they lowered the box of what was left of Maeve and his da *and* his ma into the ground, Jamie had sworn on their coffins that he'd lay a werewolf pelt in front of his fireplace before he left this world. *That* was why Jamie had traveled to Salamanca—to be ordained the Hunter. He'd fought and trained harder than any of them; he'd sat in the chapel in the middle of many a freezing-cold night and more boiling-hot ones—Christ, Spain was like hell!—and begged sweet Mother Mary to put the mark of the Hunter on his brow. And he'd sworn on the memories of his murdered family that the second he'd drunk that elixir down, he'd go back to Belfast and rid his folk of vampires and werewolves, too.

But not only had he *not* become the Hunter, he'd been persuaded to stay in Salamanca to fight as part of a bleedin' hunting *team*. It went against all hunting custom and tradition, and if Father Juan had been the only master to put a team together, Jamie would have suspected Juan of working with the English to make sure Belfast remained defenseless. Jamie was positive that the English government had made a backroom deal with the Cursed Ones—*We'll let you have the Irish, if you leave us English alone.*

The local Cursers in his rough west Belfast neighborhood still ran with the same pack of wolves who had ripped Maeve limb from limb. Still carted off little girls and old men, leaving the tourists alone (if any were fool enough to wander into west Belfast), which gave additional weight to Jamie's conspiracy theory.

"I know you're angry," Father Juan said "But she is

one of us. We don't leave our own behind. Ever. She needs our help."

Jamie gulped down half his scaldy, sending a boiling river of tea down his throat. It barely registered, he was fuming so. If he, Jamie, was going to gallivant off and take care of anyone's sister—well, Belfast was full of good Catholics with sisters and daughters and mothers who needed saving.

"Our American needs more help than we can give her," Jamie snapped. "First she bollockses up the Cuevas job; now we're leaving our home base—leaving *Europe*, for God's sake—because she couldn't even keep her own sister safe from the locals. . . ."

"Papeles," said a uniformed man who came to a standstill in front of Jamie. Papers. With a jowly face and black sideburns, he was wearing the new Civil Forces uniform—dark blue dress jacket, black trousers, and an insignia on his shoulder of an eagle holding a sword. Before the war lots of Spanish battalions had featured crosses. As vampires could not abide crosses, the images had all been redrawn as swords. To show courtesy, it was said. But it was appeasement, pure and simple.

Father Juan figured it was only a matter of time before the vampires moved against the Church, whether or not they got humans to help them with that. On that day mankind would truly be doomed.

Beside Jamie, Father Juan moved the pointer and

middle finger of his left hand and moved his lips. Casting another spell.

Jamie reached into the inside pocket of his jacket and pulled out his forged passport. It was still Irish-issued, wine-colored pleather stamped with a gold Irish harp—no sense trying to deny that Jamie, with his heavy accent, was anything but *feckin' oirish*.

Jamie's hand was steady as he handed the passport to the soddin' traitor to his species, and the Spaniard made a show of examining it, staring at Jamie's photo and then at Jamie himself as if he were memorizing the answers to a test. Then the guard handed it back as if himself was doing Jamie the greatest of favors and dipped his head respectfully at Father Juan.

"*Buenos días, Padre,*" the man said, and moved on.

Once he was out of earshot Jamie turned to Father Juan. "What the bloody shite was that all about?"

"You invite scrutiny because of your negative energy," Father Juan said simply. A public announcement in Spanish echoed through the speakers, and he put the lid back on his coffee. "That's our flight."

Father Juan rose and looked down expectantly at Jamie, who finished his tea—what the hell, he had no nerve endings left in his throat anyway—and stood his ground.

"I'm waiting here for Eriko," he declared, crossing his leg over his knee.

Father Juan sighed. "You're boarding now, my son." He

raised his hand and made the sign of the cross over Jamie, then over himself. "Let's go."

At that moment Holgar and Antonio walked up side by side, and Jamie boiled over. The two supernaturals of the group, and *they* were allowed to hang out together?

He glared first at the Curser, and then at the wolf. Once Holgar had been outed, rumors about his bestial nature flew. Scandinavian werewolves were said to possess more than a few drops of Viking berserker blood—but the Dane had won over most of the students with his so-called quick wit. Jamie found nothing quick about him except his damnable speed and ability to heal himself. And if ever the Dane slowed down in a place where no one else was about . . .

"Woof," Holgar whispered, his blue eyes twinkling, as if he could read Jamie's mind. Antonio just kept gazing at Jamie, very neutral, as if he had never met him in his life. Vampires were cunning liars.

We're really doing this because of Antonio, Jamie realized. *He's the Church's pet vampire, and he has the hots for our little Jenn. Father Juan wants to keep Antonio happy . . . so the rotter will stay on our side. He knows about us, could tell the opposition so many lovely things. He probably already has. Why we haven't staked him is beyond me.*

Jamie balled his fists, hating Antonio even more, if that was remotely possible. If Father Juan wanted negative energy, Jamie had buckets of it. Rivers.

And then some.

*   *   *

As Father Juan settled into his seat on the plane, he kept a close eye on his team. He knew that while they were sympathetic to Jenn's plight, most didn't understand why they were going to help.

He had prayed and worked magicks almost nonstop since Jenn's departure from Spain. He had known something was going to happen, though he hadn't known what it was until she had called on her way to the airport. The one thing the visions had told him was that when she called, they must respond.

Of all the hunter teams, he knew that his was the most fractious. Salamanca was the one academy that drew people from all over. His hunters had so little in common, sharing neither creed nor culture with each other. The fighting they did amongst themselves made them weak. It was only by embracing their differences that they would ever be strong enough to handle what was coming.

He was loath to leave the new first-year students, who had been at the academy less than two months. He wasn't teaching any of the classes this time; his duties with the hunter team precluded it. It was probably just as well. He couldn't afford to be distracted. Besides, he had left the school in the capable hands of his faculty, which included the nine graduates of the team's class who had not been selected.

There were two cohorts of students: those who would graduate in one year, and those who would finish in two—if they didn't wash out, if they survived. Each new class was divided into nine teams of ten students, designated only by a number—1, 2, 3, up to 9. There were no fanciful or inspiring names for the teams or the dorms they shared. That was by design; becoming a hunter was hard, brutal work with an early death as its most likely reward. Training at Salamanca was not romantic or cute.

The 180 were taught by twelve priests, nine former military men, and three civilians with what the world saw as acute disabilities. Each instructor brought his or her own strengths to the table. The soldiers taught hand-to-hand combat, weapons, field medicine, and tactics. It was their job to harden the students' bodies and make them lethal weapons. The priests taught world history, vampiric history, and critical-thinking skills, and otherwise prepared the students' minds and souls for battle. It was one thing to take a life; it was quite another to be at peace with it and to be able to do it without hesitation.

Most of the students followed some variant of Christianity, but they also had some Jews and two Muslims. There was Eriko, their Buddhist, and some atheists and agnostics. The students were sometimes surprised to learn that vampires recoiled from symbols of any faith—crosses, images of Buddha, pentagrams. But as Salamanca belonged to the Church, all potential hunters carried crosses and holy water in their training kits.

By far, though, some of the most valuable training they

received came from those who were neither priests nor warriors. Susanna Elmira, a matronly former kindergarten teacher, blind from birth, trained the students to fight what they could not see, to sense and respond to movements that were lightning fast. The final exam for her class pitted a blindfolded student against three sighted adversaries with wooden swords called bokkens.

Jorge Escobar, a young man who had been unable to use his lower body since a car accident when he was four, taught students to fight no matter how badly injured they were, and how to defend themselves even when they were on the ground. He taught them to hone their strengths to near superhuman levels. He himself could crush the bones in a grown man's wrist using only two fingers.

José Trujillo, an old man with acute obsessive-compulsive disorder who had spent much of his life institutionalized, had found a home at the academy as well. He taught students how to have a heightened awareness of their environment, to see patterns, no matter how obscure, and to recognize when something or someone didn't belong. Two years before, he had been the only instructor to realize on the first day of classes that Holgar was a werewolf. Fortunately, he had come to Father Juan, who already knew the truth, and had not just blurted out his discovery in a way that would cause panic. Holgar managed to do that, with his howling. While most students had learned immeasurably from the old man's classes, Father Juan was convinced that those lessons had made Jamie even more paranoid than he was when he arrived at the academy.

The nine graduates were at a bit of a disadvantage, as they were seen as washouts. But they humbled themselves in order to continue serving the cause. Their dedication gave Father Juan hope for humanity.

These, then, were the brave men and women who sacrificed much to train hunters. They had done their jobs well. Even Antonio and Holgar had found themselves challenged and had learned to heighten their already acute senses.

They're a good team, he reminded himself.

The last passenger boarded the plane, flight attendants barring the door behind him. The man made his way down the aisle and to his seat next to Father Juan. He sat down, and Father Juan could smell blood.

"Pull the shade, please," the man asked.

Father Juan stiffened and glanced sideways just in time to see a glimpse of fangs. He slowly pulled down the shade, weighing his options. His team was scattered through the plane. There could be other vampires present, or sympathizers. Were they following the hunters? Or simply traveling on the plane for other reasons, other plans?

Up front the flight attendant called for attention as the plane pulled away from the gate. As she began to explain the safety features of the airplane, Father Juan prayed they wouldn't have to use them.

*　　*　　*

Skye felt squished. She was in the middle seat in a row of three. The aging man sitting to her right, next to the window, was extremely overweight. The guy sitting to her left, on the aisle, looked like he could play professional American football. Holgar was in the row in front of her, on the aisle, and she wished she could have been seated next to him.

"Buenos días," the football guy said to her.

"Hi," she answered.

"You speak English?"

"Yes," she said, keeping her eyes focused forward. It was going to be a long flight. She wondered if she could do a little magick, just a small spell to avert his interest. She glanced at the man on her right, who was watching, seemingly having nothing better to do.

She bit her lip. She was already spreading herself thin trying to keep the team from attracting attention. Five rows behind and to her left, Antonio also sat in an aisle seat, far enough away from the windows to avoid the sun. Eriko was on the opposite side of the plane toward the front, Father Juan sat toward the back. Jamie slouched in the very last row in the middle section, muttering about leg room and blood clots. Skye didn't like it. She felt exposed, vulnerable.

Ay, mi amor, do you miss me? a voice seemed to whisper inside her head. A chill shot down her spine, and she shivered. It always whispered when she was alone, vulnerable.

She saw Holgar's head turn slightly, as though sensing

something was wrong. She took a deep, calming breath, willing both of them to relax.

Mr. Football began to talk about himself, and she tried to tune most of it out. She tried to focus instead on dispelling her mounting feelings of dread. There was a weird energy that seemed to be crackling through the plane, like that which preceded an oncoming storm. The longer they were in the air, the more intense it grew.

We shouldn't be here, she thought suddenly, the certainty of that overwhelming her. Mr. Football leaned in close, and she jumped.

"Oh, come on. One little kiss won't hurt you," he said.

Holgar stood and turned around. "Leave my girl alone," he said, his voice a low, rumbling growl. Skye always thrilled to the sound of it.

The man snickered. "Oh, I'm sorry, is she your girl?"

Holgar growled again.

The petite dark-skinned female passenger beside Holgar gave a little cry. "Um, miss?" She reached up and jabbed the call button. "Hello?"

Football brushed an icy finger across Skye's cheek. From the way Holgar's eyes opened wide, she knew that he hadn't detected the vampire either until that moment, had missed the scent in the confusion of so many odors. His eyes swept the rest of the plane, and she saw his lips curl back. *Goddess, no!* She could tell from his expression that there was more than one vampire on the plane.

Holgar's eyes began to glow. He growled again, low in his throat, menacing.

"What's the problem?" Jamie said as he strode up the aisle. A flight attendant barred his way.

"Sir, the fasten-seat-belt sign is on," she said nervously.

"Yeah, sorry," Jamie said, easing the attendant into the row of seats and pushing his way past her.

"Sir!" she protested.

Jamie ignored her and kept going until he reached Skye's row. He grabbed the vampire's hand.

"You bleedin' piece of shite!" Jamie bellowed.

"I'm getting the captain," the flight attendant yelled.

"Do that! Get the co-captain, too! He was going to bite her!" Jamie shouted. Then back at the vampire, "You feckin' sucker!"

At that, several more passengers rose from their seats. Skye counted five. Their eyes were glowing, their fangs extending.

She closed her eyes and tried to conjure a calming spell. Her heart was pounding; she was too scared to concentrate.

"Joining the party?" Jamie said, and she blinked her eyes open to find Antonio hovering beside Jamie, wearing his monstrous mask of bloodlust. He had revealed his vampiric identity to everyone on the plane.

They couldn't start a fight, not with so many innocents in the way, not in a plane that could so easily come crashing down, killing them all.

"No, no," Skye murmured, and closed her eyes again. *Goddess, make me a channel of your peace. . . .*

And she felt Father Juan's essence joining in her chant, which for him was a prayer, the Prayer of St. Francis of Assisi:

Where there is hatred, let me sow love; Where there is injury, pardon . . .

Working together with the priest, who had once served the Goddess—the peculiar man who seemed so ageless, and yet so careworn and tired. But in this moment she sensed the golden halo of his soul, which had lived before, and the dreams of his heart, which had yet to live.

And together they poured balm on the anger, and the football vampire's bloodlust.

When she came out of her trance the plane was landing, and everyone was back in their seats. As they deplaned, Father Juan came up to her and bobbed his head.

"I hope no one saw Antonio," he murmured. "No one who should not have seen."

"We can work some magicks about that, too," she offered.

He smiled. "Or ask God to work some for us."

Skye remembered the whispered words inside her mind. She hadn't heard them for a long time and had begun to believe that the one who whispered them had lost track of her. Right then, right there, she got ready to tell him what she'd been hiding all this time. She had a stalker, and he was someone who was bad, mad, and dangerous to know. But

Jamie bounded up with a duffel over his shoulder and said, "Let's get out of here, before I tear that Curser apart."

The moment was lost. *Another time,* Skye promised herself. Then she smiled briefly at Holgar, who was carrying her duffel. During the fracas he'd kept his cool.

"Well, that was fun," he drawled.

Father Juan smiled faintly. "As they say, you ain't seen nothing yet."

"Bring it on." Jamie jutted out his chin and grabbed Skye's duffel from Holgar. Then he stomped toward the exit, stopped, and turned around.

"You coming?"

They left.

Outside Biloxi
Jenn

"You look tired, honey," Modean said to her at breakfast. The two women were alone at the table. "But good news. They've reopened the border. We'll be on our way as soon as Oral wakes up."

It took another hour, but at last they hit the road. As it turned out, the Bethunes knew how to bribe the border guard to ignore their sweet little gal Jackie, who didn't have the proper papers to get into Louisiana. They stopped for lunch, making plans to drive Jenn straight to her *maw-maw*'s. So, with regret, Jenn slipped out the window of the restaurant bathroom and flew down the road.

Then it was just Jenn and her thumb, and a trucker who had picked her up. As they neared New Orleans, he became increasingly agitated.

The grizzled sixtysomething man pushed back his New Orleans Saints ball cap and looked down at her like a sad angel. He was wearing a denim jacket over a faded dark blue T-shirt, and ragged jeans and work boots. Touching the crucifix hanging from the mirror, the trucker grimaced and gave his head a shake.

"You shouldn't be doing this, *cher*," he said in a twangy accent. "New Orleans don't belong to us anymore. It's *theirs*. I grew up there, and I am *gone*. Trucking company offered me triple to go into town; I said I am *gone*. That place is pure evil. Folks that are left are owned lock and stock by *them*. They don't take kindly to strangers. They'd sooner slit your throat than ask you what your name is."

Jenn was shocked. Things back in Spain were so different; she traveled with the group on missions but lived behind the walls of the university. They'd heard nothing about how bad it must be in New Orleans, if what the trucker was saying was true.

"Why don't they just leave?" she asked.

"Half of 'em can't. Bloodsuckers won't let 'em. The other half won't. Lots of vampire groupies moved here when they took over the city. They can hypnotize you, did you know that? Make you walk off a cliff if they want to."

"Thanks for the warning," Jenn said, even though she already knew what he was telling her.

He pulled over to the side of the road. "This is as far as I go."

She climbed out of the refrigerated cab with her duffel over her shoulder. Outside, the early-afternoon sky was drizzling warm rainwater. Her boots sank into the boggy earth, and she grimaced, pulling her right foot out of the muck and looking for higher, drier ground. The bayou air was a wet slap against her chilled face.

"That's the quickest way in, right?" she asked him. That was what he'd told her.

"*Oui.* They watch the highway, but the bayou will hide you." He raised a hand off the big steering wheel and pointed to the trees. "But I don't know, *cher*. It don't look good to me, now that we're here. It's dark enough in there for them to be out. For all we know, *un Maudit*—a Cursed One—is sharpening his fangs right now, just waiting for someone like you to walk on in. You ever seen a person after those suckers got hold of them?"

"Yes," she said softly. "That's why I'm here."

His face softened with pity, the crosshatches of leathery lines growing more shallow as he pursed his lips; after a beat, unshed tears glistened in his eyes. "So you're here for revenge? There ain't nothing you can do, *cher*. Ain't nothing anybody can do. Government's sold us down the river, just like they did when Hurricane Katrina hit. Letting the vampires chew on us so they'll leave the big shots alone."

He sounds like Jamie, she thought. *Or . . . Dad . . .*

A wave of nausea hit her. Biting her lower lip, she forced back tears. If she stared crying, she would never stop. She couldn't think about her father, not now. Maybe not ever.

"I can do something. And I will."

"I tried too," he said. Then he gathered up the neck of his T-shirt and yanked it down, exposing his collarbone. A thick, jagged, purple scar ran from one side of his neck to the other. "Nearly got me killed."

She sucked in her breath at the clear evidence of a vampire attack. Some said a vampire's bite was the most painful experience imaginable. Others that it was a taste of heaven.

"My brother, he come up behind that vampire and staked him. The *Maudit* turned to dust, right on my chest." He pulled his shirt back up and patted his chest. "You should have seen all the blood."

"I'm glad you were saved," she said sincerely.

He tapped his finger against the large black crucifix dangling from the mirror, making it swing. "Jesus Christ saves. I was *rescued*."

"I'm glad for that, too." She moved to shut the door.

"Don't go to the city," he begged her, but she slammed shut the door and took a step back as she waved at him. He pointed to the crucifix again, and she nodded, unsure exactly what he was trying to say, but she would accept any and all good wishes and blessings.

His air brakes squealed as he left. Once he'd rolled back onto the highway proper, she reached into the top of the duffel for a stake and hefted it in her hand. It was the sharpest one she had. In the hands of Eriko or any of the others, it was a formidable weapon. In her hands . . .

"You're a trained hunter," she said to herself. "You can do this." There were five fewer vampires in Oakland as proof of that. Still, she knew that most of that had been luck. She just hoped her luck held, because at this point she was Heather's only hope. If it wasn't already too late.

I hate you, Dad. You might as well have painted a bull's-eye on her chest. . . .

You've killed her.

She couldn't think like that. That vampire — Aurora — had promised to keep Heather alive until Mardi Gras, which was nine days away. But there was a lot Aurora could do to Heather in the meantime besides killing her outright. Torturing her, draining her bit by bit.

Jenn forced herself to remain calm and in control. She couldn't think like a big sister right now. She had to be a hunter, 100 percent, inside and out.

She pulled out her cell phone and saw one bar. Hoping for a connection anyway, she dialed first Father Juan, and then Antonio, and got no service. She hoped they were en route, coming to help her as Father Juan had promised.

But they weren't there now. She was alone, aware that Heather was bait and that she was doing exactly what Aurora wanted her to. Why? Surely bagging one Salamancan wasn't worth all this effort, especially when Aurora could have killed her already. Jenn had spent the last several hours wondering why Aurora had walked away instead of finishing things. She was sure the Cursed One had a reason, and she was equally sure she wasn't going to like it when she found out what it was.

Squaring her shoulders, Jenn gripped the stake and opened a Velcro pocket, pulling out a glass vial of holy water. If a Cursed One came after her, she could break open the vial against a tree trunk. Holy water burned vampires like acid—vampires, that is, except for Antonio. Wasn't that proof enough for him that he really did possess a soul?

The bayou sloshed, although the rain had stopped. The sun struggled through the low-hanging clouds and the lacy cypress trees. Weird gray wooden stumps rose from the swirling water. Alligators? Vampires in those little Cajun canoes she'd read about somewhere?

She squinted into the gloom, smelling mud and an undercurrent of rot. Live oaks surrounded the bayou, then extended left to right before her like a marching army— a barrier and a trap. She started walking parallel, hoping to skirt around them. There was a stretch of two-lane road farther on—the "highway" road into New Orleans that the trucker had refused to take. The one he said was too dangerous to take. In the center of the pitted tarmac, a burned-out, rusted Infiniti lay on its side like the skeleton of a dead animal. No one had taken that road in a long time.

Still, the sun shone brighter there, so she kept walking toward the blacktop, stake at the ready, slinging her fingers through her duffel in such a way that she could immediately drop it if she had to. Everyone else on the team could use a bag like that as a weapon, but Jenn didn't have enough upper-body strength to manage it.

She reached the road and hesitated; more burned, abandoned vehicles stretched down the pavement. The sun beat down on the twisted metal, and she swallowed, bracing herself in case she ran across a dead body. She had not yet become accustomed to seeing corpses. But the wrecks had disintegrated so badly that she guessed years must have passed since they'd caught fire, or been torched; if anything was left of the people who had ridden in them, they would be clean bones by now. The thought did little to comfort her, but she walked on. Behind her, crickets scraped and frogs croaked; a bird cawed. So there was life in New Orleans. Lots of it.

The buzz of something like a dragonfly vibrated against her ear; the sound grew louder as she passed the Infiniti. She felt a vibration against the soles of her boots. It was the roar of an engine coming up behind her on the long-deserted road.

She turned, shielding her eyes against the glare. About fifty yards from her a black panel van swerved around a rusted tow truck, brakes squealing. The windshield was dark, and so was the driver's-side window. Tinted? A chill ran down her back. The patrol the trucker had warned her about? Was it Cursed Ones, daring to drive in the sun? No vampire she'd ever encountered had tried something so risky.

The van gunned its motor, picked up speed, and angled straight for her. Dropping the duffel, she broke into a run. The van kept coming. The engine was racing. She moved faster. The whine became a roar that vibrated against her bones.

The trees, she thought. It wouldn't be able to follow her into the tangle of oaks at the side of the road. But was that what they wanted her to do? Were more vampires crouched on branches and leering behind trunks, waiting? And if so, what should she do next?

Hunters learned to process situations strategically. Top priority was getting away from the van. If it hit her, it would kill her for certain. She had to do the first thing most likely to keep her alive. For the moment, that meant the trees.

The van roared toward her as she whirled on her heel and sprinted for the nearest oak. Sweat slicked her hands; she gripped the stake, her only one, and kept hold of the vial of holy water in her sweaty left hand. Her heart pounded wildly, and she forced herself not to pant, but to breathe regularly through her exertion—a hunter's technique for increasing stamina. Her eyes couldn't make a quick enough adjustment from the bright sun to the darkness of the woods, and she knew she had to slow down, or the impact when she ran into a tree would knock her out. Spanish moss hanging from a branch scratched her forehead as she put on a burst of speed.

Then the van slammed to a stop. She listened hard, dropping to a crouch and grinding her fist against her mouth so whoever got out of the van wouldn't hear her gulping in air. Sweat stung her eyes, and she wiped her brow with her forearm. It stung, and she realized she was covered with fine scratches from blasting through the crisscrosses of branches.

"It was a chick," someone—it sounded like a guy—shouted. *"Vite!"*

A shrill whistle followed.

Vite was French for "first"—it could also mean "hurry." Jenn had learned a few words from a student at the academy. Simone had washed out, walking away disappointed but free. She was lucky. Most students who left the academy did so in body bags.

But now Jenn was trapped. Her heartbeat stuttered, and adrenaline gushed into her system. Through a supreme act of will she made herself breathe slowly again. Her eyes still hadn't adjusted; she was blind, for all intents and purposes.

Another whistle pierced her eardrums, startling her so badly she almost fell forward onto her hands. If that happened, she would break the vial. Shifting her weight, she closed her eyes, fighting to adjust.

The whistle was answered . . . from somewhere *behind*

her. Her eyes flew open. The second whistler was *in* the forest. With her.

Antonio, she thought, because each time she faced death, her last thought was of him. His face blazed into her mind. She remained stock-still, afraid the scent of her fear would carry despite the sultry, leaden air.

Footfalls crashed closely behind her. Could be a vampire, could be a human. Given the sunlight, whoever had gotten out of the van was more likely human, unless the van had rolled into shadow. And the guy had spoken to someone, so there were at least two of them. Maybe they were surrounding her.

Finally, the dim shapes of trees took form, their ropes of Spanish moss hanging like nooses. Half straightening, she glided as silently as she could behind the trunk of the nearest oak. She craned her neck around it, straining to see in the half-light.

"Gotcha," someone said, as a blow crashed down on the back of her head.

NEW ORLEANS
FATHER JUAN, JAMIE, ERIKO, HOLGAR, SKYE, AND ANTONIO

"Thank God for basements," Father Juan said as Antonio stepped from the service elevator and the door closed. They hefted their gear. No one had checked baggage. Everything they had brought, they carried on their backs. That meant they were seriously lacking in weapons of any kind.

"There's a door leading to the maintenance tunnel, and from there, the sewer." Father Juan gave Jamie a look. "No smoking."

Jamie huffed and put his cigarettes away. Everyone was tired and dirty, including Antonio. The sun pulled hard on him. When their plane had been delayed in New York, the danger that he would have to walk in the sun had escalated. Luckily the companionways both in New York and New Orleans had been indoors, shielding him.

Eriko walked with Father Juan toward a gray metal door. Antonio glanced at Skye to see if she sensed any nearby vampires, then at Holgar to see if he smelled anything out of the ordinary. He himself had not. Everyone was tense. Father Juan's contact in New Orleans had e-mailed information designed to help them connect with the local band of fighters, but refused to meet them in person. He said it was too dangerous, that he'd already risked too much by helping them at all. The only reason he had gotten involved was because Father Juan was a Catholic priest, like him.

"So far, so good," Father Juan announced as Eriko held open the door. "He said there would be a maintenance cart. Then beyond that, we can get to the sewers."

"Brilliant," Jamie groused. He glared at Holgar. "You'll like that, won't you, wolfman? Sloggin' about in a big stream of shite?"

Holgar ignored him.

"And they'll find us in the sewers?" Skye prompted.

"That's the plan," Father Juan replied.

"Ambush us, more like," Jamie said.

"Please, be quiet," Eriko said.

They found the cart and wound their way through the warren of service tunnels, moving deeper into darkness and away from the airport. It was Mardi Gras season. Antonio had never been, but the traffic in the terminal had seemed sparse for such a festive occasion. People were afraid to come to New Orleans.

He thought of Jenn all alone, working her way here, and felt a clutch at his unbeating heart. She was a fully trained hunter, chosen by Father Juan, but she was so much more to him. And he had been born to a time when men took care of their women.

Yet you failed the woman who looked to you for protection, he thought. *And now she is dead.*

He pushed away his guilt and concentrated on moving the team to their rendezvous point. But he couldn't push away his fear.

For Jenn.

The hours stretched; Antonio determinedly brought up the rear as they kept going. Then he smelled death, and glanced at Holgar, who nodded.

"We're underneath one of those cemeteries," Holgar told him. "They bury their dead in those little houses. What do they call them in English?"

"Tombs," Antonio said.

"So they won't wash away in the gutters," Jamie groused, avoiding the fetid water trickling down the center of the tunnel they were in. "Bloody hell, this is worse than the catacombs."

Then Father Juan jerked, and cocked his head. Antonio watched him, listening to someone's strangely pounding heartbeat. Except . . . it wasn't a heartbeat. He squinted, concentrating.

"Voodoo drums," Father Juan said. "In the cemetery above us."

"Magicks," Skye affirmed. "They raise the dead."

"As zombies," Jamie added. "We got nothing to fear from 'em. Can barely move. We'll mow them down."

"*Alors*, stop right there," a voice rang out in the darkness.

The sharp *click* of a weapon echoed close behind it.

"Friend or foe?" Father Juan said loudly.

There was no answer.

The bayou outside New Orleans
Jenn

As the blow to the back of her head propelled Jenn against the tree trunk, she pushed with the flats of her hands and tilted her head, slamming it into the face of her assailant. She heard him grunt and felt him stagger backward, and she executed a sharp round kick as she whirled to face him. Her boot caught the side of his head.

He was a tall, dark-skinned black man, and as he crashed to the ground, she threw herself on top of him, capturing his left arm with her right leg. Straddling him, she pushed on his right shoulder and jabbed his chest with her stake, hard enough to make a dent but not to break the skin.

"No, no, no!" he screamed, flailing at her with his unpinned arm. "I'm human!"

"You *attacked* me," she reminded him, realizing that that might not make sense to him. What she meant was that her vow not to harm humans went out the window if she needed to defend herself.

"That's enough," said someone to her right. It was the voice of the man she'd heard getting out of the truck. "I got a rifle aimed at your head."

She was a hunter. Hunters didn't surrender.

"I've got a stake pressed against his heart," she said, raising up on her knees and allowing her body weight to push on the stake. Now the skin did break. As he screamed, she rolled off him, then yanked him up to a sitting position like a rag doll and draped him over her chest. She repositioned the sharp point against his carotid artery, straining to make out the figure of the other man. But it was too dark. If he could see her well enough to shoot her, it was likely he was a vampire—or he had a nightscope.

"If it goes in, he'll bleed to death!" she yelled.

"Oh, *merde, merde,*" the black man whispered. "Lucky, stop!"

"What are you doing here?" the other man—Lucky—demanded. "No one comes here."

"Drop the gun!" she bellowed, grabbing her prisoner under the chin and holding his head still. *"Now!"*

"Shit," her prisoner rasped. "Lucky, just do it!"

"Wait, stop, everybody." The voice belonged to a third person—a woman. "Lucky, I think . . . I think she's a Hunter. She's got a patch from Salamanca. They have an academy, don't they?"

They'd found her duffel. Her jacket with her Salamanca patch was folded inside.

A flashlight winked on, washing her and her captive with yellow light. She didn't stand down, keeping the stake pressed against the side of his neck. He looked at her with huge eyes.

"Is that true?" he ground out. "You're a Hunter?"

She didn't answer. But he started to cry.

"Merci," he whispered. *"Merci,* God."

"If you're a Hunter, you're among friends," said the woman. "I swear it."

The light whirled against the trees, then came to rest on the faces of a young woman and a guy—Lucky. Neither of them looked older than early twenties, maybe younger. The woman had hennaed red hair pulled up into two pom-pom ponytails. She was wearing tattered blue jeans and a black T-shirt silk-screened with a Japanese geisha face, and Jenn's duffel was in her arms. Lucky looked mildly gothy, with kohl-rimmed eyes and rings on all his fingers. His ears were pierced multiple times.

"Look," the woman said to Lucky, holding up Jenn's jacket.

Lucky showed Jenn his rifle and laid it on the ground, stretching out his hands and slowly straightening, his arms above his head. The woman held the flashlight steady with her right hand and dangled the jacket from her fist.

The fourth stranger, a man, approached Jenn from behind. In the glow from his flashlight, she saw that he was taller, with gray hair. He appeared to be unarmed.

The quartet looked at her. She lifted the stake away from her captive's throat and got to her feet. She still didn't entirely trust them. But as Father Juan often said, one had to go by one's instincts. She lowered her weapon and raised her chin.

"Yes," she said, facing the three. "I'm a hunter."

Lucky and the woman began cheering and dancing. The man she had nearly staked turned and threw his arms around her. And the older man lowered his head.

CHAPTER ELEVEN

*Our masters have sought out one another, and
organized us into fighting bands. We are sent out where
we might do the most good—that is, cause the most
harm to our common enemy. But creating teams of
hunters is a new concept; working with other bands is
just as new, and we have tensions and problems equal
to those of our older, supposedly wiser, elite fighting
forces. Many who have heard of us have protested our
very existence, calling us children on a crusade.*

—from the diary of Jenn Leitner

New Orleans
Jenn

"There are tunnels beneath most of New Orleans. They've
been here for ages," the redheaded woman told Jenn, as the

older man squeezed the black panel van into a narrow alley behind a beautiful three-story apartment building laced with wrought-iron balconies. "Pirates, bootleggers, kids have all used 'em. Now it's us. And the vampires."

The woman's name was Suzy, and she was from Ohio. She'd been working in Le Pirate, a restaurant in the beautiful and historic Vieux Carré, or French Quarter, of New Orleans. They'd been allowed to stay open because, after all, people had to eat.

It turned out that Jenn's "friend" the trucker had seen the foursome patrolling, and he'd pulled over and told them about his passenger and her odd behavior. There were prices on all their heads—they were outlaws, rebelling against the current government of their city—and people did terrible things to each other these days. That made her highly suspect, worth checking out. They'd accidentally struck gold, capturing a hunter.

"Let me carry that for you, Hunter," Matt, the driver, offered, as Jenn climbed out of the back, hoisting her duffel over her shoulder.

"Thanks," she said, allowing him to take it from her. If he took care of the duffel, she'd have her hands free for battle. Besides, she was massively exhausted. She had barely recovered from her last concussion, and she hoped that she didn't have a new one thanks to the latest head blow.

Moving stealthily, the others climbed out. Bernard, her former attacker, was their leader. While they pressed against the wall, he sidled down the alley, scanning left, right, and nodded at Lucky, who was a runaway sixteen-year-old from Tampa. Life had clearly aged him; he looked older. Jenn gathered by their dark humor that "Lucky" was the most ironic of nicknames. He'd run away from home to New Orleans, for God's sake.

They advanced a few feet, then paused beneath a sickly sweet magnolia tree. Engulfed in its perfume, Jenn almost sneezed, but she managed to hold it, her chest constricting painfully. With the others she watched Lucky dart to the center of the street and scan the area. She wanted to tell him that his furtive behavior was an attention grabber for sure; there really was no way to casually slide back a manhole cover, but he was raising more red flags than necessary. As the heavy cover scraped against the street, Lucky nodded once. Then he climbed down.

Jenn tapped Bernard's shoulder. "It's too dark down there. They'll be able to attack."

"They've got eyes and ears everywhere," Bernard whispered back. "Among the humans, I mean. If we go on the surface streets, we'll get picked up."

Monumentally uneasy, she debated leaving. She had only their word that they were fighting the vampires and the corrupt local human government. For all she knew, they were going to deliver her to Aurora.

Was this how Papa Che had felt? Constantly wondering who he could trust, knowing that at any turn he could be betrayed? Maybe that was why he had always been so good at reading people, their hearts, their intentions. If she had only had half his skill, she could have more easily read her father's intentions before he betrayed her.

"It's asking for it, going down there," Jenn insisted.

Suzy sidled up beside her. She ducked her head and nodded. "We're taking stupid chances. We know it," she whispered. "We just . . . we're getting tired. Everyone is looking for us. The vampires live in the houses, and so do the people who worship them. That leaves the sewers for the rats. And for us."

"We have a safe house down there," Bernard put in.

"Nothing is safe in the dark," Jenn countered. "The only reason I would ever go down there is to save someone."

"You'll be saving *us*," Suzy said under her breath as she hunched her shoulder beneath the tree. "There used to be more of us. The police came. . . ." Her voice trailed off, and she caught her lower lip. "We've never heard from Stan and Debbie again."

"She's telling you the truth, her," Bernard said. "It's all topsy-turvy here. New Orleans is a closed city. No one gets out. They'd warn people, tell 'em what's really going on. Cell phones don't work. Private citizens' use of Internet is blocked. It's like the Middle Ages."

She blinked, and Bernard continued. "People who protest get taken away. They never come back. There were terrible shortages for a while, but the C.O.'s have started getting supplies in. New Orleanians have gotten the message: Toe the line, you'll live and you'll eat. Complain, and you disappear."

She thought of her father. Gave a nod. "So they do it. Toe the line."

Suzy nodded. "Oh, hells yeah, they do it. And they smile while they do it. Of course, a lot of 'em also drink a lot, take drugs. There's a lot of post-traumatic stress disorder. And then there's people who pretend it's life as usual. That it's no big deal." She smiled sourly. "Denial is big here in the Big Easy."

"Then there's you," Jenn said. She was getting worried about Lucky. Then his head popped back up and he made the "okay" sign.

"There's us," Bernard agreed. "And you'd be amazed how many people hate us. They say we're going to get everyone killed. Say if we want to help, we should help the suckers—bring in more supplies, repair levees, things like that."

It sounded very familiar. "That's so messed up." Jenn looked at the tunnel. It was a death trap.

"Look, we've got a place where you can rest, send out the call for your people. On the streets . . ." He made a face.

"But she's a Hunter," Matt reminded them. "She'll be okay."

"Please come with us." Suzy took her hand. "It *is* dangerous down there. And scary."

252

Suddenly Jenn saw the situation differently: Here was a human asking a hunter for help. Had she not stood with the team, on New Year's Eve, and sworn to protect human life? Didn't her word count for something? Wasn't that what she had become a hunter for? Not just for her sister, but for all people?

"Please?" Suzy begged, her face small and very young.

In that moment Jenn realized she had no choice. She couldn't turn these people down.

"All right," she said, and Suzy gave her a quick hug.

They scurried to the manhole and climbed down into the tunnel, one at a time. It was colder beneath the ground, and it stank worse than the bayou. The echo of dripping water punctuated the rapid-fire rhythm of her heartbeat, and a couple of inches of foul-smelling liquid covered the floor of the tunnel.

"We live in an abandoned convent," Suzy told her, as they made so many rights and lefts that Jenn lost track. "It's supposed to be haunted."

"It is," Lucky blurted, then looked down at his hands.

"How do you know that?" Jenn asked him, but he hunched farther over, his body language screaming that he didn't want to talk about it. She could see the bones of his spine through his T-shirt, as if he wasn't getting enough to eat, or had a chronic illness. He wouldn't be much good in a fight. And as for Suzy, a waitress, Sarah Connor she wasn't. Were these the best fighters this group had?

Assessing their ability to defend themselves, she eyed Lucky's rifle. She knew Bernard was carrying a pistol, but neither of those weapons would inflict much damage on a vampire—and nothing permanent. She made sure her grip on her stake was good and firm.

As calmly as she could, she pulled out her phone. Of course it wouldn't work belowground, but she still hoped a delayed message would have come through by now.

"Like I said, there's no decent cell-phone reception in New Orleans anymore," Suzy murmured. "The mayor says it's something to do with the cell towers, but we know better." She frowned. "That's not happening in Spain?"

Jenn frowned and shook her head. They had cell phone reception in Spain. As hunters they kept pretty low profiles. Father Juan kept them sheltered from the day-to-day concerns of the war—and, apparently, the world. It bothered her that she was out of touch. But then again, what did it really matter?

"We should cut the chatter," Bernard warned them. "We're moving deep into enemy territory."

As if on cue Jenn's flashlight shone on a bloody handprint on the wall. She swallowed down a frisson of fear and looked carefully around, gazing into the shadows. Even if vampires lived in the houses, they would still need the tunnels to move about during the day. Bernard turned off his flashlight, and the others did the same.

"Vampires can see pretty well in the dark," she said.

There was silence. Then Bernard said gently, "But people can't see at all."

A reminder that they also had human enemies. "Right," she said, and extinguished hers as well. In Spain it wasn't that way. They were always hailed as the salvation of the citizens. She had never had to watch her back around humans before. Maybe if she had, this wouldn't have happened.

She shook her head. Her dad and she had never been close. It had been Papa Che who taught her to ride a bicycle, Papa Che who had encouraged her to take risks, even though it infuriated her father.

Still, she had never truly understood how deep the schism was between her father and *his* father until the night of the fight. Papa Che and Gramma had come over for dinner, and during dessert the conversation had turned to the vampires. Papa Che had denounced them, and her father had grown irate, saying he wouldn't have him speak that way in his house, didn't want to hear talk of war. In the end he had ordered Papa Che to leave, and Gramma had gone with him.

No sooner had the door closed behind them then Jenn had spoken up. Two girls at her school had gone missing, and she was sure that they had been killed by vampires. There were so many evil things happening; how could her father turn a blind eye to them?

He had accused her of being tainted by Papa Che, said that she sounded like a revolutionary.

"One of us should," she had accused. And something that had been buzzing in the back of her mind for weeks came to the front. She declared that she was going to go to Spain and study to become a Hunter.

Her father had totally lost it, screaming at her about what a daughter of his would and wouldn't do. She had left, stopping by her room just long enough to grab her passport—which bore a lone Canada stamp—the money she had earned working at the movie theater over the summer, and a jacket.

Twenty-four hours later she had landed in Madrid. A week after that and she was officially enrolled at the academy in Salamanca, part of the new entering class of almost ninety teenagers from around the world. At sixteen she wasn't the youngest by a long shot. There were others who were older, too. The cut-off age was twenty-one. Unless, of course, you were like Antonio and were nineteen going on ninety.

As Jenn and the small Resistance group sloshed through the water, they grew quieter, edgier. Soon they moved in utter silence. They walked for so long that Jenn began to suspect they were lost. She pulled out her phone and cupped the display while she checked the time. It was two fifty-five in the afternoon. The trucker had let her out at nine in the morning, and she was light-headed with hunger. There were some protein bars and a couple of water bottles stashed in her duffel bag.

She was just about to ask for the bag when the group

stopped moving. She didn't know if Bernard had given them a signal that she hadn't caught, or if they'd reached their destination. Bernard flicked on his flashlight. Suzy moved closer to Jenn.

Bernard painted a flight of rotten wooden stairs with the beam of light. The banisters were cracked and peeling, and the staircase itself was littered with Styrofoam takeout food containers, rotted newspapers, and beer bottles. It didn't appear to have been used in years. But as she watched, Suzy and Lucky grabbed the left corner of what appeared to be a long swath of camouflage netting beneath the layer of trash and folded it in half, revealing a much cleaner staircase. The trash had been deliberately attached to the netting. She was impressed by the clever trick, and filed it away as something the Salamancans might be able to imitate at a future date.

Her cheeks burned. It was so hard to think of a future. If something had happened to Heather, time in her world would stop, forever—to the moment that her father had betrayed them. Betrayed them *both*, when he thought he was saving his "good" daughter by sending his bad one to her death.

She began to shake. She couldn't think about it now. She wouldn't ever be able to think about it. As she averted her head and wiped her eyes, Bernard climbed the staircase and rapped on a wooden door in a special code—*rap-rap-rap, pause, rap, pause, rap-rap*. If these people were smart, they'd change it up at least once a day.

The door cracked open, and a low, quiet voice spoke in

French. Bernard replied. Jenn, who had never been to New Orleans before, hadn't realized how many New Orleanians used French as their first language. It was like being in a foreign country.

"*Bon*, come in," said the speaker, as he held the door open.

On the other side a young man with dark hair beneath a black cap held out a cross, and another, a slightly older redhead, held a submachine gun against his shoulder, aimed squarely at her. She kept her hands in plain sight, understanding—and approving of—their caution.

"Jenn," said Antonio, stepping from around the two men.

"Antonio!" she cried. "How'd you get here ahead of me?"

Oblivious of all else, she ran to him and threw her arms around him. He held her tightly and murmured in Spanish, so softly and rapidly she couldn't understand what he was saying. She didn't care. The words weren't important. Eyes pressed tightly shut, she laid her cheek against his chest and felt his strong arms around her, as the walls she had built around herself ever since Aurora had taken Heather crumbled.

"How could he, how could he?" she blurted as she began to cry. "My father." She wept harder, losing herself now that he had found her.

"*Sí*," he whispered. "*Sí, mi amor.*"

She gave into her grief and her rage, not caring who saw. She cried until she had exhausted herself. Then she heard him hiss, like a sigh against her cheek, and his arm muscles flexed as his chest expanded. He eased her away and turned his head. From her vantage point she could see the glowing washes of red in his eyes. Affected by her presence as much as she had been by his, he was changing.

Deflecting attention from him, she embraced Father Juan as he walked toward her with Eriko and Holgar. He kissed her forehead, then made the sign of the cross over her and handed her a tissue.

"Thank God you're safe," he said as she wiped her eyes. "We caught a flight right away, and after we made contact with Marc we tried to reach you, but cell phones don't work here."

"This place is a death trap," Jamie said, unknowingly echoing her exact thoughts. He leaned against the pitted wall, glowering at her as if that were her fault. He was white-knuckling a bottle of Rabid Bat beer.

"Any word?" she asked Father Juan, as Eriko gave her a hug and Holgar squeezed her forearm.

"*Sí,*" Father Juan said. "We have learned a few things about Aurora. She's a very old vampire. We don't know how old. We don't know who her sire is, or why she came here. The vampires here were expecting her."

"For Mardi Gras?" Jenn asked.

"Who knows?" Father Juan shrugged. "But we believe we have found a way to locate her."

"Really?" Her voice rose along with her excitement. "Then let's go."

"Yeah, right," Jamie said, stepping forward. "Let this Aurora have us all in one neat little gift-wrapped package. *There's* a good idea."

"It seems that this is a team of hunters," the redheaded man said to Bernard. "It's something they're doing in Europe."

"A team?" Bernard whistled under his breath and looked at Suzy, Matt, and Lucky, who were just coming through the door. Jenn assumed they'd stayed behind to replace the staircase camouflage.

Suzy reached on her tiptoes to kiss the redheaded man, whose name was Andrew. He smiled at her and pressed his fingertip against one of her pompom ponytails. Jenn thought they might be brother and sister, and she felt a terrible tug on her heart.

Suzy looked at Jenn and said, "You said you were the Hunter."

"Flying under false colors?" Jamie muttered as he raised his eyes toward the ceiling, drinking his beer.

"No," Jenn snapped at him.

"She is *a* hunter," Father Juan elaborated. "Eriko is their leader. But they are all hunters."

The man who had opened the door looked at Jenn with heavily-lidded, slightly drooping eyes, as if he had seen too many sad things in this world.

"I am Marc Dupree," he told her, "the head of this antivampire group. In another war people like us were called—"

"The Resistance," Antonio murmured, gazing with far-away eyes. "In World War Two." He lowered his head. "I had family who died fighting for the Resistance."

"True heroes, then," Marc said, inclining his head in deference. "It's an honor to have you stay with us. *All* of you hunters," he added, as if for Jamie's sake. "We know why you've come—that the vampire queen named Aurora has taken your little sister." He nodded once at Jenn. "We'll help you all we can. We can't allow another vampire like her into our city."

"We'll get her," Eriko said simply, as if in her mind there was no doubt of success.

"*Merci*, Marc," Father Juan said. "Now, if you please, Jenn has had a terrible shock. Her own father betrayed her to the Cursed Ones, and she was nearly killed. You've met the rest of our team; we can go into the other room and strategize while Jenn rests."

"No," Jenn protested. "I don't need to rest."

As Father Juan opened his mouth to reply, Jamie huffed and finished off his beer.

"Father," he said, "if it was one of us who'd been taken—Holgar, say—would you tell her to rest? She's part of this team, and if she wants *my* help, she'd better damn well pull her own weight."

"She *is*," Antonio gritted, moving toward the Irishman so quickly that Jenn didn't see him do it. Neither did Jamie, who jerked backward, running into Holgar.

"Woof," Holgar drawled, grinning faintly.

Jamie clenched his jaw and doubled his fists, and Jenn's heart skipped a beat. Jenn wondered if the strangers had been told that Antonio was a vampire. As if he could read her mind, Antonio gave his head a quick shake and looked at her with his normal, dark eyes.

"Please, enough," Father Juan said, glancing at their hosts and throwing Antonio a warning look. Tempers were short. The tension in the room was thick, and everyone was on edge. "We have a plan, and it's already in play."

Jenn exhaled slowly as Marc Dupree looked long and hard at Antonio. Then she realized that one of them was missing.

"Where's Skye?" she asked.

"She's the plan," Father Juan replied.

SAMHAIN (HALLOWEEN NIGHT) OUTSIDE LONDON TWO YEARS AGO, THE HELL FIRE CAVES SKYE

"Put on the mask, *borachín*," Estefan said to Skye as he held out the black-velvet half mask decorated with purple and black laces and feathers. A silver pentagram shimmering with amethysts gleamed in the center of the mask's forehead. Estefan had told her the pentagram had once belonged to Lord Dashwood himself, the aristocratic sorcerer who had created the secret ritual caves on his estate in 1740.

"Don't call me that," Skye snapped. His Spanish nickname for her was "little drunk one," in honor of the night they had met, four months before, on Midsummer's Eve, at her sister Melody's handfasting ceremony just outside Stonehenge.

The Yorks were powerful witches, highly respected, and Melody York's joining with the Highfall witch family was the event of the season. Everyone needed a good time—London was overrun by the Cursed Ones, and witches everywhere were going into hiding, as they had in other eras of oppression, the worst having been the Burning Times in the sixteenth century. Many had decreed that Melody's handfasting would be the last time they attended a public witch function.

At the party after the joining ritual, Skye had had too much spiced wine to drink—she wasn't accustomed to drinking at all—and she had flirted outrageously with a visitor from out of town, the witch Estefan Montevideo. The Spaniard had worn a fantastic black tux with a black rosebud, all bad-boy shadow against the frou-frou light green dress that Melody had forced Skye to wear as her honor attendant. With her crown of pastel flowers and ribbons, Skye had looked like an escapee from a Renaissance fair. But it was a look Estefan had liked. A lot.

After he'd come up to her with a glass of wine, she'd decided not to go and immediately change into her black leather corset, red petticoats, and black buckled boots, which had been her original plan. Before she even knew what was happening, she was dancing the tango—and she *never* danced—in the silver high heels she had sworn to burn as soon as Melody and Llewellyn Highfall had sworn to be faithful to one another as long as love would last.

Then Estefan uncorked the bottle of Spanish *orujo* he'd brought, and soon she was hiding behind one of the large Stonehenge stones, throwing back shots with him and his three Coven brothers from Spain. They were from Cádiz. Estefan said magick was so common there that there was a pentagram on the floor of the Catholic church. The way he talked—relaxed, fun-loving, and filled with life—Skye could almost forget that the Cursed Ones were taking over the world and that they hated witches, whom they feared. He made her parents' plans to stop using magick sound ridiculous.

"It is only through our magick that we'll be safe from *los Malditos*," he insisted. He stared hard at her. "And I would use every bit of magick I have to keep you safe, *cielito*." Little sky.

It was such a macho, exciting thing to say. The magicks of love and desire swirled in the summer breezes that wafted around Stonehenge, and Skye fell for him, hard. With his sexy Spanish accent and his buff, cut body, he was impossible to resist. They spent the last hour of the party making out. She was not even fourteen—she hadn't even been on a date—and her parents would have gone ballistic if they'd known he was eighteen.

That was reason enough to keep their relationship a secret. On the next full moon Estefan had revealed to her that he was what White Witches termed a Dark Witch—a witch who served Pan, god of the forest, and not the Goddess. She was shocked, but also thrilled by just how inappropriate he was. Besides, she was so in love with him that he could have been a full warlock and she wouldn't have cared.

Of course, she'd had to hide their relationship from her parents. It was easy: The Yorks were distracted by the increasing threat the Cursed Ones posed on Witchery— since witches could detect the presence of vampires—and, curiously, gave Skye more freedom than she was used to. So she saw more of Estefan, who kept pressuring her to worship the moon with his coven brothers and himself.

Since Estefan's transplanted coven celebrated Moon later in the evening than Skye's, she had time to finish her obligation and then join him. His coven met in the woods, under cover of darkness, all masked. White Witches never wore masks, but Estefan told her that masks were traditional, because centuries before, the White Witches had persecuted the Dark Witches—in fact, the White had originated the term "Dark"—and they had been as intolerant of the worship of Pan as the Catholic Church had been of witchcraft.

The ritual had been almost identical to Skye's, except that Pan received the honors instead of the Lady Goddess. She had remained silent during the chants, and no one had minded. When Estefan had called her the next morning, he had told her she'd been *magnífica*. She felt *magnífica* . . . blissful and filled with light, not darkness.

Magnífica. Every time she was with him, her feet barely touched the ground, and she'd been so happy she would nearly burst into tears. He drove her around London in a Jaguar, and he was beyond rich. Skye's parents believed that the blessing of magickal powers could be used only to benefit others, and not oneself. They lived off what her parents made at mundane jobs—her father was a software engineer, and her mother owned a bakery. Estefan said that was ridiculous. The only traditional rule of witchcraft was "An it harm none, do what thou wilt." What would it hurt anyone to become wealthy?

So he had used magick to get rich—she wasn't sure exactly how—and he showered her with presents: very high-end goth clothes; a bit of steampunk; and fabulous boots, shoes, and a magick wand said to have belonged to Iphigenia de la Tour, a famous witch who had lived in Paris during the Belle Epoque—the early part of the twentieth century. She squirreled it all away so her parents wouldn't ask questions. He adored her, loved her; she superheated his Spanish blood. He wanted her to handfast with him so that he could protect her from the Cursed Ones. She could still live at home with her parents; who had to know that they were joined? These were wild times, calling for wild work.

Her two best girlfriends, the twins Soleil and Lune,

CRUSADE

could hardly stand how jealous they were. What magicks had she woven at Midsummer Moon to snag such a hottie?

Then it was September, and she snuck out to celebrate the vernal equinox with Estefan. But this time she didn't remember what had happened. She woke up in her bed, having no memory of getting there, and she had a tattoo at the small of her back—a Valentine's heart carried in the mouth of a gargoyle. It was about two inches by two inches, and it was similar to the symbol used by the Cursed Ones— a flying bat carrying a heart.

She called Estefan, who laughed. "You wanted it. You asked for it, *borachín*," he'd told her. Little drunk one. "We went to a tattoo shop."

She was horrified. Soleil and Lune tried to erase it with magicks, but nothing worked, and it itched terribly as it healed.

Next she began to have horrible nightmares about masked balls that she and Estefan attended, in dank underground caves decorated with scarlet tapestries and lit with torches. She was dressed in full black-and-purple ball gowns, and he wore all black. Everyone else there was a vampire . . . and Estefan drank blood with them, and tried to force her to do it, too.

Each time he brought the cup to her lips, she woke up. At home. In her own bed. The tattoo on her back burning.

After a week of nightmares she was exhausted, and she looked horrible—circles under her eyes, her face breaking out. Having no idea of the cause, Melody and her parents performed healing spells on her, but nothing worked. Soleil and Lune told her that if she didn't break up with Estefan, they would tell her parents about him.

Desperate, still in love, she went to Estefan and told him what was happening. He wound his arms around her waist and pulled her close. He whispered in her ear, "In these dreams of yours, what would happen if you *did* drink the blood, *mi amor*?" And his teeth against her earlobe pricked a bit sharply.

And she *knew*, then, that his magicks were entwined with the Cursed Ones. She didn't know exactly how, but she knew he wasn't just a bad boy. He was a bad man, and dangerous, and she had to get away from him.

But somehow there she was, in front of the Hell Fire Caves of her dreams, dressed in a tight purple corset laced with black, over black petticoats trimmed in purple, a black ritual cape wadded in her arms. Her thick-soled boots came up over her knees. The other girls present were much sexier, in plunging black gowns and high, spiked heels. They already had on their masks, and she didn't know if she knew any of them. That was the point. None of the girls from her coven should be here. She could admit the truth—this was not even dark magick; it was black.

I shouldn't have come, Skye thought miserably, holding the cape against her chest as she studied the mask. *I should have broken up with him over the phone.*

But the truth was, she'd been afraid to. If she pissed him off, what would he do?

"Tonight," he said, as he placed the mask against her face and tied it in place with black ribbons. "We'll handfast. Let me help you with your cloak."

The others grinned at her as they glided past into the entrance of the cave. Anticipation swirled in the night air; the moon glowed down on Estefan's blue-black hair, and for an instant, crimson light danced in his eyes. His teeth . . . were they long and sharp?

Oh, my Goddess, she thought, *is he a vampire?*

Wouldn't she know? Couldn't witches sense the presence of Cursed Ones as vampires in turn sensed them? Wasn't that why the vampires hated them?

"Vámonos, mi amor," he murmured lustily. "Let's make it happen."

"Make wh-what happen?" Her voice rose shrilly, and she glanced in the direction of the cave. Red and orange lights lit up the entrance like the gate to hell. She stumbled backward, afraid. "Estefan? What's going on?"

He narrowed his eyes, and suddenly the handsome male witch was something else entirely, something she had suspected lay beneath his charm. It was as if *he* had taken off a mask and finally shown her his true face. And it was evil.

"We really went, didn't we?" she whispered. "To those parties."

He slid his black half mask, the twin of hers, over his face as he walked toward her. "It won't hurt," he said.

Her heart pounded as she stumbled backward. She knew to the depths of her soul that he was lying. It *would* hurt. A lot.

Something moved in her peripheral vision. Three hooded, masked figures were emerging from the cave, carrying torches. She recognized their silhouettes—they were Estefan's Spanish coven mates, coming to help him, coming for her. Had this been the plan all this time?

Estefan took her hand. "You'll be safe," he said.

"Because I'll be one of them?" Cold dread flooded through her. She could feel herself going frozen, unable to move as he cast a spell on her. Summoning her own magick, she fought his mesmerizing touch, concentrating on the danger she was in.

"We won't be Cursed Ones exactly. They want magick users on their side, helping them. We'll be changed, but not converted." He seemed unaware of the spell she was desperately weaving. Could it be that he was so much more powerful than she was that her magicks were beneath his notice?

"*Ay, hermosa, mi dulce, mi alma,*" he whispered, all the sweet nothings he'd whispered in her ear those past months, softening her up, making her believe that he *loved* her.

"Did you . . . did you make some kind of deal?" She wouldn't look at him. He could bewitch her more fully if he could catch her gaze.

"*Sí*, but it will benefit you, too," he replied. His hand tightened around her hand, sliding up to encircle her wrist. "*Escúchame.* Listen to me. They're going to take over this world. It's inevitable. But those of us who side with them, who become like them, we'll be okay." She heard the certainty in his voice.

"No, oh, no." She tugged on his hand. "No, please."

He touched her hair with his free hand. "It will be over very fast. I promise."

"It's over *now*," she said. And from somewhere deep inside her, fury boiled up in a seething geyser of magick. She could almost see it as it traveled through her physical body, then into the immaterial plane where magick acquired its force.

To her astonishment it manifested as a ball of fire that burst from her free hand and slammed into his masked face. The flames danced across the black velvet, and Estefan released her, shrieking and grabbing at the fabric.

His coven brothers raced toward them. Skye screamed and turned on her heel, running away as fast as she could, begging the Goddess to help her, save her. Balls of fire crashed to her left and right, and at her heels, but she kept running, whispering to the Lady in Latin, "*Conservate me! Conservate me! Conservate me!*"

Protect me.

Heaving, her lungs stinging, she reached the main road and hitched a ride home. As soon as she crossed the threshold of her family's ivy-covered brick cottage, her cell phone rang.

"Better run," Estefan ground out in a hoarse, wounded voice. "Run fast. And far."

THE PRESENT: NEW ORLEANS
SKYE

And she had run . . . to Salamanca, for protection. She figured that the Spanish Academia would be the best place to hide from a Spanish Dark Witch, and that she would learn how to protect herself with new magicks. She hadn't fully understood what the training entailed—hadn't realized that she would become the target of even more enemies once she became a member of a hunting team.

Worse, on the first night she was there, he had come to her in a dream. They were at a glittering masked ball, illuminated with candles and torchlight, and he held up the cup . . .

She woke up panting. A week later she received a postcard from Cádiz. When she read it, she heard his voice—a bit of magick: *"I won't give up, mi amor. I still love you."*

Gasping aloud, she ripped the postcard into dozens of pieces and fed each one to a votive candle flame placed before the statue of the Virgin Mary in the university chapel. The Virgin was the Goddess, in her eyes. And the Goddess would help her become the Hunter, able to fend off any attack Estefan might launch.

Because he didn't love her. He wanted to use her.

A month later a second postcard had arrived:

"Love never dies."

Six months later another postcard, whispering threats cloaked as words of love. *"I will come for you."*

A year later another.

"Para siempre." Forever.

But he never attempted to approach her, and she hadn't heard from him in eight months. She figured she'd been right—there *was* safety in numbers.

Her parents had neither understood nor approved when she'd left to join the academy. Like Jenn's parents, they'd been against it. Witches didn't fight people, and they certainly didn't participate in wars. They remained neutral, focusing on healing the wounds to bodies and souls, to the ether of magick, and to Mother Earth. It was anathema to a witch to do violence. If Skye's parents had known about the fireball she'd flung at Estefan, they might have gone as far as to disown her. In their eyes conjuring weapons was that wrong.

She was the only witch ever known to have studied at the academy. Antonio had helped her study old magicks from spell books they found in the dusty archives of the library. Centuries old, the vellum pages crackled with incantations written by Spanish witches—many of whom the Inquisition had burned at the stake.

Both Antonio and Father Juan assured Skye that

although she hadn't become the Hunter, she was just as valuable. Word of a White Witch Salamancan got around, and she was contacted by the Circuit, a loose international confederation of younger witches—some White, some Dark, and even some who followed the Black Arts—who believed that a neutral position regarding the vampires was in itself a harmful act. They couldn't stand passively by while the Cursed Ones toppled governments and murdered people. Soleil and Lune had also joined, and they sent Skye updates on her parents.

She wanted to tell Antonio about Estefan, but one of the questions put to applicants to the academy was "Do you have any enemies who might blackmail you or otherwise pressure you to turn against the cause?" And she had lied and said no. Now she was ashamed to confess it, which was one of the reasons she kept her distance from Father Juan. He scared her a little. Actually, a lot. And she was halfway certain that he already knew much more about her than she'd ever wanted him to. She hadn't told him about the Circuit, either, because the witches had promised to keep it secret from the world.

But Antonio was kind to her and spent hours coaching her with her magicks. He was religious in the extreme—he had been studying to become a Catholic priest when he'd been converted; the irony was not lost on her—but he wasn't all mystical and mysterious like Father Juan. He told her that he prayed for each person on the team every night, and she believed that his prayers did keep them safe. She felt a bond with him. She didn't love him the way she loved Jamie—a love she couldn't really explain—and that, actually, was one of the reasons she liked Antonio so much. Trusted him.

And now, in the sewer of the French Quarter, she had placed her trust in these two members of the Circuit, previously just names in a chat room: the dusky-hued White Witch named Mikhu, and Theo, a hot voodoo *bokor*—practitioner—who both lived in New Orleans and confirmed that a new vampire *doyenne*—queen—was in town. They didn't know if her name was Aurora, but they did know she was here for a reason, and they were helping Skye get ready to meet her. As prickles of magick darted over her skin, she envisioned the triple face of the Goddess—maid, matron, and crone—visible in a multitude of aspects from butterflies to rainbows, and held the image of her own face changing in response to her own need.

"Okay, you look great, which means that you look hideous," said Mikhu, as she and Theo stood back and admired their work. Skye had conjured the original glamour spell on herself, and the witch and the *bokor* had given it a boost. She would need all the magickal help she could get to pass as a vampire in a vampire stronghold.

"Now the final test," Theo said, holding up a mirror. "Work it, *cher*."

Skye summoned energy all around her, willing a barrier of seeing between herself and the glass. It worked. No reflection appeared — or rather, there was a reflection there, but no one could see it. She lowered the spell, and her face appeared, sweetheart-shaped, her Rasta braids intact.

Once she had fled a man who wanted to turn her into a vampire, or something very nearly resembling one. But now she magickally forced a red glow into her eyes and willed her teeth to lengthen. With the full force of White magick behind her, she assumed the appearance of a Cursed One with the bloodlust on her.

Then, with the help of her two friends, she wove an attraction spell, encouraging anyone near, be they human or vampire, to seek her out.

"Whew, I feel it," Mikhu told her. "Hey, *femme magique*, take a walk on the wild side?"

Skye grinned feebly. She raised her eyes at Theo, who let his tongue hang out of his mouth.

"You got the juice, *cher*," he assured her. "You are a total everything magnet."

"Okay. Well," she said. She took a deep breath. "I'd better get going."

Theo held up a finger. "Don't breathe. Or at least don't look like you're breathing."

"Got it. No breathing," she said. She blanched. "I hope I can pull this off."

"Goddess be with you," Mikhu said, as they both dropped kisses on her forehead. "We'll alert the Circuit to give prayers for one of our own in danger."

"But no details," Skye said.

"Zero," Theo promised.

Then they walked into the shadows. She listened to their receding footsteps, tempted to call them back a dozen times. But she had to do this. She had volunteered for the mission, and she was the one most likely to pull it off.

She glanced down at her silver thumb ring and wondered if she should have taken it off. It was shaped like a crescent moon wrapped around a moonstone. She wore it as a constant reminder of who she was, so she wouldn't risk losing herself again. And now here she was trying to lose herself. A moment later she smiled grudgingly. Vampires had every reason to worship the moon as much as witches. The thought gave her the strength not to call the others back and instead to start walking.

As she walked alone, trembling, she prayed that Estefan would not be among those who gravitated toward her now. That he'd finally given up, or was still back in Europe, or — best of all — that he had died. How horrible, to wish someone's death. *An it harm none, do what thou wilt.*

Fingers crossed that the new vampire in town was Aurora.

Fingers crossed that the vampire staring out of the

shadows with demonic red eyes right now could lead Skye to her.

The vampire hissed at her. Chills tickled Skye's shoulder blades and down her spine. *Goddess, protect me, I charge you,* she prayed. *I am your daughter. I am in your care.*

And then she hissed back.

CHAPTER TWELVE

Witches, wolves, and mortal friend
There is a horror that does not end
War is waged and battles fought
But have you stopped to count the cost?
We are the ones backed by right
We must strike with bold and might
The Cursed Ones blameless be
Warn them of the Hunters you see

NEW ORLEANS
FATHER JUAN, JENN, HOLGAR, ERIKO, JAMIE, AND ANTONIO

Father Juan escorted the team to the chapel of the abandoned convent. With its secret stairway from the tunnel, said to have been used by escaped slaves and pirates, the convent didn't feel like a very safe safe house. Marc and his group had pooh-poohed Jenn's follow-up questions about why Lucky had said the place was haunted. She'd wanted to ask more questions when Lucky refused to join them in the chapel for Mass but asked Father Juan to hear his confession later. Unnerved, she was sure that they were hiding something. Maybe they were afraid that if the hunters found out what it was, the Salamancans would leave.

There was no electricity in the building, and all the windows had been painted with black paint, then boarded over to hide evidence that it was being lived in. In addition, they didn't use the outer rooms, only those with no windows at all. It was cold and damp, and Jenn didn't know how to describe it in any other way except "unfriendly."

The corridor to the chapel was pitch-dark, and as they made their way with flashlights, Jenn remained hyperalert for movement, for attack. Antonio carried a flashlight too, although he didn't really need it. Passing beneath a stone arch into the icy room, Jenn smelled old dust and incense. She thought about the ghosts of nuns in black and white habits, gliding through the darkness.

The chapel held a blank-eyed stone statue of the Virgin, and an empty place on the wall behind the altar where a crucifix must once have hung. Jenn started uneasily at the blank spot, looking around for more crosses. Vampires had taken over churches all over the world, tossing out any offending religious symbols.

The priest lit a candle and placed it on the altar as Marc hastily cleaned the once-sacred space with a dish towel. Gently, Father Juan stopped him, and Marc joined the row of five at the front pew, which was half rotted away, the splintered wood crumbling beneath Jenn's hand as she stood beside Antonio. Father Juan raised his hands, and the six—Jenn, Antonio, Jamie, Eriko, Marc, and Bernard—knelt on bed pillows to protect their knees from the cold. Jenn swayed beside Antonio, shivering, wishing for body heat. But Antonio had no physical warmth to give her.

Since she wasn't a baptized Catholic, she didn't take communion, but Antonio did. She watched, fascinated, as Father Juan placed the host on Antonio's tongue, then offered him the cup. Any other vampire she'd ever seen would have screamed in agony. But Antonio closed his eyes and crossed himself, then lowered his head over his hands and prayed.

Father Juan talked about patience. He quoted 2 Corinthians 6:4, first in Latin—"'*sed in omnibus exhibeamus nosmet ipsos sicut Dei ministros in multa patientia in tribulationibus in necessitatibus in angustiis*'"—and then in English: "'But in all things approving ourselves as the ministers of God, in much patience, in afflictions, in necessities, in distresses. . . .'"

Jenn was sure he had chosen the verse—and the sermon—for her. Despite the frigid temperature she was sweating bullets. It was all she could do to keep from jumping to her feet and bursting outside, running down the streets of the French Quarter, and screaming Heather's name. It seemed so wrong to be praying, essentially doing nothing.

Then, with his nearly magickal sense of knowing what she was thinking, Antonio laid his left hand over her right and laced his fingers through hers, assuming a gesture of prayer.

"This *is* doing something," he whispered, in a voice so low only she could hear it. "You believe in magick spells, *sí*? What are they but prayers?"

She didn't answer him. How many millions of people had prayed for the defeat of the Cursed Ones? For loved ones who had been butchered, or converted? When spoken by a witch, a magikc spell *worked*.

And violence *worked*.

While Suzy and Lucky prepared a dinner of dirty rice and sausage, Father Juan offered a demonstration of Krav Maga, a street-combat martial art practiced by the Mossad, the special forces of Israel. It was the first form of self-defense offered at the academy.

"It builds on basic street fighting," Father Juan explained to Marc as Jamie assumed a starting position—legs apart and loose, hands up in front of his face.

Marc mirrored Jamie, ready to do battle. He was taller than Jamie, and possibly more muscular—Jamie was wiry, Marc more beefed up—and light on his feet. Eriko and

Father Juan had set up the demonstration in the convent's former common dining room, lit with battery-powered fluorescent camping lanterns. Half-decomposed tables and shabby wooden chairs, pushed to the walls, were bathed in stark bluish-white light.

Beside Antonio, Jenn studied the priest, who sat in a chair with a dark blue blanket over his lap, drinking a glass of wine. His resemblance to the statue of St. John of the Cross that guarded the university gates was diminished — he seemed like a regular person — and Jenn reconsidered all the stories she'd heard about Father Juan. Maybe people needed him to be special, magickal, because then he would train hunters that really would save them.

"Anyone can use Krav Maga," Eriko began, standing between the two potential combatants. "Older people, those with no martial arts training. Krav Maga exploits people's natural defensive reactions and shows how to use them as weapons. Jamie will show you." She moved her hands together and stepped backward, signaling the beginning of the bout.

"The idea is not to dance some fancy dance, but to walk away alive," Jamie said, advancing and striking at Marc's jaw, pulling his punch but making sure it was clear that what he'd done would have resulted in Marc's teeth being knocked out.

"You'd know best," Holgar said from his place in the corner, gesturing to Jamie's two front teeth, which were actually a bridge. Jamie had lost his original teeth in a practice session three months after joining the academy. He was supposed to have been wearing a mouth guard, but he'd been too macho to use it. Tisha, the girl who had bested him, had lost her life to a vampire on the night of their final exam.

Jamie and Marc went through a few more moves. Jenn watched distractedly, obsessively pulling out her cell phone and checking the time since she couldn't receive any messages. No one knew when and if Skye would get in contact. Bursting with anxiety, barely able to sit still, she wanted to go out and search for Aurora too, not watch Jamie showing off.

"This is great," Marc said, slicking back his hair as Eriko announced that the bout was over and awarded Jamie all the points. Marc obviously didn't care that he'd lost. Drenched with sweat, he was pumped. "We can really use this. We have access to a gym a few streets over. Would you be willing to run some training sessions for us there?"

How can you be talking about this now? Jenn wanted to scream. *Aurora has my sister! And we don't know if Skye's alive or — worse.*

"I think we could manage that," Father Juan said, lifting his wine glass as Marc guzzled down a sports bottle of water. "To peace."

"To the war," Marc countered.

Jenn looked down at her cell-phone face again. One

minute had passed since the last time she'd checked it. A shadow crossed over it; Antonio stood up and walked over to Father Juan, looking down at him, and it was obvious to Jenn that something was wrong. Waves of anxiety were rolling off him; his dark hair framed his hooded eyes and clenched jaw, and his usually full lips pursed into a thin white line. His fists were balled at his sides.

He leaned over and said something in the priest's ear. Father Juan listened carefully, then finished his wine and rose. Antonio glanced over at Jenn but didn't meet her eyes. Shame pinched his features.

"Antonio and I need to discuss a few things," Father Juan said to the group. "We'll meet you at dinner."

"Yeah, you do that," Jamie drawled. Then Holgar and Eriko both stared at the Irishman, and he turned on his heel and grabbed his towel, which was hanging off the back of a chair. He wiped his face and muttered something, then turned back around as Antonio and Father Juan walked out of the room.

"They lie," Jamie said straight to Jenn. "Remember your manual?"

"What?" Marc asked, making crinkling noises with his empty water bottle as he squeezed it in his fist. "What does *that* mean?"

"Nothing," Eriko said. She stretched her hands over her head, then bent from the waist and touched her toes. The next time Jenn could track her, Eriko was on the floor in a wide split, resting her head on the floor. She glanced over at Marc, who was gaping at her in admiration. Being around Eriko was like getting stuck with an older, hotter sister. Heather thought Jenn was a hero, but as soon as Marc's group had found out that Eriko was the capital-*H* Hunter, most of their attention had shifted to her. It was not lost on Jenn that Eriko didn't like the limelight. Jenn wouldn't have, either; she didn't want to be fussed over. She just wanted to feel like she had a real place among the Salamancans.

And to find her sister.

"Have you heard anything about Japan, Marc? My family live in Kyoto," Eriko said, sounding British. Her English shifted between slangy American and what she'd learned in school, which was the English of the British upper classes.

"Kyoto is such a beautiful city," Marc said, causing Eriko to lift her head and look at him. He smiled.

"Ah so desuka," Eriko said, smiling back very wanly. *"Hai."*

"Both sides—vampires and humans—tried hard to preserve the treasures there. I traveled in Asia before the war. I was an art student."

Before the war. Everyone had been something else, before the war.

Except for Antonio.

Father Juan is feeding him. She'd known it when they left the room together. She had never seen Antonio feed. He'd never permitted it. And as for feeding off her . . . once she had tried to offer, and he'd cut off her words so forcefully, practically shouting at her, that she'd never offered again.

She'd been intensely relieved.

If he needed my blood, I would give it to him, she told herself. It was what she always told herself. But the mere thought sent her reeling. It made her feel sick and dizzy. Could she really love him, if that was her honest reaction? Wasn't the fact that he had refused her offer proof that he loved her?

Suzy stuck her head into the room, breaking Jenn's thoughts. "Dinner's ready," she announced.

Eriko was up and at the door before Jenn saw her again. She bowed and waited for Marc to go first, which, after a moment's hesitation, he did. Jamie glowered at Marc's back, and Eriko, unaware, also left.

Then Jenn got up and crossed the room. As she passed Jamie, he followed so closely behind her that she could feel his warmth—the warmth that had been missing from Antonio, back in the chapel.

"They lie," Jamie whispered viciously. "Wait and see."

New Orleans
Skye

"Sorry to do this, but you can't be too careful, you know?" the vampire told Skye as they moved through the sewers beneath the French Quarter.

Skye could see perfectly well through the ebony silk blindfold the vampire, whose name was Nick, had wrapped over her eyes before leading her to Aurora's lair. She'd dared to perform a seeing spell, hoping that the vampires still hadn't acquired the ability to detect the use of magicks. He'd had no clue, and she was weak with relief. If things got dicey, she had a vast arsenal of things she could do to protect herself—all of which went against the most sacred tenet of her beliefs, which was to do no harm.

Nick reminded her a little of Jamie—young, bald, but no tattoos, and with a California-surfer sort of accent. He was new to Aurora's court, having proven his worth in the attack on Jenn and Heather. Nick boasted that he'd been the one to drag "the sister of the Hunter" by her hair and push her into a cage, then had helped load it onto Aurora's private jet. Skye masked her reaction and told him she wished she'd been there.

"I've never seen a Hunter," she'd lied.

"Trust me, you don't want to," he'd answered.

Now, her cold hand in his equally cold hand, Nick led her out of the sewer and into the moonlight. She was shocked to see that night had fallen; she had no idea what time it was. His face was bleached like bone by the watery light. The air was fresh, and she had to fight not to inhale deeply.

Steadily, without pausing to check if he was seen, he led her up a flight of concrete stairs onto a walkway bordered by oak trees, then through a charming oval courtyard punctuated with a spiral staircase of white wrought iron, leading to an upper apartment bordered by two white columns.

On the cobblestone ground floor, elegant alabaster urns brimmed with hot pink and deep pumpkin-orange flowers. Keeping the pretext that the blindfold was working, she pretended to knock her toe against the riser, making him mutter, "Oops, sorry, step up."

Their feet clanged on the wrought iron. The door opened before Nick reached it, and another vampire stood on the other side, surrounded by darkness. Vampires had excellent hearing, but anyone could have heard that racket. Either Nick had been announcing their arrival, or the vampires didn't care who knew where they were staying. If so, then, why the blindfold?

The vampire at the door was a young girl with purple hair trailing over a black bustier and steampunk olive-green pants decorated with black leather straps and bronze buckles. She was smoking, which was impressive, since vampires had to consciously force air into and out of their lungs, making smoking more challenging. Her fingernails were painted black, overlaid with red slashes, and her lips were the same shade of purple as her hair.

"Who's this?" the vampire asked Nick, narrowing her black-rimmed eyes.

Skye had used magicks to muffle her heartbeat and make her skin feel clammy to the touch. She prayed she'd done enough.

"Her name's Brianna. She's a local," Nick replied. "Well, sort of. She's an orphan."

Black eyelashes met as she studied Skye. "Oh?" She ticked her gaze to Nick. "Your sire was murdered?"

"I'm not certain I'm an orphan," Skye replied, using her own voice, her own accent. She'd decided to use as much of her real self as she could, in order to be able to concentrate on the effects of the glamour. No need to worry about a foreign accent on top of everything else. "I—Desmond attacked me in Toronto. I was visiting my aunt."

"He converted you, you mean," the vampire prompted, "to the true religion."

"Yes." Skye nodded, even though she didn't understand exactly what she meant by that. She was unbelievably nervous, terrified she was going to make a muddle of things and get her throat torn out for the trouble—and Heather's, too, if she was here.

"And you wound up here because . . . ," the vampire said suspiciously. She gave Nick a sharp nod.

There was a pause, and the blindfold loosened from around Skye's head. Skye stared straight into the burning red eyes and long, sharp fangs as the vampire studied her. Then Nick appeared at the vampire's shoulder, moving with exaggerated speed. Despite all her magicks Skye couldn't do the same, but she could cast spells that caused other people to lose track of bursts of time, giving the illusion that she was moving at a faster pace. Of course, all magicks cost her in concentration and energy; she would have to be as sparing as possible.

"I've been looking for Desmond," she said, crossing her fingers that that would sound reasonable. "I found another vampire he'd converted on the Internet, and Jon—that's his name—said Desmond had been seen here."

"I haven't heard of any Desmond. Did you get permission to stay in the French Quarter? You have to ask to stay on someone else's property. This part of the city is owned by Christian Gaudet. *My* sire." Straightening her shoulders, she tossed her hair.

Then her eyes bulged, and she made a gagging sound. Nick gasped and scurried back across the threshold just as the vampire girl burst into dust, coating Skye, who forced back a cough and held onto Nick.

A beautiful vampire swept into view, her sharp features accentuated by shiny black hair pulled tight into a bun and massive chandelier earrings brushing her jawline. Her eyes were crimson, her fangs extended. She was wearing a plunging scarlet sweater over black leather trousers and black boots with four-inch heels. On her right ring finger she wore a simple gold band decorated with a single ruby; there was something about it that seemed familiar to Skye.

"Christian Gaudet does *not* own the French Quarter," the vampire decreed.

She glared at Nick, who dropped to his knees, then at Skye, who was so terrified that her legs gave way, leaving her with the semblance of curtseying.

"Au-Aurora?" Skye managed.

"Of course." Aurora threw back her head.

Skye had prepared herself for this moment—for standing face-to-face with Aurora—but she wasn't prepared. Menace radiated from Aurora like an exotic perfume. Skye felt as if she were suffocating, and the urge to cough seized her again. She clamped her hand over her mouth, then made a show of brushing the dust that had been the vampire off her face and clothes.

Aurora stepped back into the shadows, her burning eyes seemingly floating in space. Skye waited to be invited in, although it wasn't true that vampires needed an invitation to enter a place. She simply didn't want to wind up stabbed through the heart.

"Bring her in here," Aurora said to Nick, and Skye almost screamed as Nick gripped her arm and propelled her forward, as if to prove that he was a badass vampire thoroughly loyal to his imperious new leader. He pushed Skye into the black room. Her spell of seeing was fading, and she was terrified she might accidentally run into something that was hidden in the darkness—a table, a chair, or Aurora herself.

She heard rustling ahead and pretended to stumble to give herself time to adjust. She wanted to boost her spell, but she was afraid to use up her magickal reserves. Her life depended on maintaining her vampire glamour.

"So, you're looking for the sire who abandoned you," Aurora said with a lilt in her voice. "Do you think your sire has an obligation toward you?"

What answer would please Aurora? Skye's stomach clenched and she licked her lips, nearly pricking her tongue as she ran it across her fangs. "I—I don't know," she said. "All I know is that it's hard to live among humans, without a family."

"Where's your friend, this Jon?" Aurora demanded. "Why didn't he come with you?"

"He's afraid," she replied. "It's been tough."

Aurora regarded her closely. Skye fought hard not to react.

Finally, the vampire said, "You're lying."

New Orleans
Father Juan, Jenn, Antonio, Eriko, Jamie, and Holgar

What just touched me?

Jenn jerked to a stop as she moved along the corridor to the little nun's cell Antonio had claimed as his own. Had something kissed her cheek?

Something that was not there?

With a soft cry she stumbled backward, shining her flashlight into the darkness. The beam quivered; she was shivering as hard as if she had been plunged into an icy river.

"Antonio," she whispered, but her voice was dry as bone dust.

Did a darker shape hang in the space before her? A

sense of menace washed over her in waves, cold and thick, like hands running down her face and chest.

"*Aaaah,*" something whispered, or was it her own voice, whispering for Antonio?

"Jenn?"

That *was* Antonio, sticking his head out of his room. She ticked her glance from the center of the corridor to his face; frowning, he came out of the room and hurried toward her, walking directly through the darkness.

"Go," she urged, grabbing his hand.

He closed his own around hers and pulled her back toward his room; she dug in her heels, not wanting to pass through the hall. Throwing her a quizzical look, he stopped.

"*¿Que tienes?*" he asked her in Spanish.

"I don't know. I thought something touched me. On my cheek." She didn't tell him that she'd thought it was a kiss. Why, she didn't know. But she licked her lips and took a slow breath. "I'm too scared to move," she confessed.

"Where did it happen?" he asked, gazing around.

"Where you're standing," she whispered.

"It's just me." He wrapped both his hands around her wrists, squeezing, and took her into his room. He shut the door and leaned against it while she hugged herself, trying to get warm again.

"Describe it."

"I heard something and I—I felt something. I think this place *is* haunted." She sat down on his bed, which had a very thin mattress and an even thinner blanket on top of it. She gathered up the blanket and put it around her shoulders, wincing as Antonio opened the door again and went into the hall.

"I see nothing, Jenn," he told her. She made herself look through the open door; her flashlight beam caught Antonio in bold relief as he made the sign of the cross and murmured words in Latin. Then he came back into the room and shut the door.

"*Nada*," he said as he sat beside her on the bed and put his arm around her. "Did you feel threatened?"

"Yes," she replied, sinking her head onto his shoulder. Eriko wouldn't have done that. She would have attacked the darkness and yelled for backup.

"It's all right. I'm here," Antonio said, and she shut her eyes tightly to hold back fresh tears. She was mortified. All she did these days was cry.

"Antonio," she began, but he pressed her head against his shoulder, and she surrendered to her need to be comforted.

"We'll tell Father Juan about it," he said, but if he really thought something was out in the hall, he'd rush off to alert everyone. He didn't believe her. He probably thought she'd imagined the whole thing.

Maybe she had.

No, she thought fiercely. *It was there.*

"We should tell him now," she insisted.

Antonio hesitated. Then he said, "Father Juan is resting for a bit. In a few minutes you can take him some of the evening meal, and then you can tell him."

Her stomach clenched. Father Juan was resting because he had given Antonio his blood. Sometimes she felt her mind struggling to bolt from the truth of what Antonio was, but it always wormed its way back into her consciousness. He was a vampire. He had to drink fresh human blood from the veins of human beings—not animal blood, not refrigerated or from a blood bank. If he didn't, he would die.

"Okay," she said weakly.

Something changed in him; he shifted, and his hand around hers tightened. His thigh, pressed against hers, flexed. Tension flowed through him like electricity.

"You know," he began, "that I was a seminarian when I was converted. I was studying to be a priest. And I never . . . I have never *been* with anyone."

She hadn't either.

"But if I could, Jenn . . ." He kissed the crown of her hair, and her lips parted. Tingles skittered through her, and her face felt hot.

Silence fell between them. His fingers stroked the back of her hand, caressing her skin, and maybe he was unaware of just how deeply it affected her. Why Antonio? She had wondered about him all through their two years of training. Crammed into tight living quarters, undergoing brutal, rigorous training, the students of Salamanca had reacted to the pressure in many ways, including hooking up and breaking up, then getting together with someone else. Except Jenn never had. She had always wanted Antonio, but she'd assumed he didn't return her feelings. He'd remained aloof, never anything more than friendly in a polite, almost courtly way.

On the night they had graduated, Father Juan had paired them as fighting partners, and it was only then that everyone had learned his secret: He was the enemy. Except he was one of them. A hunter.

When he saw that she still loved him even though she knew, he had moved to close the gap between them. And then stepped away again, convinced that it was his devotion to the Blessed Virgin and all the saints that kept him from behaving like a monstrous, ravening beast. That he must seek holiness, and pureness, by embracing the vows of the holy orders of the Church: poverty, chastity, and obedience.

She knew she tempted him, and since she wasn't religious, she didn't believe that being with her would change him.

Most of the time, at any rate.

But on nights like this, when ghosts wafted in dark corridors and Heather was so far away, all she knew was that she didn't know anything.

"Haven't you ever had a girlfriend?" she asked, then flushed because it sounded so high school.

"I had someone who loved me," he replied. And there it was, the despair. The horrible sorrow that lived deeply inside him.

"What happened to her?" She wrapped her hand around his and gave it a squeeze. "Maybe if you talked about it . . ."

"No one has ever heard the story," he said. "God alone knows what I have done."

She tried to raise her head, and he placed a careful hand across it, keeping her as she was.

"But if you're a Catholic, and Father Juan is your priest, you should tell him. He can forgive you. Isn't that how it works?"

He was silent for a long time. Against any other guy's chest like this, she would have heard his heartbeat. But the silence between them lengthened. And if she had been afraid of the dark before, she was even more afraid now.

"I'm not sure what Father Juan is," he said at last. "And he can't forgive me. He can only absolve me. Only God forgives."

"Is that what you believe?"

"I believe there is a divine plan," he said quietly.

"But you don't *know* that." Her voice was almost fierce.

"I know that I would die for you."

Then he turned toward her, and gazed at her, his crimson eyes filled with love.

His fangs lengthening with bloodlust.

"Before I let anything happen to you, I would die first."

298

New Orleans
Aurora, Skye, and Heather

"You're lying about everything," Aurora said to Skye. "You've heard. You know about the plan. And you want to be on the winning side."

"I—I," Skye stammered. *What plan? The plan to use Heather as bait?*

"That's a good move. A wise move. You impress me."

"Thank you." Skye made herself smile. "I confess. I heard you were coming here. So I said we should join—ask to join you. My sire was too scared of you."

"A wise move as well." Aurora cocked her head. "What can you offer me?"

"My allegiance?" Skye asked.

"Are you a good hunter?"

The question threw her off balance. Did Aurora know? Was she taunting her?

"Yes, I am." Skye met her gaze.

"Well, I wish someone would hunt *him*. I can't wait until he's dead. Still, he served his purpose. The war was an excellent distraction. Then again, so is this 'peace.'" She made air quotes. "While *we* get on with the *real* work."

Skye knew she was hearing something important. Her training in interrogation—both as subject and as interrogator—kicked in. She had to let Aurora think she knew something, anything, about "the real work."

"Solomon," she said.

"Poor Solomon." Aurora smirked, clearly having no sympathy for Solomon at all.

"Come," Aurora said—to Nick, apparently. His fingers dug into Skye's arm, and he walked her forward, turning sharply to the right without warning. She pretended to stumble again.

"What's wrong with you? Are you sick?" Aurora asked.

Could vampires get sick? Skye had never heard anything that would indicate that. She filed that away and cleared her throat.

"Just hungry."

Oh, Goddess, *why* had she said *that*? What if Aurora—

"Then feed, *mi dulce*," Aurora said.

There was a hiss, and a whiff of sulphur; then she saw Aurora's face in the glow of match light. The vampire was lighting a long white taper. And in the warm glow Skye suddenly smelled a terrible stench. Then, as Aurora raised the candle high, the light fell on a rusty cage on the other side of an octagonal room furnished in Victorian antiques. Something moved inside the cage.

Aurora walked toward it. As the light from the candle fell across the bars, Skye saw eyes. Big blue eyes.

Heather Leitner had blue eyes.

Skye fought hard not to react. *It's her. It's got to be her.* She heard a whimper, and panting; then the cage rocked as the person inside it scrambled backward, back into the darkness. And then a strange wheezing, as if Heather was having trouble breathing. Maybe *she* was sick. Maybe she was dying.

"Do you know who this is?" Aurora asked Skye, looking supremely happy. The smudge of dust on her high cheekbone was the only evidence that she had just staked a boastful vampire. Beside Aurora, Nick moved jerkily, like a windup toy, as if he was barely keeping it together. Skye back-burnered all thought as Aurora glided closer to the cage, moving like a snake. Skye's gorge rose, all her witchly protective instincts warring with her self-preservation.

"This is the sister of the Hunter," Aurora declared. "She's delicious." She licked the tip of her own forefinger like a lollipop, then held it out to Skye. Gazing at Skye with a sly little smile on her face, she said in a thick, low voice, "Would you like a taste?"

BOOK THREE
BARON SAMEDI

In the happy night,
In secret, when none saw me,
nor I beheld aught,
Without light or guide,
save that which burned in my heart.

—St. John of the Cross,
sixteenth-century mystic of Salamanca

CHAPTER THIRTEEN

Salamanca Hunter's Manual: The Hunter
The Hunter stands apart and unchanging, committed to the mission: the death of the foe. Though the world changes, you must not. Like an avenging angel you must not be deflected, distracted, or distressed. The battle between vampire and Hunter must rage until the demons are wiped from the earth. This is your charge and your burden. It cannot be lifted from you— and if you are indeed the Hunter, you will not wish it to be.

(translated from the Spanish)

New Orleans
Skye and Heather

Heather felt her throat close up as Aurora offered her to the new vampire with the blond braids. She moved as far away as her cage would permit and shook with fear. She could hear herself wheezing, but she dared not reach for her inhaler. She was sure they would take it from her if they found it. It was running low, too, and she had to save it for emergencies.

The new vampire moved closer, approaching the cage with teeth bared and eyes glowing. Heather heard herself make a whimpering sound. Then the vampire was standing next to the cage, staring at her hard.

And Heather knew her.

From her nightmares.

Heather began to scream. She had seen the other girl's face dozens of times in her dreams. She had always been covered in blood and standing in a circle of dead bodies.

The nightmare-come-true wrinkled her nose in distaste and turned back to Aurora. "She smells sick to me. Thank you, but I can push off the hunger a little longer."

Heather felt a ray of hope. Aurora had killed others for less. Maybe she would kill this one, and those nightmares would never ever come true.

Aurora smiled. "Very good. You're right; she is sick. Nick, take her out hunting."

The surfer vampire nodded, grabbed the new vampire by the elbow, and steered her from the room.

NEW ORLEANS
FATHER JUAN, ANTONIO, AND JENN

Antonio walked Jenn into Father Juan's room. Their master was lying fully dressed in a narrow bed, two pillows beneath his head, which was cradled in his palms. A hunk of gauze had been taped to the inside of his left wrist—the wound Antonio had left behind.

Three votive candles in red glasses flickered on a chair pulled up beside the bed. A rosewood rosary lay coiled beside a plate containing a half-eaten powdered-sugar donut and a glass of what smelled like apple juice. Father Juan was replacing sugar after his blood loss.

"Jenn thought she saw something in the hall," Antonio told the priest. "Like a," he thought a moment, "a *fantasma*."

"A ghost?" Father Juan sat up. "Can you describe it, Jenn?"

She was terrified all over again. He believed her. Which meant that he believed in ghosts.

"Dark. I think it touched me." She gestured to her cheek. "It was cold."

"Padre?" Antonio said, raising his brows.

"It could be magick," Father Juan said, swinging his legs over the side of his bed. "Some sort of seeing." He reached in his pocket and pulled out a rough, rectangular piece of murky, pinkish-white crystal. "I've been hoping that Skye would send us some images. But there's nothing yet."

Then light danced in the crystal, and all three of them bent toward it. Antonio squeezed Jenn's hand as images blurred and stretched, then took shape.

Aurora's face filled the surface of the prism. Antonio jerked, and Jenn instinctively drew back as Father Juan held up a hand.

"She can't see you," he reminded them.

Aurora moved to the right, and a cage was revealed. It was too dark to see who was inside, but Jenn knew. She knew.

She grabbed the crystal from Father Juan and stared hard into it, straining to see if Heather was still alive. But the picture went gray, and then winked out.

"Oh, God," Jenn whispered. "Oh, please, please, God."

"Amen," Antonio and Father Juan said in unison, crossing themselves.

Eriko, Matt, Bernard, and Father Juan investigated the hallway while the others sat in the dining room at the cracked and peeling oval table. Old stained-glass mosaics hung on the walls, so chipped and faded they looked like weathered coloring-book pages. Saints with halos, lambs, flaming hearts.

The Catholic imagery reminded Jenn of her grandparents' collection of old vinyl rock albums with their psychedelic covers. She wondered what lies her father had told her grandmother about her two missing granddaughters. If he thought Gramma would never find out the truth. And she wondered where her grandmother and her mother had gone.

Her eyes glazed over for a moment as she stared at a sword-wielding knight in a halo about to attack a dragon. There were rumors that Father Juan had been an exorcist before he became director of the academy and, from there, master of the Salamancans. It frightened her badly to think that Antonio didn't entirely trust their master. But there again she was working overtime to trust in someone, something. And that always ended badly.

Candlelight flickered across taut, tired faces as hunters and underground rebels drank wine and got to know each other. Jenn was exhausted, dozing in the corner despite all her attempts to stay awake. Ghost or no ghost, she was just about to go to bed—with flashlights and candles blazing—when three more members of the Resistance arrived: two women and a guy. They were tired and shaken. New Orleans PD had spotted them and shot at them, but they'd successfully eluded the police, arriving at the safe house after doubling back two miles out of their way. They brought word that Aurora had formed an alliance with Christian Gaudet, the vampire king of the French Quarter. There was movement in the air, excitement. Something big was going to happen, and Aurora had a hand in it.

"What do you mean, Tina?" Marc asked the woman—Tina. Right. Jenn had been introduced. She was too tired to remember much of anything. "What 'big'?"

"The vampires are laying claim to territories," Tina replied. "We think they're throwing down. Like *they're* going to have a war between themselves, now that they've defeated us."

"That would be good for us," Holgar said. "They divide; we conquer."

"We don't conquer shite," Jamie muttered.

Tina's cheeks reddened. "We still don't know Aurora's location, but she's somewhere in the French Quarter."

"*That's* helpful," Jamie groused.

The others shifted, probably as tired of his snarking as Jenn was. Tina continued her report. There was no information on Heather, and no one had seen Skye. Antonio showed them the crystal—more properly called a scrying stone—and they discussed Aurora's Mardi Gras deadline.

"Have you heard anything about why she would set a deadline like that?" Marc asked.

"Why do any of it?" Jamie countered, pushing his chair backward and leaning up against the wall on the rear two rungs. He'd had a lot to drink. "Why not kill the Hunter—even though, of course, Jenn's not actually *the* Hunter—but why not kill her in San Francisco? Maybe the girl is a birthday present for Christian Gaudet or some nonsense."

"Her name is Heather," Jenn said through clenched

teeth. She wanted to slap him. He was arrogant and mean.

"I was referring to *you*," Jamie shot back, giving her a hard look. "She expects you to come to the rescue. She's waiting for all of us. I mean, *please*. It's pretty clear she wants six heads on her wall, not just one. Sorry, make that seven, with the sister."

"Maybe the deadline was imposed by someone else," Holgar suggested. "Her chieftain, or whatever they have."

"They're not *Vikings*," Jamie retorted

"Or her lord or her king. Her CEO. Perhaps Aurora has to prove something," Holgar said. "You know how that goes, Jamie."

Jamie glared at him. Slamming his chair legs onto the hardwood floor, he reached for the bottle of red wine on the table and poured himself another glass.

"I doubt Aurora has to prove anything to anyone, a bossy bitch like her." He guzzled down the entire glass like water and let out a small burp.

"Stop drinking so much. If we are attacked tonight, you'll be no good to us," Antonio snapped at him.

"Don't get your knickers in a twist, Spain," Jamie said, unsteadily setting his empty glass back on the table. "You know me. Always ready." His eyes narrowed. "Same as you."

Marc cleared his throat. "If I may say, *mes amis*, for a team you don't seem very . . . teamlike."

"We're new at it," Holgar told him.

"And we *suck* at it," Jamie drawled, pulling a pack of cigarettes from the pocket of his black leather jacket. "Smoke, Antonio?"

Jenn studied the faces of the Resistance fighters with anxiety as they watched the Salamancans. Distrust. Unease. *Why* did Jamie bait Antonio? Did he want them to realize that Antonio was a vampire? Did he hate him so much that he'd jeopardize their chances of rescuing Heather?

Jamie put his lips around a cigarette and drew it out of the pack. Then he reached for a candle on the table and lit the end. Awkward silence settled around the room. Jenn's head drooped forward onto her chest. She began to sink into sleep, hearing the talk around her. She began to dream of St. John of the Cross in his dark cell, praying.

> *Where have you hidden yourself,*
> *And abandoned me in my groaning, O my Beloved?*
> *You have fled like the hart,*
> *having wounded me;*
> *I ran after you, crying; but you were gone.*
> *Antonio de la Cruz, where is your soul?*

*   *   *

Antonio carried Jenn into the nun's cell that Suzy had fixed for her. A battery-powered lantern sat on a small table beside the cot, and Suzy had wiped down the white plaster walls. Fresh floral sheets—the top sheet decorated with red roses, the bottom sheet a field of purple violets—and a soft white blanket dressed the mattress; there was also a fluffy pillow in a white case. A plain cross hung over the bed. He liked the uncluttered look of their lodgings. In his life Antonio had grown up with stark simplicity. It hadn't been much of a stretch to embrace a vow of poverty when he'd entered the seminary in Salamanca.

But celibacy was another matter. He gazed down hungrily at the young girl in his arms, then gave his head a shake and laid her gently on the bed. She let out a sigh but didn't wake up. He moved tendrils of dark red hair from her forehead and resisted the urge to kiss the worry lines away. Her eyes were sunken. She was under so much strain. He remembered how it had been, leaving home to join the seminary, his mother so proud of him, joy and sorrow warring in her gaze as she gave him a blessing. Her only grown son. Spain was tearing herself apart in a civil war, and the young men were leaving the villages to fight.

Except for Antonio de la Cruz, called by the Holy Spirit to Salamanca to become a priest. Many criticized him—with his father dead, he was the man of the family. How could he desert his mother and siblings when the world was collapsing?

He had struggled. Night after night he had prayed for guidance. And each night his answer had been the same. He had to go to Salamanca and become a priest.

"God is calling you," his mother said to him, as she

made the sign of the cross and reached on tiptoe to kiss his cheek. His six sisters stared wide-eyed from the doorway. The oldest, Beatriz, was holding his only brother, Emilio, named for their father. Beatriz wore a black veil over her hair; her fiancé had died in a skirmish in the mountains. She had sworn never to marry, and if the family could have managed it, she would have left after his funeral to become a nun. But her money from sewing was desperately needed. Everyone in the family worked, except for Emilio. Raquel, the littlest girl, gathered sticks to sell as firewood.

They all told him to go. All, that is, except Rosalita Hernandez.

Rosa, newly from Mexico, with her shiny twin black braids looped and pinned to her head and held in place with enormous satin flowers, and with her outlandishly embroidered Mexican clothes—all ruffles and ribbons. Rosa, Rosalita, Lita.

She sang and twirled like a pinwheel when she walked, sixteen and so lovely, so fair. Lita was their neighbors' niece, and he had no idea why she'd come to Spain, because anyone with relatives in Mexico was moving to the New World to escape the war in the Old. But Lita came alone. Shy yet wanting to become part of the community. Eager to fit in.

All the men wanted her. He wanted her too. And Lita— he was the only one to call her Lita—dragged him behind the barn and kissed him, took his hands and wrapped them around her waist, and giggled at his astonishment. He'd been so shocked. None of the other girls he knew behaved like that around him. He was off-limits, the village son promised to God. They treated him like a eunuch.

But she teased him, and whispered to him about how sweet it would be, although they had never done any of the things she told him she wanted to do.

"How can you leave to become a priest, *mi amor*?" she whispered into his ear as he came to say good-bye to her in private. "God wants you to be with me. He wants you to enjoy the pleasures of a wife."

"*Ay, niña*, stop," he begged her.

He went hot as she giggled and nibbled at his earlobe. "Oh, you're so innocent, *cariñoso*, so precious. Let me sully you a bit so God won't be so insistent about stealing you away from me."

"Lita," he said, gasping, telling himself to walk back around the barn and leave, just leave.

"You think I'm so forward," she guessed. "You're shocked. But if *I* don't make the first move, nothing will happen. You're not a priest *yet*, 'Tonio."

"But I already belong to God," he replied, and she shook her head.

"If you were, you wouldn't have come to see me alone. You knew what I would do." Her dark eyes glittered. Her lips were full and moist, and her fingertips tickled the sides of his neck. She looked upward. "I'm fighting You for him," she said to the sky.

"Lita, no," he begged. "Don't make fun. God will strike you down."

"Antonio de la Cruz, don't be silly. God is a bigger person than that."

He was at the seminary when the bombs of Spain's civil war fell on his village. They didn't suffer, he was told. They didn't have time. There would have been nothing he could have done to save them, and he would have died with them. His confessor, Father Francisco, had suggested that perhaps God's voice had called him so insistently for the purpose of saving his life.

Father Francisco put his hand on Antonio's shoulder. "He called you to serve him, *mi hijo*, with all your heart, your soul, and your life. Be a good priest. A wonderful priest. Take your vows, and keep them."

He was keeping that vow now—never to let harm come to another woman who loved him, whether that harm came from her enemies or from him. He was unclean, a Cursed One, but God had granted him grace. At least, that was his belief. He hadn't been able to save Lita, but he could save Jenn—or at least die trying.

As awful as it was to contemplate, he did believe that God had saved him by calling him to Madrid. He did believe that he had escaped Sergio to serve a larger purpose in the divine plan. And he suspected Father Juan knew more about those plans than he was willing to say.

But he knew, somehow, that that plan concerned Jenn. How, he couldn't yet say.

He withdrew his hand from her forehead, stood and turned, nearly running into Father Juan, who had been watching him from the doorway. If vampires could blush, Antonio would have. As it was, he gave his shoulders a little shrug and raised an eyebrow.

"Which temptation is the stronger?" Father Juan asked, ticking his glance from Antonio to Jenn and back again.

"I'm not hungry," he replied. "Thanks to you."

The priest cocked his head and gestured to the hall. The two left Jenn's room, Antonio closing the door quietly behind him. Then he crossed his arms over his chest, waiting to hear what the priest wanted.

"Why are you angry with me?" Father Juan asked point-blank.

"I'm not," Antonio replied, and then he realized it was true. He was angry. "Because she shouldn't be here. She's not strong enough—"

"She *should* be here," Father Juan countered. "Have you lost so much faith in me?"

"I . . ." He trailed off. "Did you find anything in the hall?"

"No. Answer me, please."

"Maybe it's I who shouldn't be here," Antonio said.

Father Juan made a fist and pretended to sock him in the jaw. Then he grew serious. "Is the call of the Cursed Ones too strong for you to withstand?"

"There is no call," Antonio said. "But Father, I think this team is a mistake. There's too much rancor. I half expect to be staked from behind." He looked hard at Father Juan, as if it should be obvious that the group was, as Jamie himself would say, "all arseways."

"When I found you, you had lived in the catacombs beneath the chapel for how long?" Father Juan asked him. "You're new to the world again, Antonio." His eyes took on a faraway gleam. "While I've been in the world much too long."

"Who are you?" Antonio demanded. "Who are you, really?"

The priest shrugged. "Maybe I'm a ghost who likes to frighten young girls in hallways."

"Don't patronize me." Antonio ran his hands through his hair. "I trained these people for you. I'm loyal to the human race, and hunted by my sire because of it. If there's lack of trust between us, it's that you don't trust me with the truth."

Father Juan extended his arm, showing Antonio the gauze dressing on his wrist. "Every time I allow you to feed, *mi hijo*, I trust you with the truth." He patted Antonio's shoulder. "In due time, 'Tonio." Then he patted his chest. "For now, trust me."

New Orleans
Aurora, Heather, and Skye

Aurora turned to Christian Gaudet as he moved out of the shadows and prodded the captive girl through the bars of her cage with his bare foot. Bare-chested, with amber hair cut into a shag and then pomaded, Christian was wearing a pair of black jeans and a single silver earring in his left ear.

Like most vampires who had achieved a certain status and had sired others, he was arrogant. Christian fancied himself the lord of New Orleans. It both amused and offended Aurora.

Christian hadn't seen what she had done to his little brat at the door. She contemplated letting him live a while longer. He had his uses, and even though they had the run of the city, he and his had not grown as lazy as the vampires in San Francisco.

"She's wheezing again," he told Aurora. Then he glanced at the front door, which had just closed behind Skye and Nick. "Are you sure those two can be trusted?"

"No," she replied easily. "But then, no one can." She reached behind herself with her left hand and felt for the extra-sharp stake as she extended her right hand to him. If he moved wrong, if he blinked wrong, he was dust.

He blinked.

She moved.

"Ah, too bad," she whispered, when it was done. She picked the silver earring up out of the ashes and tossed it into Heather's cage.

"For you, my pet," she said.

"Yo, I'm sorry," Nick said half an hour later, as he and Skye emerged from the sewer next to one of the levees by the Mississippi River. "I know you want to join her court. But I'm never going back there. She's crazy. You look at her cross-eyed, and—" He pantomimed being staked. "So, like, good luck, dudette."

Then he bolted and ran into the late-night traffic. Car horns blared, and she winced as she watched him weave across the road. She was relieved beyond the telling that he had bailed on her. Ever since they had left the lair, she'd been working overtime on how to get rid of him without staking him. Despite the fact that he was a bloodsucking monster, she kind of liked him. That made her a bad hunter, she supposed.

I've always liked the bad boys, she thought, smiling grimly as he reached the other side of the road, turned, and waved. Unlike Estefan, this Cursed One at least wore his evil for all the world to see. There were hours yet until dawn, and he might feed. He might not be the kind of vampire who left his victims alive. She should have staked him.

She was equally relieved that she'd been able to avoid drinking Heather's blood. It was only after Aurora had agreed that Heather smelled sick that Skye had realized that the invitation to drink had been a test—one that she had mercifully passed.

Skye pulled out her scrying stone and conjured energy to power it. As she gazed into the surface, the pale light built inside. Then she held it up and panned her surroundings. Scrying stones were ancient tools of the craft, but once GPSs and cell phones had been invented, they'd been relegated as quaint and ineffective. She thanked the Goddess for her extremely traditional parents, who had raised her to know all the old ways. Those old ways were serving her well now.

As were the traces of magick she had scattered down in the sewer. They would lead her back to the vampire lair so the Salamancans could rescue Heather—after they rested up for the rest of the night, so they could go in fresh with the sun. She hugged herself, pleased that she'd pulled this off. Maybe Jamie would notice, and finally be impressed with her instead of mooning after Eriko, the unattainable ice goddess. Maybe that was why he lusted after her—because he knew he could never have her. That made her safe. Jamie was so guarded, and so bitter. Beside him Nick was a puppy.

"We're all so dysfunctional," she murmured aloud. What mad plan did Father Juan have, force-fitting such mismatched personalities together? They'd only been a team for a few months, and in her opinion it wasn't working out at all.

As a white NOPD squad car with the star and crescent logo slowed, she slipped into the shadows on the banks of the river. New Orleans was under a curfew. It would be beyond ironic if Father Juan had to come down to a police station to bail her out for being out on the mundane city streets, after she had successfully snuck into and out of a vampire lair.

The cruiser crept slowly down the road as the passenger window rolled down and a flashlight passed over the top of the bushes she hid behind. Reluctantly summoning more magickal energy, Skye created a version of the spell of seeing she'd used to prevent her reflection.

A tingle at the back of her neck made her blink. It traveled up her neck and over her head. She felt her face with her right hand, then stopped moving as the flashlight froze on the swaying leaves.

She held her breath. *Goddess, protect me,* she thought.

The light winked off. The patrol car moved on.

Thank you, Lady.

Lightning flashed overhead, followed by a rumble of thunder across the rushing black waters of the river. Gazing up at the scudding black clouds, she made magicks over the scrying stone, murmuring the address of the safe house. With any luck she would—

"Skye," came the whisper on the wind.

Still squatting, she whirled around. The lights across the river twinkled, and the river rushed on. Then the sky cracked open, and rain rushed down hard, like rain on the moors back home. Tensing, she squinted through it, seeing nothing but the sudden, violent storm as it dervished around her. With a cry she got to her feet and dashed for the closest shelter, the underside of a balcony tumbling with ferns and geraniums.

Then the rain became a torrent, rocketing water crashing down with unnatural force. A cascade of water sluiced over the pavement and shot into the gutters, curling in waves toward the storm drains.

Magick? she wondered. Was this normal for New Orleans? And had she really heard a voice calling her name?

His voice?

Holding the top of her coat firmly closed, she whirled on her heel and broke into a run. Her boots clattered on cobblestones; her breath came in grunts, and she ran faster, as fear mounted on fear.

New Orleans
Team Salamanca

"Jenn, *despierte.* Wake up," Antonio murmured, gently shaking her.

She jerked and opened her eyes, bolting upright as he put his hand on her shoulder. He was holding a flashlight, and the room was dark. His eyes were nearly black, and he looked very serious.

"There's a heavy rain. The sewer tunnel's filling up. We have to leave."

"What?" She slung her feet over the side of the bed and stood as he helped her up.

"We're moving to higher ground," he said.

Eriko stuck her head in the door. She had on a dark blue raincoat, and a black baseball cap concealed her eyes. "Let's *move*," she ordered. *"Now."*

Jenn was muzzy with sleep. Usually in the midst of a mission—which was what this was—she would wake right up; she figured this time she was exhausted from traveling so hard. She stumbled as she stepped into her boots and buckled them shut, then rummaged in her pocket for her cell phone. The charge was nearly gone. She tucked it back into the pocket and followed Antonio out of the room as he hoisted her duffel over his back.

"Let me carry it," she insisted, flushing as she trotted behind Eriko. He gave it to her, and for a moment she thought about changing her mind. It was heavy and she was tired.

Antonio took up the rear. They assembled in the same room where Jamie and Marc had sparred. Outnumbered by rebels, her teammates were slapping on body armor and knee pads, lacing and buckling their boots. The patches of Team Salamanca were blurs of color among all the shadowy shades of black.

And there was Skye, sopping wet in her heavy black

maxi coat, her skirts and boots, pushing past Bernard and Lucky. When she saw Jenn, she ran to her and threw her arms around her.

"I found her. She's okay. Well, pretty okay." Skye pushed her wet braids away from her face as she looked at Jenn. They looked like blond spider legs. "Aurora keeps her in a cage. She was kind of wheezing."

"Oh, God." Jenn felt dizzy. "She's got asthma. Did you see an inhaler?"

"Are you *mad*? Yeah, and Aurora's vaccinated her against the flu as well," Jamie sniped. He came up to Skye and patted her shoulder. "Good work, witchy."

Scowling, Skye moved her shoulders as if to bat him away. "God, Jamie, you don't need to be so harsh. She's Jenn's sister."

"Yeah, I got the memo."

"Were they . . . did they . . . ?" Jenn began, and what she wanted to ask, but couldn't, was, *Did you?*

"I can't lie to you, Jenn," Skye said. "Yes. They had been drinking from her. But they've stopped because she's sick."

Jenn swayed. Skye gripped her arm. "We're going to get her out."

Jamie jerked his head at Eriko. "What are we going to do, a dozen people running out the front door? I'm sure the locals will think it's a bunch o' lads having a session." He mimed drinking a beer. "*Laissez les bons temps rouler*, eh, gents?"

"We're going down into the tunnel." Marc turned to the Salamancans and addressed them all. "Which is why we have to leave now. The water level is rising."

"In the feckin' *sewer*?" Jamie cried. "I don't see why we have to leave at all. Even if the sewer fills up, you've got the ground floor to bivouac in, and none the wiser." He looked at Skye. "You can put up some of them spells—"

"Hush," Skye gritted, as Marc's people stirred and looked at Skye. Silence fell like a house over the room.

"Spells? She can use magick?" Marc asked, halfway to slinging a submachine gun over his head. He looked from Skye to Father Juan and then to Eriko. Silence.

Then Father Juan said, "Yes," not adding that he could use magick, too.

"And you were not going to mention it?" Marc's voice thrummed with tension and fear.

"It's only for defense," Skye said quickly, her face turning red. Water dripped from her hair down the side of her face, and she shook it off like a poodle. "I can't hurt anyone with it. But I can make us harder to notice while we're all escaping."

Pursing his lips, Marc walked to an open box of ammo on the table and stuffed some clips into the pockets of his jacket. Jamie joined him, examining the boxes of ammunition and breaking one open, then holding a round up to the artificial light.

"I thought you knew that was why we sent her," Eriko said, crossing to Jamie and yanking the clip out of his hand.

326

"She had the best chance to infiltrate, because she can use magicks."

"I missed that." Marc's voice was icy with anger. The others were very quiet.

"Then how did you figure we got her in?" Eriko asked, genuinely confused.

"We've pulled off an infiltration now and then. Going undercover," Marc said, gritting his teeth. Lucky and Bernard nodded.

"What, you just walk in?" Jamie asked admiringly. "Lad, you got a pair."

"We've got a *cause*," Lucky cut in.

Marc glared at Eriko, then at Father Juan. "When we leave this place, we'll become a hundred times more vulnerable. We're wanted. No doubt the word's out on you, as well, so we're even more vulnerable because of you."

"They still think I'm a vampire," Skye said. "And Aurora is planning something big. They're going to kill Solomon."

"What?" came a chorus of voices, faces staring at Skye.

"Yes. She thought I'd come to New Orleans because of her. She's at the center of something."

"Well, *ja*, you did come because of her," Holgar reminded her. He grinned faintly. "Just not in the way that she thinks."

Marc exhaled. "*Merde.* I don't want *more* suckers in my city. Is there anything *else* we need to know about?"

Eriko gestured to the ammo. "We don't use guns."

"Well, *we* sure the hell do," Bernard informed her.

"We don't know much about hunters. Do you have some kind of prohibition about killing human beings?" Suzy sounded forced, as if she was trying to keep the peace.

"Yeah, stupidly," Jamie cut in. "We only do it as a last resort. Kill 'em, I mean."

"We go on missions," Eriko elaborated. "Our objectives are defined. We're sent out by our master." She lowered her head in Father Juan's direction.

"I send them where I think they'll do the most good," Father Juan elaborated. "They're secret missions, of course."

"Except someone's been spilling a few deets." Jamie gave Father Juan a look. "For all we know, they told Aurora we're here."

"Aurora didn't sound like she knew," Skye said. "She said that Heather was *the* Hunter's sister."

"Back to these missions," Marc said. "We do the same thing."

"Most of the time there are no humans on the other side," Eriko replied.

"That we know of," Jamie muttered.

"*Pardon?*" Marc said, frowning. "What does that mean?"

"It means that if you have extra weapons, my team will take them." Father Juan stepped forward with his hand extended. "With thanks." He looked at Jenn. "We'll do whatever it takes to save your sister."

"That's a slippery slope, Father," Jamie said. Father Juan didn't react.

"Thank you, Master." Jenn's voice was strained. She was afraid she was going to burst into tears, and she'd cried enough.

Jamie grunted and slid a glance toward Eriko. "A word?"

Eriko raised her chin as if bracing herself to deal with Jamie. The two walked a bit apart. Antonio narrowed his eyes, and Jenn could tell he was eavesdropping on them. As they talked, Suzy left the room and then returned, hefting two overstuffed backpacks.

"This one is water. The other one is protein bars and beef jerky," she said. "We've still got a lot of trail mix too."

"You should jumble them up," Jenn told her. "If you lose one, you won't lose all your water or all your food."

Suzy blinked, nodded. "Good idea."

Lucky held out a submachine gun to Jenn. He was already wearing one around his shoulders. "Do you know how to use this?" he asked her.

"I'm a little rusty," she admitted as she put the strap around her neck and hefted the weapon, "but we did have basic weapons training at the academy." She grasped the barrel and the hilt. "This is an Uzi, and it has an open-bolt design. That helps with the balance. But we should keep them decocked as much as possible, to prevent contamination. Such as sewer water."

She gazed at him. "Also, it's good to rest between bursts and lower your weapon. *Bam-bam-bam*, rest. Otherwise you might wind up shooting at the moon."

Lucky whistled. "You should open up more academies, Father. You could train more fighters."

"*Oui,*" Marc said. "Why be so elitist? What do these hunters possess that sets them so much apart?" When Marc spoke, he looked at Jenn, and she could feel her cheeks burning.

"We usually engage in hand-to-hand combat. As you know, guns don't work on vampires. We'll teach you all we can," Father Juan said.

"Including magick?" Lucky asked, moving to stand beside Marc. "I've never met anyone who could do magick. That's so freaky." He smiled over at Skye. "Can you do, like, love spells and stuff like that?"

"I can't," Skye blurted quickly, suddenly busy with a satchel containing sharp-tipped stakes and vials of holy water.

"Can you make our phones work?" Marc asked.

"I tried while I was gone. And I tried to cast protective spells over your place, here. I couldn't tell if they formed properly." Jenn's training in scanning for what was out of place kicked in. Skye was acting fragmented. Torn, literally. Something was very wrong.

"We have another safe house in the Quarter," Marc said. "We'll regroup there, and then we'll leave."

Jamie and Eriko rejoined the group. Eriko cleared her throat and said, "I want to discuss the plan more fully. We're carrying a lot of gear. We'll have to stow it before we launch our rescue attempt."

"I say leave it here," Jamie insisted, stuffing ammo clips into his Velcro pockets. "There's no point bogging ourselves down. The higher floors should be okay." Jamie grabbed an Uzi with one hand and a Magnum .457 in the other. He looked like a kid at Christmas.

"You weren't here," Marc said, "when Katrina hit."

"It's only *raining*," Jamie said.

"This is New Orleans. We're below sea level," Marc countered.

"There should be two teams," Holgar piped up. "One to move things, one to rescue Jenn's sister." He raised his hand. "I'll help with the rescue."

"You should go with the gear. You'd make a proper *beast* of burden," Jamie drawled.

Holgar narrowed his eyes. "I'm keeping score, you know."

"And it's a hundred thousand to zero, by my count," Jamie replied.

"Well, I'm the one who can follow the magick traces I left," Skye said, "so I have to go."

"Vale, vale," Antonio said. "Of course Jenn and I are going." He stood closely beside her.

Jamie turned to Eriko. "What do you say, ducks?"

Eriko nodded and stood beside her fighting partner. "But you should be careful loading your pockets," she said, wrinkling her forehead. "It will be difficult for you to reach your stakes and holy water if the ammo clips are in the way."

"I used to carry a lot more than this in Belfast," he retorted, patting the breast pocket of his olive green jacket. "And that was to go to the shop and buy me da a pint."

"Northern Ireland is a good analogy," Marc said. "Or Paris, after the Nazis conquered France. The vampires have taken over, and they're very brazen. They have terrorized the police and the mayor into submitting to them. No human can expect justice. For vampires it's close to paradise."

"Closer to hell," Jamie said.

"Maybe that's why Aurora brought your sister here," Bernard added, nodding at Jenn. "If she wants to put down roots, it says a lot about her strength if she can snatch a family member from under the nose of a hunter."

"To underscore my point," Marc cut in, "the people here do what the Cursed Ones want. Some of them are too afraid not to. But the truth is that many of them have better lives since the vampires came. Poor people, the powerless—the vampires are using them against us. And they're happy to be used."

"It makes them feel useful," Holgar ventured.

"It does." Marc apparently wasn't in a joking mood. "There are prices on our heads. We're worth a lot dead. It is more than likely that humans will shoot at you."

"Bring it on," Jamie said, cocking the Magnum.

"The Uzi is a good weapon," Antonio said, looking at Father Juan. "When we get home, perhaps we should reconsider our way of doing things."

"We're hunters," Eriko said. "Not commandos."

Marc rested his arms on his Uzi. "Yeah, well, you define the mission to match your enemy, not the other way around, eh?"

"*Sensei?*" Looking flustered, Eriko bowed in Father Juan's direction.

Jenn took a step toward Eriko. "My sister is in mortal danger." She picked up another Magnum .457 and held it out to Eriko, but it was so heavy that her arm swung in an arc until she grabbed it with her other hand. That definitely took the edge off her challenging gesture.

Father Juan hesitated. Then he said, "I'm sorry, Eriko, but please take the gun. We'll sort this out when we get home."

When we get home. Jenn licked her lips and swallowed hard. *When, not if.*

"Let's move out," Marc said.

CHAPTER FOURTEEN

Though our flesh is pale and cold
We are beautiful to behold
Love us for our peaceful way
And never once our trust betray
For to harm us is to harm your own
To cut the flesh and break the bone
For with us gone you soon would find
You'd be lost both in body and mind

New Orleans
The Resistance and the hunters of
Salamanca

With Eriko beside him Marc opened the convent door that led to the sewer and immediately panned the area with his Uzi, while she painted the darkness with her flashlight.

Gazing over Eriko's shoulder, Jenn saw rushing water where, before, there'd been a trickle from the French Quarter's storm drains. Despite the increase in the amount of water, it didn't smell any worse than the first time she'd been down there. But she wondered how they would be able to move through the tunnel—it would be waist-high on her, and rising.

Marc nodded at Bernard, Matt, and Lucky, who climbed down the stairs, then disappeared behind them. They reappeared a few seconds later with the first of four flat-bottomed boats, each approximately ten feet long, with benches stretching horizontally between the two sides of the hull.

"These are called pirogues," Marc announced. "Cajun boats. There are seventeen of us. Bernard, Lucky, Suzy, and I will go with the extraction team. That makes eleven. The rest of my people will take the gear to the safe house in shifts. We'll meet there."

Suzy looked a little uncomfortable as she made room for Skye on her bench as Suzy climbed aboard. She had taken out her pom-pom ponytails and pulled her hair back with an elastic band. Skye was twisting the silver ring on her thumb, her face pale, her Rasta braids fuzzy and unkempt.

The atmosphere had changed as soon as Skye's witch identity had been revealed, and had worsened when Eriko had protested their arming themselves with conventional weapons. Now that they were on the move, it was even worse. The Resistance was uneasy around them now, and that was bad. Marc's people wanted to get rid of Aurora. Jenn wanted to save her sister's life. But the Resistance had no compunctions about killing humans in order to serve the greater good. If Heather got in the way, and it came down to Jenn's sister or their vampire target, what would Marc's soldiers do?

Antonio, Jenn, and Father Juan climbed into a boat.

"If I may," Marc said, pushing off their boat, then gracefully climbing aboard, wet up to his knees. A wooden pole about six feet long lay along the right side of the benches, and he picked it up and thrust it into the water. "This is how we steer in shallow water," he explained.

The current caught them, and they glided away from the convent entrance. One rider in each boat turned on a flashlight, guiding the captain. In Jenn's boat Father Juan was the light keeper.

The tunnel became narrower, and darker; the flashlights played over the beady eyes of the rats that squeaked from moss-covered, trash-strewn crevices in the walls and then scurried away. On Marc's order everyone ducked their heads as the tunnel ceiling dropped, making it harder to watch where they were going—and to see any potential attackers.

"One time I was down here alone," Marc murmured, "and a vampire fell on me from overhead. They use the manholes same as us."

"Is it so bad up there that we have to travel like this?" Jenn asked.

"For us? *Mais oui*," he replied. "We're known. But if you walked outside like a person, no, it wouldn't look so bad. People smile. They're celebrating Mardi Gras. Vampires are charmers. And killers."

"You sound angry."

He looked at her, really looked. She saw lines around his face. "You're very smart, Jenn. I am angry. We're risking our lives to get rid of the suckers, and most of the people on the street hate us. They'll do what they can to survive."

"But you'd rather die."

"Hell, no, I don't want to die. But they may as well be real zombies. They're not living. They're just treading water."

He fell silent. Jenn took her cue from him and asked no more questions. Her back ached from hunching over, and sweat was stinging her eyes.

Antonio's lips grazed her neck; they were cool against her throbbing vein. She jerked, hard, shocked and frightened. She tried to turn her head to look at him, but just then the boat dropped about five feet, creating a splash as it slammed back down, and Antonio caught her arm, steadying her.

"Sorry, should have warned you," Marc murmured.

Antonio wrapped his hand around hers and squeezed it.

Was he apologizing? Had he meant to touch her like that? Her heart thundered as she warily gripped the edge of the bench. Then, as carefully as she could, she looked in his direction.

Red eyes flickered like flames dancing on the water. Deep, crimson, smoldering. She caught her breath. If Marc saw, he would know Antonio's secret. What would he do? She fingered her Uzi. What would *she* do?

She reached out and found Antonio's hand again; lacing her fingers with his, she gripped him, hard, giving him a quick shake.

He hissed.

"What was that?" Marc whispered. "Father Juan, move your flashlight around."

She heard the hesitation in Father Juan's voice. "Very well."

Their master knew the hiss was from Antonio. Father Juan knew that Antonio had changed. Jenn began to tremble. Joining forces had been a terrible mistake. They should have stayed on their own. Now they had to worry about the vampires *and* the Resistance.

"Estoy bien," Antonio whispered against her ear. I'm fine. He had taken command of himself. She hazarded a look and saw nothing. Then Father Juan's flashlight bounced off a wall, and she dimly traced Antonio's profile. His eye was no longer glowing. *"Lo siento."* I'm sorry.

"We're here," Marc announced. "Father, please aim

your flashlight straight up. It's our code, signaling that we're friends. In case any of our people are about."

Marc extended his pole in front and pushed downward at an angle, using it as a braking mechanism. The yellow light played over a graveled slope that reached upward into the blackness. Rats chattered and disappeared. With a whoosh of water, the bow of the pirogue scraped onto the gravel; the boat jerked forward, and then Marc jumped out. Father Juan followed suit, and then Jenn and Antonio.

Soon the other boats were lined up beside Jenn's. Marc took the flashlight from Father Juan, passing the beam over two tunnels ahead of them. Skye came up beside him, holding her scrying stone.

"From what you described, I think we need to take the tunnel to the left," Marc said.

"Yes," she said. "I should lead."

"You don't have a weapon."

"I'll concentrate on my magick trail," she replied, and Jenn heard a strange catch in Skye's voice. She looked at Antonio again, but his face was shrouded in darkness.

"I'll cover you, since you'll be unarmed," Jamie said. "Me and Eriko. We've both got Uzis."

"*Hai hai.*" Eriko was speaking in Japanese. She was stressing. She'd lost control of the mission, and they weren't doing it her way.

Please, you guys, please keep it together. This is my sister, Jenn thought.

"Father Juan," Antonio murmured. "I thought I heard something in the other tunnel."

"Let's investigate," Father Juan said quickly. To Marc, "We'll check it out and catch up."

"No, it's too dangerous," Eriko cut in. "Don't leave the group."

"*Yes*. We should make sure there are no vampires there," Father Juan replied smoothly. But Jenn heard the tension.

Antonio can't stop his transformation. She clenched her hands around her submachine gun. This was going badly. All these guns, all around them, Eriko losing control, Antonio losing control.

"*Vite,*" Marc said to Father Juan. Dark shapes shifted around Jenn; she caught a flash of red—Antonio's eyes—and then she saw nothing more; he must have turned away. She took a tentative step in his direction; then the pressure of a hand stopped her, and someone bent to whisper in her ear.

"Let 'em go. No fussin'." It was Jamie. So he'd seen too. She nodded, turning away, and he followed after her.

"Be cool. Act cool," Jamie said.

She was grateful for his steadying voice.

"If you can," he muttered.

Maybe not so grateful.

"There's a problem," Skye said in a low voice. "I can't find my magick trail. Are you sure this is the correct tunnel?"

Boots shifted on gravel. Jenn watched as Father Juan and Antonio walked into the other tunnel, Father Juan holding a flashlight down low, although Antonio could have guided him in the darkness. But they had to maintain appearances.

"You started out beneath Decatur Street, *oui*?" Marc said. "In front of Jackson Square? You saw the statue of Andrew Jackson on the horse?"

"Yes, that's where I went down into the tunnel, but we—I—came out a different way. I wound up by the levee," she replied.

Jenn blinked. *Did I just hear her say "we"?*

"Then either way you would have had to walk through the other end of this tunnel. That's where the tunnels intersect," Marc said. "Maybe we're too far away from your 'bread crumbs.' Let's head into the tunnel."

She heard clacking—weapons being reslung over necks, soldiers checking their ammo clips. Boots clumped on the damp gravel. Flashlights grazed the fighters as they entered the tunnel. Jenn saw the look on Skye's face—worried, frustrated—as the witch murmured and waved her free hand across the surface of the stone. She walked slowly, and Jenn hurried over to her.

"Can you do something like put a glamour on Antonio?" she asked in a low voice. "He's having trouble."

"Oh, my Goddess," Skye breathed, staring at her. "I don't know if I can, Jenn. I mean, I'm not sure if I can do it in the first place. But right now my magicks are being blocked."

Jenn caught her breath. "But you were able to put a glamour on yourself so you could pass as a vampire. *That* worked."

Skye hesitated. Then she said, in a voice so low that Jenn could hardly hear her, "I had help."

We, Jenn thought. So she had heard her correctly. Had no one else?

"Help?" Jenn cocked her head. "Like other witches?"

Skye made fists with both her hands and pounded her forehead. "Bloody hell, I just broke my vow. We're sworn to secrecy. What we're doing is so *wrong* in the eyes of Witchery."

Her shoulders rounded, and she shook her head. "And I'm doing things witches are forbidden to do: fighting, using weapons. With *bullets.* And now I've gone and told you about the others."

Jenn put her hand on Skye's shoulder. "You're trying to keep my sister from dying. Or worse." Her voice cracked. "You have to tell Father Juan about these other witches. We need their help. How many are there?"

"I can't tell you that," Skye said tightly. "I misspoke, Jenn."

"Maybe you can ask them to help us." Jenn kept her voice as even as she could, but she wanted to shake Skye until her teeth rattled. *How could you not tell us?* she wanted to scream at her. *How could you keep something like that from us?*

"I *have* asked. They were willing to help me as long as I promised not to reveal their existence." She puffed a braid off her forehead. "So I may have just lost all my allies."

"But if they know a human life is at stake," Jenn argued, "then—"

"The vampires of New Orleans have someone from the magickal world who is helping them." Skye's voice shook. She was scared. "I think whoever it is is blocking me right now. And maybe they're casting a spell on Antonio as well."

Jenn gaped at her. "Do you mean that someone is *making* Antonio change?"

"I don't know," Skye whispered back. "I've heard it said that some can. But my scrying stone is drawing a blank. That shouldn't be. It should respond to me. My magick trail should appear in the stone, and it should glow more strongly the closer we get to it."

Skye thought a moment, then spoke rapidly in Latin, creating a ball of bluish-white light about the size of her thumb that drifted ahead of her.

"*That* worked, at least. I'm going to talk to Marc."

"But you won't say anything," Jenn said. "Not about Antonio."

"*Or* my fighting partner, Holgar," Skye huffed. "Do you think I'm an idiot?"

Jenn bit her tongue.

"And you need to keep quiet about my friends," Skye added.

"You *have* to tell Father Juan, at least," Jenn begged.

"Look, I just told you that I've already asked them to help us. They're doing what they can. They won't come forward. What they're doing now is it, Jenn."

Skye minced away on the balls of her boots, a stealthy version of stomping her feet, and tapped Marc on the shoulder. He stopped, and they conferred. He turned his head toward the group, then looked back at Skye. They walked about ten feet farther away and craned their necks over Skye's scrying stone. They walked another ten feet into the tunnel, then twenty, taking the light with them.

Her hand cupped over a flashlight, Suzy caught up to Jenn. "Did she create that light?" she asked. "With magick?"

Jenn didn't know what to say. She wasn't used to explaining the actions of the group to outsiders. And what Skye had revealed had shocked her. Not only did Skye have a secret life, but it was pretty clear to Jenn that she wasn't as powerful a witch as Jenn had assumed. Father Juan might be similarly dismayed.

Father Juan must be told.

Her spine stiffened as Skye and Marc headed back toward them. Then Eriko moved around Jenn, placing herself between Jenn and Marc, trying to re-establish herself as the person in charge.

"Something's not right," Marc said to the Hunter. "Skye says her stone isn't working."

Eriko shrugged. "Maybe sometimes it doesn't work."

"No," Jenn put in. "That's the thing about magick. If it doesn't work, there's a reason." *Unlike prayer.*

"My best guess is that there's someone else using magicks to keep me blind," Skye said. She licked her lips as if she were about to say something more, then pursed them, looked over at Jenn, and gazed down at the stone. "Maybe there are spells all over the city. Maybe that's why your cell phones don't work."

Bernard's dark skin looked purple in Skye's bluish light. "That may be. There's also technology that can jam cell phone usage, though. And the Internet," he added, before anyone could interrupt.

"So what is magick and what is technology?" Marc murmured.

"If they're keeping you from using magick, then why does your light thingie work?" Suzy asked Skye.

Skye shifted her weight. "Magick is a force, like electricity. A spell caster shapes it. If someone turned off the lights in a room, for example, your iPod wouldn't stop working. It would take a very powerful spell, or set of spells, to dampen all my spells. Whoever blocked my trail is doing it to protect Aurora."

There's more to Skye's freak-out than that, Jenn thought, studying her teammate. *She's not just worried; she's terrified.* Skye's eyes were darting left and right, almost as if she were bracing herself for something to happen.

As if she were waiting for someone to show up.

And suddenly, Jenn had the surest sense that they were in terrible danger. It felt like insects crawling all over her, or tiny electrical shocks.

"We should get out of here *now*!" Jenn cried.

The tunnel roared to life like a living monster as shapes dropped from the ceiling and crashed hard on the gravel. Skye's light blinked out, and in the darkness the *ratatatatat* staccato of machine-gun fire slammed against Jenn's eardrums.

"Hold your fire!" Eriko bellowed. "You might shoot one of us!"

The noise roared all around Jenn, thrusting her into chaos and bedlam; then something hit her in the face, and she fell backward, smacking the back of her head against the sharp rocks. Rolling to the left, she reached in the pocket along her thigh for a stake while she grabbed a plastic vial of holy water out of her jacket. Unable to see, she flung the blessed water in an arc, and was rewarded with a sharp hiss. She followed through, throwing the vial, then pushing herself and jabbing into the darkness with her stake. The sharp end penetrated something—or someone—but her assailant kicked her hard in the ribs. Her body armor helped absorb the shock.

What if it's Antonio? she thought, flinging herself toward her attacker.

More machine-gun fire blasted through the tunnel like exploding dynamite, and her eardrums closed. The world shattered into a soundless void as Jenn punched, kicked, and stabbed empty air. The vampire had moved away. It knew where she was, but she couldn't say the same. She whirled in a circle, blind, deaf, stabbing at nothing.

Something hit her hard. She didn't know where. Icy numbness spread through her body as her legs gave way and she collapsed to the ground. With a grunt she fought to get back up—nothing was holding her down—but her muscles began to quiver. She was spinning, freezing.

I'm wounded. She couldn't tell if she'd been shot or hit or what. That wasn't the issue. She was out of the fight. *Get up,* she ordered herself. *Now.*

"Antonio," she murmured, although she couldn't hear the word. Where was he? What was happening to him?

Then someone scooped her up, and she was either floating or they were carrying her; gradually, she began to hear words, and they were Spanish and Latin mixed together. In her dazed mind it sounded like a lullaby. It was Antonio, praying over her. Her head lolled on his chest, and she slid her arm around his neck.

"Jenn," he said. "Jenn, I have you." His voice shook.

"Oh, God, I feel so cold."

Chilly air hit her cheeks, and she listened to the rhythm of his footfalls. He was running faster than anyone could, except for Eriko. He was outing himself; someone would notice, and ask questions.

"Antonio, slow down," she said.

He didn't answer. Then he shifted her weight to one arm and climbed up a metal ladder. Rain poured down on them. Other hands took her — Holgar — and he raced with her across the street, around a building, and down a small alley strewn with purple and green banners. There was a large poster for Mardi Gras; they flashed past it so quickly she couldn't read it.

"What happened?" she asked, as a purple door flew open and Holgar carried her inside. In murky light the foyer was grimy and loaded with mailboxes, trash, and two stacks of office chairs piled one on top of another. Rounding a corner, they went through a doorway of peeling white wood, and Father Juan ushered Holgar to an unfolded sleeping bag on the floor.

"You passed out. We couldn't find you. Antonio went back," Holgar said, as he laid her down. He looked at Father Juan. "This is crazy, Master. There is nothing safe about this safe house. We had to run across the street. A dozen vampires could have seen us."

"Or informers," Jamie chimed in. He leaned over Holgar and gazed down at Jenn. "Want some whiskey? It'll dull the pain."

"Yes," she replied, surprising both herself and everyone else.

"Have at it, then." As Holgar helped her sit up, Jamie put the bottle to her lips. It seared her throat and flashed into her bloodstream. She stifled a cough; Jamie saw it and grinned, putting the bottle to his lips.

"How are the rest of the team?" she asked. "Where are Skye and Eriko?"

"Skye's helping the wounded. Eriko's walking the perimeter. She doesn't like this place either," Father Juan replied.

"Ground floor. It's feckin' arseways," Jamie muttered. "We should get out of here *now*. We're not far enough away from the sewer. They'll smell all the blood."

"But no one was killed," Father Juan added, answering Jenn's question.

"Was I shot?" she asked.

"Let's find out," he said, placing his hands on her arm. She looked down and gasped at the amount of blood that had soaked her jacket. She was still bleeding.

He looked at Jamie. "Would you please ask Skye to come here, *mi hijo*?"

"Where's Antonio?" She lifted her head, feeling dizzy.

"He's staying in the tunnel for a bit," her master told her. He gave her a hard look, as if warning her not to say anything. Troubled, she obeyed.

The front door opened. Heavy footfalls sounded in the hall, and Marc and Eriko leaned into the room. Marc said, "We've rounded up transportation. Let's go."

Father Juan knit his brows. "This hunter has been hurt."

"I'm sorry about that," Marc said directly to Jenn. "We were surprised."

"There were no human attackers in that tunnel." Eriko ran her hand over her hair. "Just vampires. So the bullets caused only harm."

"We didn't *know* that when we opened fire," Marc replied.

Jamie glared at Marc. "We have to go. It's not safe here."

"We *are* going," Marc replied. "We're getting out of the city." He looked down at Jenn. "We have to make a stop first."

The roar of an approaching vehicle covered Jenn's cry as Father Juan helped her sit up. Now she did hurt. Everything hurt. Her arm throbbed, and she felt sick to her stomach. She took a deep steadying breath as Father Juan raised her to her feet. She swayed.

"Come on, Jenn." Holgar picked her up in his arms, grinning down at her. "You need to go on a diet."

"I'll see to Lucky," Father Juan said.

Then everyone was barreling back out of the building and into the heavy rain—except for Lucky, who was carried out on two pieces of wood bound together to make a stretcher. Marc had one end and Father Juan the other. Wrapped in a dark green blanket, Lucky was groaning, and his face was dead white. Skye walked beside him, making circles with her hands. Her forehead was furrowed with concentration.

"Oh, no," Jenn murmured, as two vans rolled to a stop and their doors slid back. One was the black van that had nearly run her down, black with tinted windows. The other was white, with black paint on the windows. Bernard was behind the wheel of the white one, and Suzy was driving the other. "What happened to him?"

"Gut shot," Jamie said. "Looks bad. Of course, they can't take him to a hospital."

"A doctor will be meeting up with us," Marc said.

Jamie shook his head. "Listen to me. You shouldn't move him. He's going to die if you do."

"We have no other choice." Marc scowled at him. "You want war? This is Belfast during the Troubles, before you and I were born. This is tanks moving in on innocent people in their pajamas."

"This happened because of the guns," Eriko said as she looked left, then right, and jerked her head at Holgar. "Get Jenn inside one of the vans."

"Where's Antonio?" she asked.

"I'm here," he replied quietly, as Holgar half carried, half slid her into the black van with the tinted windows. There were no seats, only the floor, which was crammed with more blankets and weapons, and a large first-aid kit. Antonio had gathered up a dry blanket, and he gently wrapped it around Jenn. Her arm felt as if it had been set on fire, and she sucked in her breath.

"*Bien, bien, mi amor,*" he said, wiping her forehead with a trembling hand, gazing down at her with his dark Spanish eyes. They held no fire; he'd gotten himself under control. Or else, in his fear, the fire had gone out.

351

"Am I dying?" she asked.

His lips parted. "No, never." He grabbed her hand, squeezing so tightly she winced. He studied her face, his eyes half closed, and she felt herself slide farther away, as if she were in an elevator. She was cold.

"Hey, how'd you get in here so fast?" Marc demanded, poking his head into the van. Then he was distracted, murmuring, "Easy with Lucky." He left and went ahead to the white van.

Father Juan climbed in next, then Holgar. Holgar slid the door shut, and the two vehicles rolled. Less than a minute had elapsed. By the light from the windows Jenn could see that dawn was approaching. Fighting not to whimper from the pain, she studied Antonio, who had wrapped himself in a blanket. The gathered material around his head looked like a monk's hood.

Holgar raised up on his knees, gazing out the tinted window. *"Hold kaeft,"* he said in Danish. Hazy with pain, Jenn grunted weakly. It was the Danish equivalent of "Holy shit," and he hadn't said it in a long time.

"There are soldiers everywhere," Holgar announced. "Heavily armed."

"And police officers," Suzy said from the driver's seat. "So you see, Marc wasn't wrong." She cleared her throat as if she knew she should change the subject. "When we get on the main road, you'll see the billboards."

The van bumped along. Jenn was getting a headache,

and she felt sick to her stomach. Antonio held her hand very tightly—too tightly, almost as if he was pinning her down rather than comforting her. She was bleeding. What was that doing to him?

"*Ja*, I see the big road signs," Holgar reported. "With slogans written in huge letters. This one says 'Friends.' And it shows a man and woman with big fangs smiling at an old lady and a kid."

"See that one? 'Peace for All,'" Father Juan read, craning his neck. "*Por el amor de Dios*, look at that. A vampire with his arms spread, like Christ."

Antonio grunted.

"'Stand Up to the Resistance,'" Suzy intoned over her shoulder, as if she knew all the slogans by heart. "We're the bad guys, hurting the nice vampires. Now that it's pretty obvious that *they're* the bad guys, no one has the guts to say any different."

Holgar growled low in his throat. "The world has gone mad."

The van hit another bump, then a pothole, and Jenn groaned. Antonio cupped her cheek. His skin was even colder than hers.

"'Tonio," she said, "this is messed up."

"No," he began, and then he looked down at her. Points of scarlet light danced in his eyes. "*Sí*, Jenn, you're right. It's very messed up."

And hearing him say that made it worse. Wounded,

scared, despairing, she began to weep. His fingertips were gentle against her face.

"Oh, God, Antonio, what's going to happen to my sister?" She dissolved into tears.

He squeezed her hand as he stroked her forehead, her temple, her cheek. *"Yo sé."* I know. "God has a plan. I'm sure that He does."

"That does nothing," she said between sobs, "to make me feel better."

"He is here, with His hands out, if you just take them."

And so am I, Antonio thought.

But what he was was a vampire. A vampire who had served in the court of his sire and lord, Sergio. One of Sergio's many vampiric subjects, who had savaged street girls and the waifs of Madrid for their blood. Unable to control his desires, his needs. Watching as a disobedient *Maldito* was tied to a pyre like a victim of the Inquisition, waiting for the sun to take him, finally, from the earth. Learning of the Cursed Ones' gods, such as the one Sergio followed—Orcus, bringer of light, punisher of those who broke their vows. Hell gods, who promised to bring light to the darkness—like Lucifer, chief of all the gods of hell, the luminous one. Who, if he was seen in this life, would burn his witness to death. Blinded by the light—not by angels, but by demons. That was why vampires burned in daylight, or so it was said. And why humans burned too, only much more slowly.

The van rolled on, as the sky lightened, and Antonio gazed down at Jenn. If he gave up his vows, if he let go of his rigid self-control . . .

He would walk into the brightest day on the sunniest spot on the planet first. He'd face the light gladly, ashes to ashes, dust to dust, scattered on the wind.

CHAPTER FIFTEEN

It is a crusade, at least for most of us. A holy cause.
We are dedicated to it. We will give our lives for it.
We fight with the idealism of the young and struggle
with the emotions and confusions of growing up at the
same time. For us love and hatred can spin into life or
death, especially for me, Jenn Leitner.

And for some of us, death can never come.
Which means this war can rage on . . .
. . . forever.

—*from the diary of Jenn Leitner*

NEW ORLEANS
THE HUNTERS AND THE RESISTANCE

The van picked up speed, bumping and swerving, as Jenn drowsed. She dreamed she was walking along the beach, with Heather, warning her about the sharks.

They can smell you, she said.

And dream Heather replied, *I know. I'm a shark now too.*

Jenn shouted herself awake. Antonio and Holgar were leaning over her, and the van door was open.

"It's all right," Antonio soothed. His face was pinched with concern, and he looked very much the way she remembered him from her first day at the academy, hair long and curly, his face earnest. He wore his single earring with the ruby cross. His physical appearance was that of an older teen. That hadn't changed.

Father Juan had introduced him as a seminarian, a man studying to be a priest. He'd neglected to mention that Antonio had been a seminarian for over seventy years.

"We're parked in the shade," Holgar said quietly. "So Antonio won't get a *sunburn.*"

She flashed them both a wan, weepy smile and sat up, surprised to find that her shirtsleeve had been pushed up around her elbow and her jacket slung across her shoulders. Her forearm had been bandaged and put in a sling that went around her neck, same as the submachine gun that was now gone.

At her questioning expression Antonio said, "I did it. Field dressing."

"Let's go," Father Juan told them, poking his head into the van. "Antonio, the roof should shelter you, but go inside and move to the center of the house."

"*Sí, Padre.* Take care of her."

Holgar helped Jenn climb out of the van while Antonio waited. Her arm throbbed. They had parked beneath the overhang of an enormous ruined mansion. It was three stories tall, and blue and white paint flaked off graceful balconies encircling each floor, half destroyed by time and weather. Three dormer windows were centered in the sloping roof, which had caved in in many places. The rain had stopped, and clouds blanketed the sky. Antonio cautiously emerged next, ducking beneath the awning and positioning Jenn's good arm over his shoulders.

A door stood open, and Holgar held back, allowing Antonio to get inside. He looked uncomfortable—even the small amount of sun was too much for him. Moving swiftly into a corridor, he leaned against the wall and closed his eyes.

Holgar walked Jenn across a parquet floor gaping with holes to a burgundy-upholstered settee, the kind with a tilted headrest and a single padded side, made for lying on one's side and reading, daydreaming. It was in beautiful condition, belying the ruins of the mansion it furnished. Jenn scrunched herself up so that her boots stayed off the upholstery, hanging in midair. It was supremely uncomfortable.

She lay quietly, dozing, feeling weak, aware that she was the only hunter who had been wounded in the attack. She hadn't moved fast enough, or been observant enough, or something. Closing her eyes, she spared thoughts for Lucky, even if she didn't exactly pray.

Why don't I pray? Why can't I believe? Crosses and holy water hurt them. He prays, and he's untouched. Isn't that proof enough that Antonio's god is involved in this?

Footsteps jerked her awake. Antonio was sitting with his back against the edge of the settee, keeping watch. Shadows had slid along the wall and spread across the floor.

"Is this my other patient?" asked a plump, mocha-skinned woman. She was wearing a billowing black, purple, and white muumuu-like dress that concealed her feet. Her hair was caught up in a purple-and-black kerchief, and she wore large hoop enamel earrings decorated with big black crosses. A necklace of what had to be animal bones and chicken feet hung down over ample breasts.

"Are you the doctor?" Antonio blurted, sounding incredulous.

The woman smiled. "Doctor and *voudou mambo*. Voo-doo woman," she translated. "And let me tell you, *cher*, the drums are talking."

"How's Lucky?" Jenn and Antonio asked in the same breath.

The woman sighed and crossed herself. Antonio did the same.

"Not good," she confessed. "Father Juan is with him."

"Is he giving him last rites?" Antonio asked her. "What that means is—"

"I know what last rites are," she said. "I don't know if he has . . . yet."

She cleared her throat. "But I'm here now for *you, cher.* You've waited a long time to see me."

The woman untied Jenn's sling from behind her neck. The muscles in Jenn's forearm seized as the woman straightened her arm and began to unwrap the dressing.

"Nice work," she said, and Antonio lowered his head. "You did it? Are you a paramedic?"

"Of a sort," he said.

"I'm Alice Dupree, Marc's *maw-maw.* That's grand-mother to you folks."

"Antonio de la Cruz, *a sus órdenes,*" he replied, inclining his head.

"I'm just Jenn. Leitner," Jenn said, flashing with anger as she remembered Aurora's mocking tone. "Is this your house?"

Alice sighed. "Oh, no, Just Jenn. *Les Maudits* took my house years ago. Killed Marc's wife, too."

"I'm sorry for your losses," Jenn said through clenched teeth, trying not to show how much pain she was in.

"Maw-maw," Marc said, striding into the room, plant-ing a kiss on her cheek. He nodded to Antonio and Jenn. "How is she?"

"Can't say yet. Where you been?" she asked him.

"Making sure everybody's safe. We have to stay by here for a while. It's too hot for us in the Quarter. And we got bad *voudou* after us. Hope you can lend a hand."

Alice frowned as she inspected Jenn's arm. "How do you know you got *voudou*?"

"Did you see the blonde with the crazy braids? Her name is Skye. She says she's a witch, and I saw her make a ball of light. She was going to lead us to the new *doyenne* vampire in town, but she said something was blocking her. Then a bunch of vampires attacked us, and I'm wondering if they were tracking us through her."

Alice tsk-tsked and pursed her lips. "Could be. I'll make some talk tonight, see what I can come up with. You help me, *petit*?"

"*Oui*, Maw-maw, you know I will." Marc watched a moment. "Bullet?"

"Don't know, baby; get my bag," she said to Marc. "I'm a physician," she assured Jenn. "I had a practice in Algiers, across the river. Mayor shut me down, said I was patching up the rebels." She winked. "I was. Still am."

"Oh," Jenn said.

Marc left, returning with a large black leather bag, just like doctors had in old-timey movies, and Alice opened it.

"I heard you are all from Spain. You don't sound like you're from Spain. Why don't you tell me about it?" Alice asked Jenn.

"I'm from California," Jenn began. Then she felt a prick by her elbow, and her arm went numb from the funny bone down.

"That's just Lidocaine," Alice said. "Now I'll take a look around."

Marc leaned in closely. "Was she bitten?"

"Or shot?" Antonio asked.

"Doesn't look like either. I'd say cut. I'm cleaning it out. Then a few stitches."

"Does she need a blood transfusion?" Antonio asked.

"We don't have any units here." Alice's voice was tight.

Oh, God, she knows Antonio is a vampire, Jenn thought, tensing.

"That boy, Lucky, lost a lot of blood," Alice murmured. "He's very young . . ."

Of course, that was why she sounded so stressed. Not because of Antonio, but because a young boy might die. Jenn had to get a grip.

Not until we have Heather back.

"There, done. You'll need to rest," Alice told her, managing a small smile as scissors flashed and she held up a large needle and black suture thread. "Do you need something to help you sleep?"

"*Sí*, she does," Antonio broke in. "She's been under a lot of strain, and she's overtired."

"*Jenn?*" Alice asked pointedly, looking straight at her.

If vampires attacked tonight, she had to be ready. She couldn't be drugged. But Antonio had a point, patronizing as he was. She *was* overtired. She couldn't stop worrying about Heather.

"Can I have just a little something?" she asked. "Not to make me groggy, just to help me get to sleep. I might be needed."

"Yes, you might," Alice replied. She rummaged in her black bag. "Here."

"I'll get her some water," Antonio said.

He came back with a water bottle, and Alice gave her a small blue pill. She started to get sleepy almost immediately.

"Thank you," Jenn said faintly.

Jenn's eyelashes fluttered shut, and Antonio made the sign of the cross over her. Then he unfastened the Crusaders' cross Father Francisco had blessed and given to him the night he had fallen half dead into the Salamanca chapel back in 1942, begging for sanctuary—and put it around Jenn's neck. His fingers brushed her pulsing vein there, and he shut his eyes against the wave of intense desire that roared through him. It didn't have a shape—it wasn't physical lust or a craving for her blood—he simply *wanted*.

Antonio drew up a chair for a while, keeping vigil over Jenn as he had so many nights at the Academia. He was probably embarrassing her; she wore her insecurity about her role as a hunter like a patch on her sleeve. She tried hard to appear the equal of the others; didn't she know that she was?

Like the convent, the mansion had no electricity or running water, but as it had been used as a safe house for some time, there were battery-powered lights throughout. In the kitchen there was a propane stove and a refrigerator, and Suzy got to work preparing dinner. The mundane tasks attended to, Eriko, Marc, and Father Juan assembled to discuss strategy while Alice gathered together the ritual objects she needed to conduct her voodoo ceremony.

There was a lot of coming and going, with most rebels checking in with Marc. Marc was the leader of the Resistance, but there were dozens of small cells of threes and fours all over New Orleans and its surroundings, making it harder to kill the movement if a safe house were discovered.

Sighing, Antonio pulled his rosary from his pocket and held his beads, praying for Jenn, and the team, and the victory of humanity over his brethren.

Though he had been changed, he had not converted in the religious sense: He had not embraced the faith of his vampire sire, Sergio Almodóvar, who worshipped Orcus, lord of the underworld and punisher of those who broke their oaths. In the eyes of Sergio, Antonio had broken the most basic of vampiric oaths—absolute loyalty to one's maker. Instead he clung to the One True Faith, unsure if he could be saved from the fires of hell. The religion of Cursed Ones was not something understood or even heard of by most humans. Orcus was just one of the gods worshipped. It seemed as if each vampire worshipped a different one, fiercely loyal to that one alone. It was almost always the same god worshipped by their sire.

Someone behind him cleared his throat; Antonio turned to find Father Juan standing respectfully with his head bowed. He raised a brow, and Father Juan crooked his finger, beckoning him to follow. Antonio wrapped his rosary beads around his fist and rose.

"Señora Dupree is about to hold her voodoo ceremony," Father Juan said. "In my experience such rituals hold great power. I have a fear that her *loa* may expose you and Holgar."

Antonio pondered that. "Father, you've told me many times that the truth of God is like a prism, refracted in these various faiths. And it is our belief—yours and mine—that the faith we follow offers the clearest view."

"'For now we see through a glass, darkly,'" Father Juan confirmed, quoting Corinthians. "That's why I invite you to say Divine Office with me during the ceremony. As we pray together, perhaps your patron saint will shield you from scrutiny."

"And Holgar?" Antonio asked.

He smiled mischievously. "Maybe Saint Jude will watch out for him." St. Jude was the patron saint of lost causes.

"St. Jude is Jamie's patron saint," Antonio retorted.

"Let's go a bit apart," Father Juan suggested.

AD 1591, Peñuela, Spain
St. John of the Cross

John of the Cross was born Juan de Yepes Álvarez, and he was a converso: born as a son of the Jews, confessed as a child of the Church. His bed was hard, and the room was filled with light, and as he died, he made a final request:

Oh, my soul, take flight, live on, and do the work of my Heavenly Father. Live on, on the wings of the wind, in the beams of the sun. Bless and repair the world.

And as he sighed out all the troubles of the earthly world, he felt the goodness that he had been fly on the wings of angels, like God's own magick.

AD 1941, southwest France,
on the border with Spain
Antonio de la Cruz

The lowering clouds blanketed the rocky hills as Antonio and the survivors of his band fled the barrage of mortar and machine-gun fire down the steep slopes. One by one they disappeared into the scrubby maquis, underbrush, that had given them their name: the Maquis, freedom fighters. The Cross of Lorraine, the symbol of the Free French Forces, which he had joined as a volunteer, was stitched onto Antonio's rough woolen sweater. Now he was a Maquis—a maverick. Spain lay in tatters, pretending to be neutral, but the Spanish dictator Franco's loyalties lay with Adolf Hitler and his allies, Japan and Italy.

Antonio had fought against Franco at the very end of the civil war, which had ended two years before, in 1939. Now his targets were foreign invaders. In both instances he had disobeyed his spiritual advisor, Father Francisco, who had forbidden him to fight.

"God's people need prayers, not bullets," the old man had insisted as Antonio knelt before him in their little lady chapel. A statue of the Blessed Mother held out her arms, attired in a brown robe and a rope belt, like a friar. Father Francisco was tonsured, wearing a thin line of hair around his otherwise bald head, while Antonio retained the silky curls Beatriz had always complained were wasted on him.

"God's people need victories," Antonio had replied, sliding his hands into his robe as he bowed his head. He was nineteen—far too young to serve Mass for the ever-increasing numbers of Spanish widows and orphans, but the perfect age to take up a rifle on their behalf. His stomach was tight; he was trying to do the right thing. He hadn't taken his final vows—he was years from that—but he was committed to becoming a priest. Some days he felt as if his fatherless family had died as a sacrifice to his vocation. If he left Salamanca and joined the Free French Forces, would their deaths become meaningless?

"I do not release you to go," Father Francisco insisted.

Antonio considered. Fascinated that his last name—

de la Cruz—was the same name that St. John of the Cross had adopted upon becoming a Catholic, Antonio had studied the life of the saint, and he knew that St. John had been imprisoned and tortured by other Catholic priests for his beliefs. St. John had not submitted. He had escaped. And so one night, when Antonio's brothers in Christ were at vespers, Antonio left the seminary. He walked out the side door wearing a thin green shirt, dark brown canvas trousers, and boots. In the way of the Maquis he pulled his hair back in a ponytail and wore a black beret.

Before nightfall he also wore a carbine slung over his shoulder, and he had accepted a sweater pressed on him by a woman he met in a tavern called El Cocodrilo—the crocodile. The Free French Forces patch with its double cross was new and clean and had just been sewn on—for the woman's husband, who would never need it, as he had been executed against a brick wall three days before.

Antonio took the gift as a sign from God—the symbol of the Free French Forces was a cross topped with a smaller crossbar, and was also the symbol of Joan of Arc. The distraught, drunken woman had kissed him, thrusting her tongue into his mouth, and begged him to go to bed with her.

He thought of Lita and refused, as gently as he could.

Now he was here, in the dust and the dirt, fleeing the Germans, who steadily advanced like the unfeeling machines he believed them to be. All bloodless efficiency, routing the undesirables from their society—the very undesirables he, as a priest, wished to serve. Not only Jews, but the handicapped, the weak, and the defenseless. Soon Hitler would find all Spaniards and all Frenchmen undesirable. Of that Antonio had no doubt.

He ducked behind a juniper tree as bullets strafed his position. Ducking out, he shot back, rewarded with a cry.

Go to God, he told the soul of the fallen enemy.

And then there was a cry on his side—a shriek of agony. There were four other Maquis with him, fighting their way into the valley. They were all French, he the only Spaniard; two were brothers near his own age, the third a boy of twelve, and the last one, at seventy-four, was too old to fight. The old man's name was Pierre Louquet, and Antonio feared that it had been he who had been hit.

"Alors! Vite, Père Espagne!" called one of the brothers, probably Gaston. Father Spain—that was Antonio's nickname.

He pushed away from the juniper tree. Bullets whizzed past him; he could feel their heat. The brothers raced twenty feet ahead of him, each with a hand around the wrist of the boy, whom they called *Frère Jacques*—Brother John, as if they were family members.

He pushed off, practically flying right over Old Pierre, who was lying on his side, groaning. His wrinkled face and white hair were matted with dirt and blood.

Without a moment of hesitation Antonio bent down,

gathered him up, and slung him over his shoulders. The old man groaned in protest and muttered in French.

The extra weight made Antonio's descent unwieldy, and he could do nothing to protect himself or Old Pierre. If death came, then it came. He wasn't fearless—he didn't want to die—but if he died now, he felt that he would pass in a state of grace with the Lord of Heaven, saving the life of another.

But he hoped that he wouldn't die that day—or at the least, that it wouldn't hurt.

Perhaps in another world the French brothers and the boy would have berated him for weighing himself down with the dying old man. But this was the "good war," where the lines had been clearly drawn—freedom and life pitted against tyranny and death camps. A world reeling beneath evil, reaching hands to heaven for rescue.

And so the brothers and Jacques, who were good men, helped carry Old Pierre into the valley, and as the sun went down and it began to get cold, they took off their jackets and covered him with them. He'd been shot in the side, and there was no way to extract the bullet without making him suffer more, and he was already panting with pain. He was bleeding so badly that he probably wouldn't live the night. It was good that the dark was falling like a curtain; the Germans wouldn't be able to see the blood all over the branches and the ground.

The Maquis couldn't make a fire. The flames and smoke

would give them away. As quietly as they could, they broke out their food—bread, hard cheese, hard salami wrapped in brown paper. The men were all Catholic, and Antonio said the blessing. It was so dark, and so cold, and little Brother Jacques was thin, tired, and hungry. Antonio thought of his lost family, his sisters and Emilio, and of Lita, who would never have children, and a lump formed in his throat. So much innocence, destroyed. He gave Jacques his salami, telling the boy that he had eaten meat last Friday—an infraction of the rules, for good Catholics did not eat meat on Fridays—and so wished to do penance now. The brothers knew he was lying. Maybe Jacques did too, but he was too hungry to argue. He gobbled it down.

As was their custom, one man stood watch while the others tried to rest. All were aware of the enemy creeping through the forest. Antonio kept vigil beside Old Pierre. Scudding clouds freed the moon, and Antonio saw the man's closed eyes, his deeply sunken cheeks, the grizzle on his chin. His breathing was labored. Did Antonio have dispensation to give the man extreme unction, last rites? He did not. He was only a seminarian.

Old Pierre opened his eyes. His lips moved. His heart thundering, Antonio bent low.

"Confession," the man managed to say.

I'm not a priest. I can't do this, Antonio thought. But he reached in his pocket and retrieved his rosary, which he kissed and wrapped around the gnarled fingers. Then he made the sign of the cross over the wispy white head and said, *"Oui, mon fils."* Yes, my son.

"I killed . . . I . . ." The man began to cough. Gaston, who was keeping watch, looked at Antonio and wildly shook his head.

As gently as possible Antonio covered Old Pierre's mouth. The man stopped coughing. Antonio took his hand away, leaning toward the chapped, thin lips.

". . . a man . . . not in wartime . . ."

The creeping in the forest was louder. *Whoosh, whoosh,* like the mistral wind. *Germans.* Jacques sat up, his pinched face wide with terror. Gaston, their sentry, pointed with the barrel of his rifle toward the trees. The brothers and Antonio looked somberly at each other, and then, like three fathers, at Jacques.

Antonio murmured to them in French, *"Allez-y."* Go. "Leave Old Pierre and me here."

"Père Espagne, non," whispered the little boy, his eyes huge as saucers.

The brothers wanted to argue. Everyone knew there was no time. Antonio would remain behind, with the dying old man. Silently, the other three rose, and Père Espagne blessed them, for what would be the last time. Then they melted into the junipers and beeches.

Antonio heard a bird trill, and gazed up at the moon. He crossed himself and wished desperately for some oil. He spied the brown paper wrapping for the salami and pressed his fingertips against it. Tentatively he tapped his thumb against his forefinger, hoping that some residue of fat had been transferred to his skin. Then he took a breath and found courage in the ancient rite of his faith, intoning the blessing for the dying in the language of popes and monks. Closing his eyes to find the light within, the light of his soul, he began:

"Per istam sanctam unctionem, et suam püssimam misericordiam indulgeat tibi Dominus quidquid deliquisti per visum, auditum, odoratum, gustum et locutionem, tactum et gressum."

"Ah, ah," Old Pierre groaned, and Antonio opened his eyes. The wounded man was staring past Antonio with a look of pure horror. Antonio knew there was someone behind him.

A German, he thought. *And now I meet my Lord.*

He was partially right.

CHAPTER SIXTEEN

We are strong of mind and heart
Mesmerism our deadly art
We can seduce even the most pure
From our control there is no cure
So resist us now if you can
Declare your loyalty only to man
But in the night you'll beg and crawl
On your knees you soon will fall

AD 1941, SOUTHWESTERN FRANCE
ANTONIO AND SERGIO

The invader in the forest was not a German, and he didn't wear the uniform of a soldier or a Maquis. Although Antonio didn't know it then, the stranger was, however, dressed for battle. Clad in darkest black from his turtleneck sweater to his wool trousers, boots, and heavy wool coat, he sought to charm his victim. Raven-black hair like Antonio's hung loose over his shoulders, and beneath heavy eyebrows fringed with thick black lashes his eyes burned with hellfire. When he smiled, his two long, white fangs extended over his upper lip.

"*Buenas noches*, little priest," he said. "Don't let me interrupt you."

Antonio couldn't move. He stared in uncomprehending horror at the man, the demon.

. . . *un vampiro.*

Time stopped. For how long he couldn't say. Then a breath shot into his lungs, shaking him from his reverie. He crossed himself and murmured, "*Madre de Dios, Santa Maria, me protege.*"

The vampire drew back slightly, then folded his arms over his chest and cocked his head, looking down at Old Pierre, who gasped and gargled.

"He's suffering," he said. "Your god must be very happy."

"The angels are waiting for him," Antonio said, and his voice cracked like a little boy's. Nothing at the seminary, nothing on the earth or in the heavens, had prepared him for this moment. A vampire. A vampire.

A vampire.

"I can end his suffering," *el vampiro* said. His voice was low, very soothing, as he glided toward Antonio. His red eyes shimmered in the night. "For a price."

"His soul belongs to God," Antonio replied, putting his arms around Old Pierre, covering the old man's body with his.

"I wasn't speaking of his soul. I was speaking of yours," the vampire said in a deep, resonant voice. "That is my price."

Not understanding, Antonio remained silent.

"Let me begin again." He swept a bow. "I am Sergio Almodóvar, and I am the king of the vampires of Spain."

Antonio didn't reply. The vampire gestured to Old Pierre.

"I can turn him into one of my own. And *sí*, most assuredly, when I do that, his soul will be taken, and sent down to my lord, Orcus, whom I worship. He rules the underworld, where all our souls await us."

"No," Antonio said, protecting Old Pierre with his body. He pressed his lips against Old Pierre's ear and whispered the last line of the prayer for the dying: *"Benedicat te omnipotens Deus, Pater, et Filius, et Spiritus Sanctus."* May almighty God bless you, Father, and Son, and Holy Spirit.

"Amen," the vampire said, sounding amused. "Oh, my poor priest, no one is listening."

"Someone is," Antonio insisted.

"Very well. Believe your pretty little story."

"It's not just a story. It is the *truth*. Unlike your ugly nightmare," Antonio said. "We both know who rules the underworld."

"*I* do, because I serve him," the vampire replied. "And I have met him."

"Then you're both mad *and* evil."

"Scrappy. You're in the full bloom of your youth, as *I* was, before I was blessed with eternal life. I was freed on my twentieth birthday." He squared his shoulders and lifted his chin. Sharp profile, noble nose, firm jaw. "And so I'll remain, while other men age, wither, and turn to dust."

"And they will be reborn into the fullness of the Holy Spirit," Antonio countered.

"It's sad. You seem intelligent. But now, hear the rest of the bargain."

The demon unfolded his arms, and the air around him seemed to harden with evil. "I will take that man while you watch, and turn him into a vampire. I will deliver his soul unto Orcus, and he will run with me. Or I will spare him and turn *you* into a vampire."

Antonio blinked. He was suddenly very cold. Shivering, he tightened his arms around Old Pierre, then lowered him to the ground and grabbed the crucifix around the old man's hand.

"No," Antonio said, showing it to the vampire.

The vampire averted his gaze. There was something in his bearing that was very noble, ancient, and graceful. He was no ravening minion of the Devil. An aristocrat, with manners.

"Think a moment," the vampire said, raising his hand to shield his view. "You became a priest to secure a place in heaven for your soul. Everything you do is a bargain with God, calculated to prove that you've behaved well enough to dwell with the saints and the angels forever."

He lifted one of his dark brows. Despite the way he carried himself, he did look very young—even younger than Antonio, who was careworn from the fight.

"Don't you find it the least bit mortifying, all this cajoling and keeping track? Three Hail Marys, one Our Father . . . don't you wish to conduct yourself with more dignity?"

"No. I've heard the Word, and it's my pleasure to obey," Antonio said. *Except I did not obey,* he thought. *I left the seminary. Was that truly God's will, or my own?*

"If I turn you into a vampire, you will never see your supposed God in heaven. *Never.* And all this effort—the poverty, the chastity, the obedience, endless prayers, Masses, fasting, everything—will have been for nothing, because you'll go to hell anyway. This I don't simply believe—

"I *know* it."

Antonio couldn't swallow. He could barely breathe.

"But hell is not as bad as you've been told." He chuckled. "It's actually exquisite. It is a place of light, and pleasure. And you will be free from all your religious strictures, so you can actually enjoy it. That is what I offer you, my Spanish brother."

Antonio extended his arm, dangling the crucifix from his fist.

"No."

"The cross in your hand is very small," the vampire said. "It weighs as much as a handful of sand. Nevertheless, soon your arm will tire."

This time the vampire looked Antonio full on. He took a deliberate step forward, toward Antonio. The hair on the back of Antonio's neck stood on end. The hand holding the crucifix swayed.

"No," he repeated.

"You misunderstand. There is no refusing. There is you, or him."

Antonio lifted his chin in defiance, but tears of despair welled in his eyes. The vampire was right. Antonio had never realized until that moment that the threat of damnation had hung over his head like a sword fastened to the ceiling with a strand of human hair. Was it love or fear that had motivated his search for holiness?

It doesn't matter. I'll wait him out until the sun rises, Antonio thought. *Or . . .*

He looked down.

Old Pierre was dead.

The vampire smiled.

"Know me," he said. "Serve me. I will bring you into a joyous life, one free of the fear of sin and hell. And death. Really, Padre, I'm doing you a favor."

"I would rather die."

"Sorry. My sire gave me no choice, and I thank him every day for that. The choice I gave you expired along with the old man."

Then he attacked.

THE MANSION ON THE BAYOU
TEAM SALAMANCA AND THE RESISTANCE

Eriko watched, bemused, as Marc placed bones, rocks, piles of crystals, dishes of water containing hen's eggs, and candles on a long table covered with the black and purple fabric his grandmother had handed him. So many *things*. It was very different from Buddhism, which required one to detach from possessions. To detach from *desire*. It was wanting, craving, hungering that created the suffering of the world. Weren't the vampires evidence of this? Their entire existence depended on satisfying their addiction to blood.

Devout Buddhists leaned to control even their breathing, the most necessary requirement of human life. Eriko had not started out as a devout Buddhist. She'd been a modern Japanese schoolgirl.

In the days of old Japan, the Sakamotos of Kyoto had been a proud, venerable samurai family, known for their fearlessness in battle. They hadn't been afraid to die; they'd only been afraid to do less than their best. The Sakamotos of modern Japan were also about being the best, doing their best. Despite their Buddhist beliefs, they worshipped perfectionism.

When the vampires stepped out of the shadow of Mount Fuji, Eriko and her friends had been so excited. She was ten, and it was like all her best anime shows and comic books come to life. The war never came to Japanese shores, and her parents shielded her from it anyway.

By the time of the truce her life was *fun*. Fourteen was the best year of her life. After she got home from school, she changed out of her dull navy-blue uniform and into little shocking-pink plaid skirts, pink-and-orange polka-dotted kneesocks, and big hair with ponytails, and zoomed all over downtown Kyoto with her very best friends, Yuki and Mara. Shopping, drinking coffee, flirting with boys and businessmen. Earbuds drowning out the boring world, she doodled little vampires with big red eyes all over her school notebooks and went to Eigamura, the old movie lot and theme park (like the American Universal Studios!) on Sundays to watch all the themed pop bands—the Elvises, the goths—queue around the entrance to dance and sing. To her the vampires had a lot of style, wearing their hair long over their shoulders, or up in ponytails like samurai warriors. They were very polite to the emperor on TV, bowing deeply to him. How cool was that?

She, Mara, and Yuki started a vampire-boys fan club, creating a website filled with poetry and fan art. They called the Cursed Ones the Cute Ones and wrote and recorded a song about them on their website. Then they formed a band of their own and dressed like schoolgirl vampires, in starched short skirts with red ruffles, and knee socks decorated with little red hearts, with two tiny hearts on each of their necks, fangs'-width apart. They called themselves the Vampire Three.

The Vampire Three were a huge hit. They got fan e-mails from vampires, or boys pretending to be vampires. They were building up their nerve to meet up with one of them, a guy who called himself Shell Ghost Shogun. It was going to be on a Friday night, at a club called Missing Dreams, at ten.

They were supposed to meet at Mara's at seven to get ready. But Yuki didn't show. She didn't call, didn't text.

She was missing.

The police searched everywhere; no one had a clue where to find her, what had happened to her. She became a face on a poster. Eriko wrote a haiku on their website:

Fog rolls into sea
Sea rolls into universe
Universe shatters

Mara and Eriko spent hours searching for Yuki, then days, and weeks; both of them were failing school. Both of them got grounded, and Eriko was furious. Didn't their parents *want* Yuki to be found?

She was fuming about it with Mara on Skype when Yuki showed up in Mara's bedroom. Watching Mara chat away while Yuki stalked up behind her, eyes blazing, fangs glistening, Eriko screamed at Mara to run, get out of there, now, *abunai*, danger —

Next thing Yuki grabbed Mara from behind, around her neck, throwing her to the floor. Then the vampire that had once been Yuki bent over Mara, holding her down, and tore out her throat.

Eriko couldn't stop screaming. Her face covered with blood, the vampire Yuki crawled to Mara's screen and stared into it, straight into Eriko's eyes, and grinned. Eyes to eyes. Her fangs looked like fingernails dipped in scarlet polish.

Then the screen went blank.

Eriko told her parents. She told anyone who would listen. But the Sakamotos soon learned that talking in public invited trouble. Eriko's mother found her cat, Nekko, dead in the gutter behind their house. She had not died well. A bloody handprint on their front door came next.

The police did nothing.

Then they got a visit from Mara's father, who was practically a ghost, a ghost of sorrow. He had discovered that among an elite group of samurai families, warriors called *karyuudo* had been trained for centuries, quietly battling the demonic *kyuuketsuki* — vampires — that took down emperors and peasants alike. When vampires had been a secret, so had the warriors—Hunters—who fought them.

Eriko had a brother named Kenji, and he halfheartedly volunteered to go to a training facility nearby. Eriko *begged* to go instead. Kenji looked relieved and told their parents that it was fine with him.

But their father refused. Kenji had to go. Kenji was his son.

And Eriko was just his daughter.

She didn't know why she was so shocked. A *gaijin*, a foreigner, might think Japanese attitudes toward women had changed through the centuries, but men like her father weren't that unusual. She tried to go anyway, but the *sensei*— the master of the Kyoto school—told her that she was there for the wrong reason. One did not become a vampire hunter to avenge the death of a single person.

Then she heard about the school in Spain. They took non-Spanish students. So she cut her hair in an act of mourning; in an act of defiance she went to Spain; and she trained harder than even Jamie O'Leary and studied more than Skye York and pushed and pushed and pushed, all the time remembering how Mara had struggled against her fate, and how Yuki had laughed; and if Eriko could kill every vampire in the world, it wouldn't be enough.

Kenji became the Hunter of Kyoto six months before Eriko was chosen to become the Salamanca Hunter, and he staked Yuki three nights later. Eriko's father e-mailed her in Spain and told her to come home. Her friend had been avenged. But Eriko was in too deep; she couldn't back out now, and when she drank down the elixir, she assumed a place among the samurai of Japan, at least in her mind.

It was then that she embraced Buddhism, among the extreme statues and pageantry of the Catholic church. She gave away all her plaid skirts and her Hello Kitty messenger bag and all her notebooks with anime stickers on them, and wore only black.

But something was *missing*. She didn't know how to explain it, and she didn't try. Father Juan had made his choice, yet she had a sense that it had been a mistake. She didn't feel like a true Hunter, like a samurai. She wondered if it was because Kenji had done what she wanted to do. She would never be able to stake Yuki through the heart.

"Our numbers have gone way down," Marc said, jerking her back to the moment as he helped his grandmother prepare her voodoo altar. Night had fallen two hours ago, and Bernard and Jamie were patrolling the perimeter. "A year ago, for every death in action, we'd get two new recruits. But the people around here who hate the vampires have lost hope. They don't think we can win. So they just walk the walk."

He looked at Eriko as if he wanted something. He was holding the skull of an animal in his hands—very weird, she thought.

"Do you?" he asked her, setting the skull on the altar. "Think we can win?"

"That's not how I think," she replied. "Every day I wake up, I hope I can kill a vampire. That's all I hope for."

"Oh."

She saw the intense grief behind his eyes, and felt it too. She had so many bonds with her team, but she felt that she was letting them down too, the way she had let down Mara. Maybe her father was right, and she wasn't meant to do this.

I am, she thought. Then her calf muscles cramped, and she winced.

"Are you all right?" he asked her.

"Why so many bones?" Skye asked Alice.

Marc turned and looked at Skye now—fascinated, a bit guarded. He was half in love with her. Or maybe he was just horny. Skye was oblivious; all her attention was trained on what Alice was doing. Eriko's mouth twitched; Skye's classical White-magick training had not included voodoo.

"I don't know, honey," Alice replied, scattering them on the table. "I just know I need them. My *loa* comes when I have everything proper."

"Your *loa*," Skye said, looking over her shoulder at Eriko. Eriko didn't react. Skye pursed her lips and turned back around.

Sensing she was somehow not meeting Skye's expectations, Eriko got back to business. She walked around the dimly lit room as if she were patrolling it. How had the vampires known to attack them in the tunnel? Were they outside the mansion, getting ready to attack them again?

What is our mission? she wondered. *The Salamancans. What exactly are we doing?*

Alice had picked up a long black feather and a glass filled with something that looked like colored sand. She dipped the tip of the feather in the sand and made sprinkling motions in the air. "My *loa* is like a god. The spirit that talks to me," she finally answered Skye.

"How?" Skye persisted

"Through me." Alice nodded at Marc, who walked past Eriko into the shadows, then returned with a large drum. Eriko jerked slightly; it reminded her of the drums of Obon, the festival of the dead they celebrated in Japan with dancing and cleaning the graves of their ancestors. "You will have to be my witnesses. I won't know what I'm saying."

Marc sat cross-legged on the floor to the side of the table. Alice said, "Help me, please," and handed glasses of water with eggs inside them to Skye and Eriko. "Place them around Marc."

Eriko did as instructed and then moved to the back of the room and watched as Marc began to play the drum in a steady, hypnotic rhythm. Alice stood before her altar, picking up objects and putting them down as if she were looking for something. Skye moved in closely, scrutinizing her every move, as if memorizing it. Ever since her return from Aurora's court, Skye had been very subdued. Team Salamanca had endured another surprise attack — or maybe it wasn't so surprising. Vampires knew how to look for prey.

"*Loa* are like our patron saints. My *loa* is Ma'man Brigit, patroness of cemeteries," Alice said, swaying to the drum. "She'll guard your grave . . . if there's a cross on it." She winked. "Sound familiar?"

"Really?" Skye asked, startled. "And if there's not?"

"Then your enemy could turn you into a zombie," Alice said, laying down the feather and putting a purple candle on the table. "She's the wife of Baron Samedi."

"And who is he?"

"The lord of the dead. Did you know that vampires worship different gods, same as people?" She nodded. "That's right. Not a lot of Catholics among the vampires."

"We have heard the same thing," Skye said smoothly.

"That's why they refer to their transformation as a conversion. Rising to a new way of life."

"But if the vampires of New Orleans worship Baron Samedi—"

"Lot of human folks worship him too. And Ma'man Brigit is a sweet lady. Scary-looking, but sweet. She cures people, like I do." Alice nodded. "Especially those who are close to death because of magick."

"Really?" Skye said, eyes widening. "That's brilliant. Might that include vampire attacks?"

"No." Alice added two more purple candles, and then a black one. "She also exacts revenge, if she feels it's warranted."

"Sounds like a good *loa* to have on our side," Skye said. "What do you think, Eriko?"

Though she stood in the darkness, Eriko felt as if a spotlight were being shone on her. "I'm a Buddhist," she replied. "I don't have a god, actually."

"Then what do you put your faith in, child?" Alice asked.

"My people," Eriko replied. But did she?

She ran down her team. Jamie and Antonio hated vampires as much as she did. *Or at least they pretend to.*

Jenn's sister had been kidnapped by the vampires. *If the girl Skye saw was even her sister.* Skye never expressed hatred for the vampires, and with her goth clothes and her inability to use offensive magick, she could easily be hiding a heart that beat for vampires, or one in particular. Antonio? Someone back in England? She could be so secretive.

If I can become a hunter because I wanted to kill one, she could become a hunter because she wanted to save one. Father Juan has trained us all, taught us to kill vampires. Yet he harbors one, even feeds him when we aren't watching.

And that left Holgar. The werewolf made the least sense to her. She had no idea what drove him, no idea why he wanted to be a hunter when most of his kind pledged allegiance to the Cursed Ones. Everyone liked him because he was funny, everyone except Jamie.

Maybe Jamie's right not to trust him. We really know nothing about him.

Maybe I don't have any faith, after all.

Alice watched her closely. "Faith can move mountains.

It's the worst kind of hell, not having anything to believe in."

Marc continued to play the drums. Alice struck a match and lit the purple candles. As each candle flared with a yellow flame, the shadows shifted and moved around the room, almost as if they were taking shape. The atmosphere in the room shifted too, as if the ceiling had lowered five feet, and Eriko frowned, unsure that this ritual was a good idea. If something went wrong, well, they already had enough to contend with.

Still, she watched, unsure how much time passed. It seemed like hours. The rhythm of the drumbeat picked up, and Alice, positioning herself in front of the voodoo altar, began to move her hips seductively. Eriko was a little shocked; it was very sexual. Then Skye joined Alice, facing her, mimicking her movements. The two undulated like belly dancers. Skye let her head fall back, and Alice danced around her, rocking her pelvis and rolling her shoulders.

Marc's eyes closed, and his lips parted, as if in ecstasy.

"Ah," Skye gasped, in a voice that sounded like someone having sex. From her observation post Eriko ran her hand over her hair. "Oh, ahhhh."

"Ma'man Brigit," Alice murmured, thrusting her hips and running her hands down her sides. "*Écoutez-moi.* Listen to me."

"Oh, oh," Skye cried, raising her hands over her head.

Scowling, Eriko turned on her heel and went in search of Father Juan. The drums followed her down the hall as she strode into the makeshift sickroom, the walls covered with tatters of scrolled wallpaper, the floor swept clean, where Lucky lay on a mattress covered with sheets. There was another mattress on the other side of the room, and a pair of house slippers that looked to be Alice's size.

Father Juan and Antonio knelt beside Lucky, whose face was ashen. Antonio was holding out what appeared to be a missal or a Bible of some sort so that Father Juan could read from it. The older man was wearing a black sash over his shoulders. A little dish of what appeared to be oil sat beside his knee, and a white candle. Oil glistened on Lucky's forehead. So they were conducting a ritual as well. It all seemed a little crazy to her. More than a little crazy, actually.

Father Juan stopped speaking, and he and Antonio looked up at her. She could hear the drums and Alice moaning, and her face went hot.

"Maybe the voodoo ceremony is an unusual idea," she began.

The moaning grew louder.

Father Juan glanced from her to Antonio and back again. Obviously, they both could hear what was going on, but they were looking at her as if she needed to explain herself. Abashed, she stared down at the floor. She didn't want to start something with Father Juan.

Finally, the priest said, "Voodoo is very unusual to us. But not to these people."

"*Ah so desuka*, I see," she murmured, keeping her eyes downward because in Japan that was very polite. At least that was what she told herself. Maybe it was so he couldn't see her grinding her teeth.

For a moment no one spoke. Eriko kept staring at the same square of floor.

The drumming grew louder. The cries more intense.

She wanted to die.

Father Juan cleared his throat. "Eriko, could you stay here? I think we need to talk some strategy and tactics."

Finally. Thank you, Eriko thought.

"*Hai, hai, sensei,*" she answered, bowing. Eriko sank down in the traditional Japanese *seiza* position, folding back her lower legs and resting her butt on her heels.

"I'm going to check on Jenn," Antonio said; at Father Antonio's nod, he got to his feet.

The drumming and the moans jerked Jenn awake from a terrible dream. She'd been crying in her sleep, something about Heather.

Dizzily, she sat up and slung her legs over the side of the settee. Someone had taken off her boots. She stepped into them and, without buckling them, got to her feet. She was starving. She wasn't sure where the kitchen was, but if she followed all the drumming she'd be able to find someone who could tell her.

Antonio was in the hall; he looked surprised to see her

up; then his smile faded, and she looked down at herself. Her jacket had been taken off, and her body armor as well, but her black sweater was stiff with blood.

"Jenn." Antonio drew her to him and put his arms around her. She let herself rest against him for a moment, but the groaning embarrassed her—or was it her uncertainty about how he would react to all the blood?—and she pulled away.

"Is that Alice and *Skye*?" she asked him. Her cheeks burned.

"Voodoo is a religion of ecstasy," he replied, keeping his arm loosely around her shoulders. "You must be hungry."

"Yes, but I want to see what they're doing." She made a little face. "Unless they're dancing around naked or something."

"That'd be a sight, no?" he said, smiling faintly. Living in such close quarters, Jenn had seen most of her team members in various stages of nakedness, except for Antonio. It actually made him sexier, if that were possible.

She took a step down the hall, a little surprised and disappointed when he stayed put, letting his arm slide off her shoulders. He shrugged.

"Father Juan and I thought it best for me to stay out of Alice's way. In fact," he continued, "I've been thinking that it might be better if I leave."

Now it was his turn to look surprised, as if he hadn't meant to say that. But he looked thoughtful and nodded to himself.

"*Por supuesto.* That's exactly what I should do."

"No," she said, but at the same moment something settled around her, fiery hot and exciting, something that felt so *good*, and she entwined herself around him, parting her lips. She wanted him. All of him. It would be so wonderful.

"Antonio," she breathed, turning toward him.

"Jenn." His hands caught her face. "Jenn." His eyes took on a red tint. When he looked down at her, she almost couldn't breathe. The drums vibrated through the floor and the bones in his hands.

"Antonio . . ." She couldn't say his name enough. Couldn't be close enough. The drumbeat ran up and down her spine, playing her, and pounded deep inside her bones like a pulse. It commanded the rhythm of her heart.

She put her arms around his neck and threw back her head, offering herself. And he felt warm, finally, and he was heating her blood.

"Please," she whispered.

"*Ay, no, amor, no,*" he murmured.

"Antonio." She loved him, loved his name, loved who he was.

Do you love what he is? asked a voice inside her head.

She ignored it.

"Jenn," he whispered. His lips parted, and he kissed her mouth, then her upper and lower lip. Tingles skittered through her body; his arms tightened around her. They held each other.

Wanted each other.

Do you want what he is?

Then his lips touched her throat, and he groaned. She felt as though someone had set her on fire. She wanted him to bite her.

"Yes," she whispered, clinging to him. "Yes, Antonio."

And then he hissed.

"Ay," he ground out in agony, and pushed her away from him.

She fell backward with a cry, and the world spun; as she collapsed, someone picked her up and carried her down the hall.

The corridor rocked; she moaned, dizzy and weak. And then she saw that Father Juan was the one who was carrying her.

"What happened?" she whispered.

"One more second and I would have had to kill him," the priest said tightly.

He carried her into a small room lit by a candle. Jenn's head lolled to the left. Eriko was there, huddled beside Lucky, looking grim. And Jenn knew that Lucky's luck had run out. He was dead.

"No," Jenn whispered. "No."

Her sight blurred, and she sank into the black.

CHAPTER SEVENTEEN

Salamanca Hunter's Manual: Your Duty

Know this: You are locked in combat with the forces of evil. For so long as you honor your holy calling, God's grace will shine on you as the sun on the vine. Do not waver. All vampires are evil, and they beget the sons of evil. You must never waste an opportunity to end the existence of such a one; otherwise, it is the same as if you have spilled the blood of innocents yourself.

(translated from the Spanish)

NEW ORLEANS
TEAM SALAMANCA AND THE RESISTANCE

Someone pressed a spoon to Jenn's lips; it was beef broth, and she eagerly opened her mouth. She thought she heard

Alice's voice, then Skye's. Someone was arguing. Someone else was speaking in French.

She drifted and dozed. Someone stayed with her. Someone kissed her forehead and the back of her hand. That someone had cold skin.

When she opened her eyes, she was lying in a bed against the wall of the room. Seated in a wooden chair, Antonio was staring at her, and Skye sat beside him, knitting something out of moss-green yarn.

"*Buenos tardes,*" Antonio said, and Skye looked up from her knitting. She cried out and threw her arms around Jenn.

"Oh, thank Goddess, Jenn!" She turned to Antonio. "Please tell Dr. Alice that Jenn's awake."

"*Sí,*" Antonio said, looking one last time at Jenn and then rushing from the room.

"What happened? What time is it?"

She tried to sit up, but Skye forced her down, laying a hand on her head.

"Easy, Jenn," she said. "You've had a high fever. You've been out of it for three days."

"*What?*" Jenn croaked.

"Yes." Skye reached down to a light blue plastic basin and retrieved a wet washcloth, which she wrung and then used to gently wipe Jenn's face. It was icy, and Jenn jerked away. "Do you know, Antonio's been going outside in the cold mornings, and then coming and putting his hands on your face, to bring your fever down. That's really awfully sweet, in a very strange way."

"Have we found my sister?" Jenn asked, grabbing Skye's hand and searching the witch's face. There were rings under Skye's eyes, and she was very pale.

Skye sighed heavily. "Teams have been searching for Aurora's lair. We think she must have moved. I'm so sorry, Jenn. But there's time yet." She took a deep breath. "We think."

"What do you mean?" Now Jenn did sit up, forcing Skye's hand away and frowning at her. "Tell me what's going on."

"Well, you see, what we didn't realize is that Mardi Gras is not just a one-day event here in New Orleans. They've been celebrating in the French Quarter for almost two weeks now, with smaller parades and such. We missed one the day we arrived, in fact. The biggest days are the last three, when the big parades and balls are held. There are these groups called krewes; they're like clubs, and they put on the parades—"

"Skye, *please*, get to the point."

"I'm sorry. Well, the point is, that from what you told us, Aurora threatened to convert Heather 'at' Mardi Gras." She made air quotes. "But we're wondering if she meant the actual night of Mardi Gras, or during the Mardi Gras season."

"No, she said in nine days," Jenn insisted. Then she

stopped. "Wait, I'm not sure she said that." She covered her face. "Oh, my God. What if it's already happened?"

"Jenn, I checked with the Circuit. They're trying to help, throwing the stones, doing magicks. I've been working with Alice, but we've not come up with an answer. But at night we can hear voodoo drums. And when the Resistance fighters come in, they tell us that there's increased activity in the graveyards. The voodoo sorcerers are warning their followers not to go out at night."

"Jenn," said Alice, sweeping into the room. She was wearing a purple fleece bathrobe over a white flannel night-gown. "How are you feeling? Are you in pain?"

"I was just bringing her up to date," Skye said. "It was rather upsetting, I'm afraid."

Alice pursed her lips. "I have some news. I've contacted Papa Dodi, and he's going to help us."

She looked at the two Salamancans, then tapped her forehead lightly. "Sorry. Of course you don't know who he is. He's the most respected *voudou bokor* in the state of Louisiana, and he lives in New Orleans. If *anybody* can get the *loa* to tell us where your sister is, he's the one."

"Thank you," Jenn said fervently. Then she had a vague memory of how she had behaved during Alice's voodoo ceremony, crawling all over Antonio, and flushed.

At that moment Antonio entered the room. He looked not at Jenn, but at Alice.

"One of Marc's soldiers just arrived. Andrew, the one

with the red hair? We're going to the French Quarter to try Bourbon Street again. We might have a lead."

"I'll go too," Jenn said.

"I as well," Skye offered.

"No," Antonio said, finally looking at Jenn. For less than a second. "You're too weak. And as for you, Skye, Doña Alice has told me that since Papa Dodi has offered to help, you and she should conduct another ceremony. No?" He turned to Alice for confirmation.

"That's right." Alice nodded at Skye. "Midnight tonight."

Antonio was behaving oddly; he wouldn't look at Jenn. His profile was sharp against the soft light in the room as he lowered his head.

"We'll be back before dawn," he said, and turned to go.

"Antonio?" Jenn asked in a small voice.

Then he did turn, and she saw a wash of scarlet in his eyes. From her position Alice couldn't see, but Skye could.

"Be careful," the witch said, effectively dismissing him.

He said nothing more, but simply left.

Jenn welled up, and Alice cleared her throat. "I'll see if there's something a little more substantial to eat. You need to make up for lost calories."

Jenn nodded mutely. When Alice was gone, Skye put the washcloth back in the plastic basin and dried her hands. She leaned forward and made circular motions with her hands, murmuring to herself in Latin.

"Healing spell," she said when she was done. Then she

took a breath. "I think we need to speak about Antonio. He's been having a rough time of it."

Jenn's face went hot, even though a chill centered at the base of her spine. "What do you mean?"

"Around you. You affect him too much." Jenn stiffened, and Skye leaned forward, as if needing her to pay close attention to what she was saying. "I know that you care about him. But sometimes, no matter how much you want to be with someone, it just doesn't work."

Swallowing hard, Jenn tried to clear her throat. "Do you really think this is the time to talk about this? My sister is in danger for her *life*."

"Yes, yes, I do," Skye answered. "We have a lot of strangers helping us. They've committed their lives to killing Cursed Ones. It was bad of us not to tell Marc and his fighters that I'm a witch. No one really knows about werewolves, so I don't suppose Holgar's in danger of discovery."

She bit her lower lip and dropped her gaze down to her hands. "But maybe you should think about Antonio in all this. What they would do to him if they found out that he's a vampire? Or to the rest of us?"

Then, without another word, she turned and walked out of the room—leaving Jenn staring after her, speechless, and fearing, in her heart, that Skye was right.

After Skye left her room, Jenn got up and took a walk with Father Juan up and down the hallways of the house.

She leaned on his arm, moving like an old lady.

They came to a room where several of their hosts were gathered around a radio. A thin voice was speaking, and she strained to make out the words through the static.

"It's not hopeless, but you can't give in. They have weaknesses. Sunlight, fire, beheading, wood through the heart. These can all kill vampires, as you know. Holy water, crucifixes can burn them. Take your garlic tablets. Rub garlic cloves over the skin on your throat and wrists so they will be unable to feed from you. Tattoo crosses on your body so you can burn them with a touch."

Jenn smiled faintly. Half of Jamie's tattoos had a cross of some kind in them. *Must be his long-lost twin.*

The man on the radio continued. *"The government of Cuba, the last country on this side of the ocean to keep the faith, signed a free-trade agreement with the vampires today. Rumors have it that Spain is about to recognize Solomon as the official ambassador of what is being referred to behind closed doors as the Vampire Nation."*

Everyone in the room gasped and looked at Father Juan. His face was white.

"Can that be true?" she said. "*What* vampire nation?"

"Do not despair, though. Every day people are taking back their towns, their villages, and one day soon their cities. And I have a special message now for our listeners in New Orleans."

Jenn jumped. Everyone else did as well. She moved closer, Father Juan still supporting her, and held her breath.

"Let it burn."

There were disbelieving protests all around.

"You are needed elsewhere desperately, and the city is already irretrievably lost. And now we must end this transmission. I am Kent, and you have been listening to the Voice of the Resistance."

"Who is he?" Jenn asked.

One of the men shook his head. "Nobody knows. Nobody knows where he is or how he manages to keep from getting caught."

"This type of thing happened in World War Two," Father Juan noted.

"Yeah, but this isn't the 1940s. Technology should have been able to track this guy and shut him down months ago. It's a miracle he's still doing it."

"Then we must pray that it continues," Father Juan said, pulling Jenn away from the door. They continued walking.

Let it burn. It was weird, but she almost felt like he'd been talking directly to her. She would love to leave the city, run far and fast, but she couldn't, not without Heather.

Hiding, secret transmissions—it wasn't her life. She thought of her grandparents and all that they had seen and experienced. They would have been so much better equipped to deal with this than she was.

She wished she could call her grandmother. She hoped she and her mother were safe. As for her father—

I hope the vampires killed him.

"Ow," Father Juan said. She was digging her nails as she clutched his arm. He looked at her. "Jenn?"

"I hate him," she whispered. "If he were here, I'd kill him myself."

"Then for your sake I hope you never see him again." He stopped walking, turned, and faced her. Putting both his hands on her shoulders, he cocked his head, his face softened by grief and understanding.

"Jenn, take this hatred and put it into your fight. But don't let it fester in your heart." He smoothed a tendril of her auburn hair out of her eyes. "We all try so hard to be just, and to be fair, but the truth is, we're only a heartbeat away from sin. From letting out the beast . . ."

"Hello, Mester Jens," Holgar said cheerily from the other end of the hall. He was wearing the same sweater and jeans he'd arrived in days ago. Everyone was. "Speaking of the devil, eh?" There was a strangely forced giddiness in his tone. He made claws out of his hands and showed his teeth. "I'm a beast, loaded with extra sin?"

Father Juan looked unfazed. "Holgar, you know that's not what I meant," he replied. "You should get some rest. I believe you and Jamie offered to continue training Marc and his people in Krav Maga techniques tomorrow morning?"

Holgar swept a bow. "I hear, my master, and obey." He smiled at Jenn. "Glad to see you."

"*Tak,*" she replied.

He turned to go, then turned back, looking more serious. "Master," he said, "you misspoke, *ja?*"

"Holgar," he said wearily, "I would hope you know me better than that."

The Dane stopped smiling. "Talking about sin and beasts? I'm not so sure I do." He ran his hands through his blond hair and let them drop to his sides. "See you in the morning."

"We're all on edge," Father Juan said as they both watched him go. "You see, it's as I'm saying. It's hard enough on the six of you to learn to work together, but now we're in close quarters with strangers, and there's so much we must keep hidden."

She took a breath. "That's becoming a little harder for some of us."

"I know."

"It's my fault."

"No, it's not." He studied her. "I wish I could tell you that it's going to work out fine. But there's a difference between false hope and faith."

"And what is that?" she asked.

"Faith is knowing that it will work as it should." Light seemed to fill his eyes, and she managed a flicker of a smile. That was the main quarrel she had with his religion. If things fell apart, it was God's will. If her sister died . . .

"Let's get you something to eat," he said.

New Orleans
Heather

Heather's inhaler had run out. She shook it, whimpering, her chest tight, her breath rattling in her throat. She shook the inhaler again, desperation coming over her. She brought it to her lips, depressed the plunger, and nothing.

Tears of frustration cascaded down her cheeks. She shook it a third time and tried holding it upside down. Still nothing. She tossed it on the floor of her cage, a useless piece of plastic, and tried to calm herself down.

The door to the parlor opened, and a vampire entered, carrying a bloody steak on a white china plate. Instead of moving as far away in her cage as possible, she gripped the bars tightly in her hands. "Can I have some coffee?" she asked.

Her voice was rusty from disuse, and the only thing she recognized about it was the lilting wheeze at the end.

The vampire looked surprised as he slid the plate into her cage. "Why?" he asked suspiciously.

"So I can breathe. Caffeine helps with asthma." Then, since she knew that he wouldn't do anything that would actually help her, she added, "If I don't get some, I'm going to stop being able to breathe soon. If I stop breathing, I die. Aurora wouldn't like that."

He narrowed his eyes and looked at her for a moment. She could almost see him thinking, processing what she had said. It was true. Aurora's plans for Heather would be completely spoiled if she died of asphyxiation now.

"Let me check," he said, turning and leaving the room.

She pushed at her steak absently. No fork or knife. She knew from experience that she wouldn't be able to swallow it down until her throat wasn't constricting.

Five minutes turned into ten. Ten minutes turned into twenty. Her throat tightened more until every breath was a gasp. She began to panic. She was going to die alone in a cage in New Orleans.

She thought of Jenn, coming to save her. She thought of Aurora and all the vampires like her that she wanted to kill. *It can't end like this!*

Suddenly the door to the parlor opened, and she trembled. Instead of the servant, though, Aurora herself strode into the room. She glided across the floor, resplendent in a purple bustier and a bell-shaped gown of purple and green. She had forgone her customary reds. Her black hair was piled on top of her head and held in place with glittering purple clips. A dark-skinned man accompanied her, dressed in a black caftan and a round, feathered hat. He wore a necklace of what appeared to be finger bones around his neck.

Human finger bones.

Aurora strode up to the cage, and Heather didn't have the strength to pull away from her. She was getting shaky, and her head was swimming. *Not enough oxygen; must breathe.*

Aurora took in her and the useless inhaler with a sweeping glance. "Caffeine excites the heart; it makes the blood taste different, and yours is already bitter enough. I don't permit it here."

"Please, can't breathe," Heather managed to whisper. "Inhaler." She grabbed her own throat and felt like she was choking. Something about it seemed so familiar, like it was a dream. *I'm dying,* she realized with a start. All those lectures from her parents about keeping her inhaler close had all been meant to prevent this. *But I did keep it close,* she thought wildly. *I was a good girl.*

Her thoughts began to fragment and fly apart. Aurora stood, arms crossed over her chest, looking at her with distaste.

"Maybe we could find one somewhere. We don't have to worry about inhaling."

Aurora tapped her fingernails against her fangs. "You have to last. You're part of my celebration. The sister of a Hunter, a worthy sacrifice to my lord indeed. But of course she's not even the big-ticket item. It's who's with her. Antonio de la Cruz."

Jenn was in the city! Jenn could save her!

Invisible fingers tightened their grip on her throat, and Heather sank to the floor of the cage. Aurora crouched down so that she was eye level with her. She could see the vampire's eyes, awash with red. Just like blood.

The vampire began to smile, revealing her fangs. Heather

wanted to whimper, to move away, but she couldn't. There was no strength left in her limbs. She was dying, suffocating. It hurt so bad.

"Hmm, obviously, you *aren't* going to last. It seems I must make the sacrifice, and taste your sickness. After all, what they don't know . . . will hurt them."

She gazed into Heather's eyes. "So listen to me, *bonita* Heather Leitner. I can end your torment in one of two ways. If you wish to live, nod your head. If you wish to die, do nothing."

What? What had she said? *Heather, who is Heather?* The name sounded like it should mean something, but as darkness filled her peripheral vision, even that slipped away.

The invisible fingers tightened once more, and there was no more wheezing, no more struggling, no more gasping. There was just darkness and pain.

"Nod your head if you want to live," a voice commanded her.

She should really answer the woman.

New Orleans
Antonio, Bernard, and Andrew

Dawn broke while Antonio, Bernard, and Andrew crept through the sewers below the French Quarter. Antonio felt it as a burst of heat and then a heaviness, like additional gravity pulling him toward the earth. Sergio, his vampire sire, had explained to him that the sensation was partial proof that the souls of vampires awaited them down below in the underworld. Sergio's god was Orcus, lord of the dead and punisher of those who broke their oaths.

Another oath broken. He'd lasted less than a year in Sergio's royal court, revolted by his lord's definition of pleasure. Unspeakable cruelties.

But time to get to business. As Bernard led the way, Antonio tapped Andrew on the shoulder. The man turned with his flashlight, and Antonio locked gazes with him. Andrew blinked, and Antonio turned on his charm.

"It makes sense to go on without me," he said. "We'll meet back at the mansion."

It took a little over a minute to convince him. Bernard required more effort. But soon Antonio found himself alone.

The day was long and unproductive. He saw no other vampires, and just listened to people talking in subdued voices as they walked down the sidewalks above him, worn down into submission, drowning in fear. *Them. Us. The Cops. The you-know-who. Shh, don't say that. Please, just let it go.* Just like it had been during World War II.

He had wondered all these years what had happened to the brothers and Frère Jacques.

And then:

"There's a new krewe this year, called Krewe du Sang." A pause. "And yes, it's what you think it is."

"They're having their own parade?"

"Tonight. They're taking video, seeing who shows. Taking care of anyone who does."

"What are—"

"Shh. Cops."

Antonio's mouth dropped open. *Du Sang* meant "of the blood" in French. The vampires were having their own parade during Mardi Gras?

He flew through the sewers as he returned to the mansion in the bayou. He found shortcuts through the underground tombs and managed to creep through the blackness of the bayou. But he ached, feeling scorched and exhausted. Drained by the sunlight he could not see, he forced himself to slow down as he came to the place where he would need to exit. It was behind the house, so he could walk in the shade from its overhanging roof as he went around to the front. He pulled his hood over his face, tucked his hands inside his sleeves, and blasted out of the sewer.

He could feel the burn of the sun instantly. A second and he had gained the shade next to the house. He forced himself to stop for a moment before walking slowly around the front of the house.

Marc stood just inside the house, his Uzi pointed at the door. Antonio nodded at him and came inside. Marc looked, waited, then said, "Where are Bernard and Andrew?"

"*¿Cómo?*" Antonio replied in Spanish. "What? They left. I stayed in the sewers. And I found something out. The vampires are going to have a Mardi Gras parade. Tonight."

Marc blinked, incredulous. "You're serious?"

"Krewe du Sang," Antonio replied.

"It's not on the schedule." Marc looked hard at Antonio. "No matter. We'll strike."

"What if the girl isn't with them?"

Marc set his jaw. "I'm not passing this up."

"They could retaliate and kill her. She's important to us."

Marc began to speak, but clamped his mouth shut instead. What was he going to say? That Heather wasn't important to him?

"I'm going to get something to eat," Antonio lied. "I'm starving."

"Wait." Marc grabbed his arm. "How did you get back here?"

"Hitched, and then walked. I was careful."

Marc didn't look pleased, but he nodded tersely at Antonio, and Antonio left the room. He headed for the kitchen and made himself a peanut butter and jelly sandwich and took a bite, even though he found peanut butter to be rather repulsive. Then he went in search of Father Juan and Eriko.

Jenn was standing in the hall, looking much better than when he'd left. There was even a little color in her cheeks. He wanted to take her in his arms. But he kept his distance.

"Jenn," he said, and he heard the odd mixture of measured calm and heightened anxiety in his voice as she started to walk toward him. He held up a hand. "The vampires are throwing a parade." He told her about the Krewe du Sang.

She went dead white. "Aurora said she would convert my sister at Mardi Gras."

He nodded. "I know. I think this is the break we've been looking for. Our prayers are being answered."

"Oh." She covered her mouth with her hands as tears welled. She swayed, and he wanted to catch her, hold her. But he felt his fangs lengthen, responding to the intoxicating scent of adrenaline. When she took a step toward him, he held up a hand, much as he had seen young priests ward off pretty parishioners who had crushes on them.

"Antonio, do you think, really, that we can get to the parade and rescue her?" she asked in a small voice. She broke down. *"Heather."*

He wanted to take her into his arms and smooth her wild red hair. To kiss the crown of her head, and hold her. He could feel her careful barriers crumbling as she broke down into sobs, and his own began to tumble. His fangs were sharp. He smelled her blood. Heard her heartbeat like a thundering promise. He needed blood.

But not hers. For the love of God, not hers.

"Jenn, listen to me," he said sternly. "You're a hunter. God has chosen you for this holy calling."

She shook her head. "Father Juan chose me."

"With magicks and prayer," he said, hoping that he didn't betray his own uncertainty about Father Juan's methods by his tone of voice. "This is a mission that our team has been given to fulfill."

"We weren't trained to rescue people," she said, and her body language begged for comfort—she leaned toward him, eyes huge. "We were trained to kill vampires."

"Perhaps this is God's way of expanding our mission," he said, very glad that Eriko was nowhere near to hear him talking like this. "Maybe this is a crucible, a test—"

She blinked, shocked. Her face hardened. "How can you say that? How can you believe in a God who would hurt my sister, maybe even kill her, for a *test*?"

"He's *not* hurting her. Aurora is," he countered.

And then he could no longer stay away from her as she raised her chin defiantly and tears ran down her cheeks. She backed away; he followed and gathered her in his arms. Her pulse roared.

"There is so much evil in the world," he said, "that God must do all he can to seek out the good. These things are not his doing, but he must make use of them."

"No," she whispered, "you're so wrong. You're so wrong."

He cupped the back of her head, and her red hair fanned out over her shoulders as he gazed down at her angry, terrified features. *Por Dios*, he wanted to taste her. His thirst was nearly overwhelming.

"In this I'm right: God doesn't want your sister to die. He wants us to save her. Can you do that, Jenn?"

Don't surrender, don't succumb, his mind whispered.

"Hunter," he said, "can you do that?"

He watched her struggle, and loved her for that struggle. This life, this entire world, was a crucible. It was the crusade of their times, and they were the knights, the warriors.

But last time you fought, you lost, he reminded himself, remembering the night he became a vampire. *You lost everything.*

"Yes," Jenn said, taking a deep breath. "I can do that."

Not everything, then, he thought.

Then she reached to kiss him on the lips, and he let himself have that. Soft, warm, she loved *him,* a monstrous abomination, a Cursed One. This might be all they ever had, this moment, this kiss, this love. So he gave in to it, aware that his fangs were lengthening, that by now his eyes were glowing. Hunger, want, and desire waged their own war inside him. And then he won again, prevailing as he finished the kiss and took her hand.

"We're going to save her," he promised her.

"All right." She gave his fingers a squeeze, and the sweetness of the gesture nearly broke his heart.

They went together to find Father Juan. Antonio was in the midst of filling him in when noise and shouting erupted from the front of the house. It was Bernard.

"We've bagged a sucker!"

*   *   *

Everyone came to see the captured vampire. And Skye felt a moment of panic.

"It's Nick," Skye announced, nearly overcome with shame as she had to essentially confess that she hadn't tried to stake him. "The one I left Aurora's lair with. He ran off before I could do anything."

"Yo, I've never seen you before in my life," the vampire retorted. Then he hissed. His eyes were red, and his fangs were out. He was surrounded by Salamancans and the Resistance, in the room with the settee where Jenn had lain when they'd first arrived.

Once he'd realized that Andrew and Bernard had returned with a vampire, Antonio had made himself scarce. Skye tried not to think about what would happen if Nick, detecting the presence of another vampire, denounced him to the group.

"I wore a disguise," she said. And then she realized that he might know who had magickally blocked her.

She was almost afraid to find out.

Eriko approached him, showing him a stake in her right hand and a cross in the other. He stumbled backward, then whirled around and turned his head as Holgar, now facing him, extended his stake and cross, mirroring Eriko.

"He tried to attack us," Bernard informed them, sneering at Nick. "It was the most pathetic thing I've ever seen."

"I'm weak because it's light out. And I'm hungry," Nick wheedled. "She wouldn't let me feed." He peered at Skye.

"Dude, you didn't have a heartbeat. Having no heartbeat is *not* a disguise."

Skye licked her lips. "I'm a witch. I can conjure magick spells. You've got one like me, don't you?"

"One?" Startled, he laughed. "We've got a whole pile of witchy people, from all over the world. And voodoo guys, too. We got some big kahuna coming in tonight, in fact." He saw her face fall, and he squared his shoulders. "We're, like, majorly dangerous."

"I can see that," Eriko drawled. She walked toward him. He looked from her to Holgar and back, and groaned again.

"So you went back to Aurora," Skye pushed.

"Yeah. I told her that you bailed on me and I went after you. She was really pissed off, and she said we had to move. I got in such major trouble." He shook his head. "So she says I have to 'man up' and get my own food for a while. I can't gnaw on anybo—I have to fend for myself."

"More like 'vamp up,'" Holgar said.

"It's not funny," Jamie snapped. "So, where did you move to? Tell us, and we may spare you." He glided toward Nick, unarmed, hands in the pockets of his black leather trousers. He pulled a baggie of unpeeled garlic from his left pocket. "You know what we do with this? We stuff your mouth with it until the inside of your mouth starts bleeding."

"No way," Nick said, eyes bulging. "Oh, *man.*"

"Just tell us," Eriko said, nodding at Jamie, who opened the bag.

"Oh, come on, you guys," Nick pleaded. "If I tell you . . ." Then he trailed off, as if it had just occurred to him that he was surrounded by his mortal enemies. "Whoa."

"Tell us. In detail," Eriko said.

"I'll show you. I'll take you there," he said, his voice rising. "Please?"

"And tell us about the witches with Aurora," Skye ordered him.

"Well, they're not witches, exactly. They're witch doctors. Y'know, voodoo dudes." He looked hopefully around the circle. "With the drums and stuff." He smiled hopefully at Alice, who had just swept into the room in her ceremonial black-and-purple robe.

"Traitors," she said, spitting on the floor. "When I tell Papa Dodi—"

"Oh, yeah," the vampire said, nodding like a bobble-head. "He's supposed to meet up with us for the parade."

A heavy silence crashed down around the room. Skye looked from the vampire to the voodoo sorceress and back again.

"No," Jenn whispered. In the stillness her voice echoed against the walls, down the corridors.

Alice pressed her forehead with both her hands. There was no other sound for at least five seconds. Skye moved to her and put her arm around the distraught woman.

"Maybe it's not what it looks like," Skye said. "Maybe Papa Dodi is one of us, infiltrating Aurora's group —"

"Um, we call them courts," Nick offered helpfully. "And I think he's pretty jazzed to be with us. Aurora's going to convert him." He brightened. "I'm sure she'd convert you guys if you wanted."

Glares of hatred melted him into a puddle. "Just sayin'," he muttered.

Skye glanced over at Alice. Twin tears streamed down the older woman's face. She looked hard at Eriko.

"Find out what you need to know," she bit off. Then she swept out of the room.

After the vampire had spilled his guts, they staked him. Antonio watched from the shadows, saw the clueless surfer fall to his knees, screaming and begging. Three seconds after that he was dust.

The hunters of Salamanca conferred. The freedom fighters of New Orleans did the same. Then they met at a long, rickety table, Eriko seated across from Marc. Father Juan sat at Eriko's right hand, and Bernard served as Marc's advisor.

After a while Marc and Eriko pushed back their chairs, and each went over to his or her team. Father Juan excused himself and left the room. The hunters stood near the front door, Jamie leaning against the wall with his head tilted back, as if he were supremely bored. He lowered his head when he saw Eriko walking toward them.

"So it's settled?" he asked her.

"*Hai,*" Eriko replied. "Marc will drive us back to town. Our whole team, and his core group—Bernard, Suzy, and Matt. We all go to the parade, and then our team breaks off to go to Aurora's new lair."

"I gather the rest will take on the parade," Jamie said.

"*Hai.*" She hesitated a moment, and then she went on. "Marc's objective is different from ours. The Resistance sees this as their one big chance to inflict as much damage as possible. They hope to inspire the people to help them."

"The parade spectators," Holgar said, as if to make sure he understood what she was saying.

"*Hai.*" Eriko bobbed her head. "And we will rescue Heather." Her cheeks turned pink.

She doesn't think that should be our primary objective, Jenn realized, shocked to her core. *She wants to help Marc.*

"Depending on how this goes down, Antonio might peel off and go inside the lair alone," Eriko added. Antonio nodded.

"No," Jenn blurted.

"Jenn, he's a vampire," Holgar said.

"Can you please say that a little louder?" Jamie grumbled at him.

"*I'll* go inside. Let me go. She's my sister," Jenn argued.

Eriko narrowed her eyes at Jenn. "Aurora knows you. She doesn't know Antonio."

"Are you ready?" Marc asked, striding over to them.

"We'll suit up and get weapons—and we *will* be armed—and—"

He stopped speaking as Father Juan walked into the room. His face was drawn, and his cheeks were ashen. A young man in a clerical collar was standing beside him.

"This is Father Gilbert," Father Juan announced. "He's the priest who sent us the information about Marc's group."

"Hello," Father Gilbert said. Jenn thought he didn't look old enough to be a priest. His forehead was creased and his face was drawn. "I came to find your master because we've gotten word of trouble."

He turned his attention to Father Juan, who nodded grimly.

"I have to go to Spain," he said. "Now."

CHAPTER EIGHTEEN

Humanity is on its knees
Giving us whatever we please
Lick our boots and whine like dogs
In your own demise you are the cogs
Beg us now to let you live
Tell us what else you can give
And we will laugh and tell you no
It's time for mankind to go

NEW ORLEANS
THE HUNTERS OF SALAMANCA, THE RESISTANCE, AND THE CURSED ONES

They were trundling back to the French Quarter in one larger van, all of Salamanca and Marc and his three, and Antonio was terrified. He hadn't felt that particular emotion in a long, long time. When the team needed him most, he was losing control—for some reason he couldn't fathom. Something dark and magickal was surely at work, and it had more power over his monster than he did.

Skye and Alice had worked with Father Juan to put magickal protections on the van in which they rode, masking it as a moving van. Father Juan had provided the incantations, from what arsenal of arcane and magick lore Antonio didn't know. Father Juan's magickal repertoire was uniquely his.

The spell casting hadn't been easy, and Father Juan had said a lot of things in Latin that only Antonio understood and would have blushed to repeat in any language. Father Juan had been able to verify that there was a magickal force working against them, but he couldn't confirm if it was Papa Dodi. He didn't know if it was voodoo, or White, Dark, or Black magick, either. Alice's *loa* was silent on the subject too. When the job was finally done, all six hunters had squeezed in, and Marc and his three—Matt, Bernard, and Suzy. More fighters would be driving separately, and more cells would join forces once they reached the French Quarter. Weapons were cached—guns—while the Salamancans carried everything they needed for their traditional hand-to-hand combat.

Antonio didn't know how Marc had gotten the word to the other cells, and at the moment he was too preoccupied to care. He fought to keep his bloodlust down, aware that at any moment he might burst into full feeding form with red, glowing eyes, razor-sharp fangs.

Father Juan was getting a ride from Alice to the Louis Armstrong New Orleans International Airport, or as close as they could get. Father Gilbert had left as quietly as he had arrived, still insisting that he couldn't get involved.

The streets on the parade route in the French Quarter were cordoned off to vehicles. A few quick questions at a gas station off the highway had revealed that the Krewe du Sang parade would begin on the eastern side of the Quarter, on Franklin Avenue. Marc got as close as he could; he pulled into the narrow alley of an abandoned apartment complex—there were a lot of those—and the group silently filed out. On the brick wall someone had spray-painted *VAMPIRES SUK GO TO HELL CURSED ONES*. Marc smiled grimly when he saw the words.

It was seven o'clock, time for the two groups to separate. Marc's goal: to kill as many vampires as possible. Team Salamanca's: to save Heather Leitner. Both: to make a difference.

"Bonne chance," Marc said to Eriko, including all the hunters in his wish for good luck. Marc's group was planning to rendezvous with another cell about a mile away. Others would join them. His gaze rested a moment on Antonio, and he narrowed his eyes; then they softened at the sight of Skye, who was weaving a spell on behalf of the Resistance fighters.

"The good news is that we'll create a diversion for you," Marc said. He took a deep breath, and Antonio saw the resolve on the face of the warrior. He knew that feeling. Every night that he'd been a Maquis, he had known his life was in God's hands. But on some missions the risks were greater than on others. That was when the possibility of death became the probability of death. Marc was placing his team in the column of probability.

"Banzai," Eriko said, bowing, saluting the quartet — Marc, Bernard, Suzy, Matt. Japanese tradition revered the kamikaze, the warrior prepared to die for his cause. The four bowed back, Marc bowing lowest.

"Let's go," Eriko told her people.

They left in ones and twos, going in different directions to avoid attention. The hunters wore no body armor, no jackets, nothing to call attention to themselves.

Nick had placed Aurora's new lair off Decatur Street, by the cathedral. It was on the parade route for Krewe du Sang, which the hunters would reach about half an hour after the parade started, at eight o'clock.

The Vieux Carré — the French Quarter — was festooned with purple and green garlands, and glittering ropes of beads and feathers swathed across the streets and looped along the balconies. Crowds jammed the streets, some half-dressed in black leather and lamé, others in jeans, shirts, ball caps, cowboy hats. Scores of them were carrying beer in plastic cups. Above, on the balconies, women flashed the crowds by pulling up their T-shirts, receiving strings of gold beads for their trouble.

Two belly dancers in red and purple wigs danced through the crowds to appreciative hoots and hollers. Four men dressed like Santa Claus started dancing with them.

So much of it was forced, like a performance, a show. Smiles were plastered on; people were drinking very heavily. Jenn saw a woman turn her head and begin to cry. A man hugged her, bent down, tried to reason with her. Sobbing, she wiped away her tears and took his beer. She drank it down.

But other people seemed genuinely happy. Overjoyed, even. It was so insane.

"Look," Jenn murmured.

Antonio looked in the direction she pointed. On the next balcony over, four armed members of the New Orleans Police Department stood unsmiling, watching the crowd. They wore helmets and full riot gear. The balcony directly across from them on the other side of the street contained three more officers, also suited up for action.

In fact, armed law-enforcement officers clogged the upper floors of all the rainbow-hued and brick buildings. And with each cluster of police officers, other people were holding up video cameras and cell phones, recording everything. The people below them knew it. Though they laughed and caroused, few of them looked up.

"Avestruces," Antonio muttered. "Ostriches."

"How are we going to pull this off?" Jenn asked into his ear. He jerked away from her, feeling himself change.

Wheeling around, he spotted Skye half a block down. Antonio said to Jenn, "Keep walking," and hurried through the crowd toward the witch. Half-drunk pedestrians saw him and blinked, then either laughed, cheered, or swallowed down their beer and took a step away. It was clear that they didn't know if he was a real vampire or not.

He reached Skye. She gaped at him, and he shook his head, needing her to focus.

"Can you do anything?" he asked. "If Marc's people see me like this . . ."

"I don't know." She wove her hands and whispered in an ancient language he didn't know. He began to relax, and that worried him: He needed to be alert.

"Don't fight me," she said. "There."

His fangs had retracted. He no longer felt the fire in his eyes. He said, "Thank you."

Eriko appeared at his shoulder. She raised a brow.

"I'll begin recon," he said. "See if they're still at the lair."

She inclined her head. "Good luck, Antonio." Her voice was cold. She still didn't trust him.

He turned and caught sight of Jenn in the crowd. She was gathering up her red hair into a ponytail. He saw how her hands shook. Her heart was pounding so fast he was afraid she might have a heart attack. He looked hard at her. It might be the last time he ever saw her.

Te amo, he thought. *I love you.* But he forced himself not to mouth the words. Already he could feel Skye's spell begin to weaken, so strong was his instinct to release the beast.

Staring at him, Jenn bit her lower lip and nodded at him. Was she saying "I love you, too"? He might never know.

Leaving Eriko and Skye behind, he moved through the crowd. Holgar was up one block, across the street. Antonio turned around to see Jamie sauntering beside Jenn. A flash of jealousy caught him by surprise.

He looked at the numbers on the street signs and began to cross the street. The alleyway between a gumbo shop and a stand selling Mardi Gras souvenirs was his best hope of entering into Aurora's new lair, boldly located in a brick building with a VACANT sign on it.

But as he started across, the world erupted into craziness.

Calliope music, discordant, off-tune, blasted through the night. Explosions like cannon fire shook the gaudy street decorations, and everyone screamed. Red fog or dry ice or magick rolled down the center of the street as police officers on horses trotted on either side of the unfolding cloud, ordering people back. In the confusion they obeyed, most of them well trained in Mardi Gras etiquette and safety—during a parade, you stayed on the sidewalk.

Then a voice came over dozens of loudspeakers:

"Mesdames et messieurs, ladies and gentlemen, it's time for

Mardi Gras, vampire-style! We bring you Krewe du Sang!"

And suddenly, as if they had materialized out of the night air, a gaggle of vampires wearing grotesque masks depicting full bloodlust capered and marched down the street — at least twenty. The women were dressed in elaborate ball gowns of purple and green, the men in matching satin coats and breeches, all were crowned with powdered white wigs, as from the court of Marie Antoinette in the eighteenth century in France. They were tossing throws to the audience, some of whom had frozen in horror. But as the mounted police officers trotted by on their horses, the onlookers forced smiles and laughter onto their faces and reached their hands for the loops of beads — strings of silver and gold vampire fangs. Antonio did a double take and then realized they weren't vampire fangs but actual human teeth, filed to look like fangs.

Then the first float appeared, its sides covered with swirling spirals of red roses and silver crescent moons, and a sign that read WE WERE THERE!

The float was a re-creation of a Parisian ballroom, complete with a baroque silver and crystal chandelier suspended over a wooden dance floor. Candles burned, flickering as red fog swirled up and around the dancers, who were attired in gowns and coats like the walkers before them. Harpsichord music played as they danced the minuet.

The next float showed a castle — Antonio recognized it as a Spanish-style *castillo* — and before it stood a human man dressed in a brown robe with a hood. Another man dangled, his feet barely touching the ground, his arms bound by the wrists to a gibbet—a crossbar extending from a thick column. At the base of the column human skulls had been stacked.

WE WERE THERE! the side of the float proclaimed. Antonio wondered if the onlookers knew that these two figures were humans, with heartbeats.

And if they realized that the skulls were real.

The castle rolled past him, and then the third float towered above the previous two. On one end was a re-creation of a modern city, all glass and steel skyscrapers, and on the other the brick buildings and lacy verandas of the French Quarter—combined, they made a miniature of New Orleans itself. On top of the tallest steel and glass building, rising about six feet from the bed of the float, a striking vampire dressed in a plunging green and purple gown, her black hair held in place with purple combs, smiled and tossed beads at the people.

Aurora.

The vampire who had threatened Jenn's life, and taken her sister. His enemy.

And his sister by blood.

No, he thought, feeling his face shift. *Just because we're both vampires, that means nothing. That would be like saying that Jenn and Adolf Hitler are kin, because they're both human.*

"Good evening, New Orleans!" Aurora cried over the

loudspeakers as she tossed her gold and silver strings of fangs. She had a Spanish accent. So, like his sire, Sergio, she was Spanish. And . . . like him.

Did crimson light gleam in his eyes? Or had Skye successfully masked him? Now he wished the glamour away and the startled gasp of an elderly woman dressed in a Mardi Gras T-shirt and a ruffled gauze skirt told him he was hidden no longer.

Antonio heard the heartbeats of the crowd—sporadic, accelerating. The body knew no difference between intense excitement and abject fear—adrenaline was adrenaline—and faces were taking on the desperate, overwrought thrill of a mob. Trying to please, to show that they weren't afraid. That they loved their vampire overlords.

Another cry rose up, and Antonio looked back at the float. Emerging from one of the modern buildings, a man in a business suit joined Aurora. The crowd cheered and screamed.

From one of the older buildings a black man in a caftan emerged. He was dressed as a voodoo *bokor*, with a bone necklace and a round, feathered cap. Was this Alice's Papa Dodi? He held a staff with curled horns jutting from the top; a live cobra coiled around the horns. Beside him danced a vampire who was dressed as Baron Samedi, voodoo god of death—black top hat decorated with little white skulls, bones, and feathers, a white skull mask across his face. He wore all black, and white gloves, and a necklace of human bones.

Baron Samedi was one of the dark gods of death, also worshipped by some vampires, who had as many cults and religious practices as humans. And there was Alicia's *loa*, Ma'man Brigit, the baron's wife, wearing a veil dotted with rotten flowers. Perhaps tonight Brigit was siding with the vampires as well.

"Papa Dodi!" someone shouted. "No!"

The *bokor* turned and stared into the crowd. Then he lifted the staff with the snake coiled on it and threw back his head. He shouted in a strange language. The cobra coiled around the horns of the staff, then moved faster; then it began to smoke. It shook and sizzled, as Papa Dodi continued to chant. Distant drums began to pound. The creature shuddered.

Suddenly, the cobra expanded to twice its size, then three times, and it hissed at the crowd, tongue flicking. The crowd cheered wildly, as if it were part of a performance, a crazy Hollywood special effect.

Magick. Voodoo. Evil.

The drums beat, frenetic, hollow, menacing. Something was rising, something was coming.

The float rolled past. There was no sign of a human girl. Jenn had described Heather in loving detail; Antonio felt as if he had met her. Of the vampire parade Antonio had seen enough—more than enough.

He had to get across the street, to Aurora's lair, before the parade ended. But the police were there, and the crowd was becoming more frenzied. Humans crushed around him in waves, pushing him along. They were shrieking, cheering. Kaleidoscopes of faces whirled around him. Beer sloshed on him

"Vampire, bite me!" a woman in a spangled bra cooed at him, throwing her arms around him. Then she looked past him and started shrieking.

"Look, look!" she ordered him. "She's going to convert the mayor!"

Cries and groans rose up, like a geyser of humanity's defeat, and through the scarlet smoke he saw Aurora in her full predatory appearance—her eyes of crimson and her sharp fangs. She grabbed the man in the business suit and sank her teeth into his neck.

"Oh, my God!" the woman screamed, covering her face. "It's . . . oh, God!"

He stared hard at her and said, "That's what it's really like."

"No," she said, beginning to sob, "no, it's . . . it's . . ."

"If she doesn't feed him her blood, he will be safe," Antonio added. *Dead, maybe, but not converted.*

But in that moment, Aurora gestured to the cobra. It shot downward toward her and sank its fangs into the fleshy area above her heart. She cried out as if with ecstasy.

As she held the mayor upright, she positioned her hand around the cobra's head, just behind its fangs, and yanked it free. Blood trickled from her chest. Papa Dodi took the serpent from her, and she pushed the mayor's face against the wound. He began to drink.

The man would rise again, Antonio knew.

Tears rolled down the woman's cheeks.

"Get out of here. Now," he told her.

He moved on, as the tide of the crowd changed in a moment to panic. They were surging, rioting; he couldn't see Jenn, or any of the others. They were spilling into the street, some running in the opposite direction, in sheer terror, but most of them had no idea where they were going, what they were doing.

Pushing against the sea of humanity, he got across the street.

He ran silently to the back of the brick building, debating how to go about gaining entry. He should go through the back door, up the interior stairs, and through the red door, which stood at the southern end of an interior central courtyard. Go in, assess the situation, and report back.

He heard the craziness: sirens, whistles. The screams. People losing their humanity, whether permanently, or just through mob frenzy, he couldn't say.

And he made a command decision. He wasn't going to endanger Jenn and the others. He was going to go in, grab Heather, and run for it, staking any who got in his way.

He took the stairs four at a time—as he was a vampire, he could almost, but not quite, fly. Moonlight gleamed through skylights on the courtyard, which was bursting with dead plants in large black urns, and sightless Greek statues.

There was the red front door. He wanted to get inside as

soon as possible and get Heather and leave before the sun came up. He ran up the steps, hesitated, and then twisted the knob. The door swung inward.

They were either careless or completely sure of their power over the humans of the city. He walked inside. There was no one immediately in sight.

No one, in fact, at all.

Heather wasn't there.

Swept along by the raging sea of the terrified crowd, Jenn stumbled backward, keeping her gaze fixed on the abandoned apartment building. She was freaking out: This wasn't the plan; Antonio wasn't supposed to go in by himself. She was fighting to move forward, but short of using Krav Maga on a hundred people at once, she would have to content herself with inching forward. Then Jenn spotted Skye's Rasta braids bobbing about twenty feet ahead of her.

"Skye!" she shouted.

The witch didn't hear her. Then Skye raised a hand and started through the crowd, toward the building. Jenn followed her line of sight and saw Antonio, alone.

Heather, Jenn thought. *Where is Heather?*

She started shoving people out of her way, blocking someone's fist, hunching her shoulders and lowering her head like a football player. Protests and swearing came with her efforts, but she kept pushing, and she got across the street less than ten seconds after Skye. Both Jenn and the witch stopped just short of Antonio, whose eyes were glowing.

"Not there," he said. "Never there."

"*What?*" Jenn cried.

He put his arms around their waists and drew them into the alley, out of the madness. The noise was deafening. Jenn's boots crunched on gravel. The moon—half full—gleamed on Antonio's blue-black hair. If he had been human, he would have been panting and out of breath.

"There was no scent of a human in that place. They didn't move her there. Either Nick was lying to us, or Aurora lied to him."

"Bloody hell," Skye said, clapping her hand to her face. "Then where the hell is she?"

"Oh, no, no," Jenn wailed. "No, Heather!"

"Jenn." Antonio put his hands on her shoulders and bent his knees so that he could look into her eyes. "Listen. You have to be strong. You have to stay focused. The parade is still going. Aurora is not with your sister. That means there's hope."

"No, it doesn't," Jenn said. She took a deep breath. "But you're right. I have to stay focused." She turned to Skye. "You have to try your scrying stone again." Before Skye could say anything, Jenn licked her lips and gave her a hard look. "You *have* to, Skye. And you have to make it work."

Skye made a face as she fished in her pocket and pulled out the small rectangular stone. "It didn't work before."

"We were underground. You've done voodoo since then," Antonio reminded her. "That opens up more channels of arcana. And I have continued to pray for you."

"You have to have *faith*," Jenn said. The words were out of her mouth before she'd realized she was going to say them.

"Close your eyes, Jenn and Skye, and pray with me," Antonio invited them.

Jenn hesitated. She still didn't believe, not the way he did. But she closed her eyes, tears running down her face. Time was ticking. The parade was winding through the streets of the French Quarter, and who knew what route it would take. Or if Heather was hidden in one of the floats, being savaged by Aurora.

"Amen," Antonio murmured, and the three opened their eyes.

Skye looked into her stone and gave her head a shake. Nothing.

"Una vez más," Antonio said. "One more time."

"We don't *have* time," Jenn said, grabbing the stone. She looked around. "Oh, God, we don't have time."

Gently, Antonio cupped her chin and gazed in her eyes. She jerked her head. She was done with this.

"Close your eyes," Antonio said.

"Antonio," she pleaded. "We have to *do* something." Then she huffed, remembering that they'd already had this conversation, back in the convent.

Nothing in her wanted to repeat failure, but she had no idea what else they could do except run haphazardly all over the Quarter, hoping Skye could recognize the building. Yes, they could do that.

"Shh," Antonio urged her. "For Heather."

Frustrated, scared, she closed her eyes. *Please, God, or Goddess, or luck or fate, or . . .*

The face of her beloved grandfather, Papa Che, blossomed in her mind. She could see him so clearly—the calm, dark eyes, the freckles on his nose, the bushy brows and the smile.

Oh, I loved you. I still love you, she thought. *I'll love you as long as I'm alive.*

I will fill your shoes.

And something happened. Something shifted. Something changed. Jenn felt it like a warm vibration running down the center of her body, like someone plucking the string of a harp. It thrummed through the core of her, then stilled.

"Yes!" Skye shrieked.

Jenn jumped. Then she and Antonio stared into the crystal as Skye held it out to them. Jenn leaned in, squinting at it, seeing a courtyard and, behind it, a building with a winding spiral staircase.

"That's *it*!" Skye shouted.

She turned right. The crystal dimmed. Left. It brightened.

"Let's go!" she shouted.

"Here, behind the building, in the alley," Antonio said.

He grabbed Jenn and Skye's hands, and they broke into a run. The brick alley was pitch-black, but Jenn knew he could see where to go. He dragged them along; she was running so fast she was falling over her own feet. She stumbled; he slowed. She was holding him up, and so was Skye.

"I see a name behind the staircase!" Skye shouted. "It's on Saint Peter. There are numbers: one, two, five, and another I can't read."

"Antonio, go!" Jenn shouted. "We'll follow."

Antonio's response was to let go of both of them and fly like a bat into hell.

He was there in less than a minute. Up the stairs he raced, and through the front door, breaking it off its hinges, ready to kill a hundred of his kind to save Jenn's sister.

The smell of fresh blood filled the air, and he found himself in an octagonal room furnished with antiques.

There on the far side a cage stood open, the body of a young girl draped half in, half out of it. In a moment he was staring down at the body of Jenn's sister. Rage filled him.

They were too late.

She was dead.

He bent down, and suddenly the stench of death filled his nostrils, strong, pungent, and not right. He crossed himself as he jumped backward.

"That's right; I converted her," a voice purred behind him. "I am her sire."

He spun to see Aurora staring at him, fangs bared playfully. "She tasted horrible. She was nearly dead. But she's mine now."

Antonio had no words.

"So, you're the traitor," she said, moving slowly toward him as if she were floating. "The vampire who helps the humans hunt us. I've been waiting a long time to meet you. Your sire speaks so fondly of you, Antonio de la Cruz."

Antonio hissed and lunged for her, a scream of fury shaking him.

Holgar watched as Resistance fighters threw off Mardi Gras masks and capes, brandishing submachine guns as they charged the crazy vampire floats. Bernard, Matt, Andrew, and Marc mowed down vampires and that voodoo man, Papa Dodi. From their balconies the police opened fire, shooting into the crowd. The humans were shrieking and running everywhere.

A fire erupted inside one of the buildings. Smoke billowed and rose into the sky.

Vampires flew off the floats like rats, eyes bloodred, fangs glistening. One, a man, grabbed the nearest woman and sank his teeth into her neck. The Cursed One beside him took down a huge man, dropping him to his knees. Blood streamed down the vampire's face.

Holgar pushed people out of his way, tracing the route

he'd seen Antonio, Skye, and Jenn take. He reached the end of the alley to find Jenn and Skye, but no Antonio.

"Saint Peter," Skye got out, showing him the stone.

He nodded. "Find Eriko and Jamie," he told them.

A block from his destination he crouched low as he heard a scream of fury. It was Antonio.

He threw himself toward the house, bounded up the stairs, and flew through the opened doorway.

Antonio had his hands around the throat of a female vampire, who was hissing and scratching at him. They were both clacking their fangs together, snapping them open and closed like wolves.

Holgar pulled stakes free from his pockets and tried to close in. Antonio and the woman started moving so fast, though, that he couldn't track them, let alone take a chance of missing her and killing Antonio.

He roared in frustration and spun around as he heard cursing. Half a dozen vampires entered the room. He slammed his stake into the chest of the first one, who died with a look of surprise on his face.

Eriko and Jamie found Jenn and Skye. Without a word Eriko picked up Jenn and carried her piggyback down the street. People were running everywhere, screaming. A woman with a head wound jerked past them. Machine-gun fire sounded a staccato counterpoint to the waves of sirens.

Jamie and Skye ran together. Then a vampire burst through the crowd, headed straight for Eriko.

"Hunter!" he yelled, challenging her. "You're a Hunter!"

"Put me down," Jenn told her, and Eriko complied. Jenn spared one look as Eriko pulled a stake from her trouser leg, spread her legs wide for balance, and readied for battle.

Running on, Jenn spotted the house. She put on a burst of speed from reserves she had never dreamed she possessed. Clanging up the stairs, she burst into the house with Skye and Jamie.

Aurora and Antonio were slashing at each other, and more vampires were circling, hissing, as Antonio flung a stake into the chest of one directly behind him. The Cursed One exploded.

Holgar was in the thick of the fray, scratching with his human nails and biting everything that came near him.

Past them Jenn saw her sister, and she ran toward her, despite the chaos and fighting going on around her.

One look told her everything she needed to know: Heather's throat was torn open; blood pooled around her. Her eyes were half shut.

And though there was no spark of life in them—not yet—they glowed as red as the fresh blood on her lips. Vampire blood.

She'd been converted.

"No, Heather, oh, Heather, I'm so sorry," she wept.

With a sob she fell to her knees. The room spun. She

wanted to scream and cry and beg and hate and kill, but it was too late.

Too late.

Heaving, she pulled out a stake and prepared to drive it through Heather's heart. In her mind she saw Heather and herself walking along the beach, Heather in a bright pink bikini, squealing as a wavelet snuck up on her and washed over her toes.

"It's so cold!" Heather cried.

"It's filled with sharks!" Jenn shouted back.

Shaking herself, Jenn wiped her tears away. Keening, whimpering, she lifted her arm, swung it downward . . .

. . . and Antonio grabbed it and stopped her so that the tip was just short of its mark. Behind him Eriko, Jamie, and Skye had arrived. And so had Marc, and at least a dozen Resistance fighters, shooting their weapons in the close quarters and staking the vampires.

"Antonio, Antonio, I have to do this," Jenn screamed through the noise. "They changed her."

"No, you don't," Antonio said, trying to wrest the stake out of her hand without hurting her. "I can help her. I can save her."

Around them the fight raged. Vampires went up in dust. A young revolutionary fell dead next to her, his neck broken, his dead eyes staring at her, urging her to do the right thing.

This is the test, she thought as the world seemed to go

cold and black around her. She heard none of the fighting, saw nothing but the stake in her hand and Heather's red eyes. *I am a hunter, and she's a vampire.*

Colder.

Darker.

She couldn't do it.

This is the moment of trial for you. This is when you accept your calling. This is when you do what you were born to do.

"I have to," she ground out again. "We can't take the chance."

"You have taken a chance on me," Antonio urged. "Let me at least try, for your sake and for hers."

Jenn stared at him for a moment, her heart warring with her mind. Antonio was injured; deep, bloody scratch marks covered his face and chest. A hole gaped in his shoulder where he had been stabbed with something. He was shaking, and she realized suddenly that he was close to collapse. She reached out for him.

Suddenly Eriko and Marc came to a stop before her, a vampire turning into dust between them. Marc turned, saw Antonio's fangs, and lunged toward him, screaming, "Vampire!"

Antonio was too weak to defend himself. Marc knocked him backward and knelt on his chest, swinging a stake downward. It made contact, driving deep into Antonio's chest—but missing his heart. Eriko rammed into Marc, knocking him across the room and screaming like a banshee as she followed him. She grabbed his head and slammed it into the ground.

"He's a vampire," Marc yelped, voice filled with pain. "You need to kill him! Or let *me* kill him!"

"You shall not," Eriko said, yanking a stake free and threatening Marc with it.

"Stop it!" Jenn screamed. "He's on our side; he always has been."

Marc wasn't buying it. He lunged forward, and Eriko hit him, hard, across the side of the face. Again. She brandished her stake, aiming it at his chest.

Jenn jumped to her feet, grabbing Eriko around the waist. She screamed into her ear, "Eriko, stop; you'll kill him. He's a human, an ally. Stop!"

Suddenly Eriko dropped her stake and backed up as Marc scrambled to his feet, a frightened look passing over her face. She and Marc stood, panting, four feet apart, murder in both their eyes.

Holgar shouted across the room. "Eriko! We need you over here!"

Eriko turned and headed off. Marc stared from Antonio to Jenn and back again. "He's been like this the whole time?"

"Yes."

"Merde." He spat. "You are liars!"

"Would you have helped us if we'd told you?"

Marc looked her in the eyes. "Of course not."

Jenn shrugged.

"Sorry about your sister," Marc said, before diving back into the fray. And there was such malice in his tone that she staggered backward, as if he had struck her.

Eriko must have said something to Holgar, because a minute later he came up beside her. He looked down at Antonio, who was trying to stand. The vampire was bleeding severely from wounds on his face and neck, and part of Marc's wooden stake was lodged in his chest—far from his heart, but blood bubbled up around it and dripped to the floor.

"What do you need?" Holgar asked Jenn.

She pushed her blood-streaked hair out of her eyes and wiped her nose with the back of her hand. "We've got to get Antonio out of here."

"And we're taking Jenn's sister with us," Antonio said in a raspy voice.

"Is Aurora dead?" Jenn asked.

Holgar shook his head. "She got away. She put a stake in Antonio's shoulder and ran before any of the rest of us could get her."

The wolfman slung Heather over his shoulder and helped Antonio to his feet. They fought their way to the front of the house. The battle had spilled onto the streets outside, combining with the fracas of the enraged New Orleanians.

They staggered down the stairs and found Jamie, Eriko, and Marc in the street, circling two vampires. In a flash Eriko staked them both.

The three turned and saw Jenn, Holgar, and Antonio.

Police cars screamed toward them. Overhead, the steady *whum-whum-whum* of a helicopter signaled that the allies of the vampires had taken to the air.

Skye came running out of the house and then skidded to a stop beside Jenn. She was staring fixedly at the ground. Jenn glanced down and saw a chalk drawing. It was a gargoyle with a heart in its mouth, a twin to Skye's tattoo, which she'd seen in the showers. In the center of the heart read *E+S*.

"Get out of here while you still can!" Marc shouted above the roar, pulling Jenn's attention back to the danger at hand.

"Are you sure?" Eriko asked.

"Yeah, I think we've got it covered," he said. "Thanks to you and your damn vampire." He flashed her a crazy, bombastic grin. "You people are crazy—*fou*."

Jenn raised her head and looked around. Everywhere people were pouring out of houses, carrying crosses and pieces of wood—broken bits of chair, snapped-off pieces of banisters and table legs. The streets were filling up, not with more terrified victims of mob frenzy, but with *fighters*.

We've done it; we've started a revolution, she thought, tears filling her eyes.

Then, as she gazed into the slack, undead face of her sister, she thought, *Will it matter?*

CHAPTER NINETEEN

*I was given this journal by my master, Father Juan,
the day we came back from New Orleans. He told
me to write it down, all of it—to remember each
moment so that I could go over it and learn from
it. He said that as dark as these times were, darker
times were coming.*

He was right.

*And so was I, when I wrote the first line on the
first page, which read . . .*

—from the diary of Jenn Leitner

MADRID
FATHER JUAN

As soon as Father Juan stepped outside the airport in
Madrid, he knew just how serious the summons home had

been. Diego, the bishop in charge of the entire Academia, pulled up to the curb in a tan Mercedes himself.

Juan slid into the car, and Diego accelerated quickly away from the curb. Looking at the older man, Juan noticed that he was in civilian clothes, no hint of his religious standing about him.

"They're blaming our hunters for the loss of the virus," Diego said without preliminaries.

Father Juan grunted. "The virus didn't work anyway."

Diego merged into traffic. "We know that and they know that, but that's not how they're spinning this. They're also publicizing the fight on the plane."

"What's going on?" Juan demanded, fear prickling through him.

"The government has moved to outlaw hunters."

"No." Juan's worst nightmare, come to pass.

"*Sí.*"

"What can they possibly use to rationalize this decision? The hunters do the work. They're out there killing vampires when the military can't. They're the only thing standing between the people and darkness."

"You have said a mouthful, my friend," Diego said solemnly. His face was furrowed with worry lines, and dark circles ringed his eyes. He had aged terribly since Juan had last seen him.

"They are too popular. The Spanish people see them as saviors, as doing for them what their government can not. And so, they are a threat?" Juan asked, trying to make sense of it.

Diego nodded. "Now that Spain is making overtures to the vampires, they are."

"*¡Hostia!*" Juan slammed his fist into the dashboard of the car, an outburst of anger unlike any he had demonstrated in many, many years, swearing an oath a priest should not utter.

"They *knew* we were going to fail. They were counting on it. They knew the virus wouldn't work, but they couldn't just admit that. No, instead they have to have someone to blame. They need an enemy they can actually fight in order to maintain power."

"Hunters," Diego said softly.

"Yes, hunters. Bloody hell, we've been looking for the weak link, the traitor within our ranks," Juan said, looking out the window at Spain, his Spain, where he had lived for so long, longer than anyone else could imagine. His to protect.

He was failing.

"The traitor was our own government, one of the last to stand against the vampires. Every military man, everyone on a government payroll, every contact, any of them could have seen us, betrayed us at every turn." Juan closed his eyes. How could he have been so blind?

"They must have found it more attractive to end the shadow war than to continue fighting on the losing side," Diego speculated.

"But they couldn't just snap their fingers and do it. They needed a new enemy, a new face to put before the people as the reason for all their suffering."

"*Dios.*"

"We can't allow this to stand," Juan said through clenched teeth.

"I'm not sure what the Church can do to persuade the Spanish government. But rest assured that as long as the Academia is owned and controlled by the Church, we will continue to support our hunters and to train new ones."

Juan allowed hope to flare inside himself, but the warmth was scant. "But for how long?"

Juan glanced over at Diego, who refused to meet his eyes. They had both heard the rumors for months now about a movement inside the Church herself to make a treaty with the vampires. It was outrageous, unthinkable, and now too terrifying not to be true.

"For as long as there is breath in our bodies," Diego vowed, taking his hand off the wheel and crossing himself.

Juan did likewise. "Amen."

"I will need your help to address the students. We'll have to find a way to explain the situation to them, prepare them."

"Of course." Juan exhaled slowly as the enormity of what was happening descended on his already very weary shoulders. "And I will need yours when I tell my hunters. If they return."

"You sound worried."

He leaned his head against the seat, envisioning his quarrelsome charges. Missing them. Hoping they were still alive.

"They're the right ones at the right time, but I can't get them to see that. I can't even get them to work together without bickering and fighting."

"As in the Church, so in the world," Diego said, laughing bitterly.

"The Resistance in New Orleans is a shambles, but at least there are people still willing to fight and die for what is right."

"We need more of them, and not just in America," Diego observed.

"I know. Now that Spain has fallen, there is no organized war; there is only the underground, the Resistance, to liberate us. Men and women living in fear and acting out of desperation, that's all we will have now," Juan said.

"Then that must be our starting point," Diego replied.

SALAMANCA
FATHER JUAN, HOLGAR, SKYE, JENN, ANTONIO, ERIKO, AND JAMIE

Jenn lay in her own bed and stared at the ceiling, breathing in the familiar scents of the Academia. Upon arrival they had been told that Father Juan would see them in the morning; then they had been sent straight to their rooms to sleep. All but Holgar, that is. It was going to be a full moon, and Jenn was secretly grateful that they had arrived at Salamanca two hours before nightfall. She knew he locked himself up somewhere while he changed. She just didn't want to see it.

Antonio and one of the priests had taken Heather somewhere, she didn't know where. It usually took a full twenty-four hours for a new vampire to wake up, a full cycle of day and night. It could occasionally take slightly longer, but never less.

They'd torn out of the French Quarter and down the I-10 West in Marc's van, preparing to chance a flight to Madrid. The sun had shone down on a man in a black suit, who was standing in front of a black, unmarked car stationed across their lane of traffic, his hands held out for them to stop. He'd worn sunglasses and a small black Jerusalem cross on his lapel.

"There's a private jet waiting for you," he'd said. "Father Juan sent it. Come this way."

They'd followed him to the airport and through a gate in a hurricane fence. There a matte-gray private jet sat waiting on the tarmac. Eriko walked down the covered companionway, then up into the plane, followed by Jamie, Skye, and Holgar.

As Jenn climbed out from beside Antonio, who was bundled up against the sun, she turned and looked at the man, who was holding open the car door for her. Her face was reflected in his mirrored sunglasses.

"Do you know Greg?" she asked, thinking of the man who had spoken to her at Papa Che's funeral.

The man's face was expressionless.

"That's a common name," he replied. "You'd better hurry. We had to pull some strings to make this happen."

They all made it on the plane to discover that the windows had been blacked out. Antonio had been only slightly singed in the millisecond it took him to make it from the car to the plane, hurrying ahead of Holgar, who was carrying Heather.

Once they took off, things got ugly. Accusations and recriminations flowed hot and heavy. Jamie was furious that they had brought her newly turned sister along, and frankly, she couldn't blame him. She would have felt the exact same way had it been his sister, or someone else's sister — anyone, really, except Heather.

Holgar stepped in to try and make peace, and Jamie hit him. Eriko and Skye broke it up, dragging away their respective partners.

Antonio didn't speak or look at her the entire flight. Instead he spent the time with Heather's still form, bowed over her in prayer.

In Spain the plane had landed on another private airstrip, and a limo had taken them to the university.

Jenn's thoughts kept freezing back to that moment when

she'd realized her sister had been turned, when she'd hefted the stake in her hand, prepared to do the right thing, and when Antonio had stopped her. Why had he done that? Was it really out of love for her, or because he thought he could find some sort of salvation in saving another Cursed One?

There were too many questions without answers. She had hoped to at least be able to talk to Father Juan and discover why he had left New Orleans in such a hurry. Something was wrong, she was sure of it, but she had no idea what it could possibly be. What could be so bad that it drove him to abandon them on the eve of battle?

He didn't abandon us, she reminded herself sternly, flipping onto her side so she could see the door to her room. As a child she had never been able to sleep with the door closed, always fearful that a monster lurked just on the other side. Now she could only sleep with it shut and locked, for she had seen the faces of the monsters who were just on the other side.

And I know their names, she thought, starting to drift to sleep. Her cell phone chimed, indicating that she had a text message. She reached for her phone and flipped it open. There was no time stamp, no sender information, only a single word: *Montana.*

She stared for a long time. Montana was called Big Sky Country. There weren't a lot of people there, and she guessed there were very few vampires. True to her word, her grandmother had gotten herself and Jenn's mother out of harm's way and had sent word where they were.

*   *   *

Skye tested the locks one more time as Holgar watched her from inside the cage. She couldn't stop the sick feeling in her stomach as she thought of Heather, who had also been locked in a cage like an animal.

Yet Holgar *was* an animal. Well, at least sometimes. When he smiled at her, it was full of warmth and laughter. But his eyes were always sad. She knew he carried with him a dark secret, but he shared it with no one. That was okay. She hadn't shared hers with anyone either. Jamie, Antonio, and Jenn wore their pain like badges of honor, wounds received in combat. Eriko didn't allow herself to feel. Skye and Holgar, though, buried their pain deep so no one else could see.

"Do not look so sad, *min lille heks*," Holgar said. "It's just for the night. And it's better this way. Safer."

"Safer for who?" Skye whispered.

"For all of us," he said, staring her in the eyes. He meant it. He really believed he was protecting them as well as himself. Maybe he was. But tonight she knew he could use some extra protection.

"Good night," she said softly, and then walked out of the room. She closed the door behind her and then worked her magick to create a barrier that would prevent anyone from entering the room until the morning. She hated to do it, but she was afraid of Jamie, afraid of what he might do. He was still angry, and Holgar's wolf form was the personification of everything Jamie hated.

"Be safe, Holgar," she whispered before turning and heading for her own room.

Once she had closed the door, Skye drew a circle on the floor. Normally, she preferred to go outside to perform her rituals, stand among the trees and feel the earth beneath her toes and stare up at the moon. Not tonight, though. Dark forces swirled around her, and she wasn't entirely sure that someone or something wasn't waiting out there in the darkness for her.

Estefan's face rose in her mind, and she shivered.

She opened her trunk and pulled out the tools of her trade. She needed to purge the darkness from her mind and break the bonds that seemed to be hampering her, twisting her magick in ways she did not intend.

"It has to end tonight," she whispered to the darkness.

She listened to see if it would whisper back.

Holgar watched Skye go with mixed emotions. It was best that she left, but he didn't want her to. None of his new pack had ever seen him change into the wolf. Father Juan had witnessed it, but not the others. It was something he wasn't willing to share with them yet.

But it was when he changed that he most craved contact with others. That was the wolf in him: fierce, strong, and desperately needing communion with others. The loneliness rose up to choke him, as it had every month since he had left home to train to be a hunter. It was unbearable, and he howled with the pain of it. For the first few months he had nearly quit after each transformation, convinced he could not go through the pain of isolation again.

Stay, Skye, just this once, he thought. Maybe one day he'd ask her, when he knew she could handle watching it. He hated eating alone, but it was nothing compared to how much he hated having to go through the change alone.

Three times Father Juan had stayed with him, and it had made it so much easier to bear. But the priest was under no delusions as to what Holgar was. Holgar had most of them fooled into thinking he was a nice guy. They didn't truly understand the beast in his nature, and so they couldn't be trusted to witness what happened to him when the full moon rose.

His pulse quickened suddenly, and he began to sweat as though he had a high fever. The moon was calling to her wayward son, and it was his duty to answer. He had no choice but to answer.

As his body began to change, Holgar howled again, singing to the moon, begging her for a mate.

The howl of a wolf brought Eriko wide awake from what had been a mercilessly dreamless sleep. Her head pounded, and she could hear blood rushing in her ears. Her arm was asleep, twisted underneath her, but when she tried to roll over, pain raced like fire along the nerves of her body.

She whimpered and lay still, willing the pain to stop.

Overtaxed muscles were twisting, trying to heal themselves—another effect of the elixir. She had broken five bones in her hand during the battle, and they were almost mended. Her left foot was swollen almost beyond recognition, sprained and bruised all over. It would have been so much better if she had actually broken it. She had learned from painful experience that a sprain could take five times longer to heal than a break and could be reinjured much more easily.

The wolf howled again, and it felt like the sound rattled around in her skull, pounding it from the inside.

"Why doesn't someone just shoot that wolf?" she groaned. A moment later she repented her words, as she realized that the wolf in question was probably Holgar.

Holgar. He was a great fighter, a strong member of the team. She wished he and Jamie weren't constantly at each other's throats, though. It was exhausting trying to keep them from killing each other.

Like I almost killed that man, that human, she thought. She relived again the horror of that moment and thanked any deity who would listen that she had been able to stop herself. She was well aware that she might not be so lucky the next time.

She reached out her hand and grabbed two painkillers, popping them in her mouth and swallowing them whole. She resolved that in the morning she would talk to Father Juan about going to see a doctor. She needed something stronger to manage the pain. Maybe she could get a prescription for something that would actually stop the pain. Exhausted, she fell back asleep without having moved her arm.

Jamie paced his room like a caged animal. Normally, he had no trouble falling asleep after a mission, but his blood was still boiling over everything that had happened. He had considered going to Father Juan and waking up the priest, demanding that he deal with the problems at hand, like Heather, and their pet vampire, *and that damned wolf*, he thought as in the distance Holgar howled.

He walked over to his trunk and pulled out his tools and the half-formed skeleton of a gun. His grandfather had made them the old-fashioned way, by hand, and had taught Jamie to do the same. He let out a slow breath and set to work.

Aurora knows my sire. Did Sergio send her to get me? Who is she, and what does she want?

Brooding, Antonio kept watch over Heather's body. Soon she would wake to her new life as a vampire, and he refused to miss the first moment of fluttering life. He had to help her, to save her, for Jenn's sake.

Not just for Jenn, he admitted to himself. If he could help Heather confront her beast and win, then he wouldn't be the only one; there'd be two vampires who could control their urges.

Couldn't control them in New Orleans, his mind mocked

him. That was part of what scared him so badly. For years he had fooled himself into thinking that all he had to do was be good, devote himself to God, and that everything would be okay.

He knew now that that wasn't true. Everything wouldn't be okay, because no matter how much penance he did, how many people he saved, how hard he prayed and studied, he would still be a Cursed One.

What did that mean for his chances at living a normal life, for loving, dying, or even spending eternity somewhere that wasn't hell?

It terrified him, because for some reason he had always believed that one day it would just stop. He would wake up and discover that God had smiled upon him and he could once again walk in the sunlight, eat real food, kiss Jenn without thinking about killing her. Or was the whispered promise of the Evil One tempting him?

"God," he groaned, as he bent over Heather. "Help me."

Father Juan sat in his office, perplexed about how the hunters had made it back home. He'd waited for a message to tell him about their flight home, but it had never come. And now they were back, telling the night guard some story about a man in sunglasses and a private jet.

He had sent no such jet. Maybe they had more allies than he thought. Maybe it was another danger unanticipated. Something more to do with this Aurora.

His team had sorely needed the win in New Orleans. They were fragmenting, splintering apart instead of growing closer together. Now with the added worry of the government action and the new vampire under their roof *and* a mysterious group that had somehow interceded on their behalf, he didn't know how much longer he could keep them together.

It was early. The hunters should still be asleep. He should have been too, but a message had come for him. He let the piece of paper flutter to his desk, and his heart grew heavy. The news from the States was as bad as it could be.

God, why? You know they needed this to be a victory in order to pull them together, make them see their own potential and live up to it. And yet, nothing had changed.

Jenn still refused to acknowledge her gifts, to take responsibility and assume her rightful place on the team. He had let her go to America hoping that it would strengthen her resolve and that she would find the courage she needed to be a force to be reckoned with. He had thrown the runes and said dozens of prayers and knew that she had been meant to go. Heather had to be worth the sacrifice, or they were all doomed. With Heather now a Cursed One, he didn't know what to expect of Jenn.

Antonio was growing increasingly restless, yet another cause for concern. Father Juan hadn't discouraged the relationship between Antonio and Jenn. The truth was that there was something powerful about their love—something transcendent. He could only relate it to the love of God. There was danger there too, as evidenced by Antonio's increasingly erratic behavior. It worried him that the vampire wasn't eating regularly. Forced fasts could lead to uncontrolled binges. He worried that their vampire might bite Jenn by accident, or Jamie on purpose.

Father Juan pressed his fingertips to his temples. Jamie was another problem—a powder keg waiting to blow. He had prevented Jamie from returning to Ireland not because Salamanca needed him but because Jamie needed *them*. On his own in Belfast he would be dead within a week. He was a cunning and vicious fighter, but he had no inclination to hide, preferring instead to face down the whole world on his doorstep even if it would kill him.

On top of it all Eriko couldn't lead, Holgar couldn't trust, and Skye couldn't perform even the most basic offensive spells.

At graduation the elixir had gone to Eriko. It was tradition that the best student receive it, and she had been the best. The others, including Jenn, had assumed that it meant Eriko was the leader. Father Juan wasn't so sure about that, but he had hoped the group dynamic would come together in its own time.

Father Juan sighed. His team gave him headaches, but there were others that were worse. His phone rang, and he answered.

"It's Dimitri."

He knew the voice well enough to be able to ignore the false name it gave.

"How is your trip?"

"Terrible. I got the whole family here, even the cousins."

"Is everyone playing nice?"

"They were."

From the tone of voice Father Juan knew that the rabbi on the other end had lost his teams in their joint mission in Russia.

"I'll send a care package," he whispered.

"Da."

Father Juan ended the call and then bowed his head in prayer. Two teams had gone in to fight, and now two teams were dead. What was happening in Russia could not be allowed to stand. The vampire lord there had to be stopped. He had to send his own team there, even if they weren't ready.

A knock on his door caused him to lift his head. Dressed in his customary baggy sweats, Holgar was standing in the doorway. The first rays of the morning sun were just streaming through the window behind his desk. Father Juan looked at him in surprise. Of all his people, he had spent the least amount of time with Holgar.

The werewolf looked sheepishly at him. If he'd still been in wolf form, his tail would have been tucked between his legs.

464

"What's wrong, Holgar?"

"It was the full moon last night."

"Yes, and?"

"It seems I got out of the cage."

For everyone's safety Holgar had insisted that he spend full-moon nights in a cage. Werewolves only had a measure of control when in wolf form. It varied from one to another, and could also be affected by outside factors, including sleep, hunger, stress, and environment.

"Do you remember anything of what you did?"

Holgar shook his head. "*Nej.* I've got a bad feeling, though."

"Why?"

Wincing, the young Dane shifted his weight and pursed his lips. "I woke up next to the carcass of a deer I had gutted."

So far it wasn't too bad. Father Juan, though, sensed that there was a great deal more. A priest learned these things. "And?" he prompted.

"The head was missing."

"What do you think you did with it?" Father Juan asked, incredulous. He'd never heard of a werewolf removing a head and putting it somewhere else. It wasn't a natural wolf behavior. Which meant it had to have stemmed from some urge of the human half of Holgar.

"I don't know," Holgar whispered.

Suddenly they heard the slamming of a door and running feet.

"Holgar!" Jamie shouted at the top of his lungs.

Father Juan squeezed his eyes shut. "I think I know what you did with the head."

Skye bowed her head as she sat in Father Juan's office. Holgar sat next to her, and Jamie sat on the far side of the room. She still couldn't believe that Holgar had left a deer's head in Jamie's bed. It was so *Godfather*. Jamie was so furious, he had lost the ability to speak after the initial outburst. Holgar had also turned frighteningly quiet, his usual jocularity gone and replaced with a brooding mood that scared her.

It didn't scare her half as much, though, as the look on Father Juan's face. Something terrible had happened.

"What's the news?" Eriko asked quietly.

"Not good," Father Juan revealed. "The two teams in Russia have been lost. I'll be sending you there shortly. Also, I had word this morning. The Resistance in New Orleans collapsed. With the help of the police, and the newly converted mayor, *and* their other new allies, including most of the voodoo community, the vampires retook the city. Of the human combatants there were no survivors."

"They're all dead? Marc, everyone?" Skye asked, her voice a whisper.

Father Juan bowed his head and crossed himself. So did Antonio.

"*Sí, mi'ja*, they are all dead."

Skye heard someone in the room begin to sob and after a moment realized it was her.

"There's more. The Spanish government made a treaty with the vampires this morning. They announced that hunters would cease all activities or be seen as enemies of the state. The Church will continue to sponsor and run this academy as long as it can, but things are grim."

"It's the end of the world," Skye whispered.

No one in the room disagreed with her.

They were all gathered in the chapel to think, to remember, to pray. Jenn felt numb. They had been defeated in every quarter. Her sister, locked up somewhere deep in the heart of the university, was a vampire. The people they had trained and fought with in New Orleans were dead, and the city was more tightly controlled by vampires than ever. The Spanish government had given in, and the Church was probably making a treaty with the vampires even as the Salamancans sat in the darkened chapel like sheep waiting to be slaughtered.

"I'm not a leader," Eriko said, breaking the silence. "It's not who I am. I might be the Hunter, but I can't be the one in charge."

"There's only one person here who can be," Antonio said.

Jenn looked up at him. She knew she would follow him into hell itself if he asked her.

There were murmurs for a moment, and then Skye asked, "So, Jenn, when are you going to stop running from who you are?"

"Excuse me?" Jenn asked, shocked.

"You heard her," Jamie growled.

"What are you saying?" Jenn asked.

"We need a leader, someone who can think like the enemy," Skye said, staring right through her.

"I'm just Jenn," she said, once again giving voice to what she called herself privately.

"Exactly," Holgar said. "All the rest of us are pack animals. I'm a werewolf, born and raised in a pack. Skye is a witch, born and raised in a coven. Eriko is a product of a society that values the community above the individual. Antonio has been studying for seventy damn years to be a priest. And Jamie, as much as he likes to think of himself as a lone wolf, is just as much a pack animal as I am. His pack is the IRA."

Jamie huffed but remained silent.

"You, Jenn, alone are unique," Holgar continued. "Where you grew up and the way you were raised, you're the only one who truly understands the value of the individual. Think of what you call yourself: 'just Jenn.' There is no pack for you—not your family, not even us. That makes you unique. That makes you the only one who can help us get inside the heads of the vampire masters who serve none but themselves."

Jenn stared at him in shock. She thought of all the news stories she had heard as a kid, where people talked about the breakdown of the family culture and the increasing isolation of Americans, particularly those who lived on the West Coast. Combine that with the isolation that her family had experienced for years because of her grandparents.

And she realized suddenly that what she had always thought was a bad thing might just be the thing that could save them all. Holgar was right. Had she truly been a pack person, then the doubts she had felt about herself would have forced her to actually quit the team in an attempt to save them from her ineptness. Tempting as it had been, though, it was a decision she had never been able to make.

Thank God.

Because they needed her.

Because she had a place.

Because I am special.

She put down her pen and stared at the sentence. It was the first line in her new journal—which was to be the new Hunter's Manual. The old one, Father Juan had told her, was outdated, created for such a different time, a different world.

The journal was a beautiful leather-bound book with gold edging on the heavy parchment pages. A thing of beauty, and importance. Father Juan had presented it to her after the others had filed out of the chapel.

"Write it all down, and remember it. You are not just Jenn. You are our hope."

In her room at the Academia, she was aware that Antonio patrolled outside, keeping watch. Writing by candlelight in a sort of ritual of her own, she gazed down at the line.

Because I am special.

For the moment that was all she had to say. There would be more, much more, but the four words were like four candles, or the arms of the Crusaders' cross that she wore on her sleeve.

Because I am special.

She shut the book and began to blow out the candle, before changing her mind. She sat back in her chair, and watched it glow.

It's always darkest before dawn....

The drama continues in

Damned

For the last two weeks, I've led the Salamancan hunters. What a disaster. I can't believe that Father Juan's prayers and magick spells told him I was the one for the job. I'd laugh, if I wouldn't cry first.

Sometimes I dream that I have awakened from this nightmare and there are no vampires, that I'm home and loved and safe with my sister and my parents and my grandparents. Then I wake up. The Cursed Ones are real. My grandfather is dead. My sister has been converted. She is one of them, and my father is responsible. He betrayed her. He betrayed me.

Even if the war ended tomorrow, nothing would be okay.

But, of course, the war isn't ending tomorrow. Unless we lose. I'm starting to think that's inevitable.

Humanity is fighting an unwinnable battle, and sooner or later there won't be other bands of hunters to take our place as we fall.

I can't think that way, not if I'm the leader. But I do.

I enrolled at the Sacred Heart Academy Against the Cursed Ones a little more than two years ago to learn how to kill the vampires. I come from rebel stock—my grandparents were radical protesters in the 1960s, fighting for social justice and paying for their actions by remaining underground for the rest of their lives. Esther and Charles "Che" Leitner are legendary for their bravery and sacrifice.

In honor of them I dreamed of becoming the Hunter—the warrior who would be given the sacred elixir that would endow me with super strength and speed. That honor fell to another, Eriko Sakamoto. But then our master, Father Juan, broke with tradition and gave Eriko a backup team. There are five of us, known also as hunters. She was our leader, until New Orleans fell.

Eriko never wanted to lead; the Hunter has always fought alone, and that was what she had expected. She asked Father Juan to relieve her of command. He did, and gave me her role. But of all of us I have the fewest skills—I'm not supernatural, and I had no fighting experience before I came to Salamanca. I think of myself as "just Jenn," and I feel like a fraud.

The Cursed Ones are coming down hard on us. None of our allies survived our attack on the vampires of New Orleans. During the battle, courageous New Orleanians rose up and joined the fight, but they were massacred. On the news, on the Net, there was not a word about it. But people heard; they knew: It was useless to fight the Cursed Ones. The vampires would always win, and they would show no mercy to the losers. Better to obey them to survive.

As the hunters of Salamanca, we push and we fight and we make trouble. And so the terrified people are beginning to think of us, and not the vampires, as the problem. Spain, where we live, is one of the few nations that has not signed a treaty with the Cursed Ones. Spaniards have been proud of us, calling on us to save their cities and villages from the vampires that brutalize them. But people on the streets have begun to mock us. They call us pulgas—"fleas," a nuisance, an irritant.

If the resistance fighters like us lose the trust of humanity, we lose everything. The hunters of Salamanca need a victory. Something that can make everyone feel like there's hope. We need it for the people looking to us for salvation. We need it for ourselves, to remind us that we can fight and win together as a team. And I need it for myself, so I can *be the leader that we so desperately need.*

My fighting partner, Antonio de la Cruz, says
that I need to have faith. I have no idea how he can
say that after all that's happened—to us, and to
him. I wish I could have faith. But in this world,
faith—like hope—is in very short supply.

—from the diary of Jenn Leitner,
discovered in the ashes

Pamplona, Spain
Team Salamanca: Jenn and Antonio, Skye and Holgar, and Jamie and Eriko

Where's our contact? Antonio wondered as he searched the shadows of the narrow brick alley, detecting shapes and movements only his crimson eyes could see. He spotted a few rats pillaging among the garbage cans, and a big black cat stalking them. The rats squeaked warnings to one another, but none of them ran away. They were used to cats, and humans, and vampires.

Then suddenly the rats squealed and screamed. At the same instant, the cat stiffened and yowled, then flashed past Antonio.

Antonio saw what had frightened the creatures of the night. At the other end of the alley, Holgar Vibbard stood silhouetted in his bomber jacket and jeans beneath a watery streetlamp. The Danish werewolf chuffed low in his throat, a greeting tinged with wariness. Holgar must be thinking the same thing as his vampire counterpart: *The local resistance has failed to show for our meeting. Has something else gone wrong?*

Antonio crossed himself—black cat, bad luck. He'd grown up in a small village in the Spanish countryside in the 1930s, when faith and superstition had been more tightly bound.

The absence of Moncho was another very bad omen.

It was ten o'clock at night in Pamplona, and Antonio smelled vampires everywhere. Of all the Cursed Ones the scent of death lingered most lightly on Antonio himself, or so Holgar said. Being a werewolf, Holgar had a highly developed sense of smell, better even than a Cursed One.

Ever since Antonio's escape from his sire in 1942, he had never been tempted to return to the vampire fold. His loyalties lay with humanity, hopeless though their cause might be. His love, though intended for God alone, lay with the girl walking beside him. She was Jenn Leitner, the leader of their vampire hunting team, for whose sake he had kept vigil every night for more than two years, and whose sister he had sworn to save from the stake. Heather Leitner had been changed into a vampire by their enemy, Aurora Abregón, and for the last two weeks Antonio had been attempting to reawaken Heather's humanity, if indeed it was still there. He was beginning to have his doubts.

Ay, Jenn, you're so beautiful tonight, he thought, admiring the tangles of dark red hair escaping from the black knit cap that gently brushed Jenn's jawline. Petite, deceptively delicate in appearance, she could hold her own if a band of Cursed Ones came calling. Still, every protective instinct within him remained on high alert. During her two years of training at the Academia Sagrado Corazón Contra los Malditos, the Sacred Heart Academy Against the Cursed Ones, he had looked out for her. Now he served as her unofficial bodyguard, though none knew it. Antonio had been born in a time when men fought the battles and women preserved everything worth fighting for. Traditions, culture, children. There were so many things he couldn't give Jenn, and it made him feel powerless and ashamed. The least he could do was offer his own life in place of hers, should such a moment arise. Maybe tonight would be that night.

Jenn's skin was awash with the brilliant light of a storefront window. Her face was filled with longing as she watched a young couple a few meters ahead of them pointing into the store's second window. Antonio's acute hearing picked up the threads of their conversation—the girl's birthday was coming up, and her boyfriend was going to buy her a ring. They were two Spaniards, attempting to live a normal life under the fang.

Antonio followed Jenn's gaze and saw the couple gesturing at pearl rings. In the next case rows of dangling ruby hearts were clutched in the claws of gold and silver bats— since the war against the Cursed Ones, it was the most recognizable icon on the planet, the symbol of women saving themselves for a vampire's kiss. Antonio caught Jenn's reflection in the glass as her face hardened at their sight. He, of course, cast no reflection.

Wistfulness mingled with his tension. There was no chance for them to be like that couple; he would never throw his arm around her as she tried on rings and he pretended to be dismayed by the prices. She would never giggle and rise up on tiptoe to kiss his cheek to take the sting out of his financial sacrifice. They were hunters, and he was a vampire. And he had long ago promised himself to God alone as a man intent on becoming a priest. Though he was a man no longer, his vow remained.

The couple wasn't as happy as they were pretending to be. Antonio could smell their fear, watch their eyes dart anxiously up and down the boulevard. But they were trying very hard to take joy where they could find it. Jenn wasn't even eighteen years old yet; she didn't understand how people could continue to act as if the vampires hadn't won the war. How Spain could pretend it wasn't capitulating. But Antonio knew what it was like to fight against a truth so brutal that you had to find a way to forget, even if only for a few moments, the horror of what had happened to you.

Jenn glanced at Antonio, and he gave his head a quick shake—*Nothing to concern you*. He forced down his bloodlust as she nodded back at him. She was unaware of the temptation she presented as she stood so close. He scented her, felt her heat. He wanted her. He always wanted her. But he would never have her. If he had still had the right to offer himself to her, he would have been faced with a terrible choice: break his vows of poverty, obedience, and chastity so that he could love her as men loved women; or deny the truth of his existence—that he had fallen in love with Jenn—and remain an obedient son of the Church?

Perhaps God Himself had blessed Antonio with vampirism, so that the choice would never have to be made. He balled his fists at the absurd notion. There was nothing blessed about what he had become. There was a reason vampires were called the Cursed Ones. A hundred reasons. And the God of his understanding didn't work that way. The Father of Heaven wasn't a capricious spirit, rigging tests and torturing His children to see if they deserved His love. God wanted to help. But He had to be asked.

Antonio stared at the crimson hearts reflecting a scarlet glow against Jenn's cheeks. There was no choice to be made. And yet he couldn't stop turning the question over in his head. He was obsessed with it. Vampires were known for their powers of mesmerism, able to charm their victims as men could charm cobras with the dip and lilt of a flute. Humans did it in their way—what else was flirting?—and for vampires it was just as natural and automatic. He fought constantly not to mesmerize Jenn. But had she succeeded in mesmerizing him instead?

"Antonio?" Jenn murmured softly, as if detecting his increased agitation. There was cautious distance in her voice, where before there would have been warmth.

Before Jenn's sister had been changed into a ravening monster.

Antonio had seen a similar thing happen back during the war—World War II, *his* war—when the atrocities of the Nazis had become so hideous that the people of Europe and the Americas lumped all Germans in the same category. To them every German was a Nazi, evil to a man, to be hated and feared. Now that Heather had been changed—"converted," in vampire parlance—it had become very hard for Jenn to distinguish him from the rest of *los Malditos*—the Cursed Ones—and to look upon him as the good vampire, the one she loved.

New Orleans had done this to them. Aurora Abregón, another Spanish vampire, had kidnapped Heather to lure Antonio to New Orleans, so that Aurora could present the traitorous vampire to her sire. Not only had Antonio avoided capture, but he had rescued Heather as well.

Who Aurora's sire was, Antonio did not know. All of vampiredom hated Antonio for abandoning his sire and siding with the pathetic human race. His sympathies made him a target, and he saw now how dangerous it was for him to be around the team.

Around Jenn.

"Antonio?" she said again.

"Estoy bien," he replied, assuring her that all was well with him. But it was not.

They walked past the happy pair. Antonio heard three heartbeats. The humans were going to have a baby.

To a casual observer he and Jenn looked like any other teen couple crowding the tapas bars and clubs and spilling onto the Spanish streets, though perhaps not as trendy. Jenn wore a dark gray hoodie over a black sweater and flared black jeans with clunky Doc Martens. Antonio had pulled on scuffed cowboy boots, low-slung jeans, and a simple black T-shirt. Jenn's heartbeat picked up whenever he wore the boots. So he had taken to wearing them whenever possible.

It's not good to tempt her. Or myself, he thought, but who on this earth was perfect?

Holgar's position at the far end of the alley was accounted for. Half a block up, Jamie O'Leary, another teammate, was pacing and smoking like a chimney, a seemingly endless supply of cigarettes stashed in the pockets of his black duster. He wore black jeans as well. Nearly bald and heavily tattooed, the Irish street fighter looked like the 'kicker he'd always been. He hated Antonio and Holgar both, and Antonio knew a day would come when Jamie would strike out against them. Not tonight, when Jamie had need of backup, but it would come.

Jamie's fighting partner, Eriko, had pinned a black bob wig over her two-inch spiky hair, and she wore black leather pants and a black silk T-shirt with the Chinese character for "death" embroidered in red sequins. The hunters of Salamanca had fans as well as enemies, and they could be recognized. They had opted for disguises over magickal glamours, so that the sixth member of their team, the English witch Skye York, could save her energy in the event of an emergency. And given their track record since New Orleans, there probably would be one.

Skye had gone into Gades, a club two blocks up, to look for their contact, José Ramón, also known as Moncho. Gades was Moncho's base of operations, and he was an hour late.

Father Juan, the team's teacher and master, had sent the Salamancans to Pamplona because the Cursed Ones were to hold a festival celebrating Apis, one of their gods of death. Apis had originally been worshipped in ancient Egypt as the Apis bull, symbol of the risen pharaoh, and god of the underworld. The festival was to be a mockery of Pamplona's Running of the Bulls. The real Running of the Bulls was held every July, and people—mostly men—would dress in white shirts and trousers, red sashes and kerchiefs, and run ahead of the bulls stampeding toward the bullring. Later, in the afternoon, those bulls would be killed by matadors in a highly stylized dance of death. It was said that the tradition had sprung from the practice of driving the cattle to market, but according to Father Juan, the real founders had been the bull leapers of Bronze Age Crete. Also according to Father Juan, the ancient Cretans had been plagued by vampires too.

Moncho had informed Father Juan that the vampires were rumored to be planning a running of the humans, perhaps on the feast day of St. Joseph, March 19. It was March 16, and the team had just arrived. Antonio wondered if Aurora was behind the plan, still hoping to capture Antonio himself.

Antonio touched the ruby cross that he wore in his left

earlobe. Five tiny stones in a vertical line, plus one on either side of the fourth one. To him the seven rubies represented the seven mortal sins he had committed as a Cursed One. His sire had presented them to him with great ceremony during an orgy of death and debauchery, celebrating his fledgling's fine achievement—seven murders in one week, one human death per night.

He remembered their faces, and prayed for their souls. Antonio had taken the rubies when he'd escaped, thinking to sell them to pay for lodging. Instead he had found shelter at the University of Salamanca and had had the rubies made into an earring, to remind him that he had fallen—and could fall again.

As he crossed himself, he and Jenn ambled past the entrance to another alley. Holgar was keeping pace. Ahead, Jamie dropped a cigarette to the ground. Antonio could smell the burning tobacco; the onions, garlic, and *piquillo* peppers cooking in the kitchens of the clubs and bars; wine; a dozen fragrances on the women. And vampires.

Then Jamie looked over his shoulder, turned, and straightened. Skye was flying down the street in her scarlet petticoats, black lace-up boots, and black velvet jacket.

"They're coming!" Skye screamed, her white-blond Rasta braids bouncing like coiled springs as she raced toward them waving her arms. "We've got to get the people out of here!"

"Oh, God, it's happening *now*," Jenn said.

God, protect her, Antonio thought. *Let me die for her, if need be. But keep her safe.*

ABOUT THE AUTHORS

NANCY HOLDER has published more than seventy-eight books, including novels and episode guide books about *Buffy the Vampire Slayer* and *Angel* for Simon Pulse. She has received four Bram Stoker awards for her supernatural fiction and is the coauthor of the *New York Times* bestselling Wicked series. She lives in San Diego with her daughter, Belle, their two cats, and their two Corgis. Visit her at nancyholder.com.

DEBBIE VIGUIÉ is the coauthor of the *New York Times* bestselling Wicked series and several additional Simon Pulse books, including the Once upon a Time novels *Violet Eyes* and *Midnight Pearls*. She lives in Florida with her husband, Scott, and their cat, Schrödinger. Visit her at debbieviguie.com.

Witches
Secrets
Alliances
Destiny

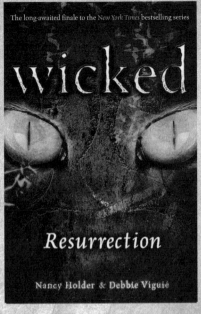

The long-awaited finale to the *New York Times* bestselling series

wicked

Resurrection

Nancy Holder & Debbie Viguié

A *New York Times*
bestselling series by
Nancy Holder
and Debbie Viguié

The first two novels in the *New York Times* bestselling series . . .

wicked

Witch & Curse

Nancy Holder & Debbie Viguié

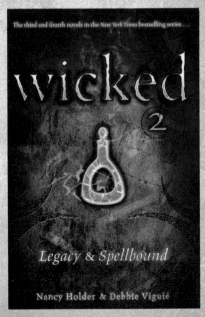

The third and fourth novels in the *New York Times* bestselling series . . .

wicked
2

Legacy & Spellbound

Nancy Holder & Debbie Viguié

From Simon Pulse
Published by Simon & Schuster

When Aura's boyfriend dies, she is devastated.
But it's hard to say good-bye to someone who is not really gone. . . .

"Hauntingly good. . . . One of my favorite reads!"
—P.C. CAST, bestselling author
of the House of Night series

Exclusive
first look at
the sequel,
Shift!

LOVE TIES THEM TOGETHER.
DEATH CAN'T TEAR THEM APART

Shade

JERI SMITH-READY

From Simon Pulse
Published by Simon & Schuster